Mary Olivier: A

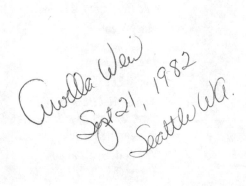

May Sinclair

MARY OLIVIER:
A LIFE

With a new introduction by
Jean Radford

The Dial Press
New York

Published by
The Dial Press
1 Dag Hammarskjold Plaza
New York, New York 10017

First published by The Macmillan Co., 1919
Manufactured in the United States of America
First printing

Library of Congress Cataloging in Publication Data

Sinclair, May.
Mary Olivier: a life.

(A Virago modern classic)
I. Title.   II. Series.
PR6037.I73M3   1982   823'.912   l82-1549
ISBN 0-385-27653-2 AACR2

INTRODUCTION

> ...since Freud has become to the run of modern writers what Butterick patterns are to the home dressmaker, I hesitate to put the thing on May Sinclair, but the line-up of her characters in *Mary Olivier* reads like a list for a clinic. (*The Little Review*, December 1919.)

The novel is not about a clinic but a family – a late Victorian, middle-class English family. As such it belongs to a set of autobiographical novels about family life which appeared in print at the beginning of the twentieth century. For Samuel Butler's *The Way of All Flesh*, Lawrence's *Sons and Lovers*, Joyce's *Portrait of the Artist as a Young Man* and Dorothy Richardson's *Pilgrimage* all have this much in common – a concern with the development of the child, the growth of consciousness from infancy to adulthood. As the private world of home and family was exposed to the scrutiny of a new generation of writers, there were some sharp reactions. Their fiction was read as an attack on the family, they were criticised for their "pathological" characters and their clinical, modernist style. But if contemporary critics were hostile, subsequent literary criticism was worse – both Richardson and May Sinclair were quietly dropped. Their characters, Miriam Henderson and Mary Olivier, were removed from the gallery, leaving Ernest Pontifex, Paul Morel and Stephen Dedalus deprived of female company and legitimate context.

May Sinclair deserves to be recovered – not as a 'forgotten genius' – but as an intelligent and talented writer deeply involved in the movements and ideas of her time. At the simplest level *Mary Olivier* is a substantial narrative of Victorian life: a protest novel thematically very close to Butler's. It deals with the role of religion and the process of socialisation in a nineteenth-century family, as the nineteen-year-old heroine makes clear when she says angrily to her brother:

MARY OLIVIER: A LIFE

None of it would have mattered if we'd been brought up right. But we were brought up all wrong. Taught that our selves were beastly... and that everything we liked was bad.

Mary Olivier is also a novel of specific interest in that it contains one of the most sustained and concentrated portraits of a mother-daughter relationship in fiction. In Mary's struggle for emotional and intellectual freedom the major opponent is not a patriarchal father but an adored mother. Mary's resistance to her mother's conception of femininity as self-suppression is the central issue in the novel. May Sinclair breaks new ground in this; in nineteenth-century fiction by women there is a curious silence about the mother-daughter relationship. In a surprising number of texts the mother is dead, usually in childbirth, but fictionally "killed off" as an active agent in her daughter's characterisation. In *Mary Olivier* the reverse is true; father, brothers, lovers fall away, one by one, leaving the two women confronting each other in a symbolic return to the mother-child relation.

The treatment of this material is certainly shaped by May Sinclair's reading of Freud and Jung. She was one of the first English novelists to use psycho-analytic ideas of repression and sublimation, dream symbolism and infantile sexuality. But the pattern which emerges is not Butterick-Freud because the work is criss-crossed by other, often contradictory, ideas. The treatment of heredity in the Olivier family bears all the traces of nineteenth-century determinist thinking, while the process of the heroine's self-development is fashioned as much in terms of Plato as of Freud. One of the fascinations of *Mary Olivier* is that so many different coloured ideological threads are woven together. In this respect, its very unevenness re-enacts something of the crisis in social and intellectual life taking place at the end of the First World War. The novel – to use the dressmaker image once more – is like a coat of many colours whose seams and patches are an integral part of its significance.

If the period was one of change and upheaval, May Sinclair was herself a very transitional figure. She was in 1919 a professional writer of more than twenty years standing, an Edwardian who had gone over to modernism. Early literary friends like Wells, Walpole and Galsworthy watched the flowering of "this prim virgin", as Arnold Bennett called her, into feminism, psycho-analysis and Imagism. This led to new friendships with poets like Pound, Lawrence and T. S. Eliot and with experimental women writers like Dorothy Richardson and H.D. She was, therefore, at the centre of some of the major literary debates of the period.

INTRODUCTION

During her association with magazines like *The Egoist* and *The Little Review*, she produced some excellent critical essays: on Eliot's "Prufrock", on H.D. and the Imagist poet, F. S. Flint. While she defended the Imagists in public, she was by no means an uncritical convert – as the private letters to Charlotte Mew, the gifted young Georgian poet, reveal:

> About the Imagists – I'm not so stupid, really, as I seem. Remember, I'm defending H.D. against what I know to be an unfair and rather spiteful attack from a writer who isn't fit to lick her boots. H.D. is the best of the Imagists (You'll observe that I don't say very much about the others) . . . I see that these young poets are doing something that *at its best* is beautiful; and it is intolerable that they should meet with ridicule and contempt because they are not doing something else.

She was a literary critic of perception and great generosity and the essay she wrote shortly before she began *Mary Olivier*, on Dorothy Richardson, provides evidence of this. It also sheds light on the "stream-of-consciousness" technique she adapted for her own novel. The article, published in *The Little Review* of April 1918 (a shorter version appeared simultaneously in *The Egoist*), was the first to use "stream-of-consciousness", a term borrowed from William James, to apply to a literary method. It was later used by critics about both Joyce and Virginia Woolf. As Walter Allen says "the essay is a classic of modern criticism and a striking instance of a wholly original talent receiving adequate critical recognition, indeed definition, from the word go."* Richardson's achievement, according to May Sinclair, was to eliminate "the wise all-knowing author" in favour of a close, immediate representation of her heroine's consciousness:

> To me these . . . novels show an art and method and form carried to punctilious perfection. In this series there is no drama, no situation, no set scene. Nothing happens. It is just life going on and on . . . In identifying herself with this life, which is Miriam's stream-of-consciousness, Miss Richardson produces her effect of being the first, of getting closer to reality than any of our novelists who are trying so desperately to get close.

It was this method, condensed and with symbolic additions that May Sinclair tried to use as she worked on *Mary Olivier* in the summer and autumn of 1918. But there were other, social as well as literary, influences in play. The war had accelerated changes in women's position; not just with new economic and social freedoms resulting from women's expanded employment, but

* See Walter Allen's reference to May Sinclair as "the brilliant woman, a fine and at present unjustly neglected novelist" in the introduction to the 1967 edition of *Pilgrimage*.

across a wide range of attitudes and assumptions. Throughout the 1914–1918 period, contemporary newspapers were full of debates on sexual morality and sex education, discussions of the increased divorce rate, illegitimacy and forms of birth control. After Armistice Day, November 18 1918, the chorus of praise for women's war-work was accompanied by their gradual replacement by men in almost every type of occupation. The House of Commons passed the second reading of the Sex Disqualification (Removal) Act, granting the equality of opportunity for which May Sinclair had campaigned before the war, just one month after *Mary Olivier* was published in June 1919. A real achievement, though May Sinclair may well have felt that, as Lady Rhondda later put it, the word "Removal" never got out of its brackets. It was from this post-war perspective that she looked back at her own Victorian childhood and wrote the story of Mary Olivier's struggle toward self-realisation as a woman.

May Sinclair, alias Mary Amelia St. Clair Sinclair, was born on August 24 1863, the youngest child and only girl in a family of five boys. The exact year of her birth varies in contemporary accounts and very little is known about her early life, except from a recent biography by T. E. M. Boll (*Miss May Sinclair: Novelist*, Fairleigh Dickinson Press, 1973). Her father, William Sinclair, was a Liverpool shipowner who married a Scots-Irish Protestant some years older than himself, called Amelia Hind. Mary Amelia began life in Rock Ferry, Cheshire, an affluent suburb for Liverpool businessmen, then after her father's bankruptcy in the 1870s, moved to Ilford, Essex where the first half of *Mary Olivier* is set. The alcoholism and heart disease in the novel appear to have been based on the author's own family; three of the Sinclair brothers died fairly young of cardiac failure, whilst their separated father died of cirrhosis of the liver in 1881.

May Sinclair was educated at home, reading widely and teaching herself French, German, and Greek from her brothers' books. In 1881 she was sent for one year to Cheltenham Ladies' College where she developed her enthusiasm for Greek and German philosophy. It was here that she met one of her most influential friends, the Principal of Cheltenham and a pioneer in women's education, Dorothea Beale. Miss Beale encouraged her to write on philosophical subjects, published her essays on Plato in the College magazine, and kept up a brisk correspondence with her former pupil until her death in 1906. A fervent but less dogmatic Christian than May Sinclair's mother, she tried to convince her that orthodox belief could be reconciled with philosophical idealism, at the same time warning her against the dangers of too much Spinoza!

INTRODUCTION

In the mid-nineties May Sinclair came to London to live in lodgings with her mother, turning her education into a means of livelihood. She did review work, German translations and wrote poetry when she had the time – her first volume of poetry *Nakiketas* had been published in 1886 under the male pseudonym Julian Sinclair. She was 33, desperately poor and imprisoned in a small flat with her difficult mother, when Blackwood published her first novel, *Audrey Craven*, in May 1897. Only after the death of her mother in 1901 did her life expand. She had her first success with her third novel *The Divine Fire* in 1904; the following year she made a visit to America, staying with the short-story writer Sarah Orne Jewett, attending Mark Twain's 70th birthday party in New York, and selling the serial rights to *The Divine Fire*. Once back in England she became involved with the Women's Freedom League, fund-raising and writing articles for *Votes for Women*. By June 1910 this rather fastidious and formal lady had taken to the streets, marching in support of the suffrage bill in the Women Writers Unit, behind a special black and white scriveners' banner inscribed with the slogan "From Prison to Citizenship".

In the next decade May Sinclair reached the height of her powers. She was writing prolifically: a series of introductions for a new edition of the Brontë novels, a pamphlet on 'Feminism' for the Women Writers Suffrage League, her major philosophical work *A Defence of Idealism*, and several novels. *Three Sisters* (1915) draws from her work on the Brontës, while her experience of the feminist movement from 1908–12 is fictionalised in *The Tree of Heaven* (1917). She also went to Europe for the first time, met Pound and through him the Vorticists, and served briefly in an ambulance unit in Belgium at the beginning of the war. In addition she became deeply interested in psycho-analytic theory through her friendship with another women's suffrage supporter, Dr Jessie Margaret Murray. Dr Murray had been a student of Pierre Janet in France, and with H. N. Brailsford, one of the early English translators of Freud, founded the Medico-Psychological Clinic in London. It was one of the first clinics in England to use psycho-analytic methods, and when it closed after the war many of its trainees went on to work for the Tavistock Square Clinic and the Institute of Psycho-Analysis under Ernest Jones. May Sinclair was a founder-member of this clinic and gave it her financial as well as her theoretical support. Her review articles of Jung's *Psychology of the Unconscious* in *The Medical Press* of August 1916 are a remarkably astute enlightened tribute to Freud and his followers, and reveal a considerable knowledge of psycho-analytic concepts. Entitled "Symbolism and Sublimation" these articles discuss the relation between Freud's theory of psychosexual processes and Jung's work on symbolism. Her comments on psychological development and its relationship to language are useful in understanding *Mary Olivier* and still extremely relevant to present-day debates.

In the 1920s, despite increasing ill-health, she continued to write, producing one of her best novels, *Life and Death of Harriett Frean* (1922). This book and *Arnold Waterlow: a Life* (1924) are especially interesting since they deal, in different ways, with some of the same themes as *Mary Olivier*. When she stopped writing in 1931, May Sinclair had published a prodigious amount: twenty-four novels, several collections of poems and short stories, two full-length philosophical studies and many miscellaneous pieces as well. She survived for another fifteen years, crippled by Parkinson's disease, dying at her home near Aylesbury on November 14 1946.

Mary Olivier is about the socialisation of a woman and the making of a poet. The tale is told, ostensibly, through Mary's consciousness but the "stream" of that consciousness is organised around key events and images, selectively presented to illustrate a Freudian theory of child development. It opens with the cot memories of the two-year-old heroine, then from the mother's breast the focus widens rapidly to the rest of the family and Mary's position within it. The author uses imagist techniques to convey her sensations and symbolism to comment on the social relations and psychic development. For the most part Mary is described in the third person (she/her etc.) but there are sudden shifts into second-person. "Mamma took her in her lap. She lowered her head to you, . . . ready to pounce if you said the wrong thing." The difficulties between mother and daughter start long before the "oedipal" rivalries over Mary's brother Mark. The heart of the matter is the mother's inferior sense of the feminine, and her pressure on her daughter to conform to her rigid conception of sexual difference. Her love for Mary is conditional on her obedience, and the effects of this conditional love on her daughter's emotional development are examined in some detail. The anger which the child cannot express is soured into hatred, and alongside the hatred we see the growth of defence mechanisms to shield them both: disavowal, idealisation and a precocious intellectualism. The social as well as the psychological implications are presented. The author suggests how particular notions of gender are transmitted from one generation to the next, how women can act as agents of other women's oppression in a patriarchal culture. The early sense of her mother's preference for her brothers, and the consequent blow to the child's self-esteem, is symbolised in the

scene in which Mary destroys her brick tower because her mother
is exclusively concerned with a brother's snowman. Not all of
May Sinclair's Freudian symbolism works as well; the funeral
phobia, modelled on the case of "Little Hans" and Aunt Charlotte's
appearances as a casualty of sexual repression, are somewhat
insistent. The representation of female sexuality through Mary
and her mother's piano playing, on the other hand, is a subtler
and more sustained use of symbolism. The piano operates as a
general metaphor for pleasure, self-expression and release in her
battles with her parents, but also to denote Mary's sexual desires
with Lindley Vickers and other potential lovers.

One of the most effective scenes representing Mary's struggle
for independence occurs in Book 3, entitled "Adolescence".
Mrs Olivier is forcing her daughter to learn the 39 articles for
confirmation and accuses her of inattention:

> 'Don't look like that,' her mother said, 'as if your wits were wool-
> gathering.'
> 'Wool?' She could see herself smiling at her mother, disagreeably.
> Wool-gathering. Gathering wool. The room was full of wool; wool
> flying about; hanging in the air and choking you. Clogging your mind.
> Old grey wool out of pew cushions that people had sat on for centuries,
> full of dirt.
> Wool, spun out, wound round you, woven in a net. You were
> tangled and strangled in a net of unclean wool. They caught you in it
> when you were a baby a month old, Mamma, Papa, and Uncle Victor.
> You would have to tug and kick and fight your way out. They were
> caught in it themselves, they couldn't get out.

The immediate application of the image is to religious dogma,
but from Mary's free associations to the word "wool" the reference
is extended to include psychological oppression within the family.
It works as a brilliant image of the power of both Church and
family – twin forces of nineteenth-century conformism – of
ideology not as imposed from above, but as a common condition.
Mary Olivier's resolve to "tug and kick" her way out echoes
Stephen Dedalus' decision in *Portrait of the Artist As a Young Man*
to "fly by those nets", and like Joyce's hero, she tries to use *writing*
as a means.

In *Mary Olivier* 'All this description of the *inner* life is as auto-
biographically accurate as I can make it' the author wrote to her
French translator, Marc Logé. Even without this admission, the
pull of the autobiographical impulse makes itself felt within the
text. The novel is too long; there are too many lovers lost, too
much detail about her philosophical reading, too many scenes
in which mother and daughter enact the same painful conflicts.
The marks of unresolved emotions, symptoms of personal tension

appear in the text as repetitions, a circling around the same emotionally charged incidents. There is also a progressive idealisation of the heroine which complicates her presentation and makes the ending enigmatic.

Mary's decision to give up the man she loves for the care of her mother, to sacrifice sexual love for her poetry and a higher sense of self, can be read in several ways. In terms of May Sinclair's Freudian argument, Mary "sublimates" her sexual energies into art and intellectual achievement. But the author's philosophical interests are also apparent here. The moments of mysticism, and the vision of "Beauty" which occurs at the end of the novel, are expressed in the terms used in Plato's *Symposium* to describe the different stages of love. Plato's *Diotima* argues that one begins with the physical love of beauty, and progresses through moral beauty to the beauty of knowledge "until from knowledge of various kinds one arrives at the supreme knowledge whose sole object is that of absolute beauty". Mary convinces herself that her renunciation of Richard Nicholson is a stage to a higher form of love, and significantly, it is only after this act that she attains her vision of "perfect happiness".

The theme of sacrifice is strong throughout May Sinclair's work, it relates to her feminism as well as to her psychological and philosophical theories. In an early poem "Helen" she had written:

> . . . for I know
> That love is not the whole of woman's life,
> Nor yet of man's, but there are higher things –
> Devotion – honour – faith – self-sacrifice.

This is of course an implicit rejoinder to Byron's "Man's love is of man's life, a thing apart,/Tis woman's whole existence". It is also fairly typical of feminists at the turn of the century who believed that women might prove their equality, their right to citizenship through their commitment to "higher things". To a modern feminist, the ending of *Mary Olivier* may well appear an elaborate rationalisation of – yet again – self-denial. The heroine's sense of liberation is based on the old solutions, sacrifice of self for others, a forced choice between love and work. Indeed, from a psychoanalytic viewpoint it is possible to read the ending not as a triumph of sublimation but as a defeat of desire by a tyrannical super-ego. Defeat or triumph, whichever way one reads it, the predicament of Mary Olivier is a moving one. It recalls the lines of another nineteenth-century intellectual feminist, Margaret Fuller, which George Eliot used to quote from memory:

> I shall always reign through the intellect, but my God –
> the life, the life – shall that never be sweet?

Jean Radford, 1980

Mary Olivier: A Life

MARY OLIVIER: A LIFE

BOOK ONE

INFANCY

1865–1869

I

THE curtain of the big bed hung down beside the cot.

When old Jenny shook it the wooden rings rattled on the pole and grey men with pointed heads and squat, bulging bodies came out of the folds on to the flat green ground. If you looked at them they turned into squab faces smeared with green.

Every night, when Jenny had gone away with the doll and the donkey, you hunched up the blanket and the stiff white counterpane to hide the curtain and you played with the knob in the green painted iron railing of the cot. It stuck out close to your face, winking and grinning at you in a friendly way. You poked it till it left off and turned grey and went back into the railing. Then you had to feel for it with your finger. It fitted the hollow of your hand, cool and hard, with a blunt nose that pushed agreeably into the palm.

In the dark you could go tip-finger along the slender, lashing flourishes of the ironwork. By stretching your arm out tight you could reach the curlykew at the end. The short, steep flourish took you to the top of the railing and on behind your head.

Tip-fingering backwards that way you got into the grey lane where the prickly stones were and the hedge of little biting trees. When the door in the hedge opened you saw the man in the night-shirt. He had only half a face. From his nose and his cheek-bones downwards his beard hung

3

straight like a dark cloth. You opened your mouth, but before you could scream you were back in the cot; the room was light; the green knob winked and grinned at you from the railing, and behind the curtain Papa and Mamma were lying in the big bed.

One night she came back out of the lane as the door in the hedge was opening. The man stood in the room by the washstand, scratching his long thigh. He was turned slant-wise from the nightlight on the washstand so that it showed his yellowish skin under the lifted shirt. The white half-face hung by itself on the darkness. When he left off scratching and moved towards the cot she screamed.

Mamma took her into the big bed. She curled up there under the shelter of the raised hip and shoulder. Mamma's face was dry and warm and smelt sweet like Jenny's powder-puff. Mamma's mouth moved over her wet cheeks, nipping her tears.

Her cry changed to a whimper and a soft, ebbing sob.

Mamma's breast: a smooth, cool, round thing that hung to your hands and slipped from them when they tried to hold it. You could feel the little ridges of the stiff nipple as your finger pushed it back into the breast.

Her sobs shook in her throat and ceased suddenly.

II

The big white globes hung in a ring above the dinner table. At first, when she came into the room, carried high in Jenny's arms, she could see nothing but the hanging, shining globes. Each had a light inside it that made it shine.

Mamma was sitting at the far end of the table. Her face and neck shone white above the pile of oranges on the dark blue dish. She was dipping her fingers in a dark blue glass bowl.

When Mary saw her she strained towards her, leaning dangerously out of Jenny's arms. Old Jenny said " Tchit-tchit! " and made her arms tight and hard and put her on Papa's knee.

Papa sat up, broad and tall above the table, all by himself. He was dressed in black. One long brown beard hung down in front of him and one short beard covered his mouth. You knew he was smiling because his cheeks swelled high up his face so that his eyes were squeezed into narrow, shining slits. When they came out again you saw scarlet specks and smears in their corners.

Papa's big white hand was on the table, holding a glass filled with some red stuff that was both dark and shining and had a queer, sharp smell.

" Porty-worty winey-piney," said Papa.

The same queer, sharp smell came from between his two beards when he spoke.

Mark was sitting up beside Mamma a long way off. She could see them looking at each other. Roddy and Dank were with them.

They were making flowers out of orange peel and floating them in the finger bowls. Mamma's fingers were blue and sharp-pointed in the water behind the dark blue glass of her bowl. The floating orange-peel flowers were blue. She could see Mamma smiling as she stirred them about with the tips of her blue fingers.

Her underlip pouted and shook. She didn't want to sit by herself on Papa's knee. She wanted to sit in Mamma's lap beside Mark. She wanted Mark to make orange-peel flowers for her. She wanted Mamma to look down at her and smile.

Papa was spreading butter on biscuit and powdered sugar on the butter.

" Sugary — Buttery — Bippery," said Papa.

She shook her head. " I want to go to Mamma. I want to go to Mark."

She pushed away the biscuit. " No. No. Mamma give Mary. Mark give Mary."

" Drinky — winky," said Papa.

He put his glass to her shaking mouth. She turned her head away, and he took it between his thumb and finger and turned it back again. Her neck moved stiffly. Her head felt small and brittle under the weight and pinch of the big hand. The smell and the sour, burning taste of the wine made her cry.

"Don't tease Baby, Emilius," said Mamma.

"I never tease anybody."

He lifted her up. She could feel her body swell and tighten under the bands and drawstrings of her clothes, as she struggled and choked, straining against the immense clamp of his arms. When his wet red lips pushed out between his beards to kiss her she kicked. Her toes drummed against something stiff and thin that gave way and sprang out again with a cracking and popping sound.

He put her on the floor. She stood there all by herself, crying, till Mark came and took her by the hand.

"Naughty Baby. Naughty Mary," said Mamma. "Don't kiss her, Mark."

"No, Mamma."

He knelt on the floor beside her and smiled into her face and wiped it with his pocket-handkerchief. She put out her mouth and kissed him and stopped crying.

"Jenny must come," Mamma said, "and take Mary away."

"No. Mark take Mary."

"Let the little beast take her," said Papa. "If he does he shan't come back again. Do you hear that, sir?"

Mark said, "Yes, Papa."

They went out of the room hand in hand. He carried her upstairs pickaback. As they went she rested her chin on the nape of his neck where his brown hair thinned off into shiny, golden down.

III

Old Jenny sat in the rocking-chair by the fireguard in the nursery. She wore a black net cap with purple rosettes above her ears. You could look through the black net and see the top of her head laid out in stripes of grey hair and pinky skin.

She had a grey face, flattened and wide-open like her eyes. She held it tilted slightly backwards out of your way, and seemed to be always staring at something just above your head. Jenny's face had tiny creases and crinkles all over it. When you kissed it you could feel the loose flesh crumpling and sliding softly over the bone. There was always about her a faint smell of sour milk.

No use trying to talk to Jenny. She was too tired to listen. You climbed on to her lap and stroked her face, and said " Poor Jenny. Dear Jenny. Poor Jenny-Wee so tired," and her face shut up and went to sleep. Her broad flat nose drooped; her eyelids drooped; her long, grey bands of hair drooped; she was like the white donkey that lived in the back lane and slept standing on three legs with his ears lying down.

Mary loved old Jenny next to Mamma and Mark; and she loved the white donkey. She wondered why Jenny was always cross when you stroked her grey face and called her " Donkey-Jenny." It was not as if she minded being stroked; because when Mark or Dank did it her face woke up suddenly and smoothed out its creases. And when Roddy climbed up with his long legs into her lap she hugged him tight and rocked him, singing Mamma's song, and called him her baby.

He wasn't. *She* was the baby; and while you were the baby you could sit in people's laps. But old Jenny didn't want her to be the baby.

The nursery had shiny, slippery yellow walls and a brown floor, and a black hearthrug with a centre of brown and yellow flowers. The greyish chintz curtains were spotted with small brown leaves and crimson berries. There were dark-brown cupboards and chests of drawers, and chairs that were brown frames for the yellow network of the cane. Soft bits of you squeezed through the holes and came out on the other side. That hurt and made a red pattern on you where you sat down.

The tall green fireguard was a cage. When Jenny poked the fire you peeped through and saw it fluttering inside. If you sat still you could sometimes hear it say " teck-teck," and sometimes the fire would fly out suddenly with a soft hiss.

High above your head you could just see the gleaming edge of the brass rail.

" Jenny — where's yesterday and where's to-morrow? "

IV

When you had run a thousand hundred times round the table you came to the blue house. It stood behind Jenny's rocking-chair, where Jenny couldn't see it, in a blue garden. The walls and ceilings were blue; the doors and staircases were blue; everything in all the rooms was blue.

Mary ran round and round. She loved the padding of her feet on the floor and the sound of her sing-song:

" The pussies are blue, the beds are blue, the matches are blue and the mousetraps and all the litty mouses! "

Mamma was always there dressed in a blue gown; and Jenny was there, all in blue, with a blue cap; and Mark and Dank and Roddy were there, all in blue. But Papa was not allowed in the blue house.

Mamma came in and looked at her as she ran. She stood in the doorway with her finger on her mouth, and she was smiling. Her brown hair was parted in two sleek bands, looped and puffed out softly round her ears, and plaited in one plait that stood up on its edge above her forehead. She wore a wide brown silk gown with falling sleeves.

" Pretty Mamma," said Mary. " In a blue dress."

V

Every morning Mark and Dank and Roddy knocked at Mamma's door, and if Papa was there he called out, " Go away, you little beasts! " If he was not there she said, " Come in, darlings! " and they climbed up the big bed into Papa's place and said " Good morning, Mamma! "

When Papa was away the lifted curtain spread like a tent over Mary's cot, shutting her in with Mamma. When he was there the drawn curtain hung straight down from the head of the bed.

II

I

WHITE patterns on the window, sharp spikes, feathers, sprigs with furled edges, stuck flat on to the glass; white webs, crinkled like the skin of boiled milk, stretched across the corner of the pane; crisp, sticky stuff that bit your fingers.

Out of doors, black twigs thickened with a white fur; white powder sprinkled over the garden walk. The white, ruffled grass stood out stiffly and gave under your feet with a pleasant crunching. The air smelt good; you opened your mouth and drank it in gulps. It went down like cold, tingling water.

Frost.

You saw the sun for the first time, a red ball that hung by itself on the yellowish white sky. Mamma said, " Yes, of course it would fall if God wasn't there to hold it up in his hands."

Supposing God dropped the sun —

II

The yellowish white sky had come close up to the house, a dirty blanket let down outside the window. The tree made a black pattern on it. Clear glass beads hung in a row from the black branch, each black twig was tipped with a glass bead. When Jenny opened the window there was a queer cold smell like the smell of the black water in the butt.

Thin white powder fluttered out of the blanket and fell. A thick powder. A white fluff that piled itself in a ridge on the window-sill and curved softly in the corner of the sash. It was cold, and melted on your tongue with a taste of window-pane.

In the garden Mark and Dank and Roddy were making the snow man.

Mamma stood at the nursery window with her back to the room. She called to Mary to come and look at the snow man.

Mary was tired of the snow man. She was making a tower with Roddy's bricks while Roddy wasn't there. She had to build it quick before he could come back and take his bricks away, and the quicker you built it the sooner it fell down. Mamma was not to look until it was finished.

"Look — look, Mamma! M-m-mary's m-m-made a tar.
And it's *not* falled down!"

The tower reached above Jenny's knee.

"Come and look, Mamma — " But Mamma wouldn't
even turn her head.

"I'm looking at the snow man," she said.

Something swelled up, hot and tight, in Mary's body and
in her face. She had a big bursting face and a big bursting
body. She struck the tower, and it fell down. Her vio-
lence made her feel light and small again and happy.

"Where's the tower, Mary?" said Mamma.

"There isn't any tar. I've knocked it down. It was a
nashty tar."

III

Aunt Charlotte —

Aunt Charlotte had sent the Isle of Skye terrier to Dank.

There was a picture of Aunt Charlotte in Mamma's
Album. She stood on a strip of carpet, supported by the
hoops of her crinoline; her black lace shawl made a pattern
on the light gown. She wore a little hat with a white
sweeping feather, and under the hat two long black curls
hung down straight on each shoulder.

The other people in the Album were sulky, and wouldn't
look at you. The gentlemen made cross faces at somebody who wasn't there; the ladies hung their heads and
looked down at their crinolines. Aunt Charlotte hung her
head too, but her eyes, tilted up straight under her forehead,
pointed at you. And between her stiff black curls she was
smiling — smiling. When Mamma came to Aunt Charlotte's picture she tried to turn over the page of the Album
quick.

Aunt Charlotte sent things. She sent the fat valentine
with the lace paper border and black letters printed on
sweet-smelling white satin that Papa threw into the fire,
and the white china doll with black hair and blue eyes and
no clothes on that Jenny hid in the nursery cupboard.

The Skye terrier brought a message tied under his chin:
" Tib. For my dear little nephew Dan with Aunt Charlotte's

fond love." He had high-peaked, tufted ears and a black-
ish grey coat that trailed on the floor like a shawl that was
too big for him. When you tried to stroke him the shawl
swept and trailed away under the table. You saw nothing
but shawl and ears until Papa began to tease Tib. Papa
snapped his finger and thumb at him, and Tib showed little
angry eyes and white teeth set in a black snarl.

Mamma said, " Please don't do that again, Emilius."

And Papa did it again.

IV

" What are you looking at, Master Daniel? " said Jenny.

" Nothing."

" Then what are you looking like that for? You didn't
ought to."

Papa had sent Mark and Dank to the nursery in disgrace.
Mark leaned over the back of Jenny's chair and rocked
her. His face was red but tight; and as he rocked he
smiled because of his punishment.

Dank lay on the floor on his stomach, his shoulders
hunched, raised on his elbows, his chin supported by his
clenched fists. He was a dark and white boy with dusty
eyelashes and rough, doggy hair. He had puckered up his
mouth and made it small; under the scowl of his twisted
eyebrows he was looking at nothing.

" It's no worse for you than it is for Master Mark," said
Jenny.

" *Isn't* it? Tib was my dog. If he hadn't been my dog
Papa wouldn't have teased him, and Mamma wouldn't have
sent him back to Aunt Charlotte, and Aunt Charlotte
wouldn't have let him be run over."

" Yes. But what did you say to your Papa? "

" I said I wish Tib *had* bitten him. So I do. And Mark
said it would have served him jolly well right."

" So it would," said Mark.

Roddy had turned his back on them. Nobody was taking
any notice of him; so he sang aloud to himself the song he
was forbidden to sing:

" John Brown's body lies a-rotting in his grave,
John Brown's body lies a-rotting in his grave — "

The song seemed to burst out of Roddy's beautiful white face; his pink lips twirled and tilted; his golden curls bobbed and nodded to the tune.

> " John Brown's body lies a-rotting in his grave,
>   As we go marching on! "

" When I grow up," said Dank, " I'll kill Papa for killing Tibby. I'll bore holes in his face with Mark's gimlet. I'll cut pieces out of him. I'll get the matches and set fire to his beard. I'll — I'll *hurt* him."

" I don't think *I* shall," said Mark. " But if I do I shan't kick up a silly row about it first."

" It's all very well for you. You'd kick up a row if Tibby was your dog."

Mary had forgotten Tibby. Now she remembered.

" Where's Tibby? I want him."

" Tibby's dead," said Jenny.

" What's ' dead '? "

" Never you mind."

Roddy was singing:

> " ' And *from* his nose and *to* his chin
>   The worms crawled out and the worms crawled in '—

" *That's* dead," said Roddy.

v

You never knew when Aunt Charlotte mightn't send something. She forgot your birthday and sometimes Christmas; but, to make up for that, she remembered in between. Every time she was going to be married she remembered.

Sarah the cat came too long after Mark's twelfth birthday to be his birthday present. There was no message with her except that Aunt Charlotte was going to be married and didn't want her any more. Whenever Aunt Charlotte was going to be married she sent you something she didn't want.

Sarah was a white cat with a pink nose and pink lips and pink pads under her paws. Her tabby hood came down in a peak between her green eyes. Her tabby cape went on along the back of her tail, tapering to the tip. Sarah crouched against the fireguard, her haunches raised, her head sunk back on her shoulders, and her paws tucked in under her white, pouting breast.

Mark stooped over her; his mouth smiled its small, firm smile; his eyes shone as he stroked her. Sarah raised her haunches under the caressing hand.

Mary's body was still. Something stirred and tightened in it when she looked at Sarah.

"I want Sarah," she said.

"You can't have her," said Jenny. "She's Master Mark's cat."

She wanted her more than Roddy's bricks and Dank's animal book or Mark's soldiers. She trembled when she held her in her arms and kissed her and smelt the warm, sweet, sleepy smell that came from the top of her head.

"Little girls can't have everything they want," said Jenny.

"I wanted her before you did," said Dank. "You're too little to have a cat at all."

He sat on the table swinging his legs. His dark, mournful eyes watched Mark under their doggy scowl. He looked like Tibby, the terrier that Mamma sent away because Papa teased him.

"Sarah isn't your cat either, Master Daniel. Your Aunt Charlotte gave her to your Mamma, and your Mamma gave her to Master Mark."

"She ought to have given her to me. She took my dog away."

"*I* gave her to you," said Mark.

"And I gave her to you back again."

"Well then, she's half our cat."

"I want her," said Mary. She said it again and again.

Mamma came and took her into the room with the big bed.

The gas blazed in the white globes. Lovely white lights washed like water over the polished yellow furniture: the bed, the great high wardrobe, the chests of drawers, the twisted poles of the looking-glass. There were soft rounds and edges of blond light on the white marble chimney-piece and the white marble washstand. The drawn curtains were covered with shining silver patterns on a sleek green ground that shone. All these things showed again in the long, flashing mirrors.

Mary looked round the room and wondered why the squat grey men had gone out of the curtains.

"Don't look about you," said Mamma. "Look at me. Why do you want Sarah?"

She had forgotten Sarah.

"Because," she said, "Sarah is so sweet."

"Mamma gave Sarah to Mark. Mary mustn't want what isn't given her. Mark doesn't say, ' I want Mary's dollies.' Papa doesn't say, ' I want Mamma's workbox.' "

"But *I* want Sarah."

"And that's selfish and self-willed."

Mamma sat down on the low chair at the foot of the bed.

"God," she said, "hates selfishness and self-will. God is grieved every time Mary is self-willed and selfish. He wants her to give up her will."

When Mamma talked about God she took you on her lap and you played with the gold tassel on her watch chain. Her face was solemn and tender. She spoke softly. She was afraid that God might hear her talking about him and wouldn't like it.

Mary knelt in Mamma's lap and said "Gentle Jesus, meek and mild," and "Our Father," and played with the gold tassel. Every day began and ended with "Our Father" and "Gentle Jesus, meek and mild."

"What's hallowed?"

"Holy," said Mamma. "What God is. Sacred and holy."

Mary twisted the gold tassel and made it dance and run through the loop of the chain. Mamma took it out of her hands and pressed them together and stooped her head to them and kissed them. She could feel the kiss tingling through her body from her finger-tips, and she was suddenly docile and appeased.

When she lay in her cot behind the curtain she prayed: "Please God keep me from wanting Sarah."

In the morning she remembered. When she looked at Sarah she thought: "Sarah is Mark's cat and Dank's cat."

She touched her with the tips of her fingers. Sarah's eyes were reproachful and unhappy. She ran away and crept under the chest of drawers.

"Mamma gave Sarah to Mark."

Mamma was sacred and holy. Mark was sacred and holy. Sarah was sacred and holy, crouching under the chest of drawers with her eyes gleaming in the darkness.

VI

It was a good and happy day.

She lay on the big bed. Her head rested on Mamma's arm. Mamma's face was close to her. Water trickled into her eyes out of the wet pad of pocket-handkerchief. Under the cold pad a hot, grinding pain came from the hole in her forehead. Jenny stood beside the bed. Her face had waked up and she was busy squeezing something out of a red sponge into a basin of pink water.

When Mamma pressed the pocket-handkerchief tight the pain ground harder, when she loosened it blood ran out of the hole and the pocket-handkerchief was warm again. Then Jenny put on the sponge.

She could hear Jenny say, "It was the Master's fault. She didn't ought to have been left in the room with him."

She remembered. The dining-room and the sharp spike on the fender and Papa's legs stretched out. He had told her not to run so fast and she had run faster and faster. It wasn't Papa's fault.

She remembered tripping over Papa's legs. Then falling on the spike. Then nothing.

Then waking in Mamma's room.

She wasn't crying. The pain made her feel good and happy; and Mamma was calling her her darling and her little lamb. Mamma loved her. Jenny loved her.

Mark and Dank and Roddy came in. Mark carried Sarah in his arms. They stood by the bed and looked at her; their faces pressed close. Roddy had been crying; but Mark and Dank were excited. They climbed on to the bed and kissed her. They made Sarah crouch down close beside her and held her there. They spoke very fast, one after the other.

"We've brought you Sarah."

"We've given you Sarah."

"She's your cat."

"To keep for ever."

She was glad that she had tripped over Papa's legs. It was a good and happy day.

VII

The sun shone. The polished green blades of the grass glittered. The gravel walk and the nasturtium bed together made a broad orange blaze. Specks like glass sparkled in the hot grey earth. On the grey flagstone the red poppy you picked yesterday was a black thread, a purple stain.

She was happy sitting on the grass, drawing the fine, sharp blades between her fingers, sniffing the smell of the mignonette that tingled like sweet pepper, opening and shutting the yellow mouths of the snap-dragon.

The garden flowers stood still, straight up in the grey earth. They were as tall as you were. You could look at them a long time without being tired.

The garden flowers were not like the animals. The cat Sarah bumped her sleek head under your chin; you could feel her purr throbbing under her ribs and crackling in her throat. The white rabbit pushed out his nose to you and drew it in again, quivering, and breathed his sweet breath into your mouth.

The garden flowers wouldn't let you love them. They stood still in their beauty, quiet, arrogant, reproachful. They put you in the wrong. When you stroked them they shook and swayed from you; when you held them tight their heads dropped, their backs broke, they shrivelled up in your hands. All the flowers in the garden were Mamma's; they were sacred and holy.

You loved best the flowers that you stooped down to look at and the flowers that were not Mamma's: the small crumpled poppy by the edge of the field, and the ears of the wild rye that ran up your sleeve and tickled you, and the speedwell, striped like the blue eyes of Meta, the wax doll.

When you smelt mignonette you thought of Mamma.

It was her birthday. Mark had given her a little sumach tree in a red pot. They took it out of the pot and dug a hole by the front door steps outside the pantry window and planted it there.

Papa came out on to the steps and watched them.

" I suppose," he said, " you think it'll *grow?* "

Mamma never turned to look at him. She smiled because it was her birthday. She said, " Of course it'll grow."

She spread out its roots and pressed it down and padded up the earth about it with her hands. It held out its tiny branches, stiffly, like a toy tree, standing no higher than the mignonette. Papa looked at Mamma and Mark, busy and happy with their heads together, taking no notice of him. He laughed out of his big beard and went back into the house suddenly and slammed the door. You knew that he disliked the sumach tree and that he was angry with Mark for giving it to Mamma.

When you smelt mignonette you thought of Mamma and Mark and the sumach tree, and Papa standing on the steps, and the queer laugh that came out of his beard.

When it rained you were naughty and unhappy because you couldn't go out of doors. Then Mamma stood at the window and looked into the front garden. She smiled at the rain. She said, " It will be good for my sumach tree."

Every day you went out on to the steps to see if the sumach tree had grown.

VIII

The white lamb stood on the table beside her cot.

Mamma put it there every night so that she could see it first thing in the morning when she woke.

She had had a birthday. Suddenly in the middle of the night she was five years old.

She had kept on waking up with the excitement of it. Then, in the dark twilight of the room, she had seen a bulky thing inside the cot, leaning up against the rail. It stuck out queerly and its weight dragged the counterpane tight over her feet.

The birthday present. What she saw was not its real shape. When she poked it, stiff paper bent in and crackled; and she could feel something big and solid underneath. She lay quiet and happy, trying to guess what it could be, and fell asleep again.

It was the white lamb. It stood on a green stand. It smelt of dried hay and gum and paint like the other toy animals, but its white coat had a dull, woolly smell, and that was the real smell of the lamb. Its large, slanting eyes stared off over its ears into the far corners of the room, so that it never looked at you. This made her feel sometimes that the lamb didn't love her, and sometimes that it was frightened and wanted to be comforted.

She trembled when first she stroked it and held it to her face, and sniffed its lamby smell.

Papa looked down at her. He was smiling; and when she looked up at him she was not afraid. She had the same feeling that came sometimes when she sat in Mamma's lap and Mamma talked about God and Jesus. Papa was sacred and holy.

He had given her the lamb.

It was the end of her birthday; Mamma and Jenny were putting her to bed. She felt weak and tired, and sad because it was all over.

" Come to that," said Jenny, " your birthday was over at five minutes past twelve this morning."

" When will it come again? "

" Not for a whole year," said Mamma.

" I wish it would come to-morrow."

Mamma shook her head at her. " You want to be spoiled and petted every day."

" No. No. I want — I want — "

" She doesn't know what she wants," said Jenny.

" Yes. I do. I *do*."

" Well — "

" I want to love Papa every day. 'Cause he gave me my lamb."

" Oh," said Mamma, " if you only love people because they give you birthday presents — "

" But I don't — I don't — really and truly — "

"You didn't ought to have no more birthdays," said
Jenny, "if they make you cry."

Why couldn't they see that crying meant that she wanted
Papa to be sacred and holy every day?

The day after the birthday when Papa went about the
same as ever, looking big and frightening, when he "Baa'd"
into her face and called out, "Mary had a little lamb!" and
"Mary, Mary, quite contrary," she looked after him sorrowfully and thought: "Papa gave me my lamb."

IX

One day Uncle Edward and Aunt Bella came over from
Chadwell Grange. They were talking to Mamma a long
time in the drawing-room, and when she came in they
stopped and whispered.

Roddy told her the secret. Uncle Edward was going to
give her a live lamb.

Mark and Dank said it couldn't be true. Uncle Edward
was not a real uncle; he was only Aunt Bella's husband, and
he never gave you anything. And anyhow the lamb wasn't
born yet and couldn't come for weeks and weeks.

Every morning she asked, "Has my new lamb come?
When is it coming? Do you think it will come to-day?"

She could keep on sitting still quite a long time by merely
thinking about the new lamb. It would run beside her
when she played in the garden. It would eat grass out of
her hand. She would tie a ribbon round its neck and lead
it up and down the lane. At these moments she forgot the
toy lamb. It stood on the chest of drawers in the nursery,
looking off into the corners of the room, neglected.

By the time Uncle Edward and Aunt Bella sent for her
to come and see the lamb, she knew exactly what it would be
like and what would happen. She saw it looking like the
lambs in the Bible Picture Book, fat, and covered with
thick, pure white wool. She saw Uncle Edward, with his
yellow face and big nose and black whiskers, coming to her
across the lawn at Chadwell Grange, carrying the lamb over
his shoulder like Jesus.

It was a cold morning. They drove a long time in Uncle

Edward's carriage, over the hard, loud roads, between fields white with frost, and Uncle Edward was not on his lawn.

Aunt Bella stood in the big hall, waiting for them. She looked much larger and more important than Mamma.

"Aunt Bella, have you got my new lamb?"

She tried not to shriek it out, because Aunt Bella was nearly always poorly, and Mamma told her that if you shrieked at her she would be ill.

Mamma said "Sh-sh-sh!" And Aunt Bella whispered something and she heard Mamma answer, "Better not."

"If she *sees* it," said Aunt Bella, "she'll understand."

Mamma shook her head at Aunt Bella.

"Edward would like it," said Aunt Bella. "He wanted to give it her himself. It's *his* present."

Mamma took her hand and they followed Aunt Bella through the servants' hall into the kitchen. The servants were all there, Rose and Annie and Cook, and Mrs. Fisher, the housekeeper, and Giles, the young footman. They all stared at her in a queer, kind way as she came in.

A low screen was drawn close round one corner of the fireplace; Uncle Edward and Pidgeon, the bailiff, were doing something to it with a yellow horse-cloth.

Uncle Edward came to her, looking down the side of his big nose. He led her to the screen and drew it away.

Something lay on the floor wrapped in a piece of dirty blanket. When Uncle Edward pushed back the blanket a bad smell came out. He said, "Here's your lamb, Mary. You're just in time."

She saw a brownish grey animal with a queer, hammer-shaped head and long black legs. Its body was drawn out and knotted like an enormous maggot. It lay twisted to one side and its eyes were shut.

"That isn't my lamb."

"It's the lamb I always said Miss Mary was to have, isn't it, Pidgeon?"

"Yes, Squoire, it's the lamb you bid me set asoide for little Missy."

"Then," said Mary, "why does it look like that?"

"It's very ill," Mamma said gently. "Poor Uncle Edward thought you'd like to see it before it died. You *are* glad you've seen it, aren't you?"

"No."

Just then the lamb stirred in its blanket; it opened its eyes and looked at her.

She thought: "It's my lamb. It looked at me. It's *my* lamb and it's dying. My *lamb's* dying."

The bad smell came again out of the blanket. She tried not to think of it. She wanted to sit down on the floor beside the lamb and lift it out of its blanket and nurse it; but Mamma wouldn't let her.

When she got home Mamma took down the toy lamb from the chest of drawers and brought it to her.

She sat quiet a long time holding it in her lap and stroking it.

The stiff eyes of the toy lamb stared away over its ears.

III

I

JENNY was cross and tugged at your hair when she dressed you to go to Chadwell Grange.

"Jenny-Wee, Mamma says if I'm not good Aunt Bella will be ill. Do you think it's really true?"

Jenny tugged. "I'd thank you for some of your Aunt Bella's illness," she said.

"I mean," Mary said, "like Papa was in the night. Every time I get 'cited and jump about I think she'll open her mouth and begin."

"Well, if she was to you'd oughter be sorry for her."

"I *am* sorry for her. But I'm frightened too."

"That's not being good," said Jenny. But she left off tugging.

Somehow you knew she was pleased to think you were not really good at Aunt Bella's, where Mrs. Fisher dressed and undressed you and you were allowed to talk to Pidgeon.

Roddy and Dank said you ought to hate Uncle Edward and Pidgeon and Mrs. Fisher, and not to like Aunt Bella very much, even if she *was* Mamma's sister. Mamma didn't really like Uncle Edward; she only pretended because of Aunt Bella.

Uncle Edward had an ugly nose and a yellow face widened by his black whiskers; his mouth stretched from one whisker to the other, and his black hair curled in large tufts above his ears. But he had no beard; you could see the whole of his mouth at once; and when Aunt Bella came into the room his little blue eyes looked up off the side of his nose and he smiled at her between his tufts of hair. It was dreadful to think that Mark and Dank and Roddy didn't like him. It might hurt him so much that he would never be happy again.

About Pidgeon she was not quite sure. Pidgeon was very ugly. He had long stiff legs, and a long stiff face finished off with a fringe of red whiskers that went on under his chin. Still, it was not nice to think of Pigeon being unhappy either. But Mrs. Fisher was large and rather like Aunt Bella, only softer and more bulging. Her round face had a high red polish on it always, and when she saw you coming her eyes twinkled, and her red forehead and her big cheeks and her mouth smiled all together a fat, simmering smile. When you got to the black and white marble tiles you saw her waiting for you at the foot of the stairs.

She wanted to ask Mrs. Fisher if it was true that Aunt Bella would be ill if she were naughty; but a squeezing and dragging came under her waist whenever she thought about it, and that made her shy and ashamed. It went when they left her to play by herself on the lawn in front of the house.

Aunt Bella's house was enormous. Two long rows of windows stared out at you, their dark green storm shutters folded back on the yellow brick walls. A third row of little squeezed-up windows and little squeezed-up shutters blinked in the narrow space under the roof. All summer a sweet smell came from that side of the house where cream-coloured roses hung on the yellow walls between the green shutters. There was a cedar tree on the lawn and a sun-dial and a stone fountain. Goldfish swam in the clear greenish water. The flowers in the round beds were stiff and shining, as if they had been cut out of tin and freshly painted. When you thought of Aunt Bella's garden you saw calceolarias, brown velvet purses with yellow spots.

She could always get away from Aunt Bella by going

down the dark walk between the yew hedge and the window of Mrs. Fisher's room, and through the stable-yard into the plantation. The cocks and hens had their black timber house there in the clearing, and Ponto, the Newfoundland, lived all by himself in his kennel under the little ragged fir trees.

When Ponto saw her coming he danced on his hind legs and strained at his chain and called to her with his loud, barking howl. He played with her, crawling on his stomach, crouching, raising first one big paw and then the other. She put out her foot, and he caught it and held it between his big paws, and looked at it with his head on one side, smiling. She squealed with delight, and Ponto barked again.

The stable bell would ring while they played in the plantation, and Uncle Edward or Pidgeon or Mrs. Fisher would come out and find her and take her back into the house. Ponto lifted up his head and howled after her as she went.

At lunch Mary sat quivering between Mamma and Aunt Bella. The squeezing and dragging under her waist had begun again. There was a pattern of green ivy round the dinner plates and a pattern of goats round the silver napkin rings. She tried to fix her mind on the ivy and the goats instead of looking at Aunt Bella to see whether she were going to be ill. She *would* be if you left mud in the hall on the black and white marble tiles. Or if you took Ponto off the chain and let him get into the house. Or if you spilled the gravy.

Aunt Bella's face was much pinker and richer and more important than Mamma's face. She thought she wouldn't have minded quite so much if Aunt Bella had been white and brown and pretty, like Mamma.

There — she had spilled the gravy.

Little knots came in Aunt Bella's pink forehead. Her face loosened and swelled with a red flush; her mouth pouted and drew itself in again, pulled out of shape by something that darted up the side of her nose and made her blink.

She thought: " I know — I know — I *know* it's going to happen."

It didn't. Aunt Bella only said, " You should look at your plate and spoon, dear."

After lunch, when they were resting, you could feel naughtiness coming on. Then Pidgeon carried you on his back to the calf-shed; or Mrs. Fisher took you up into her bedroom to see her dress.

In Mrs. Fisher's bedroom a smell of rotten apples oozed through the rosebud pattern on the walls. There were no doors inside, only places in the wall-paper that opened. Behind one of these places there was a cupboard where Mrs. Fisher kept her clothes. Sometimes she would take the lid off the big box covered with wall-paper and show you her Sunday bonnet. You sat on the bed, and she gave you peppermint balls to suck while she peeled off her black merino and squeezed herself into her black silk. You watched for the moment when the brooch with the black tomb and the weeping willow on it was undone and Mrs. Fisher's chin came out first by the open collar and Mrs. Fisher began to swell. When she stood up in her petticoat and bodice she was enormous; her breasts and hips and her great arms shook as she walked about the room.

Mary was sorry when she said good-bye to Uncle Edward and Aunt Bella and Mrs. Fisher.

For, always, as soon as she got home, Roddy rushed at her with the same questions.

" Did you let Uncle Edward kiss you? "

" Yes."

" Did you talk to Pidgeon? "

" Yes."

" Did you kiss Mrs. Fisher? "

" Yes."

And Dank said, " Have they taken Ponto off the chain yet? "

" No."

" Well, then, that shows you what pigs they are."

And when she saw Mark looking at her she felt small and silly and ashamed.

II

It was the last week of the midsummer holidays. Mark and Dank had gone to stay for three days at Aunt Bella's, and on the second day they had been sent home.

Mamma and Roddy were in the garden when they came. They were killing snails in a flower-pot by putting salt on them. The snails turned over and over on each other and spat out a green foam that covered them like soapsuds as they died.

Mark's face was red and he was smiling. Even Dank looked proud of himself and happy. They called out together, "We've been sent home."

Mamma looked up from her flower-pot.

"What did you *do?*" she said.

"We took Ponto off the chain," said Dank.

"Did he get into the house?"

"Of course he did," said Mark. "Like a shot. He got into Aunt Bella's bedroom, and Aunt Bella was in bed."

"Oh, *Mark!*"

"Uncle Edward came up just as we were getting him out. He was in an awful wax."

"I'm afraid," Dank said, "I cheeked him."

"What did you say?"

"I told him he wasn't fit to have a dog. And he said we weren't to come again; and Mark said that was all we *had* come for — to let Ponto loose."

Mamma put another snail into the flower-pot, very gently. She was smiling and at the same time trying not to smile.

"He went back," said Mark, "and raked it up again about our chasing his sheep, ages ago."

"*Did* you chase the sheep?"

"No. Of course we didn't. They started to run because they saw Pidgeon coming, and Roddy ran after them till we told him not to. The mean beast said we'd made Mary's lamb die by frightening its mother. When he only gave it her because he knew it wouldn't live. *Then* he said we'd frightened Aunt Bella."

Mary stared at them, fascinated.

"Oh, Mark, was Aunt Bella ill?"

"Of course she wasn't. She only says she's going to be to keep you quiet."

"Well," said Mamma, "she won't be frightened any more. He'll not ask you again."

"We don't care. He's not a bit of good. He won't let

us ride his horses or climb his trees or fish in his stinking
pond."

"Let Mary go there," said Dank. "*She* likes it. She
kisses Pidgeon."

"I don't," she cried. "I hate Pidgeon. I hate Uncle
Edward and Aunt Bella. I hate Mrs. Fisher."

Mamma looked up from her flower-pot, and, suddenly,
she was angry.

"For shame! They're kind to *you*," she said. "You
little naughty, ungrateful girl."

"They're *not* kind to Mark and Dank. That's why I
hate them."

She wondered why Mamma was not angry with Mark
and Dank, who had let Ponto loose and frightened Aunt
Bella.

IV

I

THAT year when Christmas came Papa gave her a red
book with a gold holly wreath on the cover. The wreath
was made out of three words: *The Children's Prize*, printed
in letters that pretended to be holly sprigs. Inside the holly
wreath was the number of the year, in fat gold letters: 1869.

Soon after Christmas she had another birthday. She was
six years old. She could write in capitals and count up to
a hundred if she were left to do it by herself. Besides
"Gentle Jesus," she could say "Cock-Robin" and "The
House that Jack Built," and "The Lord is my Shepherd"
and "The Slave in the Dismal Swamp." And she could
read all her own story books, picking out the words she
knew and making up the rest. Roddy never made up. He
was a big boy, he was eight years old.

The morning after her birthday Roddy and she were sent
into the drawing-room to Mamma. A strange lady was
there. She had chosen the high-backed chair in the middle
of the room with the Berlin wool-work parrot on it. She
sat very upright, stiff and thin between the twisted rosewood
pillars of the chair. She was dressed in a black gown made
of a great many little bands of rough crape and a few

smooth stretches of merino. Her crape veil, folded back over her hat, hung behind her head in a stiff square. A jet necklace lay flat and heavy on her small chest. When you had seen all these black things she showed you, suddenly, her white, wounded face.

Mamma called her Miss Thompson.

Miss Thompson's face was so light and thin that you thought it would break if you squeezed it. The skin was drawn tight over her jaw and the bridge of her nose and the sharp naked arches of her eye-bones. She looked at you with mournful, startled eyes that were too large for their lids; and her flat chin trembled slightly as she talked.

"This is Rodney," she said, as if she were repeating a lesson after Mamma.

Rodney leaned up against Mamma and looked proud and handsome. She had her arm round him, and every now and then she pressed it tighter to draw him to herself.

Miss Thompson said after Mamma, "And this is Mary."

Her mournful eyes moved and sparkled as if she had suddenly thought of something for herself.

"I am sure," she said, "they will be very good."

Mamma shook her head, as much as to say Miss Thompson must not build on it.

Every weekday from ten to twelve Miss Thompson came and taught them reading, writing and arithmetic. Every Wednesday at half-past eleven the boys' tutor, Mr. Sippett, looked in and taught Rodney "*Mensa*, a table."

Mamma told them they must never be naughty with Miss Thompson because her mother was dead.

They went away and talked about her among the gooseberry bushes at the bottom of the garden.

"I don't know how we're going to manage," Rodney said. "There's no sense in saying we mustn't be naughty because her mother's dead."

"I suppose," Mary said, "it would make her think she's deader."

"We can't help that. We've got to be naughty some time."

"We mustn't begin," Mary said. "If we begin we shall have to finish."

They were good for four days, from ten to twelve. And at a quarter past twelve on the fifth day Mamma found Mary crying in the dining-room.

" Oh, Mary, have you been naughty? "

" No; but I shall be to-morrow. I've been so good that I can't keep on any longer."

Mamma took her in her lap. She lowered her head to you, holding it straight and still, ready to pounce if you said the wrong thing.

" Being good when it pleases you isn't being good," she said. " It's not what Jesus means by being good. God wants us to be good all the time, like Jesus."

" But — Jesus and me is different. He wasn't able to be naughty. And I'm not able to be good. Not *all* the time."

" You're not able to be good of your own will and in your own strength. You're not good till God makes you good."

" Did God make me naughty? "

" No. God couldn't make anybody naughty."

" Not if he tried *hard?* "

" No. But," said Mamma, speaking very fast, " he'll make you good if you ask him."

" Will he make me good if I don't ask him? "

" No," said Mamma.

II

Miss Thompson —

She was always sure you would be good. And Mamma was sure you wouldn't be, or that if you were it would be for some bad reason like being sorry for Miss Thompson.

As long as Roddy was in the room Mary was sorry for Miss Thompson. And when she was left alone with her she was frightened. The squeezing and dragging under her waist began when Miss Thompson pushed her gentle, mournful face close up to see what she was doing.

She was afraid of Miss Thompson because her mother was dead.

She kept on thinking about Miss Thompson's mother. Miss Thompson's mother would be like Jenny in bed with

her cap off; and she would be like the dead field mouse that
Roddy found in the lane. She would lie on the bed with
her back bent and her head hanging loose like the dear little
field mouse; and her legs would be turned up over her stomach like his, toes and fingers clawing together. When you
touched her she would be cold and stiff, like the field mouse.
They had wrapped her up in a white sheet. Roddy said
dead people were always wrapped up in white sheets. And
Mr. Chapman had put her into a coffin like the one he was
making when he gave Dank the wood for the rabbit's house.

Every time Miss Thompson came near her she saw the
white sheet and smelt the sharp, bitter smell of the coffin.

If she was naughty Miss Thompson (who seemed to have
forgotten) would remember that her mother was dead. It
might happen any minute.

It never did. For Miss Thompson said you were good if
you knew your lessons; and at the same time you were not
naughty if you didn't know them. You might not know
them to-day; but you would know them to-morrow or the
next day.

By midsummer Mary could read the books that Dank
read. If it had not been for Mr. Sippett and "*Mensa:* a
table," she would have known as much as Roddy.

Almost before they had time to be naughty Miss Thompson had gone. Mamma said that Roddy was not getting on
fast enough.

V

I

THE book that Aunt Bella had brought her was called
The Triumph Over Midian, and Aunt Bella said that if she
was a good girl it would interest her. But it did not interest her. That was how she heard Aunt Bella and Mamma
talking together.

Mamma's foot was tapping on the footstool, which showed
that she was annoyed.

" They're coming to-morrow," she said, " to look at that
house at Ilford."

" To live? " Aunt Bella said.

" To live," Mamma said.

" And is Emilius going to allow it? What's Victor thinking of, bringing her down here? "

" They want to be near Emilius. They think he'll look after her."

" It was Victor who *would* have her at home, and Victor might look after her himself. She was his favourite sister."

" He doesn't want to be too responsible. They think Emilius ought to take his share."

Aunt Bella whispered something. And Mamma said, " Stuff and nonsense! No more than you or I. Only you never know what queer thing she'll do next."

Aunt Bella said, " She was always queer as long as I remember her."

Mamma's foot went tap, tap again.

" She's been sending away things worse than ever. Dolls. Those naked ones."

Aunt Bella gave herself a shake and said something that sounded like " Goo-oo-sh! " And then, " Going to be married? "

Mamma said, " Going to be married."

And Aunt Bella said " T-t-t."

They were talking about Aunt Charlotte.

Mamma went on: " She's packed off all her clothes. Her new ones. Sent them to Matilda. Thinks she won't have to wear them any more."

" You mustn't expect me to have Charlotte Olivier in my house," Aunt Bella said. " If anybody came to call it would be most unpleasant."

" I wouldn't mind," Mamma said, tap-tapping, " if it was only Charlotte. But there's Lavvy and her Opinions."

Aunt Bella said " Pfoo-oof! " and waved her hands as if she were clearing the air.

" All I can say is," Mamma said, " that if Lavvy Olivier brings her Opinions into this house Emilius and I will walk out of it."

To-morrow — they were coming to-morrow, Uncle Victor and Aunt Lavvy and Aunt Charlotte.

II

They were coming to lunch, and everybody was excited.
Mark and Dank were in their trousers and Eton jackets,
and Roddy in his new black velvet suit. The drawing-
room was dressed out in its green summer chintzes that
shone and crackled with glaze. Mamma had moved the big
Chinese bowl from the cabinet to the round mahogany table
and filled it with white roses. You could see them again
in the polish; blurred white faces swimming on the dark,
wine-coloured pool. You held out your face to be washed
in the clear, cool scent of the white roses.

When Mark opened the door a smell of roast chicken
came up the kitchen stairs.

It was like Sunday, except that you were excited.

"Look at Papa," Roddy whispered. "Papa's excited."

Papa had come home early from the office. He stood by
the fireplace in the long tight frock-coat that made him look
enormous. He had twirled back his moustache to show his
rich red mouth. He had put something on his beard that
smelt sweet. You noticed for the first time how the frizzed,
red-brown mass sprang from a peak of silky golden hair
under his pouting lower lip. He was letting himself gently
up and down with the tips of his toes, and he was smiling,
secretly, as if he had just thought of something that he
couldn't tell Mamma. Whenever he looked at Mamma she
put her hand up to her hair and patted it.

Mamma had done her hair a new way. The brown plait
stood up farther back on the edge of the sloping chignon.
She wore her new lavender and white striped muslin.
Lavender ribbon streamed from the pointed opening of her
bodice. A black velvet ribbon was tied tight round her
neck; a jet cross hung from it and a diamond star twinkled
in the middle of the cross. She pushed out her mouth and
drew it in again, like Roddy's rabbit, and the tip of her nose
trembled as if it knew all the time what Papa was thinking.

She was so soft and pretty that you could hardly bear it.
Mark stood behind her chair and when Papa was not looking
he kissed her. The behaviour of her mouth and nose gave
you a delicious feeling that with Aunt Lavvy and Aunt
Charlotte you wouldn't have to be so very good.

The front door bell rang. Papa and Mamma looked at each other, as much as to say, "*Now* it's going to begin." And suddenly Mamma looked small and frightened. She took Mark's hand.

"Emilius," she said, "what am I to say to Lavinia?"

"You don't say anything," Papa said. "Mary can talk to Lavinia."

Mary jumped up and down with excitement. She knew how it would be. In another minute Aunt Charlotte would come in, dressed in her black lace shawl and crinoline, and Aunt Lavvy would bring her Opinions. And something, something that you didn't know, would happen.

III

Aunt Charlotte came in first with a tight, dancing run. You knew her by the long black curls on her shoulders. She was smiling as she smiled in the album. She bent her head as she bent it in the album, and her eyes looked up close under her black eyebrows and pointed at you. Pretty — pretty blue eyes, and something frightening that made you look at them. And something queer about her narrow jaw. It thrust itself forward, jerking up her smile.

No black lace shawl and no crinoline. Aunt Charlotte wore a blue and black striped satin dress, bunched up behind, and a little hat perched on the top of her chignon and tied underneath it with blue ribbons.

She had got in and was kissing everybody while Aunt Lavvy and Uncle Victor were fumbling with the hat stand in the hall.

Aunt Lavvy came next. A long grey face. Black bands of hair parted on her broad forehead. Black eyebrows; blue eyes that stuck out wide, that didn't point at you. A grey bonnet, a grey dress, a little white shawl with a narrow fringe, drooping.

She walked slowly — slowly, as if she were still thinking of something that was not in the room, as if she came into a quiet, empty room.

You thought at first she was never going to kiss you, she was so tall and her face and eyes held themselves so still.

Uncle Victor. Dark and white; smaller than Papa, smaller than Aunt Lavvy; thin in his loose frock-coat. His forehead and black eyebrows were twisted above his blue, beautiful eyes. He had a small dark brown moustache and a small dark brown beard, trimmed close and shaped prettily to a point. He looked like something, like somebody; like Dank when he was mournful, like Dank's dog, Tibby, when he hid from Papa. He said, " Well, Caroline. Well, Emilius."

Aunt Charlotte gave out sharp cries of " Dear! " and " Darling! " and smothered them against your face in a sort of moan.

When she came to Roddy she put up her hands.

" Roddy — yellow hair. No. No. What have you done with the blue eyes and black hair, Emilius? That comes of letting your beard grow so long."

Then they all went into the dining-room.

It was like a birthday. There was to be real blancmange, and preserved ginger, and you drank raspberry vinegar out of the silver christening cups the aunts and uncles gave you when you were born. Uncle Victor had given Mary hers. She held it up and read her own name on it.

MARY VICTORIA OLIVIER

1863.

They were all telling their names. Mary took them up and chanted them: " Mark Emilius Olivier; Daniel Olivier; Rodney Olivier; Victor Justus Olivier; Lavinia Mary Olivier; Charlotte Louisa Olivier." She liked the sound of them.

She sat between Uncle Victor and Aunt Lavvy. Roddy was squeezed into the corner between Mamma and Mark. Aunt Charlotte sat opposite her between Mark and Daniel. She *had* to look at Aunt Charlotte's face. There were faint grey smears on it as if somebody had scribbled all over it with pencil.

A remarkable conversation.

" Aunt Lavvy! Aunt Lavvy! Have you brought your Opinions? "

" No, my dear, they were not invited. So I left them at home."

" I'm glad to hear it," Papa said.

" Will you bring them next time? "

" No. Not next time, nor any other time," Aunt Lavvy said, looking straight at Papa.

" Did you shut them up in the stair cupboard? "

" No, but I may have to some day."

" Then," Mary said, " if there are any little ones, may I have one? "

" May she, Emilius? "

" Certainly not," Papa said. " She's got too many little opinions of her own."

" What do you know about opinions? " Uncle Victor said.

Mary was excited and happy. She had never been allowed to talk so much. She tried to eat her roast chicken in a business-like, grown-up manner, while she talked.

" I've read about them," she said. " They are dear little animals with long furry tails, much bigger than Sarah's tail, and they climb up trees."

" Oh, they climb up trees, do they? " Uncle Victor was very polite and attentive.

" Yes. There's their picture in Dank's Natural History Book. Next to the Ornythrincus or Duck-billed Plat-i-pus. If they came into the house Mamma would be frightened. But I would not be frightened. I should stroke them."

" Do you think," Uncle Victor said, still politely, " you *quite* know what you mean? "

" *I* know," Daniel said, " she means opossums."

" Yes," Mary said. " Opossums."

" What *are* opinions? "

" Opinions," Papa said, " are things that people put in other people's heads. Nasty, dangerous things, opinions."

She thought: " That was why Mamma and Papa were frightened."

" You won't put them into Mamma's head, will you, Aunt Lavvy? "

Mamma said, " Get on with your dinner. Papa's only teasing."

Aunt Lavvy's face flushed slowly, and she held her mouth

tight, as if she were trying not to cry. Papa was teasing Aunt Lavvy.

"How do you like that Ilford house, Charlotte?" Mamma asked suddenly.

"It's the nicest little house you ever saw," Aunt Charlotte said. "But it's too far away. I'd rather have any ugly, poky old den that was next door. I want to see all I can of you and Emilius and Dan and little darling Mary. Before I go away."

"You aren't thinking of going away when you've only just come?"

"That's what Victor and Lavinia say. But you don't suppose I'm going to stay an old maid all my life to please Victor and Lavinia."

"I haven't thought about it at all," Mamma said.

"*They* have. *I* know what they're thinking. But it's all settled. I'm going to Marshall and Snelgrove's for my things. There's a silver-grey poplin in their window. If I decide on it, Caroline, you shall have my grey watered silk.

"You needn't waggle your big beard at me, Emilius," Aunt Charlotte said.

Papa pretended that he hadn't heard her and began to talk to Uncle Victor.

"Did you read John Bright's speech in Parliament last night?"

Uncle Victor said, "I did."

"What did you think of it?"

Uncle Victor raised his shoulders and his eyebrows and spread out his thin, small hands.

"A man with a face like that," Aunt Charlotte said, "oughtn't to *be* in Parliament."

"He's the man who saved England," said Papa.

"What's the good of that if he can't save himself? Where does he expect to go to with the hats he wears?"

"Where does Emilius expect to go to," Uncle Victor said, "when his John Bright and his Gladstone get their way?"

Suddenly Aunt Charlotte left off smiling.

"Emilius," she said, "do you uphold Gladstone?"

"Of course I uphold Gladstone. There's nobody in this country fit to black his boots."

"I know nothing about his boots. But he's an infidel.
He wants to pull down the Church. I thought you were a
Churchman?"

"So I am," Papa said. "I've too good an opinion of the
Church to imagine that it can't stand alone."

"You're a nice one to talk about opinions."

"At any rate I know what I'm talking about."

"I'm not so sure of that," said Aunt Charlotte.

Aunt Lavvy smiled gently at the pattern of the tablecloth.

"Do you agree with him, Lavvy?" Mamma had found
something to say.

"I agree with him better than he agrees with himself."

A long conversation about things that interested Papa.
Blanc-mange going round the table, quivering and shaking
and squelching under the spoon.

"There's a silver-grey poplin," said Aunt Charlotte, "at
Marshall and Snelgrove's."

The blanc-mange was still going round. Mamma watched
it as it went. She was fascinated by the shivering, white
blanc-mange.

"If there was only one man in the world," Aunt Charlotte
said in a loud voice, "and he had a flowing beard, I wouldn't
marry him."

Papa drew himself up. He looked at Mark and Daniel
and Roddy as if he were saying, "Whoever takes notice
leaves the room."

Roddy laughed first. He was sent out of the room.

Papa looked at Mark. Mark clenched his teeth, holding
his laugh down tight. He seemed to think that as long as
it didn't come out of his mouth he was safe. It came out
through his nose like a loud, tearing sneeze. Mark was sent
out of the room.

Daniel threw down his spoon and fork.

"If he goes, I go," Daniel said, and followed him.

Papa looked at Mary.

"What are *you* grinning at, you young monkey?"

"Emilius," said Aunt Charlotte, "if you send another
child out of the room, I go too."

Mary squealed, "Tee-he-he-he-he-*hee!* Te-*hee!*" and
was sent out of the room.

She and Aunt Charlotte sat on the stairs outside the dining-room door. Aunt Charlotte's arm was round her; every now and then it gave her a sudden, loving squeeze.

"Darling Mary. Little darling Mary. Love Aunt Charlotte," she said.

Mark and Dank and Roddy watched them over the banisters.

Aunt Charlotte put her hand deep down in her pocket and brought out a little parcel wrapped in white paper. She whispered:

"If I give you something to keep, will you promise not to show it to anybody and not to tell?"

Mary promised.

Inside the paper wrapper there was a match-box, and inside the match-box there was a china doll no bigger than your finger. It had blue eyes and black hair and no clothes on. Aunt Charlotte held it in her hand and smiled at it.

"That's Aunt Charlotte's little baby," she said. "I'm going to be married and I shan't want it any more.

"There — take it, and cover it up, quick!"

Mamma had come out of the dining-room. She shut the door behind her.

"What have you given to Mary?" she said.

"Butter-Scotch," said Aunt Charlotte.

IV

All afternoon till tea-time Papa and Uncle Victor walked up and down the garden path, talking to each other. Every now and then Mark and Mary looked at them from the nursery window.

That night she dreamed that she saw Aunt Charlotte standing at the foot of the kitchen stairs taking off her clothes and wrapping them in white paper; first, her black lace shawl; then her chemise. She stood up without anything on. Her body was polished and shining like an enormous white china doll. She lowered her head and pointed at you with her eyes.

When you opened the stair cupboard door to catch the opossum, you found a white china doll lying in it, no bigger than your finger. That was Aunt Charlotte.

In the dream there was no break between the end and the beginning. But when she remembered it afterwards it split into two pieces with a dark gap between. She knew she had only dreamed about the cupboard; but Aunt Charlotte at the foot of the stairs was so clear and solid that she thought she had really seen her.

Mamma had told Aunt Bella all about it when they talked together that day, in the drawing-room. She knew because she could still see them sitting, bent forward with their heads touching, Aunt Bella in the big arm-chair by the hearth-rug, and Mamma on the parrot chair.

END OF BOOK ONE

BOOK TWO

CHILDHOOD

1869–1875

BOOK TWO

CHILDHOOD

VI

I

WHEN Christmas came Papa gave her another *Children's Prize*. This time the cover was blue and the number on it was 1870. Eighteen-seventy was the name of the New Year that was coming after Christmas. It meant that the world had gone on for one thousand eight hundred and seventy years since Jesus was born. Every year she was to have a *Children's Prize* with the name of the New Year on it.

Eighteen-seventy was a beautiful number. It sounded nice, and there was a seven in it. Seven was a sacred and holy number; so was three, because of the three Persons, the Father, the Son and the Holy Ghost, and because of the seven stars and the seven golden candlesticks. When you said good-night to Mamma you kissed her either three times or seven times. If you went past three you had to go on to seven, because something dreadful would happen if you didn't. Sometimes Mamma stopped you; then you stooped down and finished up on the hem of her dress, quick, before she could see you.

She was glad that the *Children's Prize* had a blue cover, because blue was a sacred and holy colour. It was the colour of the ceiling in St. Mary's Chapel at Ilford, and it was the colour of the Virgin Mary's dress.

There were golden stars all over the ceiling of St. Mary's Chapel. Roddy and she were sent there after they had had chicken-pox and when their whooping-cough was getting better. They were not allowed to go to the church at Bark-

41

ingside for fear of giving whooping-cough to the children in
Dr. Barnardo's Homes; and they were not allowed to go to
Aldborough Hatch Church because of Mr. Propart's pupils.
But they had to go to church somewhere, whooping-cough
or no whooping-cough, in order to get to Heaven; so Mark
took them to the Chapel of Ease at Ilford, where the Virgin
Mary in a blue dress stood on a sort of step over the door.
Mamma said you were not to worship her, though you might
look at her. She was a graven image. Only Roman Catholics worshipped graven images; they were heretics; that
meant that they were shut outside the Church of England,
which was God's Church, and couldn't get in. And they
had only half a Sunday. In Roman Catholic countries Sunday was all over at twelve o'clock, and for the rest of the
day the Roman Catholics could do just what they pleased;
they danced and went to theatres and played games, as if
Sunday was one of their own days and not God's day.

She wished she had been born in a Roman Catholic
country.

Every night she took the *Children's Prize* to bed with her
to keep her safe. It had Bible Puzzles in it, and among
them there was a picture of the Name of God. A shining
white light, shaped like Mamma's vinaigrette, with black
marks in the middle. Mamma said the light was the light
that shone above the Ark of the Covenant, and the black
marks were letters and the word was the real name of God.
She said he was sometimes called Jehovah, but that was not
his real name. His real name was a secret name which
nobody but the High Priest was allowed to say.

When you lay in the dark and shut your eyes tight and
waited, you could see the light, shaped like the vinaigrette,
in front of you. It quivered and shone brighter, and you
saw in the middle, first, a dark blue colour, and then the
black marks that were the real name of God. She was glad
she couldn't read it, for she would have been certain to let
it out some day when she wasn't thinking.

Perhaps Mamma knew, and was not allowed to say it.
Supposing she forgot?

At church they sang " Praise Him in His name Jah and
rejoice before Him." Jah was God's pet-name, short for

Jehovah. It was a silly name — Jah. Somehow you couldn't help thinking of God as a silly person; he was always flying into tempers, and he was jealous. He was like Papa. Dank said Papa was jealous of Mark because Mamma was so fond of him. There was a picture of God in the night nursery. He had a big flowing beard, and a very straight nose, like Papa, and he was lying on a sort of sofa that was a cloud. Little Jesus stood underneath him, between the Virgin Mary and Joseph, and the Holy Ghost was descending on him in the form of a dove. His real name was Jesus Christ, but they called him Emmanuel.

> " There is a fountain filled with blood
>   Drawn from Emmanuel's veins;
> And sinners plunged beneath that flood
>   Lose all their guilty stains."

That was another frightening thing. It would be like the fountain in Aunt Bella's garden, with blood in it instead of water. The goldfishes would die.

Mark was pleased when she said that Sarah wouldn't be allowed to go to Heaven because she would try to catch the Holy Ghost.

Jesus was not like God. He was good and kind. When he grew up he was always dressed in pink and blue, and he had sad dark eyes and a little, close, tidy beard like Uncle Victor. You could love Jesus.

Jenny loved him. She was a Wesleyan; and her niece Catty was a Wesleyan. Catty marched round and round the kitchen table with the dish-cloth, drying the plates and singing:

> " ' I love Jesus, yes, I do,
>   *For* the Bible tells me *to!* ' "

and

> " ' I am so glad that my Father in Heaven
>   Tells of His love in the book He has given —
> I am so glad that Jesus loves me,
>   Jesus loves me,
>   Jesus loves even me! ' "

On New Year's Eve Jenny and Catty went to the Wesleyan Chapel at Ilford to sing the New Year in. Catty talked about the Old Year as if it was horrid and the New Year as if it was nice. She said that at twelve o'clock you ought to open the window wide and let the Old Year go out and the New Year come in. If you didn't something dreadful would happen.

Downstairs there was a party. Uncle Victor and Aunt Lavvy and Aunt Charlotte were there, and the big boys from Vinings and the Vicarage at Aldborough Hatch. Mark and Dank and Roddy were sitting up, and Roddy had promised to wake her when the New Year was coming.

He left the door open so that she could hear the clock strike twelve. She got up and opened the windows ready. There were three in Mamma's room. She opened them all.

The air outside was like clear black water and very cold. You couldn't see the garden wall; the dark fields were close — close against the house. One — Two — Three.

Seven — When the last stroke sounded the New Year would have come in.

Ten — Eleven — Twelve.

The bells rang out; the bells of Ilford, the bells of Barkingside, and far beyond the flats and the cemetery there would be Bow bells, and beyond that the bells of the City of London. They clanged together and she trembled. The sounds closed over her; they left off and began again, not very loud, but tight — tight, crushing her heart, crushing tears out of her eyelids. When the bells stopped there was a faint whirring sound. That was the Old Year, that was eighteen sixty-nine, going out by itself in the dark, going away over the fields.

Mamma was not pleased when she came to bed and found the door and windows open and Mary awake in the cot.

II

At the end of January she was seven years old. Something was bound to happen when you were seven.

She was moved out of Mamma's room to sleep by herself on the top floor in the night nursery. And the day nursery was turned into the boys' schoolroom.

When you were little and slept in the cot behind the curtain Mamma would sometimes come and read you to sleep with the bits you wanted: " The Lord is my Shepherd," and " Or ever the silver cord be loosed or the golden bowl be broken, or the pitcher be broken at the fountain or the wheel broken at the cistern," and " the city had no need of the sun, neither of the moon, to shine in it; for the glory of God did lighten it, and the Lamb is the light thereof."

When you were frightened she taught you to say, " He that dwelleth in the secret place of the Most High shall abide under the shadow of the Almighty. . . . He shall cover thee with His feathers and under His wings shalt thou trust. . . . Thou shalt not be afraid for the terror by night." And you were allowed to have a night-light.

Now it was all different. You went to bed half an hour later, while Mamma was dressing for dinner, and when she came to tuck you up the bell rang and she had to run downstairs, quick, so as not to keep Papa waiting. You hung on to her neck and untucked yourself, and she always got away before you could kiss her seven times. And there was no night-light. You had to read the Bible in the morning, and it always had to be the bits Mamma wanted, out of Genesis and the Gospel of St. John.

You had to learn about the one God and the three Persons. The one God was the nice, clever, happy God who made Mamma and Mark and Jenny and the sun and Sarah and the kittens. He was the God you really believed in.

At night when you lay on your back in the dark you thought about being born and about arithmetic and God. The sacred number three went into eighteen sixty-nine and didn't come out again; so did seven. She liked numbers that fitted like that with no loose ends left over. Mr. Sippett said there were things you could do with the loose ends of numbers to make them fit. That was fractions. Supposing there was somewhere in the world a number that simply wouldn't fit? Mr. Sippett said there was no such number. But queer things happened. You were seven years old, yet you had had eight birthdays. There was the day you were born, January the twenty-fourth, eighteen sixty-three, at five o'clock in the morning. When you were born you weren't any age at all, not a minute old, not a second, not half a second.   But there was eighteen sixty-two and there was January the twenty-third and the minute just before you were born.   You couldn't really tell when the twenty-third ended and the twenty-fourth began; because when you counted sixty minutes for the hour and sixty seconds for the minute, there was still the half second and the half of that, and so on for ever and ever.

You couldn't tell when you were really born.   And nobody could tell you what being born was.   Perhaps nobody knew. Jenny said being born was just being born.   Sarah's grand-children were born in the garden under the wall where the jasmine grew.   Roddy shouted at the back door, and when you ran to look he stretched out his arms across the doorway and wouldn't let you through.   Roddy was excited and frightened; and Mamma said he had been very good because he stood across the door.

There was being born and there was dying.   If you died this minute there would be the minute after.   Then, if you were good, your soul was in Heaven and your body was cold and stiff like Miss Thompson's mother.   And there was Lazarus.   " He hath been in the grave four days and by this time he stinketh."   That was dreadfully frightening; but they had to say it to show that Lazarus was really dead. That was how you could tell.

" ' Lord, if thou hadst been here our brother had not died.' "

That was beautiful.   When you thought of it you wanted to cry.

Supposing Mamma died?   Supposing Mark died?   Or Dank or Roddy?   Or even Uncle Victor?   Even Papa?

They couldn't.   Jesus wouldn't let them.

When you were frightened in the big dark room you thought about God and Jesus and the Holy Ghost.   They didn't leave you alone a single minute.   God and Jesus stood beside the bed, and Jesus kept God in a good temper, and the Holy Ghost flew about the room and perched on the top of the linen cupboard, and bowed and bowed, and said, " Rook-ke-heroo-oo!   Rook-ke-keroo-oo! "

And there was the parroquet.

Mark had given her the stuffed parroquet on her birth-

day, and Mamma had given her the Bible and the two grey
china vases to make up, with a bird painted on each. A
black bird with a red beak and red legs. She had set them
up on the chimney-piece under the picture of the Holy
Family. She put the Bible in the middle and the parroquet
on the top of the Bible and the vases one on each side.

She worshipped them, because of Mamma and Mark.

She said to herself: "God won't like *that*, but I can't
help it. The kind, clever God won't mind a bit. He's much
too busy making things. And it's not as if they were graven
images."

III

Jenny had taken her for a walk to Ilford and they were
going home to the house in Ley Street.

There were only two walks that Jenny liked to go: down
Ley Street to Barkingside where the little shops were; and
up Ley Street to Ilford and Mr. Spall's, the cobbler's. She
liked Ilford best because of Mr. Spall. She carried your
boots to Mr. Spall just as they were getting comfortable;
she was always ferreting in Sarah's cupboard for a pair to
take to him. Mr. Spall was very tall and lean; he had thick
black eyebrows rumpled up the wrong way and a long nose
with a red knob at the end of it. A dirty grey beard hung
under his chin, and his long, shaved lips curled over in a
disagreeable way when he smiled at you.

When Jenny and Catty went to sing the New Year in
at the Wesleyan Chapel he brought them home. Jenny
liked him because his wife was dead, and because he was a
Wesleyan and Deputy Grand Master of the Independent
Order of Good Templars. You had to shake hands with him
to say good-bye. He always said the same thing: "Next
time you come, little Missy, I'll show you the Deputy
Regalia." But he never did.

To-day Jenny had made her stand outside in the shop,
among the old boots and the sheets of leather, while she and
Mr. Spall went into the back parlour to talk about Jesus.
The shop smelt of leather and feet and onions and of Mr.
Spall, so that she was glad when they got out again. She

wondered how Jenny could bear to sit in the back parlour with Mr. Spall.

Coming home at first she had to keep close by Jenny's side. Jenny was tired and went slowly; but by taking high prancing and dancing steps she could pretend that they were rushing along; and once they had turned the crook of Ley Street she ran on a little way in front of Jenny. Then, walking very fast and never looking back, she pretended that she had gone out by herself.

When she had passed the row of elms and the farm, and the small brown brick cottages fenced off with putty-coloured palings, she came to the low ditches and the flat fields on either side and saw on her left the bare, brown brick, pointed end of the tall house. It was called Five Elms.

Further down the road the green and gold sign of The Green Man and the scarlet and gold sign of the Horns Tavern hung high on white standards set up in the road. Further down still, where Ley Street swerved slightly towards Barkingside, three tall poplars stood in the slant of the swerve.

A queer white light everywhere, like water thin and clear. Wide fields, flat and still, like water, flooded with the thin, clear light; grey earth, shot delicately with green blades, shimmering. Ley Street, a grey road, whitening suddenly where it crossed open country, a hard causeway thrown over the flood. The high trees, the small, scattered cottages, the two taverns, the one tall house had the look of standing up in water.

She saw the queer white light for the first time and drew in her breath with a sharp check. She knew that the fields were beautiful.

She saw Five Elms for the first time: the long line of its old red-tiled roof, its flat brown face; the three rows of narrow windows, four at the bottom, with the front door at the end of the row, five at the top, five in the middle; their red brick eye-brows; their black glassy stare between the drawn-back curtains. She noticed how high and big the house looked on its slender plot of grass behind the brick wall that held up the low white-painted iron railing.

A tall iron gate between brown brick pillars, topped by stone balls. A flagged path to the front door. Crocuses, yellow, white, white and purple, growing in the border of the grass plot. She saw them for the first time.

The front door stood open. She went in.

The drawing-room at the back was full of the queer white light. Things stood out in it, sharp and suddenly strange, like the trees and houses in the light outside: the wine-red satin stripes in the grey damask curtains at the three windows; the rings of wine-red roses on the grey carpet; the tarnished pattern on the grey wall-paper; the furniture shining like dark wine; the fluted emerald green silk in the panel of the piano and the hanging bag of the work-table; the small wine-red flowers on the pale green chintz; the green Chinese bowls in the rosewood cabinet; the blue and red parrot on the chair.

Her mother sat at the far end of the room. She was sorting beads into trays in a box lined with sandal wood.

Mary stood at the doorway looking in, swinging her hat in her hand. Suddenly, without any reason, she was so happy that she could hardly bear it.

Mamma looked up. She said, "What are you doing standing there?"

She ran to her and hid her face in her lap. She caught Mamma's hands and kissed them. They smelt of sandal wood. They moved over her hair with slight quick strokes that didn't stay, that didn't care.

Mamma said, "There. That'll do. That'll do."

She climbed up on a chair and looked out of the window. She could see Mamma's small beautiful nose bending over the tray of beads, and her bright eyes that slid slantwise to look at her. And under the window she saw the brown twigs of the lilac bush tipped with green.

Her happiness was sharp and still like the white light.

Mamma said, "What did you see when you were out with Jenny to-day?"

"Nothing."

"Nothing? And what are you looking at?"

"Nothing, Mamma."

"Then go upstairs and take your things off. Quick!"

She went very slowly, holding herself with care, lest she
should jar her happiness and spill it.

One of the windows of her room was open. She stood
a little while looking out.

Beyond the rose-red wall of the garden she saw the flat
furrowed field, stripes of grey earth and vivid green. In
the middle of the field the five elms in a row, high and
slender; four standing close together, one apart. Each held
up a small rounded top, fine as a tuft of feathers.

On her left towards Ilford, a very long row of high elms
screened off the bare flats from the village. Where it ended
she saw Drake's Farm; black timbered barns and sallow
haystacks beside a clump of trees. Behind the five elms, on
the edge of the earth, a flying line of trees set wide apart,
small, thin trees, flying away low down under the sky.

She looked and looked. Her happiness mixed itself up
with the queer light and with the flat fields and the tall,
bare trees.

She turned from the window and saw the vases that
Mamma had given her standing on the chimney-piece. The
black birds with red beaks and red legs looked at her. She
threw herself on the bed and pressed her face into the pillow
and cried " Mamma! Mamma! "

IV

Passion Week. It gave you an awful feeling of something going to happen.

In the long narrow dining-room the sunlight through the
three windows made a strange and solemn blue colour in
the dark curtains. Mamma sat up at the mahogany table,
looking sad and serious, with the Prayer Book open before
her at the Litany. When you went in you knew that you
would have to read about the Crucifixion. Nothing could
save you.

Still you did find out things about God.˙ In the Epistle
it said: " ' Wherefore art thou red in thine apparel and thy
garments like him that treadeth the wine-fat? I have trodden the wine-press alone, and of the people there was none
with me: for I will tread them in my anger, and trample

them in my fury, and their blood shall be sprinkled upon my garments, and I will stain all my raiment.' "

The Passion meant that God had flown into another temper and that Jesus was crucified to make him good again. Mark said you mustn't say that to Mamma; but he owned that it looked like it. Anyhow it was easier to think of it that way than to think that God sent Jesus down to be crucified because you were naughty.

There were no verses in the Prayer-Book Bible, only long grey slabs like tombstones. You kept on looking for the last tombstone. When you came to the one with the big black letters, THE KING OF THE JEWS, you knew that it would soon be over.

" ' They clothed him with purple, and platted a crown of thorns and put it on his head. . . .' " She read obediently: " ' And when the sixth hour was come . . . and when the sixth hour was come there was darkness over the whole land until the ninth hour. And at the ninth hour Jesus cried out with a loud voice. . . . And Jesus cried with a loud voice . . . with a loud voice, and gave up the ghost.' "

Mamma was saying that the least you could do was to pay attention. But you couldn't pay attention every time. The first time it was beautiful and terrible; but after many times the beauty went and you were only frightened. When she tried to think about the crown of thorns she thought of the new hat Catty had bought for Easter Sunday and what Mr. Spall did when he ate the parsnips.

Through the barred windows of the basement she could hear Catty singing in the pantry:

> " ' I am so glad that Jesus loves me,
>   Jesus loves me,
>   Jesus loves me. . . .' "

Catty was happy when she sang and danced round and round with the dish-cloth. And Jenny and Mr. Spall were happy when they talked about Jesus. But Mamma was not happy. She had had to read the Morning Prayer and the Psalms and the Lessons and the Litany to herself every morning; and by Thursday she was tired and cross.

Passion Week gave you an awful feeling.

Good Friday would be the worst. It was the real day that Jesus died. There would be the sixth hour and the ninth hour. Perhaps there would be a darkness.

But when Good Friday came you found a smoking hot-cross bun on everybody's plate at breakfast, tasting of spice and butter. And you went to Aldborough Hatch for Service. She thought: "If the darkness does come it won't be so bad to bear at Aldborough Hatch." She liked the new white-washed church with the clear windows, where you could stand on the hassock and look out at the green hill framed in the white arch. That was Chigwell.

> " ' There is a green hill far a-a-way
> Without a city wall — ' "

The green hill hadn't got any city wall. Epping Forest and Hainault Forest were there. You could think of them, or you could look at Mr. Propart's nice clean-shaved face while he read about the Crucifixion and preached about God's mercy and his justice. He did it all in a soothing, inattentive voice; and when he had finished he went quick into the vestry as if he were glad it was all over. And when you met him at the gate he didn't look as if Good Friday mattered very much.

In the afternoon she forgot all about the sixth hour and the ninth hour. Just as she was going to think about them Mark and Dank put her in the dirty clothes-basket and rolled her down the back stairs to make her happy. They shut themselves up in the pantry till she had stopped laughing, and when Catty opened the door the clock struck and Mark said that was the ninth hour.

It was all over. And nothing had happened. Nothing at all.

Only, when you thought of what had been done to Jesus, it didn't seem right, somehow, to have eaten the hot-cross buns.

v

Grandmamma and Grandpapa Olivier were buried in the City of London Cemetery. A long time ago, so long that even Mark couldn't remember it, Uncle Victor had brought

Grandmamma in a coffin all the way from Liverpool to London in the train.

On Saturday afternoon Mamma had to put flowers on the grave for Easter Sunday, because of Uncle Victor and Aunt Lavvy. She took Roddy and Mary with her. They drove in Mr. Parish's wagonette, and called for Aunt Lavvy at Uncle Victor's tall white house at the bottom of Ilford High Street. Aunt Lavvy was on the steps, waiting for them, holding a big cross of white flowers. You could see Aunt Charlotte's face at the dining-room window looking out over the top of the brown wire blind. She had her hat on, as if she had expected to be taken too. Her eyes were sharp and angry, and Uncle Victor stood behind her with his hand on her shoulder.

Aunt Lavvy gave Mary the flower cross and climbed stiffly into the wagonette. Mary felt grown up and important holding the big cross on her knee. The white flowers gave out a thick, sweet smell.

As they drove away she kept on thinking about Aunt Charlotte, and about Uncle Victor bringing Grandmamma in a coffin in the train. It was very, very brave of him. She was sorry for Aunt Charlotte. Aunt Charlotte had wanted to go to the cemetery and they hadn't let her go. Perhaps she was still looking over the blind, sharp and angry because they wouldn't let her go.

Aunt Lavvy said, "We couldn't take Charlotte. It excited her too much last time." As if she knew what you were thinking.

The wagonette stopped by the railway-crossing at Manor Park, and they got out. Mamma told Mr. Parish to drive round to the Leytonstone side and wait for them there at the big gates. They wanted to walk through the cemetery and see what was to be seen.

Beyond the railway-crossing a muddy lane went along a field of coarse grass under a hedge of thorns and ended at a paling. Roddy whispered excitedly that they were in Wanstead Flats. The hedge shut off the cemetery from the flats; through thin places in the thorn bushes you could see tombstones, very white tombstones against very dark trees. There was a black wooden door in the hedge for you to go in

by. The lane and the thorn bushes and the black door
reminded Mary of something she had seen before somewhere. Something frightening.

When they got through the black door there were no
tombstones. What showed through the hedge were the tops
of high white pillars standing up among trees a long way off.
They had come into a dreadful, bare, clay-coloured plain,
furrowed into low mounds, as if a plough had gone criss-
cross over it.

You saw nothing but mounds. Some of them were made
of loose earth; some were patched over with rough sods that
gaped in a horrible way. Perhaps if you looked through
the cracks you would see down into the grave where the
coffin was. The mounds had a fresh, raw look, as if all
the people in the City of London had died and been buried
hurriedly the night before. And there were no stones with
names, only small, flat sticks at one end of each grave to
show where the heads were.

Roddy said, " We've got to go all through this to get to
the other side."

They could see Mamma and Aunt Lavvy a long way on in
front picking their way gingerly among the furrows. If
only Mark had been there instead of Roddy. Roddy *would*
keep on saying: " The great plague of London. The great
plague of London," to frighten himself. He pointed to a
heap of earth and said it was the first plague pit.

In the middle of the ploughed-up plain she saw people in
black walking slowly and crookedly behind a coffin that
went staggering on black legs under a black pall. She tried
not to look at them.

When she looked again they had stopped beside a heap
that Roddy said was the second plague pit. Men in black
crawled out from under the coffin as they put it down. She
could see the bulk of it flattened out under the black pall.
Against the raw, ochreish ground the figures of two mutes
stood up, black and distinct in their high hats tied in the
bunched out, streaming weepers. There was something
filthy and frightful about the figures of the mutes. And
when they dragged the pall from the coffin there was something filthy and frightful about the action.

"Roddy," she said, "I'm frightened."

Roddy said, "So am I. I say, supposing we went back? By ourselves. Across Wanstead Flats." He was excited.

"We mustn't. That would frighten Mamma."

"Well, then, we'll have to go straight through."

They went, slowly, between the rows of mounds, along a narrow path of yellow clay that squeaked as their boots went in and out. Roddy held her hand. They took care not to tread on the graves. Every step brought them nearer to the funeral. They hadn't pointed it out to each other. They had pretended it wasn't there. Now it was no use pretending; they could see the coffin.

"Roddy — I can't — I can't go past the funeral."

"We've got to."

He looked at her with solemn eyes, wide open in his beautiful face. He was not really frightened, he was only trying to be because he liked it.

They went on. The tight feeling under her waist had gone; her body felt loose and light as if it didn't belong to her; her knees were soft and sank under her. Suddenly she let go Roddy's hand. She stared at the funeral, paralysed with fright.

At the end of the path Mamma and Aunt Lavvy stood and beckoned to them. Aunt Lavvy was coming towards them, carrying her white flower cross. They broke into a stumbling, nightmare run.

The bare clay plain stretched on past the place where Mamma and Aunt Lavvy had turned. The mounds here were big and high. They found Mamma and Aunt Lavvy standing by a very deep and narrow pit. A man was climbing up out of the pit on a ladder. You could see a pool of water shining far down at the bottom.

Mamma was smiling gently and kindly at the man and asking him why the grave was dug so deep. He said, "Why, because this 'ere lot and that there what you've come acrost is the pauper buryin' ground. We shovel 'em in five at a time this end."

Roddy said, "Like they did in the great plague of London."

"I don't know about no plague. But there's five coffins in each of these here graves, piled one atop of the other."

Mamma seemed inclined to say more to the grave-digger; but Aunt Lavvy frowned and shook her head at her, and they went on to where a path of coarse grass divided the pauper burying ground from the rest. They were now quite horribly near the funeral. And going down the grass path they saw another that came towards them; the palled coffin swaying on headless shoulders. They turned from it into a furrow between the huddled mounds. The white marble columns gleamed nearer among the black trees.

They crossed a smooth gravel walk into a crowded town of dead people. Tombstones as far as you could see; upright stones, flat slabs, rounded slabs, slabs like coffins, stone boxes with flat tops, broken columns; pointed pillars. Rows of tall black trees. Here and there a single tree sticking up stiffly among the tombstones. Very little trees that were queer and terrifying. People in black moving about the tombstones. A broad road and a grey chapel with pointed gables. Under a black tree a square plot enclosed by iron railings.

Grandmamma and Grandpapa Olivier were buried in one half of the plot under a white marble slab. In the other half, on the bare grass, a white marble curb marked out a place for another grave.

Roddy said, "Who's buried there?"

Mamma said, "Nobody. Yet. That's for —"

Mary saw Aunt Lavvy frown again and put her finger to her mouth.

She said, "Who? For who?" An appalling curiosity and fear possessed her. And when Aunt Lavvy took her hand she knew that the empty place was marked out for Mamma and Papa.

Outside the cemetery gates, in the white road, the black funeral horses tossed their heads and neighed, and the black plumes quivered on the hearses. In the wagonette she sat close beside Aunt Lavvy, with Aunt Lavvy's shawl over her eyes.

She wondered how she knew that you were frightened when Mamma didn't. Mamma couldn't, because she was brave. She wasn't afraid of the funeral.

When Roddy said, "She oughtn't to have taken us, she

ought to have known it would frighten us," Mark was angry with him. He said, " She thought you'd like it, you little beast. Because of the wagonette."

Darling Mamma. She had taken them because she thought they would like it. Because of the wagonette. Because she was brave, like Mark.

VI

Dead people really did rise. Supposing all the dead people in the City of London Cemetery rose and came out of their graves and went about the city? Supposing they walked out as far as Ilford? Crowds and crowds of them, in white sheets? Supposing they got into the garden?

" Please, God, keep me from thinking about the Resurrection. Please God, keep me from dreaming about coffins and funerals and ghosts and skeletons and corpses." She said it last, after the blessings, so that God couldn't forget. But it was no use.

If you said texts: " Thou shalt not be afraid for the terror by night." " Yea, though I walk through the City of London Cemetery." It was no use.

" The trumpet shall sound and the dead shall arise . . . Incorruptible."

That was beautiful. Like a bright light shining. But you couldn't think about it long enough. And the dreams went on just the same: the dream of the ghost in the passage, the dream of the black coffin coming round the turn of the staircase and squeezing you against the banister; the dream of the corpse that came to your bed. She could see the round back and the curled arms under the white sheet.

The dreams woke her with a sort of burst. Her heart was jumping about and thumping; her face and hair were wet with water that came out of her skin.

The grey light in the passage was like the ghost-light of the dreams.

Gas light was a good light; but when you turned it on Jenny came up and put it out again. She said, " Goodness knows when you'll get to sleep with *that* light flaring."

There was never anybody about at bedtime. Jenny was

dishing up the dinner. Harriet was waiting. Catty only ran up for a minute to undo the hooks and brush your hair.

When Mamma sent her to bed she came creeping back into the dining-room. Everybody was eating dinner. She sickened with fright in the steam and smell of dinner. She leaned her head against Mamma and whimpered, and Mamma said in her soft voice, " Big girls don't cry because it's bed-time. Only silly baby girls are afraid of ghosts."

Mamma wasn't afraid.

When she cried Mark left his dinner and carried her upstairs, past the place where the ghost was, and stayed with her till Catty came.

VII

I

" MINX! Minx! Minx! "

Mark had come in from the garden with Mamma. He was calling to Mary. Minx was the name he had given her. Minx was a pretty name and she loved it because he had given it her. Whenever she heard him call she left what she was doing and ran to him.

Papa came out of the library with Boag's Dictionary open in his hand. " ' Minx: A pert, wanton girl. A she-puppy.' Do you hear that, Caroline? He calls his sister a wanton she-puppy." But Mamma had gone back into the garden.

Mark stood at the foot of the stairs and Mary stood at the turn. She had one hand on the rail of the banister, the other pressed hard against the wall. She leaned forward on tiptoe, measuring her distance. When she looked at the stairs they fell from under her in a grey dizziness, so that Mark looked very far away.

They waited till Papa had gone back into the library — Mark held out his arms.

" Jump, Minky! Jump! "

She let go the rail and drew herself up. A delicious thrill of danger went through her and out at her fingers. She flung herself into space and Mark caught her. His body felt hard and strong as it received her. They did it again and again.

That was the "faith-jump." You knew that you would be killed if Mark didn't catch you, but you had faith that he would catch you; and he always did.

Mark and Dan were going to school at Chelmsted on the thirteenth of September, and it was the last week in August now. Mark and Mamma were always looking for each other. Mamma would come running up to the schoolroom and say, "Where's Mark? Tell Mark I want him"; and Mark would go into the garden and say, "Where's Mamma? I want her." And Mamma would put away her trowel and gardening gloves and go walks with him which she hated; and Mark would leave Napoleon Buonaparte and the plan of the Battle of Austerlitz to dig in the garden (and he loathed digging) with Mamma.

This afternoon he had called to Mary to come out brook-jumping. Mark could jump all the brooks in the fields between Ilford and Barkingside, and in the plantations beyond Drake's Farm; he could jump the Pool of Siloam where the water from the plantations runs into the lake below Vinings. Where there was no place for a little girl of seven to cross he carried her in his arms and jumped. He would stand outside in the lane and put his hands on the wall and turn heels over head into the garden.

She said to herself: "In six years and five months I shall be fourteen. I shall jump the Pool of Siloam and come into the garden head over heels." And Mamma called her a little humbug when she said she was afraid to go for a walk with Jenny lest a funeral should be coming along the road.

II

The five elm trees held up their skirts above the high corn. The flat surface of the corn-tops was still. Hot glassy air quivered like a thin steam over the brimming field.

The glazed yellow walls of the old nursery gave out a strong light and heat. The air indoors was dry and smelt dusty like the hot, crackling air above the corn. The children had come in from their play in the fields; they leaned out of the windows and talked about what they were going to be.

Mary said, " I shall paint pictures and play the piano and ride in a circus. I shall go out to the countries where the sand is and tame zebras; and I shall marry Mark and have thirteen children with blue eyes like Meta."

Roddy was going to be the captain of a cruiser. Dan was going to Texas, or some place where Papa couldn't get at him, to farm. Mark was going to be a soldier like Marshal McMahon.

It was Grandpapa and Grandmamma's fault that he was not a soldier now.

" If," he said, " they'd let Papa marry Mamma when he wanted to, I might have been born in eighteen fifty-two. I'd be eighteen by this time. I should have gone into the French Army and I should have been with McMahon at Sedan now."

" You might have been killed," Mary said.

" That wouldn't have mattered a bit. I should have been at Sedan. Nothing matters, Minky, as long as you get what you want."

" If you were killed Mamma and me would die, too, the same minute. Papa would be sorry, then; but not enough to kill him, so that we should go to heaven together without him and be happy."

" Mamma wouldn't be happy without him. We couldn't shut him out."

" No," Mary said; " but we could pray to God not to let him come up too soon."

III

Sedan — Sedan — Sedan.

Papa came out into the garden where Mamma was pulling weeds out of the hot dry soil. He flapped the newspaper and read about the Battle of Sedan. Mamma left off pulling weeds out and listened.

Mark had stuck the picture of Marshal McMahon over the schoolroom chimney-piece. Papa had pinned the war-map to the library door. Mark was restless. He kept on going into the library to look at the war-map and Papa kept on turning him out again. He was in a sort of mysterious disgrace because of Sedan. Roddy was excited about Sedan. Dan followed Mark as he went in and out; he was furious with Papa because of Mark.

Mamma had been a long time in the library talking to Papa. They sent for Mark just before dinner-time. When Mary ran in to say good-night she found him there.

Mark was saying, " You needn't think I want your beastly money. I shall enlist."

Mamma said, " If he enlists, Emilius, it'll kill me."

And Papa, " You hear what your mother says, sir. Isn't that enough for you? "

Mark loved Mamma; but he was not going to do what she wanted. He was going to do something that would kill her.

IV

Papa walked in the garden in the cool of the evening, like the Lord God. And he was always alone. When you thought of him you thought of Jehovah.

There was something funny about other people's fathers. Mr. Manisty, of Vinings, who rode along Ley Street with his two tall, thin sons, as if he were actually proud of them; Mr. Batty, the Vicar of Barkingside, who called his daughter Isabel his " pretty one "; Mr. Farmer, the curate of St. Mary's Chapel, who walked up and down the room all night with the baby; and Mr. Propart, who went about the public roads with Humphrey and Arthur positively hanging on him. Dan said Humphrey and Arthur were tame and domestic because they were always going about with Mr. Propart and talking to him as if they liked it. Mark had once seen Mr. Propart trying to jump a ditch on the Aldborough Road. It was ridiculous. Humphrey and Arthur had to grab him by the arms and pull him over. Mary was sorry for the Propart boys because they hadn't got a mother who was sweet and pretty like Mamma and a father called Emilius Olivier. Emilius couldn't jump ditches any more than Mr. Propart; but then he knew he couldn't, and as Mark said, he had the jolly good sense not to try. You couldn't be Jehovah and jump ditches.

Emilius Olivier was everything a father ought to be.

Then suddenly, for no reason at all, he left off being Jehovah and began trying to behave like Mr. Batty.

It was at dinner, the last Sunday before the thirteenth. Mamma had moved Roddy and Mary from their places so that Mark and Dan could sit beside her. Mary was sitting at the right hand of Papa in the glory of the Father. The pudding had come in; blanc-mange, and Mark's pudding with whipped cream hiding the raspberry jam. It was Roddy's turn to be helped; his eyes were fixed on the snow-white, pure blanc-mange shuddering in the glass dish, and Mamma had just asked him which he would have when Papa sent Mark and Dan out of the room. You couldn't think why he had done it this time unless it was because Mark laughed when Roddy said in his proud, dignified voice, " I'll have a little piece of the Virgin's womb, please, first." Or it may have been because of Mark's pudding. He never liked it when they had Mark's pudding. Anyhow, Mark and Dan had to go, and as they went he drew Mary's chair closer to him and heaped her plate with cream and jam, looking very straight at Mamma as he did it.

" You might have left them alone," Mamma said, " on their last Sunday. They won't be here to annoy you so very long."

Papa said, " There are three days yet till the thirteenth."

" Three days! You'll count the hours and the minutes till you've got what you want."

" What I want is peace and quiet in my house and to get a word in edgeways, sometimes, with my own wife."

" You've no business to have a wife if you can't put up with your own children."

" It isn't my business to have a wife," Papa said. " It's my pleasure. My business is to insure ships. And you see me putting up with Mary very well. I suppose she's my own child."

" Mark and Dan are your own children first."

" *Are* they? To judge by your infatuation I should have said they weren't. ' Mary, Mary, quite contrary, how does your garden grow? Silver bells and cockle shells, and chocolate creams all in a row.' "

He took a large, flat box of chocolates out of his pocket

and laid it beside her plate. And he looked straight at Mamma again.

" If those are the chocolates I reminded you to get for — for the hamper, I won't have them opened."

" They are *not* the chocolates you reminded me to get for — the hamper. I suppose Mark's stomach *is* a hamper. They are the chocolates I reminded myself to get for Mary."

Then Mamma said a peculiar thing.

" Are you trying to show me that you're not jealous of Mary? "

" I'm not trying to show you anything. You know I'm not jealous of Mary. And you know there's no reason why I should be."

" To hear you, Emilius, anybody would think I wasn't fond of my own daughter. Mary darling, you'd better run away."

" And Mary darling," he mocked her, " you'd better take your chocolates with you."

Mary said: " I don't want any chocolates, Papa."

" Is that her contrariness, or just her Mariness? "

" Whatever it is it's all the thanks *you* get, and serve you right, too," said Mamma.

She went upstairs to persuade Dan that Papa didn't mean it. It was just his way, and they'd see he would be different to-morrow.

But to-morrow and the next day and the next he was the same. He didn't actually send Mark and Dan out of the room again, but he tried to pretend to himself that they weren't there by refusing to speak to them.

" Do you think," Mark said, " he'll keep it up till the last minute? "

He did; even when he heard the sound of Mr. Parish's wagonette in the road, coming to take Mark and Dan away. They were sitting at breakfast, trying not to look at him for fear they should laugh, or at Mamma for fear they should cry, trying not to look at each other. Catty brought in the cakes, the hot buttered Yorkshire cakes that were never served for breakfast except on Christmas Day and birthdays. Mary wondered whether Papa would say or do anything. He couldn't. Everybody knew those cakes were sacred. Catty set them on the table with a sort of crash and ran out of the room, crying. Mamma's mouth quivered.

Papa looked at the cakes; he looked at Mamma; he looked at Mark. Mark was staring at nothing with a firm grin on his face.

"The assuagers of grief," Papa said. "Pass round the assuagers."

The holy cakes were passed round. Everybody took a piece except Dan.

Papa pressed him. "Try an assuager. Do."

And Mamma pleaded, "Yes, Dank."

"Do you hear what your mother says?"

Dan's eyes were red-rimmed. He took a double section of cake and tried to bite his way through.

At the first taste tears came out of his eyes and fell on his cake. And when Mamma saw that she burst out crying.

Mary put her piece down untasted and bit back her sobs. Roddy pushed his piece away; and Mark began to eat his, suddenly, bowing over it with an affectation of enjoyment.

Outside in the road Mr. Parish was descending from the box of his wagonette. Papa looked at his watch. He was going with them to Chelmsted.

And Mamma whispered to Mark and Dan with her last kiss, "He'll be all right in the train."

It was all over. Mary and Roddy sat in the dining-room where Mamma had left them. They had shut their eyes so as not to see the empty chairs pushed back and the pieces of the sacred cakes, bitten and abandoned. They had stopped their ears so as not to hear the wheels of Mr. Parish's wagonette taking Mark and Dan away.

Hours afterwards Mamma came upon Mary huddled up in a corner of the drawing-room.

"Mamma — Mamma — I *can't* bear it. I can't live without Mark. And Dan."

Mamma sat down and took her in her arms and rocked her, rocked her without a word, soothing her own grief.

Papa found them like that when he came back from Chelmsted. He stood in the doorway looking at them for a moment, then slunk out of the room as if he were ashamed

of himself. When Mamma sent Mary out to say good-bye
to him, he was standing beside the little sumach tree that
Mark gave Mamma on her birthday. He was smiling at
the sumach tree as if he loved it and was sorry for it.

And Mamma got a letter from Mark in the morning to
say she was right. Papa had been quite decent in the train.

V

After Mark and Dan had gone a great and very remarkable change came over Papa and Mamma. Mamma left off
saying the funny things that Mary could not understand,
and Papa left off teasing and flying into tempers and looking
like Jehovah and walking by himself in the cool of the
evening. He followed Mamma about the garden. He
hung over her chair, like Mark, as she sat sewing. You
came upon him suddenly on the stairs and in the passages,
and he would look at you as if you were not there, and
say, " Where's your mother? Go and tell her I want her."
And Mamma would put away her trowel and her big leather
gloves and go to him. She would sit for hours in the
library while he flapped the newspaper and read to her in
a loud voice about Mr. Gladstone whom she hated.

Sometimes he would come home early from the office,
and Mamma and Mary would be ready for him, and they
would all go together to call at Vinings or Barkingside
Vicarage or on the Proparts.

Or Mr. Parish's wagonette would be ordered, and Mamma
and Mary would put on their best clothes very quick and
go up to London with him, and he would take them to St.
Paul's or Maskelyne and Cooke's, or the National Gallery
or the British Museum. Or they would walk slowly, very
slowly, up Regent Street, stopping at the windows of the
bonnet shops while Mamma picked out the bonnet she would
buy if she could afford it. And perhaps the next day a
bonnet would come in a bandbox, a bonnet that frightened
her when she put it on and looked at herself in the glass.
She would pretend it was one of the bonnets she had wanted;
and when Papa had forgotten about it she would pull all
the trimming off and put it all on again a different way,

and Papa would say it was an even more beautiful bonnet than he had thought.

You might have supposed that he was sorry because he was thinking about Mark and Dan and trying to make up for having been unkind to them. But he was not sorry. He was glad. Glad about something that Mamma had done. He would go about whistling some gay tune, or you caught him stroking his moustache and parting it over his rich lips that smiled as if he were thinking of what Mamma had done to make him happy. The red specks and smears had gone from his eyes, they were clear and blue, and they looked at you with a kind, gentle look, like Uncle Victor's. His very beard was happy.

" You may not know it, but your father is the handsomest man in Essex," Mamma said.

Perhaps it wasn't anything that Mamma had done. Perhaps he was only happy because he was being good. Every Sunday he went to church at Barkingside with Mamma, kneeling close to her in the big pew and praying in a great, ghostly voice, " Good Lord, deliver us! " When the psalms and hymns began he rose over the pew-ledge, yards and yards of him, as if he stood on many hassocks, and he lifted up his beard and sang. All these times the air fairly tingled with him; he seemed to beat out of himself and spread around him the throb of violent and overpowering life. And in the evenings towards sunset they walked together in the fields, and Mary followed them, lagging behind in the borders where the sharlock and wild rye and poppies grew. When she caught up with them she heard them talking.

Once Mamma said, " Why can't you always be like this, Emilius? "

And Papa said, " Why, indeed! "

And when Christmas came and Mark and Dan were back again he was as cruel and teasing as he had ever been.

VI

Eighteen seventy-one.

One cold day Roddy walked into the Pool of Siloam to recover his sailing boat which had drifted under the long arch of the bridge.

There was no Passion Week and no Good Friday and no Easter that spring, only Roddy's rheumatic fever. Roddy in bed, lying on his back, his face white and sharp, his hair darkened and glued with the sweat that poured from his hair and soaked into the bed. Roddy crying out with pain when they moved him. Mamma and Jenny always in Roddy's room, Mr. Spall's sister in the kitchen. Mary going up and down, tiptoe, on messages, trying not to touch Roddy's bed.

Dr. Draper calling, talking in a low voice to Mamma, and Mamma crying. Dr. Draper looking at you through his spectacles and putting a thing like a trumpet to your chest and listening through it.

" You're quite right, Mrs. Olivier. There's nothing wrong with the little girl's heart. She's as sound as a bell."

A dreadful feeling that you had no business to be as sound as a bell. It wasn't fair to Roddy.

Something she didn't notice at the time and remembered afterwards when Roddy was well again. Jenny saying to Mamma, " If it had to be one of them it had ought to have been Miss Mary."

And Mamma saying to Jenny, " It wouldn't have mattered so much if it had been the girl."

VII

You knew that Catty loved you. There was never the smallest uncertainty about it. Her big black eyes shone when she saw you coming. You kissed her smooth cool cheeks, and she hugged you tight and kissed you back again at once; her big lips made a noise like a pop-gun. When she tucked you up at night she said, " I love you so much I could eat you."

And she would play any game you liked. You had only to say, " Let's play the going-away game," and she was off. You began: " I went away to the big hot river where the rhinoceroses and hippopotamuses are "; or: " I went away to the desert where the sand is, to catch zebras. I rode on a dromedary, flump-flumping through the sand," and Catty would follow it up with: " I went away with the Good Templars. We went in a row-boat on a lake, and we landed on

an island where there was daffodillies growing. We had
milk and cake; and it blew such a cool breeze."

Catty was full of love. She loved her father and mother
and her little sister Amelia better than anything in the
whole world. Her home was in Wales. Tears came into
her eyes when she thought about her home and her little
sister Amelia.

" Catty — how much do you love me? "

" Armfuls and armfuls."

" As much as your mother? "

" Very near as much."

" As much as Amelia? "

" Every bit as much."

" How much do you think Jenny loves me? "

" Ever so much."

" No. Jenny loves Roddy best; then Mark; then Dank;
then Mamma; then Papa; then me. That isn't ever so much."

Catty was vexed. " You didn't oughter go measuring
people's love, Miss Mary."

Still, that was what you did do. With Catty and Jenny
you could measure till you knew exactly where you were.

Mamma was different.

You knew *when* she loved you. You could almost count
the times: the time when Papa frightened you; the time
when you cut your forehead; the time the lamb died; all the
whooping-cough and chicken-pox times, and when Meta,
the wax doll, fell off the schoolroom table and broke her
head; and when Mark went away to school. Or when you
were good and said every word of your lessons right; when
you watched Mamma working in the garden, planting and
transplanting the flowers with her clever hands; and when
you were quiet and sat beside her on the footstool, learning
to knit and sew. On Sunday afternoons when she played
the hymns and you sang:

> " There's a Friend for little children
> Above the bright blue sky,"

quite horribly out of tune, and when you listened while she
sang herself, " Lead, kindly light," or " Abide with me,"
and her voice was so sweet and gentle that it made you cry.
Then you knew.

Sometimes, when it was not Sunday, she played the Hungarian March, that went, with loud, noble noises:

Droom — Droom — Droom-era-room
Droom — Droom — Droom-era-room
Droom rer-room-room droom-room-room
Droom — Droom — Droom.

It was wonderful. Mamma was wonderful. She swayed and bowed to the beat of the music, as if she shook it out of her body and not out of the piano. She smiled to herself when she saw that you were listening. You said "Oh — Mamma! Play it again," and she played it again. When she had finished she stooped suddenly and kissed you. And you knew.

But she wouldn't say it. You couldn't make her.

"Say it, Mamma. Say it like you used to."

Mamma shook her head.

"I want to hear you say it."

"Well, I'm not going to."

"I love you. I ache with loving you. I love you so much that it hurts me to say it."

"Why do you do it, then?"

"Because it hurts me more not to. Just once. 'I love you.' Just a weeny once."

"You're going to be like your father, tease, tease, tease, all day long, till I'm worn out."

"I'm not going to be like Papa. I don't tease. It's you that's teasing. How'm I to know you love me if you won't say it?"

Mamma said, "Can't you see what I'm doing?"

"No."

She was not interested in the thin white stuff and the lace — Mamma's needle-work.

"Well, then, look in the basket."

The basket was full of tiny garments made of the white stuff, petticoats, drawers and nightgown, sewn with minute tucks and edged with lace. Mamma unfolded them.

"New clothes," she said, "for your new dolly."

"Oh — oh — oh — I love you so much that I can't bear it; you little holy Mamma!"

Mamma said, " I'm not holy, and I won't be called holy. I want deeds, not words. If you love me you'll learn your lessons properly the night before, not just gabble them over hot from the pan."

" I will, Mamma, I will. Won't you say it? "

" No," Mamma said, " I won't."

She sat there with a sort of triumph on her beautiful face, as if she were pleased with herself because she hadn't said it. And Mary would bring the long sheet that dragged on her wrist, and the needle that pricked her fingers, and sit at Mamma's knee and sew, making a thin trail of blood all along the hem.

" Why do you look at me so kindly when I'm sewing? "

" Because I like to see you behaving like a little girl, instead of tearing about and trying to do what boys do."

And Mamma would tell her a story, always the same story, going on and on, about the family of ten children who lived in the farm by the forest. There were seven boys and three girls. The six youngest boys worked on the farm with their father — yes, he was a *very* nice father — and the eldest boy worked in the garden with his mother, and the three girls worked in the house. They could cook and make butter and cheese, and bake bread; and even the youngest little girl could knit and sew.

" Had they any children? "

" No, they were too busy to think about having children. They were all very, very happy together, just as they were."

The story was like the hem, there was never any end to it, for Mamma was always finding something else for the three girls to do. She smiled as she told it, as if she saw something that pleased her.

Mary felt that she could go on sewing at the hem and pricking her finger for ever if Mamma would only keep that look on her face.

VIII

I

" I CAN'T, Jenny, I can't. I know there's a funeral coming."

Mary stood on the flagstone inside the arch of the open gate. She looked up and down the road and drew back again into the garden. Jenny, tired and patient, waited outside.

" I've told you, Miss Mary, there isn't any funeral."

" If there isn't there will be. There! I can see it."

" You see Mr. Parish's high 'at a driving in his wagonette."

It *was* Mr. Parish's high hat. When he put the black top on his wagonette it looked like a hearse.

They started up Ley Street towards Mr. Spall's cottage.

Jenny said, " I thought you was going to be such a good girl when Master Roddy went to school. But I declare if you're not twice as tiresome."

Roddy had gone to Chelmsted after midsummer. She had to go for walks on the roads with Jenny now at the risk of meeting funerals.

This week they had been every day to Ilford to call at Mr. Spall's cottage or at Benny's, the draper's shop in the High Street.

Jenny didn't believe that a big girl, nine next birthday, could really be afraid of funerals. She thought you were only trying to be tiresome. She said you could stop thinking about funerals well enough when you wanted. You did forget sometimes when nice things happened; when you went to see Mrs. Farmer's baby undressed, and when Isabel Batty came to tea. Isabel was almost a baby. It felt nice to lift her and curl up her stiff, barley-sugar hair and sponge her weak, pink silk hands. And there were things that you could do. You could pretend that you were not Mary Olivier but somebody else, that you were grown-up and that the baby and Isabel belonged to you and were there when they were not there. But all the time you knew there would be a funeral on the road somewhere, and that some day you would see it.

When they got into the High Street the funeral was coming along the Barking Road. She saw, before Jenny could see anything at all, the mutes, sitting high, and their black, bunched-up weepers. She turned and ran out of the High Street and back over the railway bridge. Jenny called after her, " Come back! " and a man on the bridge shouted

"Hi, Missy! Stop!" as she ran down Ley Street. Her legs shook and gave way under her. Once she fell. She ran, staggering, but she ran. People came out of their cottages to look at her. She thought they had come out to look at the funeral.

After that she refused to go outside the front door or to look through the front windows for fear she should see a funeral.

They couldn't take her and carry her out; so they let her go for walks in the back garden. When Papa came home she was sent up to the schoolroom to play with the doll's house. You could see the road through the high bars of the window at the end of the passage, so that even when Catty lit the gas the top floor was queer and horrible.

Sometimes doubts came with her terror. She thought: "Nobody loves me except Mark. And Mark isn't here." Mark's image haunted her. She shut her eyes and it slid forward on to the darkness, the strong body, the brave, straight up and down face, the steady, light brown eyes, shining; the firm, sweet mouth; the sparrow-brown hair with feathery golden tips. She could hear Mark's voice calling to her: "Minx! Minky!"

And there was something that Mamma said. It was unkind to be afraid of the poor dead people. Mamma said, "Would you run away from Isabel if you saw her lying in her little coffin?"

II

Jenny's new dress had come.

It was made of grey silk trimmed with black lace, and it lay spread out on the bed in the spare room. Mamma and Aunt Bella stood and looked at it, and shook their heads as if they thought that Jenny had no business to wear a silk dress.

Aunt Bella said, "She's a silly woman to go and leave a good home. At her age."

And Mamma said, "I'd rather see her in her coffin. It would be less undignified. She meant to do it at Easter; she was only waiting till Roddy went to school. She's waiting now till after the Christmas holidays."

Jenny was going to do something dreadful.

She was going to be married. The grey silk dress was her wedding-dress. She was going to marry Mr. Spall. Even Catty thought it was rather dreadful.

But Jenny was happy because she was going to wear the grey silk dress and live in Mr. Spall's cottage and talk to him about Jesus. Only one half of her face drooped sleepily; the other half had waked up, and looked excited; there was a flush on it as bright as paint.

III

Mary's bed stood in a corner of the night nursery, and beside it was the high yellow linen cupboard. When the doors were opened there was a faint india-rubbery smell from the mackintosh sheet that had been put away on the top shelf.

One night she was wakened by Catty coming into the room and opening the cupboard doors. Catty climbed on a chair and took something from the top shelf. She didn't answer when Mary asked what she was doing, but hurried away, leaving the door on the latch. Her feet made quick thuds along the passage. A door opened and shut, and there was a sound of Papa going downstairs. Somebody came up softly and pulled the door to, and Mary went to sleep again.

When she woke the room was full of the grey light that frightened her. But she was not frightened. She woke sitting up on her pillow, staring into the grey light, and saying to herself, " Jenny is dead."

But she was not afraid of Jenny. The stillness in her heart spread into the grey light of the room. She lay back waiting for seven o'clock when Catty would come and call her.

At seven o'clock Mamma came. She wore the dress she had worn last night, and she was crying.

Mary said, " You haven't got to say it. I know Jenny is dead."

The blinds were drawn in all the windows when she and Mark went into the front garden to look for snowdrops in

the border by the kitchen area. She knew that Jenny's
dead body lay on the sofa under the kitchen window behind
the blind and the white painted iron bars. She hoped that
she would not have to see it; but she was not afraid of
Jenny's dead body. It was sacred and holy.

She wondered why Mamma sent her to Uncle Edward
and Aunt Bella. From the top-storey windows of Chadwell
Grange you could look beyond Aldborough Hatch towards
Wanstead Flats and the City of London Cemetery. They
were going to bury Jenny there. She stood looking out,
quiet, not crying. She only cried at night when she thought
of Jenny, sitting in the low nursery chair, tired and patient,
drawing back from her violent caresses, and of the grey
silk dress laid out on the bed in the spare room.

She was not even afraid of the City of London Cemetery
when Mark took her to see Jenny's grave. Jenny's grave
was sacred and holy.

IX

I

You had to endure hardness after you were nine. You
learnt out of Mrs. Markham's " History of England," and
you were not allowed to read the conversations between
Richard and Mary and Mrs. Markham because they made
history too amusing and too easy to remember. For the
same reason you translated only the tight, dismal pages of
your French Reader, and anything that looked like an
interesting story was forbidden. You were to learn for the
sake of the lesson and not for pleasure's sake. Mamma said
you had enough pleasure in play-time. She put it to your
honour not to skip on to the more exciting parts.

When you had finished Mrs. Markham you began Dr.
Smith's "History of England." Honour was safe with Dr.
Smith. He made history very hard to read and impossible
to remember.

The Bible got harder, too. You knew all the best Psalms
by heart, and the stories about Noah's ark and Joseph and
his coat of many colours, and David, and Daniel in the
lions' den. You had to go straight through the Bible now,

skipping Leviticus because it was full of things you couldn't understand. When you had done with Moses lifting up the serpent in the wilderness you had to read about Aaron and the sons of Levi, and the wave-offerings, and the tabernacle, and the ark of the covenant where they kept the five golden emerods. Mamma didn't know what emerods were, but Mark said they were a kind of white mice.

You learnt Old Testament history, too, out of a little book that was all grey slabs of print and dark pictures showing the earth swallowing up Korah, Dathan and Abiram, and Aaron and the sons of Levi with their long beards and high hats and their petticoats, swinging incense in fits of temper. You found out queerer and queerer things about God. God made the earth swallow up Korah, Dathan and Abiram. He killed poor Uzzah because he put out his hand to prevent the ark of the covenant falling out of the cart. Even David said he didn't know how on earth he was to get the ark along at that rate. And there were the Moabites and the Midianites and all the animals: the bullocks and the he-goats and the little lambs and kids. When you asked Mamma why God killed people, she said it was because he was just as well as merciful, and (it was the old story) he hated sin. Disobedience was sin, and Uzzah had been disobedient.

As for the lambs and the he-goats, Jesus had done away with all that. He was God's son, and he had propitiated God's anger and satisfied his justice when he shed his own blood on the cross to save sinners. Without shedding of blood there is no remission of sins. You were not to bother about the blood.

But you couldn't help bothering about it. You couldn't help being sorry for Uzzah and the Midianites and the lambs and the he-goats.

Perhaps you had to sort things out and keep them separate. Here was the world, here were Mamma and Mark and kittens and rabbits, and all the things you really cared about: drawing pictures, and playing the Hungarian March and getting excited in the Easter holidays when the white evenings came and Mark raced you from the Green Man to the Horns Tavern. Here was the sudden, secret happiness you felt when you were by yourself and the fields looked beautiful. It was always coming now, with a sort of rush and flash, when you least expected it.

And *there* was God and religion and duty. The nicest part of religion was music, and knowing how the world was made, and the beautiful sounding bits of the Bible. You could like religion. But duty was doing all the things you didn't like because you didn't like them. And you couldn't honestly say you liked God. God had to be propitiated; your righteousness was filthy rags; so you couldn't propitiate him. Jesus had to do it for you. All you had to do was to believe, really believe that he had done it.

But supposing you hadn't got to believe it, supposing you hadn't got to believe anything at all, it would be easier to think about. The things you cared for belonged to each other, but God didn't belong to them. He didn't fit in anywhere. You couldn't help feeling that if God was love, and if he was everywhere, he ought to have fitted in. Perhaps, after all, there were two Gods; one who made things and loved them, and one who didn't; who looked on sulking and finding fault with what the clever kind God had made.

When the midsummer holidays came and brook-jumping began she left off thinking about God.

II

" Uneasy lies the head that wears a crown "—
The picture in the *Sunday At Home* showed the old King in bed and Prince Hal trying on his crown. But the words were not the *Sunday At Home;* they were taken out of Shakespeare. Mark showed her the place.

Mark was in the schoolroom chanting his home-lessons:

" ' Yet once more, oh ye laurels, and once more,
     Ye myrtles brown with ivy never sere ' " —

That sounded nice. " Say it again, Mark, say it again."
Mark said it again. He also said:

" ' Achilles' wrath, to Greece the direful spring
     Of woes unnumbered, heavenly goddess, sing! ' "

The three books stood on the bookshelf in the schoolroom, the thin Shakespeare in diamond print, the small brown leather Milton, the very small fat Pope's *Iliad* in the red cover. Mark gave them to her for her own.

She made Catty put her bed between the two windows, and Mark made a bookshelf out of a piece of wood and some picture cord, and hung it within reach. She had a happy, excited feeling when she thought of the three books; it made her wake early. She read from five o'clock till Catty called her at seven, and again.after Catty had tucked her up and left her, till the white light in the room was grey.

She learnt *Lycidas* by heart, and

> " I thought I saw my late espoused wife
> Brought to me like Alcestis from the grave," —

and the bits about Satan in *Paradise Lost*. The sound of the lines gave her the same nice feeling that she had when Mrs. Propart played the March in Scipio after Evening Service. She tried to make lines of her own that went the same way as the lines in Milton and Shakespeare and Pope's *Iliad*. She found out that there was nothing she liked so much as making these lines. It was nicer even than playing the Hungarian March. She thought it was funny that the lines like Pope's *Iliad* came easiest, though they had to rhyme.

" Silent he wandered by the sounding sea," was good, but the Greek line that Mark showed her went: " Be d'akeon para thina poluphloisboio thalasses "; that was better. " Don't you think so, Mark? "

" Clever Minx. Much better."

" Mark — if God knew how happy I am writing poetry he'd make the earth open and swallow me up."

Mark only said, " You mustn't say that to Mamma. Play ' Violetta.' "

Of all hateful and disgusting tunes the most disgusting and the most hateful was " Violetta," which Mr. Sippett's sister taught her. But if Mark would promise to make Mamma let her learn Greek she would play it to him twenty times running.

When Mark went to Chelmsted that autumn he left her

his brown *Greek Accidence* and Smith's *Classical Diction-*
ary, besides Macaulay's *Lays of Ancient Rome.* She
taught herself Greek in the hour after breakfast before Miss
Sippett came to give her her music lesson. She was always
careful to leave the Accidence open where Miss Sippett
could see it and realise that she was not a stupid little girl.

But whether Miss Sippett saw the Accidence or not she
always behaved as if it wasn't there.

III

When Mamma saw the Accidence open on the drawing-
room table she shut it and told you to put it in its proper
place. If you talked about it her mouth buttoned up tight,
and her eyes blinked, and she began tapping with her foot.

There was something queer about learning Greek.
Mamma did not actually forbid it; but she said it must not
be done in lesson time or sewing time, or when people could
see you doing it, lest they should think you were showing
off. You could see that she didn't believe you *could* learn
Greek and that she wouldn't like it if you did. But when
lessons were over she let you read Shakespeare or Pope's
Iliad aloud to her while she sewed. And when you could
say:

> " Lars Porsena of Clusium
> By the nine Gods he swore "—

straight through without stopping she went into London with
Papa and brought back the *Child's First History of Rome.*
A Pinnock's *Catechism of Mythology* in a blue paper cover
went with the history to tell you all about the gods and
goddesses. What Pinnock didn't tell you you found out
from Smith's *Classical Dictionary.* It had pictures in it so
beautiful that you were happy just sitting still and looking
at them. There was such a lot of gods and goddesses that at
first they were rather hard to remember. But you couldn't
forget Apollo and Hermes and Aphrodite and Pallas Athene
and Diana. They were not like Jehovah. They quarrelled
sometimes, but they didn't hate each other; not as Jehovah
hated all the other gods. They fitted in somehow. They

cared for all the things you liked best: trees and animals and poetry and music and running races and playing games. Even Zeus was nicer than Jehovah, though he reminded you of him now and then. He liked sacrifices. But then he was honest about it. He didn't pretend that he was good and that he *had* to have them because of your sins. And you hadn't got to believe in him. That was the nicest thing of all.

X

I

MARY was ten in eighteen seventy-three.

Aunt Charlotte was ill, and nobody was being kind to her. She had given her Sunday bonnet to Harriet and her Sunday gown to Catty; so you knew she was going to be married again. She said it was prophesied that she should be married in eighteen seventy-three.

The illness had something to do with being married and going continually to Mr. Marriott's church and calling on Mr. Marriott and writing letters to him about religion. You couldn't say Aunt Charlotte was not religious. But Papa said he would believe in her religion if she went to Mr. Batty's church or Mr. Farmer's or Mr. Propart's. They had all got wives and Mr. Marriott hadn't. Papa had forbidden Aunt Charlotte to go any more to Mr. Marriott's church.

Mr. Marriott had written a nice letter to Uncle Victor, and Uncle Victor had taken Papa to see him, and the doctor had come to see Aunt Charlotte and she had been sent to bed.

Aunt Charlotte's room was at the top of the tall, thin white house in the High Street. There was whispering on the stairs. Mamma and Aunt Lavvy stood at the turn; you could see their vexed faces. Aunt Charlotte called to them to let Mary come to her. Mary was told she might go if she were very quiet.

Aunt Charlotte was all by herself sitting up in a large white bed. A Bible propped itself open, leaves downwards, against the mound she made. There was something startling

about the lengths of white curtain and the stretches of white
pillow and counterpane, and Aunt Charlotte's very black
eyebrows and hair and the cover of the Bible, very black,
and her blue eyes glittering.

She was writing letters. Every now and then she took
up the Bible and picked out a text and wrote it down. She
wrote very fast, and as she finished each sheet she hid it
under the bed-clothes, and made a sign to show that what
she was doing was a secret.

"Love God and you'll be happy. Love God and you'll
be happy," she said.

Her eyes pointed at you. They looked wise and solemn
and excited.

A wide flat piece of counterpane was left over from Aunt
Charlotte. Mary climbed up and sat in it with her back
against the foot-rail and looked at her. Looking at Aunt
Charlotte made you think of being born.

"Aunt Charlotte, do *you* know what being born is?"

Aunt Charlotte looked up under her eyebrows, and hid
another sheet of paper. "What's put that in your head all
of a sudden?"

"It's because of my babies. Catty says I couldn't have
thirteen all under three years old. But I could, couldn't I?"

"I'm afraid I don't think you could," Aunt Charlotte
said.

"Why not? Catty *won't* say why."

Aunt Charlotte shook her head, but she was smiling and
looking wiser and more solemn than ever. "You mustn't
ask too many questions," she said.

"But you haven't told me what being born is. I know
it's got something to do with the Virgin Mary."

Aunt Charlotte said, "Sh-sh-sh! You mustn't say that.
Nice little girls don't think about those things."

Her tilted eyes had turned down and her mouth had
stopped smiling. So you knew that being born was not
frightening. It had something to do with the things you
didn't talk about.

And yet — how could it? There was the Virgin Mary.

"Aunt Charlotte, don't you *wish* you had a baby?"

Aunt Charlotte looked frightened, suddenly, and began
to cry.

"You mustn't say it, Mary, you mustn't say it. Don't tell them you said it. They'll think I've been talking about the babies. The little babies. Don't tell them. Promise me you won't tell."

II

"Aunt Lavvy — I wish I knew what you thought about Jehovah?"

When Aunt Lavvy stayed with you Mamma made you promise not to ask her about her opinions. But sometimes you forgot. Aunt Lavvy looked more than ever as if she was by herself in a quiet empty room, thinking of something that wasn't there. You couldn't help feeling that she knew things. Mamma said she had always been the clever one, just as Aunt Charlotte had always been the queer one; but Aunt Bella said she was no better than an unbeliever, because she was a Unitarian at heart.

"Why Jehovah in particular?" Aunt Lavvy was like Uncle Victor; she listened politely when you talked to her, as if you were saying something interesting.

"Because he's the one you've got to believe in. Do you really think he is so very good?"

"I don't think anything. I don't know anything, except that God is love."

"Jehovah wasn't."

"Jehovah — " Aunt Lavvy stopped herself. "I mustn't talk to you about it — because I promised your mother I wouldn't."

It was very queer. Aunt Lavvy's opinions had something to do with religion, yet Mamma said you mustn't talk about them.

"I promised, too. I shall have to confess and ask her to forgive me."

"Then," said Aunt Lavvy, "be sure you tell her that I didn't talk to you. Promise me you'll tell her."

That was what Aunt Charlotte had said. Talking about religion was like talking about being born.

XI

I

NOBODY has any innate ideas.   Children and savages and
idiots haven't any, so grown-up people can't have, Mr.
Locke says.

But how did he know?   You might have them and forget
about them, and only remember again after you were grown
up.

She sat up in the drawing-room till nine o'clock now,
because she was eleven years old.   She had taken the doll's
clothes out of the old wooden box and filled it with books:
the Bible, Milton, and Pope's Homer, the Greek Accidence,
and *Plutarch's Lives*, and the *Comedies* from Papa's illus-
trated Shakespeare in seven volumes, which he never read,
and two volumes of *Pepys' Diary*, and Locke *On the Human
Understanding*.   She wished the Bible had been bound in
pink calf like Pepys instead of the shiny black leather that
made you think of wet goloshes.   Then it would have looked
new and exciting like the other books.

She sat on a footstool with her box beside her in the
corner behind Mamma's chair.   She had to hide there because Mamma didn't believe you really liked reading.   She
thought you were only shamming and showing off.   Sometimes Mr. and Mrs. Farmer would come in, and Mr. Farmer
would play chess with Papa while Mrs. Farmer talked to
Mamma about how troublesome and independent the trades-
people were, and how hard it was to get servants and to
keep them.   Mamma listened to Mrs. Farmer as if she were
saying something wonderful and exciting.   Sometimes it
would be the Proparts; or Mr. Batty would come in alone.
And sometimes they would all come together with the aunts
and uncles, and there would be a party.

Mary always hoped that Uncle Victor would notice her
and say, " Mary is reading Locke *On the Human Understanding*," or that Mr. Propart would come and turn over
the books and make some interesting remark.   But they
never did.

At half-past eight Catty would bring in the tea-tray; the

white and grey and gold tea-cups would be set out round the bulging silver tea-pot that lifted up its spout with a foolish, pompous expression, like a hen. Mamma would move about the table in her mauve silk gown, and there would be a scent of cream and strong tea. Every now and then the shimmering silk and the rich scent would come between her and the grey, tight-pressed, difficult page.

" ' The senses at first let in particular ideas and furnish the yet empty cabinet: and the mind growing by degrees familiar with some of them, they are lodged in the memory and names got to them.'

" Then how — Then how? — "

The thought she thought was coming wouldn't come, and Mamma was telling her to get up and hand round the bread and butter.

II

" Mr. Ponsonby, do you remember your innate ideas? "

" My *how* much? " said Mr. Ponsonby.

" The ideas you had before you were born? "

Mr. Ponsonby said, " Before I was born? Well — " He really seemed to be considering it.

Mamma's chair, pushed further along the hearthrug, had driven her back and back, till the box was hidden behind the curtain.

Mr. Ponsonby was Mark's friend. Mark was at the Royal Military Academy at Woolwich now. Every Saturday Mr. Ponsonby came home with Mark and stayed till Sunday evening. You knew that sooner or later he would find you out behind Mamma's chair.

" I mean," she said, " the ideas you were born with."

" Seems to me," said Mr. Ponsonby, " I was born with precious few. Anyhow I can't say I remember them."

" I was afraid you'd say that. It's what Mr. Locke says."

" Mr. how much? "

" Mr. Locke. You can look at him if you like."

She thought: " He won't. He won't. They never, never do."

But Mr. Ponsonby did. He looked at Mr. Locke, and he

looked at Mary, and he said, "By Gum!" He even read the bits about the baby and the empty cabinet.

"You don't mean to say you *like* this sort of thing?"

"I like it most awfully. Of course I don't mean as much as brook-jumping, but almost as much."

And Mr. Ponsonby said, "Well — I must say — of *all* — you *are* — by Gum!"

He made it sound like the most delicious praise.

Mr. Ponsonby was taller and older than Mark. He was nineteen. She thought he was the nicest looking person she had ever seen.

His face was the colour of thick white honey; his hair was very dark, and he had long blue eyes and long black eyebrows like bars, drawn close down on to the blue. His nose would have been hooky if it hadn't been so straight, and his mouth was quiet and serious. When he talked to you his mouth and eyes looked as if they liked it.

Mark came and said, "Minky, if you stodge like that you'll get all flabby."

It wasn't nice of Mark to say that before Mr. Ponsonby, when he knew perfectly well that she could jump her own height.

"*Me* flabby? Feel my muscle."

It rose up hard under her soft skin.

"Feel it, Mr. Ponsonby."

"I say — *what* a biceps!"

"Yes, but," Mark said, "you should feel his."

His was even bigger and harder than Mark's. "Mine," she said sorrowfully, "will never be as good as his."

Then Mamma came and told her it was bed-time, and Mr. Ponsonby said, "Oh, Mrs. Olivier, *not* yet."

"Five minutes more, then."

But the five minutes were never any good. You just sat counting them.

And when it was all over and Mr. Ponsonby strode across the drawing-room and opened the door for her she went laughing; she stood in the doorway and laughed. When you were sent to bed at nine the only dignified thing was to pretend you didn't care.

And Mr. Ponsonby, holding the door so that Mamma

couldn't see him, looked at her and shook his head, as much as to say, " You and I know it isn't a joke for either of us, this unrighteous banishment."

III

" What on earth are you doing? "

She might have known that some day Mamma would come up and find her putting the children to bed.

She had seven. There was Isabel Batty, and Mrs. Farmer's red-haired baby, and Mark in the blue frock in the picture when he was four, and Dank in his white frock and blue sash, and the three very little babies you made up out of your head. Six o'clock was their bed-time.

" You'd no business to touch those baby-clothes," Mamma said.

⸱ The baby-clothes were real. Every evening she took them from the drawer in the linen cupboard; and when she had sung the children to sleep she shook out the little frocks and petticoats and folded them in a neat pile at the foot of the bed.

" I thought you were in the schoolroom learning your lessons? "

" So I was, Mamma. But — you know — six o'clock *is* their bed-time."

" Oh Mary! you told me you'd given up that silly game."

" So I did. But they won't let me. They don't want me to give them up."

Mamma sat down, as if it was too much for her.

" I hope," she said, " you don't talk to Catty or anybody about it."

" No, Mamma. I couldn't. They're my secret."

" That was all very well when you were a little thing. But a great girl of twelve — You ought to be ashamed of yourself."

Mamma had gone. She had taken away the baby-clothes. Mary lay face downwards on her bed.

Shame burned through her body like fire. Hot tears scalded her eyelids. She thought: " How was I to know you mustn't have babies? " Still, she couldn't give them all up. She *must* keep Isabel and the red-haired baby.

But what would Mr. Ponsonby think of her if he knew?

IV

" Mr. Ponsonby. Mr. Ponsonby! Stay where you are and look! "

From the window at the end of the top corridor the side of the house went sheer down into the lane. Mary was at the window. Mr. Ponsonby was in the lane.

She climbed on to the ledge and knelt there. Grasping the bottom of the window frame firmly with both hands and letting her knees slide from the ledge, she lowered herself, and hung for one ecstatic moment, and drew herself up again by her arms.

" What did you do it for, Mary? "

Mr. Ponsonby had rushed up the stairs and they were sitting there. He was so tall that he hung over her when he leaned.

" It's nothing. You ought to be able to pull up your own weight."

" You mustn't do it from top-storey windows. It's dangerous."

" Not if you've practised on the banisters first. Where's Mark? "

" With your Mater. I say, supposing you and I go for a walk."

" We must be back at six o'clock," she said.

When you went for walks with Mark or Mr. Ponsonby they always raced you down Ley Street and over the ford at the bottom. They both gave you the same start to the Horn's Tavern; the only difference was that with Mr. Ponsonby you were over the ford first.

They turned at the ford into the field path that led to Drake's Farm and the plantation. He jumped all the stiles and she vaulted them. She could see that he respected her. And so they came to the big water jump into the plantation. Mr. Ponsonby went over first and held out his arms. She hurled herself forward and he caught her. And this time, instead of putting her down instantly, he lifted her up in his arms and held her tight and kissed her. Her heart thumped violently and she had a sudden happy feeling. Neither spoke.

Humphrey Propart had kissed her once for a forfeit. And she had boxed his ears. Mr. Ponsonby's was a different sort of kiss.

They tore through the plantation as if nothing had happened, clearing all the brooks in a business-like way. Mr. Ponsonby took brook-jumping as the serious and delightful thing it was.

Going home across the fields they held each other's hands, like children. "Minky," he said, "I don't like to think of you hanging out of top-storey windows."

"But it's so jolly to feel your body come squirming up after your arms."

"It is. It is. All the same, promise me you won't do it any more."

"Why?"

"Because I'm going to India when I've passed out, and I want to find you alive when I come back. Promise me, Minky."

"I will, if you're really going. But you're the only person I allow to call me Minky, except Mark."

"Am I? I'm glad I'm the only person."

They went on.

"I'm afraid," she said, "my hand is getting very hot and horrid."

He held it tighter. "I don't care how hot and horrid it gets. And I think you might call me Jimmy."

It was long after six o'clock. She had forgotten the children and their bed-time. After that day she never played with them again.

V

"If I were you," Mamma said, "I should put away that box of books. You'll be no use if you read — read — read all day long."

"You oughtn't to say that, Mamma. I *am* of use. You

know I can make the sewing-machine go when you can't."

Mamma smiled. She knew it.

" And which would you rather took you over the crossing at the Bank? Me or Papa? "

Mamma smiled again. She knew she was safer with Mary at a crossing, because Papa teased her and frightened her before he dragged her over. But Mary led her gently, holding back the noses of the horses.

" There's that Locke on the human understanding," said Mamma. " Poor Jimmy was frightened when he found you reading it."

" He wasn't. He was most awfully pleased and excited."

" He was laughing at you."

" He wasn't. He wasn't."

" Of course he was laughing at you. What did you think he was doing? "

" I thought he was interested."

" He wasn't, then. Men," Mamma said, " are *not* interested in little book-worms. He told me it was very bad for you."

Shame again. Hot, burning and scalding shame. He was only laughing at her.

" Mark doesn't laugh at me," she said. The thought of Mark and of his love for her healed her wound.

" A precious deal," Mamma said, " you know about Mark."

Mamma was safe. Oh, she was safe. She knew that Mark loved her best.

VI

On the cover of Pinnock's Catechism there was a small black picture of the Parthenon. And under it was written:

" Abode of gods whose shrines no longer burn."

Supposing the candles in St. Mary's Chapel no longer burned?

Supposing Barkingside church and Aldborough Hatch church fell to bits and there were no more clergymen? And you only read in history books about people like Mr. Batty and Mr. Propart and their surplices and the things they wore round their necks?

Supposing the Christian religion passed away?

It excited you to think these things.   But when you heard the " Magnificat " in church, or when you thought of Christ hanging so bravely on the cross you were sorry and you stopped thinking.

What a pity you couldn't ever go on without having to stop.

END OF BOOK TWO

BOOK THREE

ADOLESCENCE

1876–1879

BOOK THREE

ADOLESCENCE

XII

I

MARY went slowly up the lane between the garden wall and the thorn hedge.

The air, streaming towards her from the flat fields, had the tang of cold, glittering water; the sweet, grassy smell of the green corn blades swam on it. The young thorn leaves smelt of almonds and of their own bitter green.

The five trees stood up, thin and black, in an archway of golden white fire. The green of their young leaves hung about them like an emanation.

A skylark swung himself up, a small grey ball, spinning over the tree tops to the arch of the sunset. His song pierced and shook, like the golden white light. With each throb of his wings he shrank, smaller and greyer, a moth, a midge, whirling in the luminous air. A grey ball dropped spinning down.

By the gate of the field her sudden, secret happiness came to her.

She could never tell when it was coming, nor what it would come from. It had something to do with the trees standing up in the golden white light. It had come before with a certain sharp white light flooding the fields, flooding the room.

It had happened so often that she received it now with a shock of recognition; and when it was over she wanted it to happen again. She would go back and back to the places where it had come, looking for it, thinking that any minute it might happen again. But it never came twice to the same place in the same way.

Catty was calling to her from the bottom of the lane. She stood still by the gate, not heeding Catty, holding her happiness. When she had turned from the quiet fields it would be gone.

II

Sometimes she had queer glimpses of the persons that were called Mary Olivier. There was Mrs. Olivier's only daughter, proud of her power over the sewing-machine. When she brought the pile of hemmed sheets to her mother her heart swelled with joy in her own goodness. There was Mark Olivier's sister, who rejoiced in the movements of her body, the strain of the taut muscles throbbing on their own leash, the bound forwards, the push of the wind on her knees and breast, the hard feel of the ground under her padding feet. And there was Mary Olivier, the little girl of thirteen whom her mother and Aunt Bella whispered about to each other with mysterious references to her age.

Her secret happiness had nothing to do with any of these Mary Oliviers. It was not like any other happiness. It had nothing to do with Mamma or Dan or Roddy, or even Mark. It had nothing to do with Jimmy.

She had cried when Jimmy went away, and she would cry again to-night when she thought about him. Jimmy's going away was worse than anything that had happened yet or could happen till Mark went to India. That would be the worst thing.

Jimmy had not gone to India as he had said. He had had to leave Woolwich because of something he had done, and his father had sent him to Australia. He had gone without saying good-bye, and he was never coming back. She would never in all her life see Jimmy again.

Jimmy had done something dreadful.

Nobody but Mamma and Papa and Mark knew what he had done; but from the way they talked you could see that it was one of those things you mustn't talk about. Only Mark said he didn't believe he really had done it.

Last Sunday she had written a letter to him which Mark posted:

"DEAR JIMMY, — I think you might have come to say good-bye to us, even if Papa and Mamma do think you've done something you oughtn't to. I want you to know that Mark and I don't believe you did it, and even if you did it won't make any difference. I shall always love you just the same, next best to Mark. You can't expect me to love you really best, because he will always come first as long as I live. I hope you will be very happy in Australia. I shall keep my promise just the same, though it's Australia and not India you've gone to.

"With love, ever your loving
"MINKY.

"P.S. No. 1.— I'm reading a new poet — Byron. There was a silly woman who said she'd rather have the fame of Childe Harold than the immortality of Don Juan. But I'd rather have the immortality, wouldn't you?

"P.S. No. 2.— Do you think that you will keep Kangaroos? They might help to make you happy."

III

Mary was picking French beans in the kitchen garden when Mamma and Aunt Bella came along the path, talking together. The thick green walls of the runners hid her.

"Mary is getting very precocious," said Mamma.

"That comes from being brought up with boys," said Aunt Bella. "She ought to see more girls of her own age."

"She doesn't like them."

Mary shouted "Cuckoo!" to warn them, but they wouldn't stop.

"It's high time," Aunt Bella said, "that she should learn to like them. The Draper girls are too old. But there's that little Bertha Mitchison."

"I haven't called on Mrs. Mitchison for two years."

"And why haven't you, Caroline?"

"Because I can't afford to be always hiring wagonettes to go to Woodford Bridge."

" Cuckoo! "
" Caroline — do you think she could have heard? "
" Cuckoo, Aunt Bella!   Cuckoo! "

IV

On the high road the white dust had a clear, sharp, exciting smell.   At the wet edges of the ford it thickened.

When you shut your eyes you could still see Bertha's scarlet frock on the white bridge path and smell the wet earth at the edges of the ford.

You were leaning over the white painted railing of the bridge when she began.   The water flowed from under the little tunnel across the road into the field beyond.   Deep brown under the tunnel, tawny in the shallow ford, golden patches where the pebbles showed through, and the water itself, a sheet of thin crystal, running over the colours, sliding through them, running and sliding on and on.

There was nothing in the world so beautiful as water, unless it was light.   But water was another sort of light.

Bertha pushed her soft sallow face into yours.   Her big black eyes bulged out under her square fringe.   Her wide red mouth curled and glistened.   There were yellowish stains about the roots of her black hair.   Her mouth and eyes teased you, mocked you, wouldn't let you alone.

Bertha began: " I know something you don't know."

You listened.   You couldn't help listening.   You simply had to know.   It was no use to say you didn't believe a word of it.   Inside you, secretly, you knew it was true.   You were frightened.   You trembled and went hot and cold by turns, and somehow that was how you knew it was true; almost as if you had known all the time.

" Oh, shut up!   I don't *want* to hear about it."

" Oh, don't you?   You did a minute ago."

" Of course I did, when I didn't know.   Who wouldn't? I don't want to know any more."

" I like that.   After I've told you everything.   What's the good of putting your fingers in your ears *now?* "

There was that day; and there was the next day when she was sick of Bertha.   On the third day Bertha went back to Woodford Bridge.

V

It was dreadful and at the same time funny when you thought of Mr. Batty and Mr. Propart with their little round hats and their black coats and their stiff, dignified faces. And there was Uncle Edward and his whiskers. It couldn't be true.

Yet all true things came like that, with a queer feeling, as if you remembered them.

Jenny's wedding dress. It would be true even of Jenny. Mamma had said she would rather see her in her coffin than married to Mr. Spall. That was why.

But — if it was true of everybody it would be true of Mamma and Papa. That was what you hated knowing. If only you had gone on looking at the water instead of listening to Bertha —

Mamma's face, solemn and tender, when you said your prayers, playing with the gold tassel of her watch-chain. Papa's face, on your birthday, when he gave you the toy lamb. She wouldn't like you to know about her. Mark wouldn't like it.

Mark: her mind stood still. Mark's image stood still in clean empty space. When she thought of her mother and Mark she hated Bertha.

And there was Jimmy. That was why they wouldn't talk about him.

Jimmy. The big water-jump into the plantation. Jimmy's arms, the throb of the hard muscles as he held you. Jimmy's hand, your own hand lying in it, light and small. Jimmy's eyes, looking at you and smiling, as if they said, "It's all right, Minky, it's all right."

Perhaps when Papa was young Mamma thought about him as you thought about Jimmy; so that it couldn't be so very dreadful, after all.

XIII

I

Mary was glad when Bertha went away to school.

When the new year came and she was fourteen she had

almost forgotten Bertha. She even forgot for long stretches of time what Bertha had told her. But not altogether.

Because, if it was true, then the story of the Virgin Mary was not true. Jesus couldn't have been born in the way the New Testament said he was born. There was no such thing as the Immaculate Conception. You could hardly be expected to believe in it once you knew why it couldn't have happened.

And if the Bible could deceive you about an important thing like that, it could deceive you about the Incarnation and the Atonement. You were no longer obliged to believe in that ugly business of a cruel, bungling God appeased with bloodshed. You were not obliged to believe anything just because it was in the Bible.

But — if you didn't, you were an Infidel.

She could hear Aunt Bella talking to Uncle Edward, and Mrs. Farmer and Mrs. Propart whispering: "Mary is an Infidel."

She thought: "If I *am* I can't help it." She was even slightly elated, as if she had set out on some happy, dangerous adventure.

II

Nobody seemed to know what Pantheism was. Mr. Propart smiled when you asked him and said it was something you had better not meddle with. Mr. Farmer said it was only another word for atheism; you might as well have no God at all as be a pantheist. But if " pan " meant " all things," and " theos " was God —

Perhaps it would be in the *Encyclopædia Britannica*. The Encyclopædia told you all about Australia. There was even a good long bit about Byron, too.

Panceput — Panegyric — Pantheism! There you were. Pantheism is " that speculative system which by absolutely identifying the Subject and Object of thought, reduces all existence, mental and material, to phenomenal modifications of one eternal, self-existent Substance which is called by the name of God. . . . All things are God."

When you had read the first sentence five or six times over and looked up " Subject " and " Object " and " Phenomenal," you could see fairly well what it meant. Whatever else God might be, he was not what they said, something separate and outside things, something that made your mind uncomfortable when you tried to think about it.

" This universe, material and mental, is nothing but the spectacle of the thoughts of God."

You might have known it would be like that. The universe, going on inside God, as your thoughts go on inside you; the universe, so close to God that nothing could be closer. The meaning got plainer and plainer.

There was Spinoza. (" Spinning — Spinoza.") The Encyclopædia man said that the Jewish priests offered him a bribe of two thousand florins to take back what he had said about God; and when he refused to take back a word of it, they cursed him and drove him out of their synagogue.

Spinoza said, " There is no substance but God, nor can any other be conceived." And the Encyclopædia man explained it. " God, as the infinite substance, with its infinity of attributes is the *natura naturans*. As the infinity of modes under which his attributes are manifested, he is the *natura naturata.*"

Nature naturing would be the cause, and Nature natured would be the effect. God was both.

" God is the immanent " — indwelling — " but not the transient cause of all things " . . . " Thought and Extension are attributes of the one absolute substance which is God, evolving themselves in two parallel streams, so to speak, of which each separate body and spirit are but the waves. Body and Soul are apparently two, but really one and they have no independent existence: They are parts of God. . . . Were our knowledge of God capable of present completeness we might attain to perfect happiness but such is not possible. Out of the infinity of his attributes only two, Thought and Extension, are accessible to us while the modes of these attributes, being essentially infinite, escape our grasp."

So this was the truth about God. In spite of the queer words it was very simple. Much simpler than the Trinity. God was not three incomprehensible Persons rolled into one, not Jesus, not Jehovah, not the Father creating the world in six days out of nothing, and muddling it, and coming down from heaven into it as his own son to make the best of a bad job. He was what you had felt and thought him to be as soon as you could think about him at all. The God of Baruch Spinoza was the God you had wanted, the only sort of God you cared to think about. Thinking about him — after the Christian God — was like coming out of a small dark room into an immense open space filled with happy light.

And yet, as far back as you could remember, there had been a regular conspiracy to keep you from knowing the truth about God. Even the Encyclopædia man was in it. He tried to put you off Pantheism. He got into a temper about it and said it was monstrous and pernicious and profoundly false and that the heart of man rose up in revolt against it. He had begun by talking about " attempts to transgress the fixed boundaries which One wiser than we has assigned to our intellectual operations." Perhaps he was a clergyman. Clergymen always put you off like that; so that you couldn't help suspecting that they didn't really know and were afraid you would find them out. They were like poor little frightened Mamma when she wouldn't let you look at the interesting bits beyond the place she had marked in your French Reader. And they were always apologising for their God, as if they felt that there was something wrong with him and that he was not quite real.

But to the pantheists the real God was so intensely real that, compared with him, being alive was not quite real, it was more like dreaming.

Another thing: the pantheists — the Hindu ones and the Greeks, and Baruch Spinoza — were heathen, and the Christians had tried to make you believe that the heathen went to hell because they didn't know the truth about God. You had been told one lie on the top of another. And all the time the truth was there, in the *Encyclopædia Britannica*.

Who would have thought that the Encyclopædia could have been so exciting?

The big puce-coloured books stood in a long row in the bottom shelf behind her father's chair. Her heart thumped when she gripped the volumes that contained the forbidden

knowledge of the universe. The rough morocco covers went
Rr-rr-rimp, as they scraped together; and there was the
sharp thud as they fell back into their place when she had
done with them. These sounds thrilled her with a secret
joy. When she was away from the books she liked to think
of them standing there on the hidden shelf, waiting for her.
The pages of " Pantheism " and " Spinoza " were white and
clean, and she had noticed how they had stuck together.
Nobody had opened them. She was the first, the only one
who knew and cared.

III

She wondered what Mark and her mother would say when
they knew. Perhaps Mark would say she ought not to tell
her mother if it meant letting out that the Bible said things
that were not really true. His idea might be that if Mamma
wanted to believe in Jehovah and the Atonement through
Christ's blood, it would be unkind to try and stop her.
But who on earth *would* want to believe that dreadful sort
of thing if they could help it? Papa might not mind, because as long as he knew that he and Mamma would get
into heaven all right he wouldn't worry so much about other
people. But Mamma was always worrying about them and
making you give up things to them; and she must be miserable when she thought of them burning in hell for ever and
ever, and when she tried to reconcile God's justice with his
mercy. To say nothing of the intellectual discomfort she
was living in. When you had found out the real, happy
truth about God, it didn't seem right to keep it to yourself.
She decided that she would tell her mother.
Mark was in the Royal Field Artillery now. He was
away at Shoeburyness. If she put it off till he came home
again she might never do it. When Mamma had Mark
with her she would never listen to anything you had to say.
Next Sunday was Epiphany. Sunday afternoon would
be a good time.
But Aunt Lavvy came to stay from Saturday to Monday.
And it rained. All morning Mamma and Aunt Lavvy sat
in the dining-room, one on each side of the fireplace. Aunt

Lavvy read James Martineau's *Endeavours After the Christian Life,* and Mamma read "The Pulpit in the Family" out of the *Sunday At Home.* Somehow you couldn't do it with Aunt Lavvy in the room.

In the afternoon when she went upstairs to lie down — perhaps.

But in the afternoon Mamma dozed over the *Sunday At Home.* She was so innocent and pretty, nodding her head, and starting up suddenly, and looking round with a smile that betrayed her real opinion of Sunday. You couldn't do it while she dozed.

Towards evening it rained again and Aunt Lavvy went off to Ilford for the Evening Service, by herself. Everybody else stayed at home, and there was hymn-singing instead of church. Mary and her mother were alone together. When her mother had sung the last hymn, "Lead, Kindly Light," then she would do it.

Her mother was singing:

> " ' Jesu, Lover of my soul,
>   Let me to Thy bosom fly,
> While the nearer wa-a-ters roll,
>   While the tempest still is high ' " —

She could see the stiff, slender muscles straining in her mother's neck. The weak, plaintive voice tore at her heart. She knew that her mother's voice was weak and plaintive. Its thin, sweet notes unnerved her.

> " ' Other refuge ha-ave I none:
>   Hangs my helpless soul on Thee ' " —

Helpless — Helpless. Mamma was helpless. It was only her love of Mark and Jesus that was strong. Something would happen if she told her — something awful. She could feel already the chill of an intolerable separation. She could give up Jesus, the lover of her soul, but she could not give up her mother. She couldn't live separated from Mamma, from the weak, plaintive voice that tore at her.

She couldn't do it.

IV

Catty's eyes twinkled through the banisters. She caught Mary coming downstairs and whispered that there was cold boiled chicken and trifle for supper, because of Aunt Lavvy.

Through the door Mary could see her father standing at the table, and the calm breasts of the cold chicken smoothed with white sauce and decorated with beetroot stars.

There was a book beside Papa's plate, the book Aunt Lavvy had been reading. She had left it open on the drawing-room table when she went to church. She was late for supper and they sat there waiting for her. She came in, slowly as usual, and looking at the supper things as though they were not there. When she caught sight of the book something went up and flickered in her eyes — a sort of triumph.

You couldn't help thinking that she had left it lying about on purpose, so that Papa should see it.

He stood waiting till she had sat down. He handed the book to her. His eyes gleamed.

"When you come here," he said, "you will be good enough to leave James Martineau behind you."

Mamma looked up, startled. "You don't mean to say you've brought that man's books into the house?"

"You can see for yourself, Caroline," said Aunt Lavvy.

"I don't want to see. No, Mary, it has nothing to do with you."

Mamma was smiling nervously. You would have supposed that she thought James Martineau funny, but the least bit improper.

"But look, Mamma, it's his *Endeavours After the Christian Life.*"

Her mother took up the book and put it down as if it had bitten her.

"Christian Life, indeed! What right has James Martineau to call himself a Christian? When he denies Christ — the Lord who bought him! And makes no secret of it. How can you respect an infidel who uses Christ's name to cover up his blasphemy?"

Aunt Lavvy was smiling now.

" I thought you said he made no secret of it? "

Mamma said, " You know very well what I mean."

" If you knew Dr. Martineau — "

" You've no business to know him," Emilius said, " when your brother Victor and I disapprove of him."

Emilius was carving chicken. He had an air of kindly, luscious hospitality, hesitating between the two flawless breasts.

" Dr. Martineau is. the wisest and holiest man I ever knew," said Aunt Lavvy.

" I daresay your sister Charlotte thinks Mr. Marriott the wisest and the holiest man *she* ever knew."

He settled the larger breast on Aunt Lavvy's plate and laid on it one perfect star of beetroot. He could do that while he insulted her.

" Oh — Papa — you *are* a br — "

Aunt Lavvy shook her gentle head.

" Lavinia dear " (Mamma's voice was gentle), " did you have a nice service? "

" Very nice, thank you."

" Did you go to Saint Mary's, or the Parish church? "

Aunt Lavvy's straight, flat chin trembled slightly. Her pale eyes lightened. " I went to neither."

" Then — where did you go? "

" If you insist on knowing, Caroline, I went to Mr. Robson's church."

" You went to Mr. — to the Unitarian Chapel? "

" To the Unitarian Chapel."

" Emilius — " You would have thought that Aunt Lavvy had hit Mamma and hurt her.

Emilius took up his table napkin and wiped his moustache carefully. He was quite horribly calm.

" You will oblige me by not going there again," he said.

" You forget that I went every Sunday when we were in Liverpool."

" You forget that is the reason why you left Liverpool."

" Only one of the reasons, I think."

" Can you tell me what reason you have for going now? Beyond your desire to make yourself different from other people."

" Aren't Unitarians other people? "

She poured out a glass of water and drank. She was giving herself time.

" My reason," she said, " is that I have joined the Unitarian Church."

Mamma put down her knife and fork. Her lips opened and her face turned suddenly sharp and sallow as if she were going to faint.

" You don't mean to say you've gone over? Then God help poor Charlotte! "

Emilius steadied himself to speak. " Does Victor know? " he said.

" Yes. He knows."

" You have consulted him, and you have not consulted me? "

" You made me promise not to talk about it. I have kept my promise."

Mary was sure then that Aunt Lavvy had left the book open on purpose. She had laid a trap for Emilius, and he had fallen into it.

" If you will hold infamous opinions you must be made to keep them to yourself."

" I have a perfect right to my opinions."

" You have no right to make an open profession of them."

" The law is more tolerant than you, Emilius."

" There is a moral law and a law of honour. You are not living by yourself. As long as you are in Victor's house the least you can do is to avoid giving offence. Have you no consideration for your family? You say you came here to be near us. Have you thought of us? Have you thought of the children? Do you expect Caroline to go to Victor's house if she's to meet the Unitarian minister and his wife? "

" You will be cutting yourself off completely, Lavinia," Mamma said.

" From what? "

" From everybody. People don't call on Nonconformists. If there were no higher grounds — "

" Oh — Caroline — " Aunt Lavvy breathed it on a long sigh.

" It's all very well for you. But you might think of your sister Charlotte," Mamma said.

Papa's beard jerked. He drew in his breath with a savage guttural noise. "A-ach! What's the good of talking?"

He had gone on eating all the time. There was a great pile of chicken bones on his plate.

Aunt Lavvy turned. "Emilius — for thirty-three years" — her voice broke as she quivered under her loaded anguish — "for thirty-three years you've shouted me down. You haven't let me call my soul my own. Yet it *is* my own — "

"There, please — *please*," Mamma said, "don't let us have any more of it," just as Aunt Lavvy was beginning to get a word in edgeways.

"Mamma, that isn't fair, you must let her speak."

"Yes. You must let me speak." Aunt Lavvy's voice thickened in her throat.

"I won't have any discussion of Unitarianism here," said Papa.

"It's you who have been discussing it, not I."

"It is, really, Papa. First you began. Then Mamma."

Mamma said, "If you've finished your supper, Mary, you can go."

"But I haven't. I've not had any trifle yet."

She thought: "They don't want me to hear them; but I've a right to sit here and eat trifle. They know they can't turn me out. I haven't done anything."

Aunt Lavvy went on. "I've only one thing to say, Emilius. You've asked me to think of Victor and Charlotte, and you and Caroline and the boys and Mary. Have you once — in thirty-three years — for a single minute — thought of *me?*"

"Certainly I have. It's partly for your own sake I object to your disgracing yourself. As if your sister Charlotte wasn't disgrace enough."

Aunt Lavvy drew herself up stiff and straight in her white shawl like a martyr in her flame. "You might keep Charlotte out of it, I think."

"I might. Charlotte can't help herself. You can."

At this point Mamma burst into tears and left the room.

"Now," he said, "I hope you're satisfied."

Mary answered him.

"I think *you* ought to be, Papa, if you've been bullying

Aunt Lavvy for thirty-three years. Don't you think it's about time you stopped?"

Emilius stared at his daughter. His face flushed slowly. "I think," he said, "it's time you went to bed."

"It isn't my bed-time for another hour yet."

(A low murmur from Aunt Lavvy: "Don't, Mary, don't.")

She went on. "It was you who made Mamma cry, not Aunt Lavvy. It always frightens her when you shout at people. You know Aunt Lavvy's a perfect saint, besides being lots cleverer than anybody in this house, except Mark. You get her by herself when she's tired out with Aunt Charlotte. You insult her religion. You say the beastliest things you can think of —"

Her father pushed back his chair; they rose and looked at each other.

"You wouldn't dare to do it if Mark was here!"

He strode to the door and opened it. His arm made a crescent gesture that cleared space of her.

"Go! Go upstairs. Go to bed!"

"I don't care where I go now I've said it."

Upstairs in her bed she still heard Aunt Lavvy's breaking voice:

"For thirty-three years — for thirty-three years —"

The scene rose again and swam before her and fell to pieces. Ideas — echoes — images. Religion — the truth of God. Her father's voice booming over the table. Aunt Lavvy's voice, breaking — breaking. A pile of stripped chicken bones on her father's plate.

v

Aunt Lavvy was getting ready to go away. She held up her night gown to her chin, smoothing and folding back the sleeves. You thought of her going to bed in the ugly, yellow, flannel night gown, not caring, lying in bed and thinking about God.

Mary was sorry that Aunt Lavvy was going. As long as she was there you felt that if only she would talk everything would at once become more interesting. She thrilled you with that look of having something — something that she wouldn't talk about — up her sleeve. The Encyclopædia man said that Unitarianism was a kind of Pantheism. Perhaps that was it. Perhaps she knew the truth about God. Aunt Lavvy would know whether she ought to tell her mother.

" Aunt Lavvy, if you loved somebody and you found out that their religion wasn't true, would you tell them or wouldn't you? "

" It would depend on whether they were happy in their religion or not."

" Supposing you'd found out one that was more true and much more beautiful, and you thought it would make them happier? "

Aunt Lavvy raised her long, stubborn chin. In her face there was a cold exaltation and a sudden hardness.

" No religion was ever more true or more beautiful than Christianity," she said.

" There's Pantheism. Aren't Unitarians a kind of Pantheists? "

Aunt Lavvy's white face flushed. " Unitarians Pantheists? Who's been talking to you about Pantheism? "

" Nobody. Nobody knows about it. I had to find out."

" The less you find out about it the better."

" Aunt Lavvy, you're talking like Mr. Propart. Supposing I honestly think Pantheism's true? "

" You've no right to think anything about it," Aunt Lavvy said.

" Now you're talking like Papa. And I did so hope you wouldn't."

" I only meant that it takes more time than you've lived to find out what honest thinking *is*. When you're twenty years older you'll know what this opinion of yours is worth."

" I know what it's worth to me, now, this minute."

" Is it worth making your mother miserable? "

" That's what Mark would say. How did you know I was thinking of Mamma? "

" Because that's what my brother Victor said to me."

VI

The queer thing was that none of them seemed to think the truth could possibly matter on its own account, or that anything mattered besides being happy or miserable. Yet everybody, except Aunt Lavvy, was determined that everybody else should be happy in their way by believing what they believed; and when it came to Pantheism even Aunt Lavvy couldn't live and let live. You could see that deep down inside her it made her more furious than Unitarianism made Papa.

Mary saw that she was likely to be alone in her adventure. It appeared to her more than ever as a journey into a beautiful, quiet yet exciting country where you could go on and on. The mere pleasure of being able to move enchanted her. But nobody would go with her. Nobody knew. Nobody cared.

There was Spinoza; but Spinoza had been dead for ages. Now she came to think of it she had never heard anybody, not even Mr. Propart, speak of Spinoza. It would be worse for her than it had ever been for Aunt Lavvy who had actually known Dr. Martineau. Dr. Martineau was not dead; and if he had been there were still lots of Unitarian ministers alive all over England. And in the end Aunt Lavvy had broken loose and gone into her Unitarian Chapel.

She thought: "Not till after Grandmamma was dead. Till years after Grandmamma was dead."

She thought: "Of course I'd die rather than tell Mamma."

VII

Aunt Lavvy had gone. Mr. Parish had taken her away in his wagonette.

At lessons Mamma complained that you were not attending. But she was not attending herself, and when sewing time came she showed what she had been thinking about.

"What were you doing in Aunt Lavvy's room this morning?"

She looked up sharply over the socks piled before her for darning.

" Only talking."

" Was Aunt Lavvy talking to you about her opinions? "

" No, Mamma."

" Has she ever talked to you? "

" Of course not. She wouldn't if she promised not to. I don't know even now what Unitarianism is. . . . What *do* Unitarians believe in? "

" Goodness knows," her mother said. " Nothing that's any good to them, you may be sure."

Mary went on darning. The coarse wool of the socks irritated her fingers. It caught in a split nail, setting her teeth on edge.

If you went on darning for ever — if you went on darning — Mamma would be pleased. She had not suspected anything

VIII

> " ' Full fathom five thy father lies,
>   Of his bones are coral made,
>   Those are pearls that were his eyes.
>   Nothing of him that doth fade
>   But doth suffer a sea-change
>   Into something rich and strange.' "

Between the lovely lines she could hear Mamma say, " They all scamp their work. You would require a resident carpenter and a resident glazier — "

And Mrs. Farmer's soft drawl spinning out the theme: " And a resident plumber. Yes, Mrs. Olivier, you really wou-ould."

Mr. and Mrs. Farmer had called and stayed to tea. Across the room you could see his close, hatchet nose and straggly beard. Every now and then his small, greenish eyes lifted and looked at you.

Impossible that you had ever enjoyed going to Mrs. Farmer's to see the baby. It was like something that had happened to somebody else, a long time ago. Mrs. Farmer was always having babies, and always asking you to go and see them. She couldn't understand that as you grew older you left off caring about babies.

" ' — We are such stuff
   As dreams are made of —' "

" The Bishop — Confirmation — opportunity."
Even Mamma owned that Mr. Farmer never knew when
it was time to go.

" ' As dreams are made of, and our little life
   Is rounded with a sleep — ' "

The universe is nothing but the spectacle of the dreams
of God. Or was it the thoughts of God?
" Confirmation — Parish Church — Bishop — "
Confirmation. She had seen a Confirmation once, years
ago. Girls in white dresses and long white veils, like brides,
shining behind the square black windows of the broughams.
Dora and Effie Draper. Effie leaned forward. Her pretty,
piercing face looked out through the black pane, not seeing
anything, trying greedily to be seen. Big boys and girls
knelt down in rows before the Bishop, and his sleeves went
flapping up and down over them like bolsters in the wind.
Mr. Farmer was looking at her again, as if he had an
idea in his head.

IX

The Church Service was open at the Thirty-Nine Articles.
Mamma had pushed Dr. Smith's " History of England "
away.
" Do you think," she said, " you could say the Catechism
and the Athanasian Creed straight through without stop-
ping? "
" I daresay I could if I tried. Why? "
" Because Mr. Farmer will want to examine you."
" Whatever for? "
" Because," her mother said, " there's going to be a Con-
firmation. It's time you were thinking about being con-
firmed."
" Confirmed? *Me?* "
" And why not you? "
" Well — I haven't got to be, have I? "

"You will have, sooner or later. So you may as well begin to think about it now."

Confirmation. She had never thought about it as a real thing that might happen to her, that would happen, sooner or later, if she didn't do something to stop Mr. Farmer and Mamma.

"I *am* thinking. I'm thinking tight."

Tight. Tight. Her mind, in agony, pinned itself to one point: how she could stop her mother without telling her.

Beyond that point she couldn't see clearly.

"You see — you see — I don't *want* to be confirmed."

"You don't want? You might as well say you didn't want to be a Christian."

"Don't worry, Mamma darling. I only want to stay as I am."

"I must worry. I'm responsible for you as long as you're not confirmed. You forget that I'm your godmother as well as your mother."

She *had* forgotten it. And Papa and Uncle Victor were her godfathers. "What did your godfathers and godmothers then for you? — They did promise and vow three things in my name —" they had actually done it. "First: that I should renounce" — renounce — renounce — "Secondly: that I should believe all the Articles of the Christian Faith —"

The Christian Faith — the Catholic Faith. "Which Faith except everyone do keep whole and undefiled, without doubt he shall perish everlastingly" —

—"And the Catholic Faith is this: That we worship one God in Trinity and Trinity in Unity."

They had promised and vowed all that. In her name. What right had they? What right had they?

"You're not a baby any more," her mother said.

"That's what I mean. I was a baby when you went and did it. I knew nothing about it. You *can't* make me responsible."

"It's we who are responsible," her mother said.

"I mean for your vows and promises, Mamma darling. If you'll let me off my responsibility I'll let you off yours."

"Now," her mother said, "you're prevaricating."

" That means you'll never let me off. If I don't do it now I'll have to do it next year, or the next? "

" You may feel more seriously about it next year. Or next week," her mother said. " Meanwhile you'll learn the Thirty-Nine Articles. Read them through first."

" — ' Nine. Of Original or Birth-sin. Original Sin . . . is the fault and corruption of the Nature of every man . . . whereby man is far gone from original righteousness and is of his own nature inclined to evil, so that the flesh lusteth always contrary to the spirit; and therefore in every person born into this world it deserveth God's wrath and damnation.' "

" Don't look like that," her mother said, " as if your wits were wool-gathering."

" Wool? " She could see herself smiling at her mother, disagreeably.

Wool-gathering. Gathering wool. The room was full of wool; wool flying about; hanging in the air and choking you. Clogging your mind. Old grey wool out of pew cushions that people had sat on for centuries, full of dirt.

Wool, spun out, wound round you, woven in a net. You were tangled and strangled in a net of unclean wool. They caught you in it when you were a baby a month old. Mamma, Papa and Uncle Victor. You would have to cut and tug and kick and fight your way out. They were caught in it themselves, they couldn't get out. They didn't want to get out. The wool stopped their minds working. They hated it when their minds worked, when anybody's mind worked. Aunt Lavvy's — yours.

" ' Thirteen. Of Works before Justification. Works done before the grace of Christ, and the Inspiration of His Spirit, are not pleasant to God, forasmuch as they spring not of faith in Jesus Christ . . . : yea, rather, for that they are not done as God hath willed and commanded them to be done, we doubt not but they have the nature of sin.' "

" Do you really believe that, Mamma? "

" Of course I believe it. All our righteousness is filthy rags."

— People's goodness. People's kindness. The sweet,

beautiful things they did for each other.   The brave, noble things, the things Mark did: filthy rags.

This — this religion of theirs — was filthy; ugly, like the shiny black covers of their Bibles where their fingers left a grey, greasy smear.   Filthy and frightful; like funerals. You might as well be buried alive, five coffins deep in a pit of yellow clay.

Mamma couldn't really believe it.   You would have to tell her it wasn't true.   Not telling her meant that you didn't think she cared about the truth.   You insulted her if you supposed she didn't care.   Mark would say you insulted her.   Even if it hurt her a bit at first, you insulted her if you thought she couldn't bear it.   And afterwards she would be happy, because she would be free.

" It's no use, Mamma.   I shan't ever want to be confirmed."

" Want — want — want!   You ought to want, then.   You say you believe the Christian Faith — "

Now — now.   A clean quick cut.   No jagged ends hanging.

" That's it.   I don't believe a single word of it."

She couldn't look at her mother.   She didn't want to see her cry.

" You've found that out, have you?   You've been mighty quick about it."

" I found it out ages ago.   But I didn't mean to tell you."

Her mother was not crying.

" You needn't tell me now," she said.   " You don't suppose I'm going to believe it? "

Not crying.   Smiling.   A sort of cunning and triumphant smile.

" You just want an excuse for not learning those Thirty-Nine Articles."

XIV

I

MAMMA was crying.

Papa had left the dining-room.   Mary sat at the foot of the table, and her mother at the head.   The space between was covered and piled with Mark's kit: the socks, the

pocket-handkerchiefs, the vests, the fine white pyjamas.
The hanging white globes of the gaselier shone on them.
All day Mary had been writing "M. E. Olivier, M. E.
Olivier," in clear, hard letters, like print. The iridescent
ink was grey on the white linen and lawn, black when you
stamped with the hot iron: M. E. Olivier. Mamma was
embroidering M. E. O. in crimson silk on a black sock.

Mark was in the Army now; in the Royal Field Artillery.
He was going to India. In two weeks, before the middle of
April, he would be gone. They had known this so long that
now and then they could forget it; they could be glad that
Mark should have all those things, so many more, and more
beautiful, than he had ever had. They were appeased with
their labour of forming, over and over again, the letters,
clear and perfect, of his name.

Then Papa had come in and said that Dan was not going
to live at home any more. He had taken rooms in Blooms-
bury with young Vickers.

Dan had not gone to Cambridge when he left Chelmsted,
as Mamma had intended. There hadn't been enough money.

Uncle Victor had paid for Mark's last year at Woolwich
and for his outfit now. Some day Mamma would pay him
back again.

Dan had gone first into Papa's office; then into Uncle
Edward's office. He was in Uncle Victor's office now.
Sometimes he didn't get home till after midnight. Sometimes when you went into his room to call him in the morning he wasn't there; but there were the bed-clothes turned
down as Catty had left them, with his nightshirt folded on
the top.

Her mother said: "I hope you're content now you've
finished your work."

"*My* work?" her father said.

"Yes, yours. You couldn't rest till you'd got the poor
boy out of your office, and now you've turned him out of
the house. I suppose you thought that with Mark going
you'd better make a clean sweep. It'll be Roddy next."

"I didn't turn him out of the house. But it was about
time he went. The young cub's temper is getting un-
bearable."

"I daresay. You ruined Dan's temper with your silly tease — tease — tease — from morning till night. You can't see a dog without wanting to make it snap and snarl. It was the same with all the children. And when they turned you bullied them. Just because you couldn't break Mark's spirit you tried to crush Dan's. It's a wonder he has any temper left."

Emilius stroked his beard.

"That's right. Stroke your beard as if nothing mattered but your pleasure. You'll be happy enough when Mark's gone."

Emilius left off stroking his beard.

"You say I turned him out of the office," he said. "Did he stay with Edward?"

"Nobody could stay with Edward. You couldn't yourself."

"Ask Victor how long he thinks he'll keep him."

"What do you mean, Emilius?"

He didn't answer. He stood there, his lips pouting between his moustache and beard, his eyes smiling wickedly, as if he had just found out he could torment her more by not saying what he meant.

"If Dan went to the bad," she said, "I wouldn't blame him. It would serve you right."

"Unless," she added, "that's what you want."

And she began to cry.

She cried as a child cries, with spasms of sobbing, her pretty mouth spoiled, stretched wide, working, like india-rubber; dull red blotches creeping up to the brown stains about her eyes. Her tears splashed on to the fine, black silk web of the sock and sparkled there.

Emilius had gone from the room, leaving the door open. Mary got up and shut it. She stood, hesitating. The helpless sobbing drew her, frightened her, stirred her to exasperation that was helpless too. Her mother had never been more intolerably dear.

She went to her. She put her arm round her.

"Don't, Mamma darling. Why do you let him torture you? He didn't turn Dan out of the office. He let him go because he can't afford to pay him enough."

" I know that as well as you," her mother said surprisingly.

She drew herself from the protecting arm.

" Well, then — But, oh, what a brute he is. *What* a brute!"

" For shame to talk that way of your father. *You've* no right. You're the one that always goes scot-free."

And, beginning to cry again, she rose and went out, grasping Mark's sock in her convulsive hand.

" Mary, did you hear your mother say I bullied you? "

Her father had come back into the room.

" Yes," she said.

" Have I ever bullied you? "

She looked at him steadily.

" No. You would have done if Mamma had loved me as much as she loves Mark. I wish you had. I wish you'd bullied the life out of me. I shouldn't have cared. I wish you'd hated me. Then I should have known she loved me."

He looked at her in silence, with round, startled eyes. He understood.

II

" Ubique — "

The gunner's motto. Mark's motto, stamped on all the letters he would write. A blue gun on a blue gun-carriage, the muzzle pointing to the left. The motto waving underneath: " UBIQUE."

At soldiers' funerals the coffin was carried on a gun-carriage and covered with a flag.

" *Ubique quo fas et gloria ducunt.*" All through the excitement of the evening it went on sounding in her head.

It was Mark's coming of age party in the week before he went. The first time she could remember being important at a party. Her consciousness of being important was intense, exquisite. She was Sub-Lieutenant Mark Olivier's sister. His only one.

And, besides, she looked nice.

Last year's white muslin, ironed out, looked as good as new. The blue sash really *was* new; and Mamma had lent her one of her necklets, a turquoise heart on a thin gold chain. In the looking-glass she could see her eyes shining under her square brown fringe: spots of gold darting through brown crystal. Her brown hair shone red on the top and gold underneath. The side pieces, rolled above her ears and plaited behind, made a fillet for her back hair. Her back hair was too short. She tried to make it reach to her waist by pulling the curled tips straight; but they only sprang back to her shoulder-blades again. It was unfortunate.

Catty, securing the wonderful fillet with a blue ribbon told her not to be unhappy. She would " do."

Mamma was beautiful in her lavender-grey silk and her black jet cross with the diamond star. They all had to stand together, a little behind her, near the door, and shake hands with the people as they came in. Mary was surprised that they should shake hands with her before they shook hands with Mark; it didn't seem right, somehow, when it was his birthday.

Everybody had come except Aunt Charlotte; even Mr. Marriott, though he was supposed to be afraid of parties. (You couldn't ask Aunt Charlotte because of Mr. Marriott.) There were the two Manistys, looking taller and leaner than ever. And there was Mrs. Draper with Dora and Effie. Mrs. Draper, black hawk's eyes in purple rings; white powder over crushed carmines; a black wing of hair folded over grey down. Effie's pretty, piercing face; small head poised to strike. Dora, a young likeness of Mrs. Draper, an old likeness of Effie, pretty when Effie wasn't there.

When they looked at you you saw that your muslin was not as good as new. When they looked at Mamma you saw that her lavender silk was old-fashioned and that nobody wore black jet crosses now. You were frilly and floppy when everybody else was tight and straight in Princess dresses.

Mamma was more beautiful than Mrs. Draper; and her hair, anyhow, was in the fashion, parted at the side, a soft brown wing folded over her left ear.

But that made her look small and pathetic — a wounded bird. She ought not to have been made to look like that.

You could hear Dora and Effie being kind to Mamma.

" Dear Mrs. Olivier "— Indulgence — Condescension. As if to an unfortunate and rather foolish person. Mark could see that. He was smiling: a hard, angry smile.

Mrs. Draper was Mamma's dearest friend. They could sit and talk to each other about nothing for hours together. In the holidays Mrs. Draper used to be always coming over to talk to Mamma, always bringing Dora and Effie with her, always asking Mark and Dan and Roddy to her house, always wondering why Mark never went.

Dan went. Dan seemed as if he couldn't keep away.

This year Mrs. Draper had left off asking Mark and Dan and Roddy. She had left off bringing Dora and Effie with her.

Mary wondered why she had brought them now, and why her mother had asked them.

The Manistys. She had brought them for the Manistys. She wanted Mamma to see what she had brought them for. And Mamma had asked them because she didn't care, and wanted them to see that she didn't care, and that Mark didn't care either.

If they only knew how Mark detested them with their " *Dear* Mrs. Olivier" !

Something was going on. She heard Uncle Victor saying to Aunt Lavvy, " Mark's party is a bit rough on Dan."

Dan was trying to get to Effie through a gap in the group formed by the Manistys and two young subalterns, Mark's friends. Each time he did it Mrs. Draper stopped him by moving somehow so as to fill the gap. He gave it up at last, to sit by himself at the bottom of the room, jammed into a corner between the chimney-piece and the rosewood cabinet, where he stared at Effie with hot, unhappy eyes.

Supper. Mamma was worried about the supper. She would have liked to have given them a nicer one, but there wasn't enough money; besides, she was afraid of what Uncle Victor would think if they were extravagant. That was the worst of borrowing, Mark said; you couldn't spend so much afterwards. Still, there was enough wine yet in the cellar for fifty parties. You could see, now, some advantage in Papa's habit of never drinking any but the best wine and laying in a large stock of it while he could.

Mary noticed that Papa and Dan drank the most. Perhaps Dan drank more than Papa. The smell of wine was over all the supper, spoiling it, sending through her nerves a reminiscent shiver of disgust.

Mark brought her back into the dining-room for the ice she hadn't had. Dan was there, by himself, sitting in the place Effie had just left. Effie's glass had still some wine in it. You could see him look for the wet side of the rim and suck the drops that had touched her mouth. Something small and white was on the floor beside him. Effie's pocket-handkerchief. He stooped for it. You could hear him breathing up the scent on it with big, sighing sobs.

They slunk back into the drawing-room.

Mark asked her to play something.

" Make a noise, Minky. Perhaps they'll go."

" The Hungarian March." She could play it better than Mamma. Mamma never could see that the bass might be even more important than the treble. She was glad that she could play it better than Mamma, and she hated herself for being glad.

Mark stood by the piano and looked at her as she played. They talked under cover of the " Droom — Droom — Droom-era-room."

" Mark, am I looking too awful? "

" No. Pretty Minx. Very pretty Minx."

" We mustn't, Mark. They'll hear us. They'll think us idiots."

" I don't care if they do. Don't you wish they'd go? Clever Minx. Clever paws."

Mamma passed and looked at them. Her face shrank and sharpened under the dropped wing of her hair. She must have heard what Mark said. She hated it when Mark talked and looked like that. She hated it when you played *her* music.

Beethoven, then. The " Sonata Eroica " was bound up with " Violetta," the " Guards " and " Mabel " Waltzes and the " Pluie des Perles."

" *Ubique quo fas et gloria ducunt.*" That was the meaning of the noble, serious, passionate music.

Roddy called out, " Oh, *not that* dull old thing."

No. Not that. There was the Funeral March in it: *sulle morte d'un eroe.* Mark was going away.

"Waldteufel," then. *One — two — three. One — two — three.* Sustained thrum in the bass. *One — two — three.* Thursday — Friday — *One* — two — three. Saturday — Sunday. Beat of her thoughts, beat of the music in a sort of syncopated time. *One — two — three,* Monday.

On Tuesday Mark would be gone.

His eyes made her break off to look round. Dan had come back into the room, to his place between the cabinet and the chimney-piece. He stooped forward, his head hanging as if some weight dragged it. His eyes, turned up, staring at Effie, showed half circles of blood-shot white. His face was flushed. A queer, leaden grey flush.

Aunt Lavvy sat beside him. She had her hand on his arm, to keep him quiet there in his corner.

"Mark — what's the matter with Dan?"

One — two — three. *One* — two — three. Something bumped against the glass door of the cabinet. A light tinkling crash of a broken pane. She could see slantwise as she went on playing. Dan was standing up. He swayed, feeling for the ledge of the cabinet. Then he started to come down the room, his head lowered, thrust forward, his eyes heavy with some earnest, sombre purpose.

He seemed to be hours coming down the room by himself. Hours standing in the middle of the room, holding on to the parrot chair.

"Mark!"

"Go on playing."

He went to him. Roddy sprang up from somewhere. Hours while they were getting Dan away from the parrot chair to the door beside the piano. Hours between the opening and sudden slamming of the door.

But she had not played a dozen bars. She went on playing.

"Wait a minute, Effie."

Effie was standing beside her with her hand on the door.

"I've lost my pocket-handkerchief, I must have left it in the dining-room. I *know* I left it in the dining-room," she said, fussing.

Mary got up. "All right. I'll fetch it."
She opened the door and shut it again quickly.
"I can't go — yet."

III

Friday, Saturday and Sunday passed, each with a separate, hurrying pace that quickened towards bed-time.

Mark's last night. She had left her door open so that
she could hear him come upstairs. He came and sat on her
bed as he used to do years ago when she was afraid of the
ghost in the passage.

"I shan't be away for ever, Minky. Only five years."

"Yes, but you'll be twenty-six then, and I shall be nineteen. We shan't be ourselves."

"I shall be *my* self. Five years isn't really long."

"You — you'll like it, Mark. There'll be jungles with
bisons and tigers."

"Yes. Jungles."

"And polo."

"Shan't be able to go in for polo."

"Why not?"

"Ponies. Too expensive."

They sat silent.

"What I *don't* like," Mark said in a sleepy voice, "is
leaving Papa."

"Papa?"

He really meant it. "Wish I'd been decenter to him,"
he said.

And then: "Minky — you'll be kind to little Mamma."

"Oh, Mark — aren't I?"

"Not always. Not when you say funny things about the
Bible."

"You say funny things yourself."

"Yes; but she thinks I don't mean them, so it doesn't
matter."

"She thinks I don't mean them, either."

"Well — let her go on thinking it. Do what she wants
— even when it's beastly."

"It's all very well for you. She doesn't want *you* to

learn the Thirty-Nine Articles. What would you do if she
did? "

"Learn them, of course. Lie about them, if that would
please her."

.She thought: "Mamma didn't want him to be a soldier."

As if he knew what she was thinking, he said, "She
doesn't really mind my going into the Army. I knew she
wouldn't. Besides, I had to."

"Yes."

"I'll make it up to her," he said. "I won't do any other
thing she wouldn't like. I won't marry. I won't play polo.
I'll live on my pay and give poor Victor back his money.
And there's one good thing about it. Papa'll be happier
when I'm not here."

IV

"Mark! "

"Minky! "

He had said good-night and gone to his room and come
back again to hold her still tighter in his arms.

"What? "

"Nothing," he said. "Only — good-night."

To-morrow no lingering and no words. Mark's feet quick
in the passage. A door shut to, a short, crushing embrace
before he turned from her to her mother.

Her mother and she alone together in the emptied room,
turning from each other, without a word.

V

The wallflowers had grown up under the south side of the
garden wall; a hedge of butterfly-brown and saffron. They
gave out a hot, velvet smell, like roses and violets laced with
mignonette.

Mamma stood looking at the wallflowers, smiling at them,
happy, as if Mark had never gone.

As if Mark had never gone.

XV

I

MAMMA whispered to Mrs. Draper, and Aunt Bella whispered to Mamma: "Fourteen." They always made a mystery about being fourteen. They ought to have told her.

Her thoughts about her mother went up and down. Mamma was not helpless. She was not gentle. She was not really like a wounded bird. She was powerful and rather cruel. You could only appease her with piles of hemmed sheets and darned stockings. If you didn't take care she would get hold of you and never rest till she had broken you, or turned and twisted you to her own will. She would say it was God's will. She would think it was God's will.

They might at least have told you about the pain. The knives of pain. You had to clench your fists till the finger-nails bit into the palms. Over the ear of the sofa cushions she could feel her hot eyes looking at her mother with resentment.

She thought: "You had no business to have me. You had no business to have me."

Somebody else's eyes. Somebody else's thoughts. Not yours. Not yours.

Mamma got up and leaned over you and covered you with the rug. Her white face quivered above you in the dusk. Her mouth pushed out to yours, making a small sound like a moan. You heard yourself cry: "Mamma, Mamma, you are adorable!"

That was you.

II

And as if Mark had never gone, as if that awful thing had never happened to Dan, as if she had never had those thoughts about her mother, her hidden happiness came back to her. Unhappiness only pushed it to a longer rhythm. Nothing could take it away. Anything might bring it: the smell of the white dust on the road; the wind when it came up out of nowhere and brushed the young wheat blades, beat the green flats into slopes where the white light rippled and ran like water, set the green field shaking and tossing like a green sea; the five elm trees, stiff, ecstatic dancers, holding out the broken-ladder pattern of their skirts; haunting rhymes, sudden cadences; the grave " *Ubique* " sounding through the Beethoven Sonata.

Its thrill of reminiscence passed into the thrill of premonition, of something about to happen to her.

XVI

I

POEMS made of the white dust, of the wind in the green corn, of the five trees — they would be the most beautiful poems in the world.

Sometimes the images of these things would begin to move before her with persistence, as if they were going to make a pattern; she could hear a thin cling-clang, a moving white pattern of sound that, when she tried to catch it, broke up and flowed away. The image pattern and the sound pattern belonged to each other, but when she tried to bring them together they fell apart.

That came of reading too much Byron.

How was it that patterns of sound had power to haunt and excite you? Like the " potnia, potnia nux " that she found in the discarded Longfellow, stuck before his " Voices of the Night."

πότνια, πότνια νύξ, ὑπνοδότειρα τῶν πολυπόνων βροτῶν,
ἐρεβόθεν ἴθι, μόλε, μόλε κατάπτερος
τὸν Ἀγαμεμνόνιον ἐπὶ δόμον.

She wished she knew Greek; the patterns the sounds made were so hard and still.

And there were bits of patterns, snapt off, throbbing wounds of sound that couldn't heal. Lines out of Mark's Homer.

Mark's Greek books had been taken from her five years ago, when Rodney went to Chelmsted. And they had come back with Rodney this Easter. They stood on the shelf in Mark's bedroom, above his writing-table.

One day she found her mother there, dusting and arranging the books. Besides the little shabby Oxford Homers there were an Æschylus, a Sophocles, two volumes of Aristophanes, clean and new, three volumes of Euripides and a Greek Testament. On the table a well-preserved Greek Anthology, bound in green, with the owner's name, J. C. Ponsonby, stamped on it in gilt letters. She remembered Jimmy giving it to Mark.

She took the *Iliad* from its place and turned over the torn, discoloured pages.

Her mother looked up, annoyed and uneasy, like a child disturbed in the possession of its toys.

"Mark's books are to be kept where Mark put them," she said.

"But, Mamma, I want them."

Never in her life had she wanted anything so much as those books.

"When will you learn not to want what isn't yours?"

"Mark doesn't want them, or he'd have taken them. He'd give them me if he was here."

"He isn't here. I won't have them touched till he comes back."

"But, Mamma darling, I may be dead. I've had to wait five years as it is."

"Wait? What for, I should like to know?"

"To learn Greek, of course."

Her mother's face shivered with repugnance. It was incredible that anybody should hate a poor dead language so.

"Just because Mark learnt Greek, you think *you* must try. I thought you'd grown out of all that tiresome affectation. It was funny when you were a little thing, but it isn't funny now."

Her mother sat down to show how tired she was of it.

"It's just silly vanity."

Mary's heart made a queer and startling movement, as if it turned over and dashed itself against her ribs. There was a sudden swelling and aching in her throat. Her head swam slightly. The room, Mark's room, with Mark's white bed in one corner and Dan's white bed in the other, had changed; it looked like a room she had never been in before. She had never seen that mahogany washstand and the greyish blue flowers on the jug and basin. The person sitting on the yellow-painted bedroom chair was a stranger who wore, unaccountably, a brown dress and a gold watchchain with a gold tassel that she remembered. She had an odd feeling that this person had no right to wear her mother's dress and her chain.

The flash of queerness was accompanied by a sense of irreparable disaster. Everything had changed; she heard herself speaking, speaking steadily, with the voice of a changed and unfamiliar person.

"Mark doesn't think it's vanity. You only think it is because you want to."

The mind of this unfamiliar self had a remorseless lucidity that seemed to her more shocking than anything she could imagine. It went on as if urged by some supreme necessity. "You're afraid. Afraid."

It seemed to her that her mother really was afraid.

"Afraid? And what of?" her mother said.

The flash went out, leaving her mind dark suddenly and defeated.

"I don't know what *of*. I only know you're afraid."

"That's an awful thing for any child to say to any mother. Just because I won't let you have your own way in everything. Until your will is resigned to God's will I may well be afraid."

"How do you know God doesn't want me to know Greek? He may want it as much as I do."

"And if you did know it, what good would it do you?"

She stood staring at her mother, not answering. She knew the sound patterns were beautiful, and that was all she knew. Beauty. Beauty could be hurt and frightened away from you. If she talked about it now she would expose it to outrage. Though she knew that she must appear to her mother to be stubborn and stupid, even sinful, she put her stubbornness, her stupidity, her sinfulness, between it and her mother to defend it.

"I can't tell you," she said.

"No. I don't suppose you can."

Her mother followed up the advantage given her. "You just go about dreaming and mooning as if there was nothing else in the wide world for you to do. I can't think what's come over you. You used to be content to sit still and sew by the hour together. You were more help to me when you were ten than you are now. The other day when I asked you to darn a hole in your own stocking you looked as if I'd told you to go to your funeral.

"It's time you began to take an interest in looking after the house. There's enough to keep you busy most of your time if you only did the half of it."

"Is that what you want me to be, Mamma? A servant, like Catty?"

"Poor Catty. If you were more like Catty," her mother said, "you'd be happier than you are now, I can tell you. Catty is never disagreeable or disobedient or discontented."

"No. But perhaps Catty's mother thinks she is."

She thought: She *is* afraid.

"Do you suppose," her mother said, "it's any pleasure to me to find fault with my only daughter? If you weren't my only daughter, perhaps, I shouldn't find fault."

Her new self answered again, implacable in its lucidity. "You mean, if you'd had a girl you could do what you liked with you'd have let me alone? You'd have let me alone if you could have done what you liked with Mark?"

She noticed, as if it had a separate and significant existence, her mother's hand lying on the green cover of the Greek Anthology.

"If you were like Mark — if you were only like him!"

"If I only were!"

"Mark never hurt me. Mark never gave me a minute's trouble in his life."

"He went into the Army."

"He had a perfect right to go into the Army."

Silence. "Minky — you'll be kind to little Mamma." A hard, light sound; the vexed fingers tap-tapping on the book. Her mother rose suddenly, pushing the book from her.

"There — take Mark's books. Take everything. Go

your own way. You always have done; you always will. Some day you'll be sorry for it."

She was sorry for it now, miserable, utterly beaten. Her new self seemed to her a devil that possessed her. She hated it. She hated the books. She hated everything that separated her and made her different from her mother and from Mark.

Her mother went past her to the door.

"Mamma — I didn't mean it — Mamma — "

Before she could reach the door it shut between them.

II

The library at Five Elms was very small. Emilius used it as a smoking-room; but it was lined with books. Where the rows of shelves met the shutter cases a fold of window-curtain overlapped their ends.

On the fifth shelf, covered by the curtain, she found the four volumes of Shelley's *Poetical Works,* half-bound in marble-paper and black leather. She had passed them scores of times in her hunt for something to read. Percy Bysshe Shelley. Percy Bysshe — what a silly name. She had thought of him as she thought of Allison's *History of Europe* in seventeen volumes, and the poems of Cornwall and Leigh Hunt. Books you wouldn't read if you were on a desert island.

There was something about Shelley in Byron's *Life and Letters.* Something she had read and forgotten, that persisted, struggled to make itself remembered.

Shelley's Pantheism.

The pages of Shelley were very clean; they stuck together lightly at the edges, like the pages of the Encyclopædia at "Pantheism" and "Spinoza." Whatever their secret was, you would have to find it for yourself.

Table of Contents — Poems written in 1816 — "Hymn to Intellectual Beauty." She read that first.

"Sudden thy shadow fell on me: —
I shrieked, and clasped my hands in ecstasy!"

It had happéned to Shelley, too. He knew how you felt when it happened. (Only you didn't shriek.) It was a real thing, then, that did happen to people.

She read the " Ode to a Skylark," the " Ode to the West Wind " and " Adonais."

All her secret happiness was there. Shelley knew about the queerness of the sharp white light, and the sudden still-ness, when the grey of the fields turns to violet: the clear, hard stillness that covers the excited throb-throbbing of the light.

> " Life, like a dome of many-coloured glass,
> Stains the white radiance of eternity " —

Colours were more beautiful than white radiance. But that was because of the light. The more light there was in them the more beautiful they were; it was their real life.

One afternoon Mr. Propart called. He came into the library to borrow a book.

" And what are *you* so deep in? " he said.

" Shelley."

" Shelley? Shelley? " He looked at her. A kind, con-sidering look. She liked his grey face with its tired keen-ness. She thought he was going to say something interest-ing about Shelley; but he only smiled his thin, drooping smile; and presently he went away with his book.

Next morning the Shelleys were not in their place behind the curtain. Somebody had moved them to the top shelf. Catty brought the step-ladder.

In the evening they were gone. Mr. Propart must have borrowed them.

III

" To this, then, comes our whole argument respecting the fourth kind of madness, on account of which anyone, who, on seeing the beauty in this lower world, being reminded of the true, begins to recover his wings, and, having recovered them, longs to soar aloft, but, being unable to do it, looks upwards like a bird, and despising things below, is deemed to be affected with madness."

Beauty in itself. In itself — Beauty in beautiful things. She had never thought about it that way before. It would be like the white light in the colours.

Plato, discovered in looking for the lost Shelleys, thus consoled her. The Plato of Bohn's Library. Cary's English for Plato's Greek. Slab upon slab. No hard, still sound-patterns. Grey slabs of print, shining with an inner light — Plato's thought.

Her happiness was there, too.

XVII

I

THE French nephew was listening. He had been listening for quite a long time, ten minutes perhaps; ever since they had turned off the railway bridge into Ley Street.

They had known each other for exactly four hours and seventeen minutes. She had gone to the Drapers for tea. Rodney had left her on their doorstep and he had found her there and had brought her into the dining-room. That, he declared, was at five o'clock, and it was now seventeen minutes past nine by his watch which he showed her.

It had begun at tea-time. When he listened he turned round, excitedly, in his chair; he stooped, bringing his eyes level with yours. When he talked he tossed back his head and stuck out his sharp-bearded chin. She was not sure that she liked his eyes. Hot black. Smoky blurs like breath on glass. Old, tired eyelids. Or his funny, sallowish face, narrowing to the black chin-beard. Ugly one minute, nice the next.

It moved too much. He could say all sorts of things with it and with his shoulders and his hands. Mrs. Draper said that was because he was half French.

He was showing her how French verse should be read when Rodney came for her, and Dr. Draper sent Rodney away and kept her for dinner.

The French nephew was taking her home now. They had passed the crook of the road.

" And all this time," she said, " I don't know your name."

"Maurice. Maurice Jourdain. I know yours — Mary Olivier. I like it."

"You wouldn't if you were me and your father kept on saying, 'Mary, Mary, quite contrary,' and 'Mary had a little lamb.'"

"Fathers will do these cruel things. It's a way they have."

"Papa isn't cruel. Only he's so awfully fond of Mamma that he can't think about *us*. He doesn't mind me so much."

"Oh — he doesn't mind you so much?"

"No. It's Mark he can't stand."

"Who is Mark?"

"My brother. Mark is a soldier — Royal Artillery."

"Lucky Mark. I was to have been a soldier."

"Why weren't you?"

"My mother wouldn't have liked it. So I had to give it up."

"How you must have loved her. Mark loves my mother more than anything; but he couldn't have done that."

"Perhaps Mark hasn't got to provide for his mother and his sisters. I had. And I had to go into a disgusting business to do it."

"Oh-h — "

He was beautiful inside. He did beautiful things. She was charmed, suddenly, by his inner, his immaterial beauty. She thought: "He must be ever so old."

"But it's made them love you awfully, hasn't it?" she said.

His shoulders and eyebrows lifted; he made a queer movement with his hands, palms outwards. He stood still in the path, turned to her, straight and tall. He looked down at her; his lips jerked; the hard, sharp smile bared narrow teeth.

"The more you do for people the less they love you," he said.

"Your people must be very funny."

"No. No. They're simply pious, orthodox Christians, and I don't believe in Christianity. I'm an atheist. I don't believe their God exists. I hope he doesn't. They wouldn't

mind so much if I were a villain, too, but it's awkward for
them when they find an infidel practising any of the Christian virtues. My eldest sister, Ruth, would tell you that I
am a villain."

" She doesn't really think it."

" Doesn't she! My dear child, she's got to think it, or
give up her belief."

She could see the gable end of Five Elms now. It would
soon be over. When they got to the garden gate.

It *was* over.

" I suppose," he said, " I must shut the prison door."

They looked at each other through the bars and laughed.

" When shall I see you again? " he said.

II

She had seen him again. She could count the times on
the fingers of one hand. Once, when he came to dinner
with Dr. and Mrs. Draper; once at Sunday supper with the
Drapers after Church; once on a Saturday when Mrs.
Draper asked her to tea again; and once when he called to
take her for a walk in the fields.

Mamma had lifted her eyebrows and Mrs. Draper said,
" Nonsense. He's old enough to be her father."

The green corn stood above her ankles then. This was
the fifth time. The corn rose to her waist. The ears were
whitening.

" You're the only person besides Mark who listens. There
was Jimmy. But that was different. He didn't know
things. He's a darling, but he doesn't know things."

" Who is Jimmy? "

" Mark's friend and mine."

" *Where* is he? "

" In Australia. He can't ever come back, so I shall never
see him again."

" I'm glad to hear it."

A sudden, dreadful doubt. She turned to him in the
narrow path.

" You aren't laughing at me, are you? You don't think
I'm shamming and showing off? "

"I? I? Laughing at you? My poor child — No — "

" They don't understand that you can really love words — beautiful sounds. And thoughts. Love them awfully, as if they were alive. As if they were people."

" They are alive. They're better than people. You know the best of your Shelley and Plato and Spinoza. Instead of the worst."

" I should have liked to have known *them*, too. Sometimes I pretend that I do know them. That they're alive. That they're here. Saying things and listening. They're kind. They never misunderstand. They never lose their tempers."

" You mustn't do that," he said sharply.

" Why not? "

" It isn't good for you. Talk to me. I'm alive. I'm here, I'll listen. I'll never misunderstand. I'll never lose my temper."

" You aren't always here."

He smiled, secretly, with straight lips, under the funny, frizzy, French moustache. And when he spoke again he looked old and wise, like an uncle.

" Wait," he said. " Wait a bit. Wait three years."

" Three years? " she said. " Three years before we can go for another walk? "

He shouted laughter and drew it back with a groan.

She couldn't tell him that she pretended he was there when he was not there; that she created situations.

He was ill, and she nursed him. She could feel the weight of his head against her arm, and his forehead — hot — hot under her hand. She had felt her hands to see whether they would be nice enough to put on Mr. Jourdain's forehead. They were rather nice; cool and smooth; the palms brushed together with a soft, swishing sound like fine silk.

He was poor and she worked for him.

He was in danger and she saved him. From a runaway horse; from a furious dog; from a burning house; from a lunatic with a revolver.

It made her sad to think how unlikely it was that any of these things would ever happen.

III

" Mr. Jourdain, I am going to school."

The corn was reaped and carried. The five elms stood high above the shallow stubble.

" My poor Mary, is it possible? "

" Yes. Mamma says she's been thinking of it for a long time."

" Don't be too hard on your mother till you're quite sure it wasn't my aunt."

" It may have been both of them. Anyhow, it's awful. Just — just when I was so happy."

" Just when I was so happy," he said. " But that's the sort of thing they do."

" I knew you'd be sorry for me."

XVIII

I

SHE was shut up with Papa, tight, in the narrow cab that smelt of the mews. Papa, sitting slantways, nearly filled the cab. He was quiet and sad, almost as if he were sorry she was going.

His sadness and quietness fascinated her. He had a mysterious, wonderful, secret life going on in him. Funny you should think of it for the first time in the cab. Supposing you stroked his hand. Better not. He mightn't like it.

Not forty minutes from Liverpool Street to Victoria. If only cabs didn't smell so.

II

The small, ugly houses streamed past, backs turned to the train, stuck together, rushing, rushing in from the country.

Grey streets, trying to cut across the stream, getting nowhere, carried past sideways on.

Don't look at the houses. Shut your eyes and remember. Her father's hand on her shoulder. His face, at the carriage window, looking for her. A girl moving back, pushing her to it. "Papa!"

Why hadn't she loved him all the time? Why hadn't she liked his beard? His nice, brown, silky beard. His poor beard.

Mamma's face, in the hall, breaking up suddenly. Her tears in your mouth. Her arms, crushing you. Mamma's face at the dining-room window. Tears, pricking, cutting your eyelids. Blink them back before the girls see them. Don't think of Mamma.

The Thames. Barking Creek goes into the Thames and the Roding goes into Barking Creek. Yesterday, the last walk with Roddy, across Barking Flats to the river, over the dry, sallow grass, the wind blowing in their faces. Roddy's face, beautiful, like Mamma's, his mouth, white at the edges. Roddy gasping in the wind, trying to laugh, his heart thumping. Roddy was excited when he saw the tall masts of the ships. He had wanted to be a sailor.

Dan's face, when he said good-bye; his hurt, unhappy eyes; the little dark, furry moustache trying to come. Tibby's eyes. Dank wanted to marry Effie. Mark was the only one who got what he wanted.

Better not think of Dank.

She looked shyly at her companions. The stout lady in brown, sitting beside her; kind, thin mouth, pursed to look important; dull kind eyes trying to be wise and sharp behind spectacles, between curtains of dead hair. A grand manner, excessively polite, on the platform, to Papa — Miss Lambert.

The three girls, all facing them. Pam Quin; flaxen pig-tail; grown up nose; polite mouth, buttoned, little flaxen and pink old lady, Pam Quin, talking about her thirteenth birthday.

Lucy Elliott, red pig-tail, suddenly sad in her corner, innocent white-face, grey eyes blinking to swallow her tears. Frances Elliott, hay coloured pig-tail, very upright, sitting forward and talking fast to hide her sister's shame.

Mamma's face — Don't think of it.

Green fields and trees rushing past now. Stop a tree and you'll change and feel the train moving. Plato. You can't trust your senses. The cave-dwellers didn't see the things that really moved, only the shadows of the images of the things. Is the world in your mind or your mind in the world? Which really moves? Perhaps the world stands still and you move on and on like the train. If both moved together that would feel like standing still.

Grass banks. Telegraph wires dipping and rising like sea-waves. At Dover there would be the sea.

Mamma's face — Think. Think harder. The world was going on before your mind started. Supposing you lived before, would that settle it? No. A white chalk cutting flashed by. God's mind is what both go on in. That settles it.

The train dashed into a tunnel. A long tunnel. She couldn't remember what she was thinking of the second before they went in. Something that settled it. Settled what? She couldn't think any more.

Dover. The girls standing up, and laughing. They said she had gone to sleep in the train.

III

There was no sea; only the Maison Dieu Road and the big square house in the walled garden. Brown wire blinds half way up the schoolroom windows. An old lady with grey hair and a kind, blunt face, like Jenny; she unpacked your box in the large, light bedroom, folding and unfolding your things with little gentle, tender hands. Miss Haynes. She hoped you would be happy with them, hoped you wouldn't mind sleeping alone the first night, thought you must be hungry and took you down to tea in the long dining-room.

More girls, pretending not to look at you; talking politely to Miss Lambert.

After tea they paired off, glad to see each other. She sat in the corner of the schoolroom reading the new green Shakespeare that Roddy had given her. Two girls glanced at her, looked at each other. " Is she doing it for fun? " " Cheek, more likely."

Night. A strange white bed. Two empty beds, strange

and white, in the large, light room. She wondered what
sort of girls would be sleeping there to-morrow night. A
big white curtain: you could draw it across the room and
shut them out.

She lay awake, thinking of her mother, crying now and
then; thinking of Roddy and Dan. Mysterious, measured
sounds came through the open window. That was the sea.
She got up and looked out. The deep-walled garden lay
under the window, black and clear like a well. Calais was
over there. And Paris. Mr. Jourdain had written to say
he was going to Paris. She had his letter.

In bed she felt for the sharp edge of the envelope sticking
out under the pillow. She threw back the hot blankets.
The wind flowed to her, running cold like water over the
thin sheet.

A light moved across the ceiling. Somebody had waked
her. Somebody was putting the blankets back again, pressing a large, kind hand to her forehead. Miss Lambert.

IV

" Mais — mais — de grâce! Ça ne finira jamais — jamais,
s'il faut répondre à tes sottises, Marie. Recommençons."

Mademoiselle, golden top-knot shining and shaking, blue
eyes rolling between black lashes.

> " De ta tige détachée,
> Pauvre feuille desséchée " —

Détachée — desséchée. They didn't rhyme. Their not
rhyming irritated her distress.

She hated the schoolroom: the ochreish wall-paper, the
light soiled by the brown wire gauze; the cramped classes,
the faint odour of girl's skin; girl's talk in the bedroom
when you undressed.

The queer she-things had a wonderful, mysterious life
you couldn't touch.

Clara, when she walked with you, smiling with her black-
treacle eyes and bad teeth, glad to be talked to. Clara in
bed. You bathed her forehead with eau-de-cologne, and
she lay there, happy, glad of her headache that made them

sorry for her. Clara, waiting for you at the foot of the stairs, looking with dog's eyes, imploring. "Will you walk with me?" "I can't. I'm going with Lucy." She turned her wounded dog's eyes and slunk away, beaten, humble, to walk with the little ones.

Lucy Elliott in the bathing machine, slipping from the cloak of the towel, slender and straight; sea water gluing red weeds of hair to her white skin. Sweet eyes looking towards you in the evening at sewing-time.

"Will you sit with me at sewing?"

"I'm sitting with Rose Godwin."

Sudden sweetness; sudden trouble; grey eyes dark and angry behind sudden tears. She wouldn't look at you; wouldn't tell you what you had done.

Rose Godwin, strong and clever; fourteen; head of the school. Honey-white Roman face; brown-black hair that smelt like Brazilian nuts. Rose Godwin walking with you in the garden.

"You must behave like other people if you expect them to like you."

"I don't expect them. How do I behave?"

"It isn't exactly behaving. It's more the way you talk and look at people. As if you saw slap through them. Or else as if you didn't see them at all. That's worse. People don't like it."

"Anything else?"

"Yes. It was cheeky of you to tell Mademoiselle that those French verses didn't rhyme."

"But they didn't."

"Who cares?"

"I care. I care frightfully."

"There you go. That's exactly what I mean," Rose said. "Who cares if you care? And there's another thing. You're worrying Miss Lambert. This school of hers has got a name for sound religious teaching. You may not like sound religious teaching, but she's got fifteen of us to look after besides you. If you want to be an atheist, go and be it by yourself."

"I'm not an atheist."

"Well, whatever silly thing you are. You mustn't talk about it to the girls. It isn't fair," Rose said.

"All right. I won't."
"On your honour? "
"On my honour."

V

A three-cornered note on her dressing-table at bed-time:

Sept. 20th, 1878. Maison Dieu Lodge.

"My dear Mary: Our talk was not satisfactory. Unless
you can assure me by to-morrow morning that you believe
in the Blessed Trinity and all the other truths of our most
holy religion, I fear that, *much as we love you,* we dare not
keep you with us, for your school-fellows' sake.

"Think it over, my dear child, and let me know. Pray to
God *to-night* to change your heart and mind and give you
His Holy Spirit.

"Affectionately yours,
"Henrietta Lambert."

The Trinity. A three-cornered note.

"My dear Miss Lambert: I am very sorry; but it really
isn't any good, and if it was it couldn't be done in the time.
You wouldn't like it if I told you lies, would you? That's
why I can't join in the prayers and say the Creed and bow;
in Church or anywhere. Rose made me promise not to talk
about it, and I won't.

"If you must send me away to-morrow morning, you
must. But I'm glad you love me. I was afraid you didn't.

"With love, your very affectionate
"Mary Olivier."

"P.S. — I've folded my clothes all ready for packing."

To-morrow the clothes were put back again in their drawers. She wasn't going. Miss Lambert said something
about Rose and Lucy and " kindness to poor Clara."

VI

Rose Godwin told her that home-sickness wore off. It
didn't. It came beating up and up, like madness, out of

nothing. The French verbs, grey, slender as little verses on the page, the French verbs swam together and sank under the clear-floating images of home-sickness. Mamma's face, Roddy's, Dan's face. Tall trees, the Essex fields, flat as water, falling away behind them. Little feathery trees, flying low on the sky-line. Outside the hallucination the soiled light shut you in.

The soiled light; odours from the warm roots of girl's hair; and Sunday. Sunday; stale odours of churches. You wrote out the sermon you had not listened to and had not heard. Somebody told you the text, and you amused yourself by seeing how near you could get to what you would have heard if you had listened. After tea, hymns; then church again. Your heart laboured with the strain of kneeling, arms lifted up to the high pew ledge. You breathed pew dust. Your brain swayed like a bladder, brittle, swollen with hot gas-fumes. After supper, prayers again. Sunday was over.

On Monday, the tenth day, she ran away to Dover Harbour. She had thought she could get to London with two weeks' pocket-money and what was left of Uncle Victor's tip after she had paid for the eau-de-cologne; but the ticket man said it would only take her as far as Canterbury. She had frightened Miss Lambert and made her tremble: all for nothing, except the sight of the Harbour. It was dreadful to see her tremble. Even the Harbour wasn't worth it.

A miracle would have to happen.

Two weeks passed and three weeks. And on the first evening of the fourth week the miracle happened. Rose Godwin came to her and whispered: " You're wanted in the dining-room."

Her mother's letter lay open on the table. A tear had made a glazed snail's track down Miss Lambert's cheek; and Mary thought that one of them was dead — Roddy — Dan — Papa.

" My dear, my dear — don't cry. You're going home."

" Why? Why am I going? "

She could see the dull, kind eyes trying to look clever.

" Because your mother has sent for you. She wants you back again."

"Mamma? What does she want me for?"

Miss Lambert's eyes turned aside slantways. She swallowed something in her throat, making a funny noise: qualk-qualk.

"It isn't *you?* You aren't sending me away?"

"No; we're not sending you. But we think it's best for you to go. We can't bear to see your dear, unhappy little face going about the passages."

"Does it mean that Mamma isn't happy without me?"

"Well — she *would* miss her only daughter, wouldn't she?"

The miracle. The shining, lovely miracle.

"Mary Olivier is going! Mary Olivier is going!"

Actually the girls were sorry. Too sorry. The compassion in Rose Godwin's face stirred a doubt. Doubt of the miracle.

She carried her books to the white curtained room where Miss Haynes knelt by her trunk, packing her clothes with little gentle, tender hands.

"Miss Haynes" (suddenly), "I'm not expelled, am I?"

"Expelled? My dear child, who's talking about expulsion?"

As if she said, When miracles are worked for you, accept them.

She lay awake, thinking what she should say to her mother when she got home. She would have to tell her that just at first she very nearly *was* expelled. Then her mother would believe in her unbelief and not think she was shamming.

And she would have to explain about her unbelief. And about Pantheism.

VII

She wondered how she would set about it. It wouldn't do to start suddenly by saying you didn't believe in Jesus or the God of the Old Testament or Hell. That would hurt her horribly. The only decent thing would be to let her see how beautiful Spinoza's God was and leave it to her to make the comparison.

You would have to make it quite clear to yourself first. It was like this. There were the five elm trees, and there was the happy white light on the fields. God was the trees. He was the happy light and he was your happiness. There was Catty singing in the kitchen. God was Catty.

Oh — and there was Papa and Papa's temper. God would have to be Papa too.

Spinoza couldn't have meant it that way.

He meant that though God was all Papa, Papa was not all God. He was only a bit of him. He meant that if God was the only reality, Papa wouldn't be quite real.

But if Papa wasn't quite real then Mamma and Mark were not quite real either.

If Spinoza had meant that —

But perhaps he hadn't. Perhaps he meant that parts of Papa, the parts you saw most of — his beard, for instance, and his temper — were not quite real, but that some other part of him, the part you couldn't see, might be real in the same way that God was. That would be Papa himself, and it would be God too. And if God could be Papa, he would have no difficulty at all in being Mamma and Mark.

Surely Mamma would see that, if you had to have a God, Spinoza's was by far the nicest God, besides being the easiest to believe in. Surely it would please her to think like that about Papa, to know that his temper was not quite real, and that your sin, when you sinned, was not quite real, so that not even your sin could separate you from God. All your life Mamma had dinned into you the agony of separation from God, and the necessity of the Atonement. She would feel much more comfortable if she knew that there never had been any separation, and that there needn't be any Atonement.

Of course she might not like the idea of sin being some-how inside God. She might say it looked bad. But if it wasn't inside God, it would have to be outside him, support-ing itself and causing itself, and then where were you? You would have to say that God was not the cause of all things, and that would be much worse.

Surely if you put it to her like that —? But somehow she couldn't hear herself saying all that to her mother. Supposing Mamma wouldn't listen?

And she couldn't hear herself talking about her happiness, the sudden, secret happiness that more than anything was like God. When she thought of it she was hot and cold by turns and she had no words for it. She remembered the first time it had come to her, and how she had found her mother in the drawing-room and had knelt down at her knees and kissed her hands with the idea of drawing her into her happiness. And she remembered her mother's face. It made her ashamed, even now, as if she had been silly. She thought: I shall never be able to talk about it to Mamma.

Yet — perhaps — now that the miracle had happened —

VIII

In the morning Miss Lambert took her up to London. She had a sort of idea that the kind lady talked to her a great deal, about God and the Christian religion. But she couldn't listen; she couldn't talk; she couldn't think now.

For three hours, in the train, in the waiting-room at Victoria, while Miss Lambert talked to Papa outside, in the cab, alone with Papa — Miss Lambert must have said something nice about her, for he looked pleased, as if he wouldn't mind if you did stroke his hand — in Mr. Parish's wagonette, she sat happy and still, contemplating the shining, lovely miracle.

IX

She saw Catty open the front door and run away. Her mother was coming slowly down the narrow hall.

She ran up the flagged path.

"Mamma!" She flung herself to the embrace.

Her mother swerved from her, staggering back and putting out her hands between them. Aware of Mr. Parish shouldering the trunk, she turned into the open dining-room. Mary followed her and shut the door.

Her mother sat down, helplessly. Mary saw that she was crying; she had been crying a long time. Her soaked eyelashes were parted by her tears and gathered into points.

"Mamma — what is it?"

"What is it? You've disgraced yourself. Everlastingly.

You've disgraced your father, and you've disgraced me. That's what it is."

" I haven't done anything of the sort, Mamma."

" You don't think it's a disgrace, then, to be expelled? For infidelity."

" But I'm not expelled."

" You are expelled. And you know it."

" No. They said I wasn't. They didn't want me to go. They told me you wanted me back again."

" Is it likely I should want you when you hadn't been gone three weeks? "

She could hear herself gasp, see herself standing there, open-mouthed, idiotic.

Nothing could shake her mother in her belief that she had been expelled.

" Of course, if it makes you happier to believe it," she said at last, " do. Will you let me see Miss Lambert's letter? "

" No," her mother said. " I will not."

Suddenly she felt hard and strong, grown-up in her sad wisdom. Her mother didn't love her. She never had loved her. Nothing she could ever do would make her love her. Miracles didn't happen.

She thought: " I wonder why she won't let me see Miss Lambert's letter? "

She went upstairs to her room. She leaned on the sill of the open window, looking out, drinking in the sweet air of the autumn fields. The five elms raised golden heads to a blue sky.

Her childhood had died with a little gasp.

Catty came in to unpack her box. Catty, with wet cheeks, kissed a dead child.

XIX

I

In the train from Bristol to Paddington for the last time: July, eighteen-eighty.

She would never see any of them again: Ada and Geraldine; Mabel and Florrie and little Lena and Kate; Miss Wray with her pale face and angry eyes; never hear her sudden, cold, delicious praise. Never see the bare, oblong schoolroom with the brown desks, seven rows across for the lower school, one long form along the wall for Class One where she and Ada and Geraldine sat apart. Never look through the bay windows over the lea to the Channel, at sunset, Lundy Island flattened out, floating, gold on gold in the offing. Never see magenta valerian growing in hot white grey walls.

Never hear Louie Prichard straining the little music room with Chopin's *Fontana* Polonaise. Never breathe in its floor-dust with the *Adagio* of the "Pathetic Sonata."

She was glad she had seen it through to the end when the clergymen's and squires' daughters went and the daughters of Bristol drapers and publicans and lodging-house keepers came.

("What do you think! Bessie Parson's brother marked all her underclothing. In the shop!")

But they taught you quite a lot of things: Zoology, Physiology, Paley's Evidences, British Law, Political Economy. It had been a wonderful school when Mrs. Propart's nieces went to it. And they kept all that up when the smash came and the butter gave out, and you ate cheap bread that tasted of alum, and potatoes that were fibrous skeletons in a green pulp. Oh — she had seen it through. A whole year and a half of it.

Why? Because you promised Mamma you'd stick to the Clevehead School whatever it was like? Because they taught you German and let you learn Greek by yourself with the old arithmetic master? (Ada Clark said it was a mean trick to get more marks.) Because of the Beethoven and Schumann and Chopin, and Lundy Island, and the valerian? Because nothing mattered, not even going hungry?

She was glad she hadn't told about that, nor why she asked for the "room to herself" that turned out to be a servants' garret on a deserted floor. You could wake at five o'clock in the light mornings and read Plato, or snatch twenty minutes from undressing before Miss Payne came for your candle. The tall sycamore swayed in the moonlight, tapping on the window pane; its shadow moved softly in the room like a ghost.

II

She would like to see the valerian again, though. Mamma said it didn't grow in Yorkshire.

Funny to be going back to Ilford after Roddy and Papa and Mamma had left it. Funny to be staying at Five Elms with Uncle Victor. Nice Uncle Victor, buying the house from Papa and making Dan live with them. That was to keep him from drinking. Uncle Victor was hurt because Papa and Mamma would go to Morfe when he wanted you all to live with him. But you couldn't imagine Emilius and Victor living together or Mamma and Aunt Lavvy.

Bristol to Paddington. This time next week it would be King's Cross to Reyburn for Morfe.

She wondered what it would be like. Aunt Bella said it was a dead-and-alive place. Morfe — Morfe. It did sound rather as if people died in it. Aunt Bella was angry with Mrs. Waugh and Miss Frewin for making Mamma go there. But Aunt Bella had never liked Mrs. Waugh and Miss Frewin. That was because they had been Mamma's friends at school and not Aunt Bella's.

She wondered what they would be like, and whether they would disapprove of her. They would if they believed she had been expelled from Dover and had broken Mamma's heart. All Mamma's friends thought that.

She didn't mind going to Morfe so much. The awful thing was leaving Ilford. Ilford was part of Mark, part of her, part of her and Mark together. There were things they had done that never in all their lives they could do again. Waldteufel Waltzes played on the old Cramer piano, standing in its place by the door, waltzes that would never sound the same in any other place in any other room. And there was the sumach tree. It would die if you transplanted it.

III

The little thin, sallow old man, coming towards her on the platform at Paddington, turned out to be Uncle Victor.

She had not seen him since Christmas, for at Easter he had been away somewhere on business.

He came slowly, showing a smile of jerked muscles, under cold fixed eyes. He was not really glad to see her. That was because he disapproved of her. They all believed she had been expelled from the Dover school, and they didn't seem able to forget it. Going down from Liverpool Street to Ilford he sat bowed and dejected in his corner, not looking at her unless he could help it.

"How's Aunt Charlotte?" She thought he would be pleased to think that she had remembered Aunt Charlotte; but he winced as if she had hit him.

"She is — not so well." And then: "How have you been getting on?"

"Oh, all right. I've got the Literature prize again, and the French prize and the German prize; and I might have got the Good Conduct prize too."

"And why didn't you get it?"

"Because I gave it up. Somebody else had to have a prize, and Miss Wray said she knew it was the one I could best bear to part with."

Uncle Victor frowned as if he were displeased.

"You don't seem to consider that I gave it up," she said. But he had turned his eyes away. He wasn't listening any more, as he used to listen.

The train was passing the City of London Cemetery. She thought: "I must go and see Jenny's grave before I leave. I wish I hadn't teased her so to love me." She thought: "If I die I shall be put in the grass plot beside Grandpapa and Grandmamma Olivier. Papa will bring me in a coffin all the way from Morfe in the train." Little birch bushes were beginning to grow among the graves. She wondered how she could ever have been afraid of those graves and of their dead.

Uncle Victor was looking at the graves too; queerly, with a sombre, passionate interest. When the train had passed them he sighed and shut his eyes, as if he wanted to keep on seeing them — to keep on.

As Mr. Parish's wagonette drove up Ley Street he pointed to a field where a street of little houses had begun.

"Some day they'll run a street over Five Elms. But I shan't know anything about it," he said.

"No. It won't be for ages."

He smiled queerly.

They drew up at the gate. "You must be prepared for more changes," he said.

Aunt Lavvy was at the gate. She was sweet as if she loved you, and sad as if she still remembered your disgrace.

"No. Not that door," she said.

The dining-room and drawing-room had changed places, and both were filled with the large mahogany furniture that had belonged to Grandpapa.

"Why, you've turned it back to front."

Strips of Mamma's garden shone between the dull maroon red curtains. Inside the happy light was dead.

There seemed to her something sinister about this change. Only the two spare rooms still looked to the front. They had put her in one of them instead of her old room on the top floor; Dan had the other instead of his. It was very queer.

Aunt Lavvy sat in Mamma's place at the head of the tea-table. A tall, iron-grey woman in an iron-grey gown stood at her elbow holding a little tray. She looked curiously at Mary, as if her appearance there surprised and interested her. Aunt Lavvy put a cup of tea on the tray.

"Where's Aunt Charlotte?"

"Aunt Charlotte is upstairs. She isn't very well."

The maid was saying, "Miss Charlotte asked for a large piece of plum cake, ma'am," and Aunt Lavvy added a large piece of plum cake to the plate of thin bread and butter.

Mary thought: "There can't be much the matter with her if she can eat all that."

"Can I see her?" she said.

She heard the woman whisper, "Better not." She was glad when she left the room.

"Has old Louisa gone, then?"

"No," Aunt Lavvy said. She added presently, "That is Aunt Charlotte's maid."

IV

Aunt Charlotte looked out through the bars of the old nursery window. She nodded to Mary and called to her to come up.

Aunt Lavvy said it did her good to see people.

There was a door at the head of the stairs, in a match-board partition that walled the well of the staircase. You rang a bell. The corridor was very dark. Another partition with a door in it shut off the servants' rooms and the back staircase. They had put the big yellow linen cupboard before the tall window, the one she used to hang out of.

Some of the old things had been left in the nursery school-room, so that it looked much the same. Britton, the maid, sat in Jenny's low chair by the fireguard. Aunt Charlotte sat in an armchair by the window.

Her face was thin and small; the pencil lines had deepened; the long black curls hung from a puff of grey hair rolled back above her ears. Her eyes pointed at you — pointed. They had more than ever their look of wisdom and excitement. She was twisting and untwisting a string of white tulle round a sprig of privet flower.

"Don't you believe a word of it," she said. "Your father hasn't gone. He's here in this house. He's in when Victor's out.

"He says he's sold the house to Victor. That's a lie. He doesn't want it known that he's hidden me here to prevent my getting married."

"I'm sure he hasn't," Mary said. Across the room Britton looked at her and shook her head.

"It's all part of a plan," Aunt Charlotte said. "To put me away, my dear. Dr. Draper's in it with Victor and Emilius.

"They may say what they like. It isn't the piano-tuner. It isn't the man who does the clocks. They know who it is. It isn't that Marriott man. I've found out something about *him* they don't know. He's got a false stomach. It goes by clockwork.

"As if I'd look at a clock-tuner or a piano-winder. I wouldn't, would I, Britton?"

She meditated, smiling softly. "They make them so beautifully now, you can't tell the difference.

"He's been to see me nine times in one week. Nine times. But your Uncle Victor got him away before he could speak. But he came again and again. He wouldn't take 'No' for an answer. Britton, how many times did Mr. Jourdain come?"

Britton said, "I'm sure I couldn't say, Miss Charlotte." She made a sign to Mary to go.

Aunt Lavvy was waiting for her at the foot of the stairs. She took her into her bedroom, Mamma's old room, and asked her what Aunt Charlotte had said. Mary told her.

"Poor Mary — I oughtn't to have let you see her."

Aunt Lavvy's chin trembled. "I'm afraid," she said, "the removal's upset her. I said it would. But Emilius would have it. He could always make Victor do what he wanted."

"It might have been something you don't know about."

Grown-up and strong, she wanted to comfort Aunt Lavvy and protect her.

"No," Aunt Lavvy said. "It's the house. I knew it would be. She's been trying to get away. She never did that before."

(The doors and the partitions, the nursery and its bars, the big cupboard across the window, to keep her from getting away.)

"Aunt Lavvy, did Mr. Jourdain really call?"

Aunt Lavvy hesitated. "Yes. He called."

"Did he see Aunt Charlotte?"

"She was in the room when he came in, but your uncle took him out at once."

"She didn't talk to him? Did he hear her talking?"

"No, my dear, I'm sure he didn't."

"Are you sure he didn't see her?"

Aunt Lavvy smiled. "He didn't look. I don't think he saw any of us very clearly."

"How many times did he come?"

"Three or four times, I believe."

"Did he ask to see me?"

"No. He asked to see your Uncle Victor."

"I didn't know he knew Uncle Victor."

"Well," Aunt Lavvy said, "he knows him now."

"Did he leave any message for me?"

"No. None."

"You don't like him, Aunt Lavvy."

"No, Mary, I do not. And I don't know anybody who does."

"I like him," Mary said.

Aunt Lavvy looked as if she hadn't heard. "I oughtn't to have let you see Aunt Charlotte."

v

Mary woke up suddenly. It was her third night in the spare room at Five Elms.

She had dreamed that she saw Aunt Charlotte standing at the foot of the basement stairs, by the cat's cupboard where the kittens were born, taking her clothes off and hiding them. She had seen that before. When she was six years old. She didn't know whether she had been dreaming about something that had really happened, or about a dream. Only, this time, she saw Aunt Charlotte open her mouth and scream. The scream woke her.

She remembered her mother and Aunt Bertha in the drawing-room, talking, their faces together. That wasn't a dream.

There was a sound of feet overhead. Uncle Victor's room. A sound of a door opening and shutting. And then a scream, muffled by the shut door. Her heart checked; turned sickeningly. She hadn't dreamed that.

Uncle Victor shouted down the stair to Dan. She could hear Dan's feet in the next room and his door opening.

The screaming began again: "I-ihh! I-ihh! I-ihh!" Up and up, tearing your brain. Then: "Aah-a-o-oh!" Tearing your heart out. "Aa-h-a-o-oh!" and "Ahh-ahh!" Short and sharp.

She threw off the bed-clothes, and went out to the foot of the stairs. The cries had stopped. There was a sound of feet staggering and shuffling. Somebody being carried.

Dan came back down the stair. His trousers were drawn

up over his night-shirt, the braces hanging. He was suck-
ing the back of his hand and spitting the blood out on to
his sleeve.

" Dan — was that Aunt Charlotte? "

" Yes."

" Was it pain? "

" No." He was out of breath. She could see his night-
shirt shake with the beating of his heart.

" Have you hurt your hand? "

" No."

" Can I do anything? "

" No. Go back to bed. She's all right now."

She went back. Presently she heard him leave his room
and go upstairs again. The bolt of the front door squeaked;
then the hinge of the gate. Somebody going out. She fell
asleep.

The sound of hoofs and wheels woke her. The room was
light. She got up and went to the open window. Dr.
Draper's black brougham stood at the gate.

The sun blazed, tree-high, on the flat mangold field across
the road. The green leaves had the cold glitter of wet,
pointed metal. To the north-east a dead smear of dawn.
The brougham didn't look like itself, standing still in that
unearthly light. As if it were taking part in a funeral, the
funeral of some dreadful death. She put on her dressing-
gown and waited, looking out. She *had* to look. Downstairs the hall clock struck a half-hour.

The front door opened. Britton came out first. Then
Aunt Charlotte, between Uncle Victor and Dr. Draper.
They were holding her up by her arm-pits, half leading, half
pushing her before them. Her feet made a brushing noise
on the flagstones.

They lifted her into the brougham and placed themselves
one on each side of her. Then Britton got in, and they
drove off.

A string of white tulle lay on the garden path.

END OF BOOK THREE

BOOK FOUR

MATURITY

1879–1900

BOOK FOUR

MATURITY

XX

I

THE scent of hay came through the open window of her room. Clearer and finer than the hay smell of the Essex fields.

She shut her eyes to live purely in that one sweet sense; and opened them to look at the hill, the great hill heaved up against the east.

You had to lean far out of the window to see it all. It came on from the hidden north, its top straight as a wall against the sky. Then the long shoulder, falling and falling. Then the thick trees. A further hill cut the trees off from the sky.

Roddy was saying something. Sprawling out from the corner of the window-seat, he stared with sulky, unseeing eyes into the little room.

" Roddy, what did you say that hill was? "

" Greffington Edge. You aren't listening."

His voice made a jagged tear in the soft, quiet evening.

" And the one beyond it? "

" Sarrack. Why can't you listen? "

Greffington Edge. Sarrack. Sarrack.

Green fields coming on from the north, going up and up, netted in with the strong net of the low grey walls that held them together, that kept them safe. Above them thin grass, a green bloom on the grey face of the hill. Above the thin grass a rampart of grey cliffs.

157

Roddy wouldn't look at the hill.

"I tell you," he said, "you'll loathe the place when you've lived a week in it."

The thick, rich trees were trying to climb the Edge, but they couldn't get higher than the netted fields.

The lean, ragged firs had succeeded. No. Not quite. They stood out against the sky, adventurous mountaineers, roped together, leaning forward with the effort.

"It's Mamma's fault," Roddy was saying. "Papa would have gone anywhere, but she *would* come to this damned Morfe."

"Don't. Don't—" Her mind beat him off, defending her happiness. He would kill it if she let him. Coming up from Reyburn on the front seat of the Morfe bus, he had sulked. He smiled disagreeable smiles while the driver pointed with his whip and told her the names of the places. Renton Moor. Renton Church. Morfe, the grey village, stuck up on its green platform under the high, purple mound of Karva Hill.

Garthdale in front of it, Rathdale at its side, meeting in the fields below its bridge.

Morfe was beautiful. She loved it with love at first sight, faithless to Ilford.

Straight, naked houses. Grey walls of houses, enclosing the wide oblong Green. Dark grey stone roofs, close-clipped lest the wind should lift them. On the Green two grey stone pillar fountains; a few wooden benches; telegraph poles. Under her window a white road curling up to the platform. Straight, naked houses, zigzagging up beside it. Down below, where the white road came from, the long grey raking bridge, guarded by a tall ash-tree.

Roddy's jabbing voice went on and on:

"I used to think Mamma was holy and unselfish. I don't think so any more. She says she wants to do what Papa wants and what we want; but she always ends by doing what she wants herself. It's all very well for her. As long as she's got a garden to poke about in she doesn't care how awful it is for us."

She hated Roddy when he said things like that about Mamma.

" I don't suppose the little lamb thought about it at all.
Or if she did she thought we'd like it."

She didn't want to listen to Roddy's grumbling. She
wanted to look and look, to sniff up the clear, sweet, exciting
smell of the fields.

The roofs went criss-crossing up the road — straight —
slant — straight. They threw delicate violet-green shadows
on to the sage-green field below. That long violet-green pillar was the shadow of the ash-tree by the bridge.

The light came from somewhere behind the village, from a
sunset you couldn't see. It made the smooth hill fields shine
like thin velvet, stretched out, clinging to the hills.

" Oh, Roddy, the light's different. Different from Ilford.
Look — "

" I've been looking for five weeks," Roddy said. " You
haven't, that's all. *I* was excited at first."

He got up. He stared out of the window, not seeing anything.

" I didn't mean what I said about Mamma. Morfe *makes*
you say things. Soon it'll make you mean them. You wait."

She was glad when he had left her.

The cliffs of Greffington Edge were violet now.

II

At night, when she lay in bed in the strange room, the
Essex fields began to haunt her; the five trees, the little
flying trees, low down, low down; the straight, narrow paths
through the corn, where she walked with Mark, with Jimmy,
with Mr. Jourdain; Mr. Jourdain, standing in the path and
saying: " Talk to me. I'm alive. I'm here. I'll listen."

Mark and Mamma planting the sumach tree by the front
door; Papa saying it wouldn't grow. It had grown up to
the dining-room window-sill.

Aunt Bella and Uncle Edward; the Proparts and the
Farmers and Mr. Batty, all stiff and disapproving; not
nearly so nice to you as they used to be and making you
believe it was your fault.

The old, beautiful drawing-room. The piano by the door.

Dan staggering down the room at Mark's party. Mark holding her there, in his arms.

Dawn, and Dr. Draper's carriage waiting in the road beside the mangold fields. And Aunt Charlotte carried out, her feet brushing the flagstones.

She mustn't tell them. Mamma couldn't bear it. Roddy couldn't bear it. Aunt Charlotte was Papa's sister. He must never know.

The sound of the brushing feet made her heart ache.

She was glad to wake in the small, strange room. It had taken a snip off Mamma's and Papa's room on one side of the window, and a snip off the spare room on the other. That made it a funny T shape. She slept in the tail of the T, in a narrow bed pushed against the wall. When you sat up you saw the fat trees trying to get up the hill between the washstand and the chest of drawers.

This room would never be taken from her, because she was the only one who was small enough to fit the bed.

She would be safe there with her hill.

III

The strange houses fascinated her. They had the simplicity and the precision of houses in a very old engraving.

On the west side of the Green they made a long straight wall. Morfe High Row. An open space of cobblestones stretched in front of it. The market-place.

Sharp morning light picked out the small black panes of the windows in the white criss-cross of their frames, and the long narrow signs of the King's Head and the Farmer's Arms, black on grey. The plaster joints of the walls and the dark net of earth between the cobbles showed thick and clear as in a very old engraving. The west side had the sky behind it and the east side had the hill.

Grey-white cart roads slanted across the Green, cutting it into vivid triangular grass-plots. You went in and out of Morfe through the open corners of its Green. Her father's house stood at the south-west corner, by itself. A projecting wing at that end of the High Row screened it from the market-place.

The strange houses excited her.

Wonderful, unknown people lived in them. You would see them and know what they were like: the people in the tall house with the rusty stones, in the bright green ivy house with the white doors, in the small grey, humble houses, in the big, important house set at the top of the Green, with the three long rows of windows, the front garden and the iron gate.

People you didn't know. You would be strange and exciting to them as they were strange and exciting to you. They might say interesting things. There might be somebody who cared about Plato and Spinoza.

Things would happen that you didn't know. Anything might happen any minute.

If you knew what was happening in the houses *now* — some of them had hard, frightening faces. Dreadful things might have happened in them. Her father's house had a good, simple face. You could trust it.

Five windows in the rough grey wall, one on each side of the white door, three above. A garden at the side, an orchard at the back. In front a cobbled square marked off by a line of thin stones set in edgeways.

A strange house, innocent of unhappy memories.

Catty stood at the door, looking for her. She called to her to come in to breakfast.

IV

Papa was moving restlessly about the house. His loose slippers shuffled on the stone flags of the passages.

Catty stopped gathering up the breakfast cups to listen.

Catty was not what she used to be. Her plump cheeks were sunk and flattened. Some day she would look like Jenny.

Papa stood in the doorway. He looked round the small dining-room as if he were still puzzled by its strangeness. Papa was not what he used to be. A streak of grey hair showed above each ear. Grey patches in his brown beard. Scarlet smears in the veined sallow of his eyes. His bursting, violent life had gone. He went stooping and shuffling.

The house was too small for Papa. He turned in it as a dog turns in his kennel, feeling for a place to stretch himself.

He said, " Where's your mother? I want her."

Mary went to find her.

She knew the house: the flagged passage from the front door. The dining-room on the right. The drawing-room on the left. In there the chairs and tables drew together to complain of Morfe. View of the blacksmith's house and yard from the front window. From the side window Mamma's garden. Green grass-plot. Trees at the far end. Flowers in the borders: red roses, cream roses, Canterbury bells, white and purple, under the high walls. In a corner an elder bush frothing greenish white on green.

Behind the dining-room Papa's tight den. Stairs where the passage turned to the left behind the drawing-room. Glass door at the end, holding the green of the garden, splashed with purple, white and red. The kitchen here in a back wing like a rough barn run out into the orchard.

Upstairs Catty's and Cook's room in the wing; Papa's dressing-room above the side passage; Roddy's room above Papa's den. Then the three rooms in front. The one above the drawing-room was nearly filled with the yellow birchwood wardrobe and bed. The emerald green of the damask was fading into the grey.

Her mother was there, sitting in the window-seat, reading the fourteenth chapter of St. John.

" Let not your heart be troubled: ye believe in God, believe also in me. In my Father's house are many mansions — "

Mamma was different, too, as if she had shrunk through living in the cramped rooms. She raised her head. The head of a wounded bird, very gentle.

" Why are you sitting up here all alone? "

" Because sometimes I want to be alone."

" Shall I spoil the aloneness? "

" Not if you're a good girl and keep quiet."

Mary sat on the bed and waited till the chapter should be ended.

She thought: " She talks to me still as though I were a child. What would she say if I told her about Aunt Char-

lotte? She wouldn't know what it was really like. She
wasn't there.

" I shall never tell her."

She was thrilled at the thought of her grown-up hardness,
her grown-up silence, keeping her mother safe.

Mamma looked up and smiled; the chapter was ended;
they went downstairs.

Papa stood in the doorway of his den and called to
Mamma in a queer low voice.

The letters —

She went into the dining-room and waited — ten minutes
— twenty.

Her mother came to her there. She sat down in her arm-
chair by the window-seat where the old work-basket stood
piled with socks ready for darning. She took a sock and
drew it over her hand, stretching it to find the worn places.
Mary took its fellow and began to darn it. The coarse wool,
scraping her finger-tips, sent through her a little light, creeping, disagreeable shock.

She was afraid to look at her mother's face.

" Well, Mary — poor Aunt Charlotte might have been carried away in her coffin, and we shouldn't have known if it
had been left to you to tell us."

" I didn't because I thought it would frighten you."

Mamma was not frightened. They couldn't have told her
what it was really like.

Papa's slippers shuffled in the passage. Mamma left off
darning to listen as Catty had listened.

V

On Greffington Edge.

Roddy was looking like Mark, with his eyes very steady
and his mouth firm and proud. His face was red as if he
were angry. That was when he saw the tall man coming
towards them down the hill road.

Roddy walked slowly, trying not to meet him at the
cattle-gate. The tall man walked faster, and they met.
Roddy opened the gate.

The tall man thanked him, said " Good day," looked at her as he passed through, then stopped.

" My sister — Mr. Sutcliffe."

Mr. Sutcliffe, handsome with his boney, high-jointed nose and narrow jaw, thrust out, incongruously fierce, under his calm, clean upper lip, shaved to show how beautiful it was. His black blue eyes were set as carefully in their lids as a woman's. He wore his hair rather long. One lock had got loose and hung before his ear like a high whisker.

He was asking Roddy when he was coming to play tennis, and whether his sister played. They might turn up to-morrow.

The light played on his curling, handsome smile. He hoped she liked Rathdale.

" She only came yesterday," Roddy said.

" Well — come along to-morrow. About four o'clock. I'll tell my wife."

And Roddy said, " Thanks," as if it choked him.

Mr. Sutcliffe went on down the hill.

" We can't go," Roddy said.

" Why not? "

" Well — "

" Let's. He looked so nice, and he sounded as if he really wanted us."

" He doesn't. He can't. You don't know what's happened."

" *Has* anything happened? "

" Yes. I don't want to tell you, but you'll have to know. It happened at the Sutcliffes'."

" Who *are* the Sutcliffes? "

" Greffington Hall. The people who own the whole ghastly place. We were dining there. And Papa was funny."

" Funny? Funny what way? "

" Oh, I don't know.— Like Dan was at Mark's party.'

" Oh Roddy — " She was listening now.

" Not quite so awful; but that sort of thing. We had to come away."

" I didn't know he did."

" No more did I. Mamma always said it wasn't that. But it was this time. And he chose that evening."

" Does Mamma mind frightfully? " she said.

" Yes. But she's angry with the Sutcliffes."

" Why? "

" Because they've *seen* him."

" How many Sutcliffes are there? "

" Only him and Mrs. Sutcliffe. The son's in India.

" They'll never ask him again, and Mamma won't go without him. She says we can go if we like, but you can see she'll think us skunks if we do."

" Well.— then we can't."

She had wanted something to happen, and something had happened, something that would bring unhappiness. Unhappiness. Her will rose up, hard and stubborn, pushing it off.

" Will it matter so very much? Do the Sutcliffes matter? "

" They matter this much, that there won't be anything to do. They've got all the shooting and fishing and the only decent tennis court in the place. You little know what you're in for."

" I don't care, Roddy. I don't care a bit as long as I have you."

" Me? Me? "

He had stopped on the steep of the road; her feet had been lagging to keep pace with him. He breathed hard through white-edged lips. She had seen him look like that before. The day they had walked to the Thames, to look at the ships, over the windy Flats.

He looked at her. A look she hadn't seen before. A look of passionate unbelief.

" I didn't think you cared about me. I thought it was Mark you cared about. Like Mamma."

" Can't you care about more than one person? "

" Mamma can't — "

" Oh Roddy — "

" What's the good of saying ' Oh Roddy ' when you know it? "

They were sitting on a ledge of stone and turf. Roddy had ceased to struggle with the hill.

" We're all the same," he said. " I'd give you and Dan up any day for Mark. Dan would give up you and me.

Mark would give up all of us for Mamma. And Mamma
would give up all of us for Mark."

Roddy had never said anything like that before.

" I'll stick to you, anyhow," she said.

" It's no use your sticking. I shan't be here. I shall
have to clear out and do something," he said.

On his face there was a look of fear.

VI

She was excited because they were going to the ivy house
for tea. It looked so pretty and so happy with its green
face shining in the sun. Nothing could take from her her
belief in happiness hiding behind certain unknown doors.
It hid behind the white doors of the ivy house. When you
went in something wonderful would happen.

The ivy house belonged to Mrs. Waugh and Miss Frewin.

The photographs in Mamma's old album showed how
they looked when they and Mamma were young. Modest
pose of dropped arms, holding mushroom hats in front of
them as a protection, the narrow ribbons dangling innocently.
Ellen Frewin, small and upright, slender back curved in to
the set of shawl and crinoline, prim head fixed in the com-
posure of gentle disdain, small mouth saying always " Oh."
Meta, the younger sister, very tall, head bent in tranquil
meditation, her mantle slanting out from the fall of the
thin shoulders.

They rose up in the small, green lighted drawing-room.
Their heads bent forward to kiss.

Ellen Waugh: the photographed face still keeping its
lifted posture of gentle disdain, the skin stretched like a pale
tight glove, a slight downward swelling of the prim oval,
like the last bulge of a sucked peppermint ball, the faded
mouth still making its small " oh." She was the widow of
a clergyman.

Meta, a beautiful nose leaping out at you in a high curve;
narrow, delicate cheeks thinned away so that they seemed
part of the nose; sweet rodent mouth smiling up under its
tip; blurred violet eyes arching vaguely.

Princess gowns stiffened their shawl and crinoline gestures.

"So this is Mary. She's not like her mother, Caroline. Meta, can you see any likeness?"

Miss Frewin arched her eyes and smiled, without looking at you.

"I can't say I do."

Their heads made little nodding bows as they talked. Miss Frewin's bow was sidelong and slow, Mrs. Waugh's straight and decisive.

"She's not like Rodney," Mrs. Waugh said. "And she's not like Emilius. Who is she like?"

Mary answered. "I'm rather like Dan and a good bit like Mark. But I'm most of all like myself."

Mrs. Waugh said "Oh." Her mouth went on saying it while she looked at you.

"She is not in the least like Mark," Mamma said.

They settled down, one on each side of Mamma, smiling at her with their small, faded mouths as you smile at people you love and are happy with. You could see that Mamma was happy, too, sitting between them, safe.

Mrs. Waugh said, "I see you've got Blenkiron in again?"

"Well, he's left his ladder in the yard. I suppose that means he'll mend the kitchen chimney some time before winter."

"The Yorkshire workmen are very independent," Mrs. Waugh said.

"They scamp their work like the rest. You'd need a resident carpenter, and a resident glazier, and a resident plumber —"

"Yes, Caroline, you would indeed."

Gentle voices saying things you had heard before in the drawing-room at Five Elms.

Miss Frewin had opened a black silk bag that hung on her arm, and taken out a minute pair of scissors and a long strip of white stuff with a stitched pattern on it. She nicked out the pattern into little holes outlined by the stitches. Mary watched her, fascinated by the delicate movements of the thin fingers and the slanted, drooping postures of the head.

"Do you *like* doing it?"

"Yes."

She thought:· "What a fool she must think me. As if she'd do it if she didn't like it."

The arching eyes and twitching mouth smiled at your foolishness.

Mrs. Waugh's voice went on. It came smoothly, hardly moving her small, round mouth. That was her natural voice. Then suddenly it rose, like a voice that calls to you to get up in the morning.

"Well, Mary — so you've left school. Come home to be a help to your mother."

A high, false cheerfulness, covering disapproval and reproach.

Their gentleness was cold to her and secretly inimical. They had asked her because of Mamma. They didn't really want her.

Half-past six. It was all over. They were going home across the Green.

"Mary, I wish you could learn to talk without affectation. Telling Mrs. Waugh you 'looked like yourself'! If you could only manage to forget yourself."

Your self? Your self? Why should you forget it? You had to remember. They would kill it if you let them.

What had it done? What *was* it that they should hate it so? It had been happy and excited about *them*, wondering what they would be like. And quiet, looking on and listening, in the strange, green-lighted, green-dark room, crushed by the gentle, hostile voices.

Would it always have to stoop and cringe before people, hushing its own voice, hiding its own gesture?

It crouched now, stung and beaten, hiding in her body that walked beside her mother with proud feet, and small lifted head.

VII

Her mother turned at her bedroom door and signed to her to come in.

She sat down in her low chair at the head of the curtained bed. Mary sat in the window-seat.

"There's something I want to say to you."

" Yes, Mamma."

Mamma was annoyed. She tap-tapped with her foot on the floor.

" Have you given up those absurd ideas of yours? "

" What absurd ideas? "

" You know what I mean. Calling yourself an unbeliever."

" I *can't* say I believe things I don't believe."

" Have you tried? "

" Tried? "

" Have you ever asked God to help your unbelief? "

" No. I could only do that if I didn't believe in my unbelief."

" You mean if you didn't glory in it. Then it's simply your self-will and your pride. Self-will has been your besetting sin ever since you were a little baby crying for something you couldn't have. You kicked before you could talk.

" Goodness knows I've done everything I could to break you of it."

" Yes, Mamma darling."

She remembered. The faded green and grey curtains and the yellow birchwood furniture remembered. Mamma sat on the little chair at the foot of the big yellow bed. You knelt in her lap and played with the gold tassel while Mamma asked you to give up your will.

" I brought you up to care for God and for the truth."

" You did. And I care so awfully for both of them that I won't believe things about God that aren't true."

" And how do you know what's true and what isn't? You set up your little judgment against all the wise and learned people who believe as you were taught to believe. I wonder how you dare."

" It's the risk we're all taking. We may every single one of us be wrong. Still, if some things are true other things can't be. Don't look so unhappy, Mamma."

" How can I be anything else? When I think of you living without God in the world, and of what will happen to you when you die."

" It's your belief that makes you unhappy, not me."

" That's the cruellest thing you've said yet."

"You know I'd rather die than hurt you."

"Die, indeed! When you hurt me every minute of the day. If it had been anything but unbelief. If I even saw you humble and sorry about it. But you seem to be positively enjoying yourself."

"I can't help it if the things I think of make me happy. And you don't know how nice it feels to be free."

"Precious freedom! — to do what you like and think what you like, without caring."

"There's a part of me that doesn't care and there's a part that cares frightfully."

The part that cared was not free. Not free. Prisoned in her mother's bedroom with the yellow furniture that remembered. Her mother's face that remembered. Always the same vexed, disapproving, remembering face. And her own heart, sinking at each beat, dragging remembrance. A dead child, remembering and returning.

"I can't think where you got it from," her mother was saying. "Unless it's those books you're always reading. Or was it that man?"

"What man?"

"Maurice Jourdain."

"No. It wasn't. What made you think of him?"

"Never you mind."

Actually her mother was smiling and trying not to smile, as if she were thinking of something funny and improper.

"There's one thing I must beg of you," she said, "that whatever you choose to think, you'll hold your tongue about it."

"All my life? Like Aunt Lavvy?"

"There was a reason why then; and there's a reason why now. Your father has been very unfortunate. We're here in a new place, and the less we make ourselves conspicuous the better."

"I see."

She thought: "Because Papa drinks Mamma and Roddy go proud and angry; but I must stoop and hide. It isn't fair."

"You surely don't want," her mother said, "to make it harder for me than it is."

Tears. She was beaten.

"I don't want to make it hard for you at all."

"Then promise me you won't talk about religion."

"I won't talk about it to Mrs. Waugh."

"Not to anybody."

"Not to anybody who wouldn't like it. Unless they make me. Will that do?"

"I suppose it'll have to."

Mamma held her face up, like a child, to be kissed.

VIII

The Sutcliffes' house hid in the thick trees at the foot of Greffington Edge. You couldn't see it. You could pretend it wasn't there. You could pretend that Mr. Sutcliffe and Mrs. Sutcliffe were not there. You could pretend that nothing had happened.

There were other houses.

IX

The long house at the top of the Green was gay with rows of pink and white sun-blinds stuck out like attic roofs. The poplars in the garden played their play of falling rain.

You waited in the porch, impatient for the opening of the door.

"Mamma — what *will* it be like?"

Mamma smiled a naughty, pretty smile. She knew what it would be like.

There was a stuffed salmon in a long glass case in the hall. He swam, over a brown plaster river bed, glued to a milk-blue plaster stream.

You waited in the drawing-room. Drab and dying amber and the dapple of walnut wood. Chairs dressed in pallid chintz, holding out their skirts with an air of anxiety. Stuffed love-birds on a branch under a tall glass shade. On the chimney-piece sand-white pampas grass in clear blood-red vases, and a white marble clock supporting a gilt Cupid astride over a gilt ball.

Above the Cupid, in an oval frame, the tinted crayon portrait of a young girl. A pink and blond young girl with a soft nuzzling mouth and nose. She was dressed in a spencer and a wide straw hat, and carried a basket of flowers on her arm. She looked happy, smiling up at the ceiling.

Across the passage a door opening. Voices in the passage, a smell like rotten apples, a tray that clattered.

Miss Kendal rustled in; tall elegant stiffness girded in black silk.

"How good of you to come, Mrs. Olivier. And to bring Miss Mary."

Her sharp-jointed body was like the high-backed chair it sat on. Yet you saw that she had once been the young girl in the spencer; head carried high with the remembered tilt of the girl's head; jaw pushed out at the chin as if it hung lightly from the edge of the upper lip; the nuzzling mouth composed to prudence and propriety. A lace cap with pink ribbons perched on her smooth, ashy blond hair.

Miss Kendal talked to Mamma about weather and gardens; she asked after the kitchen chimney as if she really cared for it. Every now and then she looked at you and gave you a nod and a smile to show that she remembered you were there.

When she smiled her eyes were happy like the eyes of the young girl.

The garden-gate clicked and fell to with a clang. A bell clamoured suddenly through the quiet house.

Miss Kendal nodded. "The Doctor has come to tea. To see Miss Mary."

She put her arm in yours and led you into the dining-room, gaily, gaily, as if she had known you for a long time, as if she were taking you with her to some brilliant, happy feast.

The smell of rotten apples came towards you through the open door of the dining-room. You saw the shining of pure white damask, the flashing of silver, a flower-bed of blue willow pattern cups, an enormous pink and white cake. You thought it was a party.

Three old men were there.

Old Dr. Kendal, six feet of leanness doubled up in an arm-chair. Old Wellington face, shrunk, cheeks burning in a senile raddle. Glassy blue eyes weeping from red rims.

Dr. Charles Kendal, his son; a hard, blond giant; high cheeks, raw ruddied; high bleak nose jutting out with a steep fall to the long upper lip; savage mouth under a straight blond fringe, a shark's keen tooth pointing at the dropped jaw. Arched forehead drooping to the spread ears, blond eyebrows drooping over slack lids.

And Mr. James.

Mr. James was the only short one. He stood apart, his eyes edging off from his limp hand-shaking. Mr. James had a red face and high bleak nose like his brother; he was clean-shaved except for short auburn whiskers brushed forward in flat curls. His thin Wellington lips went out and in, pressed together, trying hard not to laugh at you.

He held his arms bowed out stiffly, as if the arm-holes of his coat were too tight for him.

The room was light at the far end, where the two windows were, and dark at the door-end where the mahogany sideboard was. The bright, loaded table stretched between. Old Dr. Kendal sat behind it by the corner of the fireplace. Though it was August the windows were shut and a fire burned in the grate. Two tabby cats sat up by the fender, blinking and nodding with sleep.

"Here's Father," Miss Kendal said. "And here's Johnnie and Minnie."

He had dropped off into a doze. She woke him.

"You know Mrs. Olivier, Father. And this is Miss Olivier."

"Ay. Eh." From a red and yellow pocket-handkerchief he disentangled a stringy claw-like hand and held it up with an effort.

"Ye've come to see the old man, have ye? Ay. Eh."

"He's the oldest in the Dale," Miss Kendal said. "Except Mr. Peacock of Sarrack."

"Don't you forget Mr. Peacock of Sarrack, or he'll be so set-up there'll be no bearing him," Dr. Charles said.

"Miss Mary, will you sit by Father? "

"No, she won't. Miss Mary will sit over here by me."

Though Dr. Charles was not in his own house he gave orders. He took Mr. James's place at the foot of the table. He made her sit at his left hand and Mamma at his right;

and he slanted Mamma's chair and fixed a basket screen on its back so that she was shielded both from the fire and from the presence of the old man.

Dr. Charles talked.

"Where did you get that thin face, Miss Mary? Not in Rathdale, I'll be bound."

He looked at you with small grey eyes blinking under weak lids and bared the shark's tooth, smiling. A kind, hungry shark.

"They must have starved you at your school. No? Then they made you study too hard. Kate—what d'you think Bill Acroyd's done now? Turned this year's heifers out along of last year's with the ringworm. And asks me how I think they get it. This child doesn't eat enough to keep a mouse, Mrs. Olivier."

He would leave off talking now and then to eat, and in the silence remarkable noises would come from the arm-chair. When that happened Miss Kendal would look under the table and pretend that Minnie and Johnnie were fighting. "Oh, those bad pussies," she would say.

When her face kept quiet it looked dead beside the ruddy faces of the three old men; dead and very quietly, very softly decomposing into bleached purple and sallow white. Then her gaiety would come popping up again and jerk it back into life.

Mr. James sat at her corner, beside Mary. He didn't talk, but his Wellington mouth moved perpetually in and out, and his small reddish eyes twinkled, twinkled, with a shrewd, secret mirth. You thought every minute he would burst out laughing, and you wondered what you were doing to amuse him so.

Every now and then Miss Kendal would tell you something about him.

"What do you think Mr. James did to-day? He walked all the way to Garth and back again. Over nine miles!"

And Mr. James would look gratified.

Tea was over with the sacrifice of the pink and white cake. Miss Kendal took your arm again and led you, gaily, gaily back to the old man.

"Here's Miss Mary come to talk to you, Father."

She set a chair for you beside him. He turned his head
slowly to you, waking out of his doze.

" What did she say your name was, my dear? "

" Olivier. Mary Olivier."

" I don't call to mind anybody of that name in the Dale.
But I suppose I brought you into the world same as the
rest of 'em."

Miss Kendal gave a little bound in her chair. " Does
anybody know where Pussy is? "

The claw hand stirred in the red and yellow pocket-
handkerchief.

" Ye've come to see the old man, have ye? Ay. Eh."

When he talked he coughed. A dreadful sound, as if
he dragged up out of himself a long, rattling chain.

It hurt you to look at him. Pity hurt you.

Once he had been young, like Roddy. Then he had been
middle-aged, with hanging jaw and weak eyelids, like
Dr. Charles. Now he was old, old; he sat doubled up,
coughing and weeping, in a chair. But you could see that
Miss Kendal was proud of him. She thought him wonderful
because he kept on living.

Supposing he was *your* father and you had to sit with
him, all your life, in a room smelling of rotten apples, could
you bear it? Could you bear it for a fortnight? Wouldn't
you wish — wouldn't you wish — supposing Papa — all your
life.

But if you couldn't bear it that would mean—

No. No. She put her hand on the arm of his chair,
to protect him, to protect him from her thoughts.

The claw fingers scrabbled, groping for her hand.

" Would ye like to be an old man's bed-fellow? "

"Pussy says it isn't her bed-time yet, Father."

When you went away Miss Kendal stood on the doorstep
looking after you. The last you saw of her was a soft
grimace of innocent gaiety.

x

The Vicar of Renton. He wanted to see her.

Mamma had left her in the room with him, going out with
an air of self-conscious connivance.

Mr. Spencer Rollitt. Hard and handsome. Large face, square-cut, clean-shaved, bare of any accent except its eyebrows, its mouth a thin straight line hardly visible in its sunburn. Small blue eyes standing still in the sunburn, hard and cold.

When Mr. Rollitt wanted to express heartiness he had to fall back on gesture, on the sudden flash of white teeth; he drew in his breath, sharply, between the straight, close lips, with a sound: " Fivv-vv! "

She watched him. Under his small handsome nose his mouth and chin together made one steep, straight line. This lower face, flat and naked, without lips, stretched like another forehead. At the top of the real forehead, where his hat had saved his skin, a straight band, white, like a scar. Yet Mr. Spencer Rollitt's hair curled and clustered out at the back of his head in perfect innocence.

He was smiling his muscular smile, while his little hard cold eyes held her in their tight stare.

" Don't you think you would like to take a class in my Sunday School? "

" I'm afraid I wouldn't like it at all."

" Nothing to be afraid of. I should give you the infants' school."

For a long time he sat there, explaining that there was nothing to be afraid of, and that he would give her the infants' school. You felt him filling the room, crushing you back and back, forcing his will on you. There was too much of his will, too much of his face. Her will rose up against his will and against his face, and its false, muscular smile.

" I'm sure my mother didn't say I'd like to teach in a Sunday School."

" She said she'd be very glad if I could persuade you."

" She'd say *that*. But she knows perfectly well I wouldn't really do it."

" It was not Mrs. Olivier's idea."

He got up. When he stood his eyes stared at nothing away over your head. He wouldn't lower them to look at you.

" It was Mrs. Sutcliffe's."

" How funny of Mrs. Sutcliffe. She doesn't know me, either."

" My dear young lady, you were at school when your father and mother dined at Greffington Hall."

He was looking down at her now, and she could feel herself blushing ; hot, red waves of shame, rushing up, tingling in the roots of her hair.

" Mrs. Sutcliffe," he said, " is very kind."

She saw it now. He had been at the Sutcliffes that evening. He had seen Papa. He was trying to say, " Your father was drunk at Greffington Hall. He will never be asked there again. He will not be particularly welcome at the Vicarage. But you are very young. We do not wish you to suffer. This is our kindness to you. Take it. You are not in a position to refuse."

" And what am I to say to Mrs. Sutcliffe? "

" Oh, anything you like that wouldn't sound too rude."

" Shall I say that you're a very independent young lady, and that she had better not ask you to join her sewing-class? Would that sound too rude? "

" Not a bit. If you put it nicely. But you would, wouldn't you? "

He looked down at her again. His thick eyes had thawed slightly; they let out a twinkle. But he was holding his lips so tight that they had disappeared. A loud, surprising laugh forced them open.

He held out his hand with a gesture, drawing back his laugh in a tremendous " Fiv-v-v-v."

When he had gone she opened the piano and played, and played. Through the window of the room Chopin's Fontana Polonaise went out after him, joyous, triumphant and defiant, driving him before it. She exulted in her power over the Polonaise. Nothing could touch you, nothing could hurt you while you played. If only you could go on playing for ever —

Her mother came in from the garden.

" Mary," she said, " if you *will* play, you must play gently."

" But Mamma — I can't. It goes like that."

" Then," said her mother, " don't play it. You can be heard all over the village."

" Bother the village. I don't care. I don't care if I'm heard all over everywhere! "

She went on playing.

But it was no use. She struck a wrong note. Her hands trembled and lost their grip. They stiffened, dropped from the keys. She sat and stared idiotically at the white page, at the black dots nodding on their stems, at the black bars swaying.

She had forgotten how to play Chopin's Fontana Polonaise.

XI

Stone walls. A wild country, caught in the net of the stone walls.

Stone walls following the planes of the land, running straight along the valleys, switchbacking up and down the slopes. Humped-up, grey spines of the green mounds.

Stone walls, piled loosely, with the brute skill of earthmen, building centuries ago. They bulged, they toppled, yet they stood firm, holding the wild country in their mesh, knitting the grey villages to the grey farms, and the farms to the grey byres. Where you thought the net had ended it flung out a grey rope over the purple back of Renton, the green shoulder of Greffington.

Outside the village, the schoolhouse lane, a green trench sunk between stone walls, went up and up, turning three times. At the top of the last turn a gate.

When you had got through the gate you were free.

It led on to the wide, flat half-ring of moor that lay under Karva. The moor and the high mound of the hill were free; they had slipped from the net of the walls.

Broad sheep-drives cut through the moor. Inlets of green grass forked into purple heather. Green streamed through purple, lapped against purple, lay on purple in pools and splashes.

Burnt patches. Tongues of heather, twisted and pointed, picked clean by fire, flickering grey over black earth. Towards evening the black and grey ran together like ink and water, stilled into purple, the black purple of grapes.

If you shut your eyes you could see the flat Essex country
spread in a thin film over Karva. Thinner and thinner.
But you could remember what it had been like. Low,
tilled fields, thin trees ; sharp, queer, uncertain beauty.
Sharp, queer, uncertain happiness, coming again and again,
never twice to the same place in the same way. It hurt you
when you remembered it.

The beauty of the hills was not like that. It stayed.
It waited for you, keeping faith. Day after day, night after
night, it was there.

Happiness was there. You were sure of it every time.
Roddy's uneasy eyes, Papa's feet, shuffling in the passage,
Mamma's disapproving, remembering face, the Kendals'
house, smelling of rotten apples, the old man, coughing
and weeping in his chair, they couldn't kill it ; they couldn't
take it away.

The mountain sheep waited for you. They stood back
as you passed, staring at you with their look of wonder and
sadness.

Grouse shot up from your feet with a " Rek-ek-ek-kek! "
in sudden, explosive flight.

Plovers rose, wheeling round and round you with sharper
and sharper cries of agitation. "*Pee*-vit — *pee*-vit — *pee*-
vit! Pee-*vitt!* " They swooped, suddenly close, close to
your eyes; you heard the drumming vibration of their wings.

Away in front a line of sheep went slowly up and up
Karva. The hill made their bleating mournful and musical.

You slipped back into the house. In the lamp-lighted
drawing-room the others sat, bored and tired, waiting for
prayer-time. They hadn't noticed how long you had been
gone.

XII

" Roddy, I wish you'd go and see where your father is."

Roddy looked up from his sketch-book. He had filled it
with pictures of cavalry on plunging chargers, trains of
artillery rushing into battle, sailing ships in heavy seas.

Roddy's mind was possessed by images of danger and
adventure.

He flourished off the last wave of battle-smoke, and shut the sketch-book with a snap.

Mamma knew perfectly well where Papa was. Roddy knew. Catty and Maggie the cook knew. Everybody in the village knew. Regularly, about six o'clock in the evening, he shuffled out of the house and along the High Row to the Buck Hotel, and towards dinner-time Roddy had to go and bring him back. Everybody knew what he went for.

He would have to hold Papa tight by the arm and lead him over the cobblestones. They would pass the long bench at the corner under the Kendals' wall; and Mr. Oldshaw, the banker, and Mr. Horn, the grocer, and Mr. Acroyd, the shoemaker, would be sitting there talking to Mr. Belk, who was justice of the peace. And they would see Papa. The young men squatting on the flagstones outside the " Farmer's Arms " and the " King's Head " would see him. And Papa would stiffen and draw himself up, trying to look dignified and sober.

When he was very bad Mamma would cry, quietly, all through dinner-time. But she would never admit that he went to the Buck Hotel. He had just gone off nobody knew where and Roddy had got to find him.

August, September and October passed.

XIII

" Didn't I tell you to wait? You know them all now. You see what they're like."

In Roddy's voice there was a sort of tired, bitter triumph.

She knew them all now: Mrs. Waugh and Miss Frewin, and the Kendals; Mr. Spencer Rollitt, and Miss Louisa Wright who had had a disappointment; and old Mrs. Heron. They were all old.

Oh, and there was Dorsy Heron, Mrs. Heron's niece. But Dorsy was old too, twenty-seven. She was no good; she couldn't talk to Roddy; she could only look at him with bright, shy eyes, like a hare.

Roddy and Mary were going up the Garthdale road. At the first turn they saw Mrs. Waugh and her son coming towards them. (She had forgotten Norman Waugh.)

Rodney groaned. "*He's* here again. I say, let's go back."

"We can't. They've seen us."

"Everybody sees us," Roddy said.

He began to walk with a queer, defiant, self-conscious jerk.

Mrs. Waugh came on, buoyantly, as if the hoop of a crinoline still held her up.

"Well, Mary, going for another walk?"

She stopped, in a gracious mood to show off her son. When she looked at Roddy her raised eyebrows said, "Still here, doing nothing?"

"Norman's going back to work on Monday," she said.

The son stood aside, uninterested, impatient, staring past them, beating the road with his stick. He was thick-set and square. He had the stooping head and heavy eyes of a bull. Black hair and eyebrows grew bushily from his dull-white Frewin skin.

He would be an engineer. Mr. Belk's brother had taken him into his works at Durlingham. He wasn't seventeen, yet he knew how to make engines. He had a strong, lumbering body. His heart would go on thump-thumping with regular strokes, like a stupid piston, not like Roddy's heart, excited, quivering, hurrying, suddenly checking. His eyes drew his mother away. You were glad when they were gone.

"You can see what they think," Roddy said. "Everybody thinks it."

"Everybody thinks what?"

"That I'm a cad to be sticking here, doing nothing, living on Mamma's money."

"It doesn't matter. They've no business to think."

"No. But Mamma thinks it. She says I ought to get something to do. She talks about Mark and Dan. She can't see — " He stopped, biting his lip.

"If I were like Mark — if I could do things. That beast Norman Waugh can do things. He doesn't live on his mother's money. She sees that . . .

"She doesn't know what's the matter with me. She thinks it's only my heart. And it isn't. It's me. I'm an idiot. I can't even do office work like Dan. . . . She thinks I'll be all right if I go away far enough, where she won't see me. Mind you, I *should* be all right if I'd gone into the Navy. She knows if I hadn't had that beastly rheumatic fever I'd have been in the Navy or the Merchant Service now. It's all rot not passing you. As if walking about on a ship's deck was worse for your heart than digging in a garden. It certainly couldn't be worse than farming in Canada."

"Farming? In Canada?"

"That's her idea. It'll kill me to do what *I* want. It won't kill me to do what *she* wants."

He brooded.

"Mark did what he wanted. He went away and left her. Brute as I am, I wouldn't have done that. She doesn't know that's why I'm sticking here. I *can't* leave her. I'd rather die."

Roddy too. He had always seemed to go his own way without caring, living his secret life, running, jumping, grinning at you. And he, too, was compelled to adore Mark and yet to cling helplessly, hopelessly, to Mamma. When he said things about her he was struggling against her, trying to free himself. He flung himself off and came back, to cling harder. And he was nineteen.

"After all," he said, "why shouldn't I stay? It's not as if I didn't dig in the garden and look after Papa. If I went she'd have to get somebody."

"I thought you wanted to go?" she said.

"So I did. So I do, for some things. But when it comes to the point — "

"When it comes to the point?"

"I funk it."

"Because of Mamma?"

"Because of me. That idiocy. Supposing I *had* to do something I couldn't do? . . . That's why I shall have to go away somewhere where it won't matter, where she won't know anything about it."

The frightened look was in his eyes again.

In her heart a choking, breathless voice talked of unhappiness, coming, coming. Unhappiness that no beauty could assuage. Her will hardened to shut it out.

When the road turned again they met Mr. James. He walked with queer, jerky steps, his arms bowed out stiffly.

As he passed he edged away from you. His mouth moved as if he were trying not to laugh.

They knew about Mr. James now. His mind hadn't grown since he was five years old. He could do nothing but walk. Martha, the old servant, dressed and undressed him.

" I shall have to go," Roddy said. " If I stay here I shall look like Mr. James. I· shall walk with my arms bowed out. Catty'll dress and undress me."

XXI

I

THEY hated the piano. They had pushed it away against the dark outside wall. Its strings were stiff with cold, and when the rain came its wooden hammers swelled so that two notes struck together in the bass.

The piano-tuner made them move it to the inner wall in the large, bright place that belonged to the cabinet. Mamma was annoyed because Mary had taken the piano-tuner's part.

Mamma loved the cabinet. She couldn't bear to see it standing in the piano's dark corner where the green Chinese bowls hardly showed behind the black glimmer of the panes. The light fell full on the ragged, faded silk of the piano, and on the long scar across its lid. It was like a poor, shabby relation.

It stood there in the quiet room, with its lid shut, patient, reproachful, waiting for you to come and play on it.

When Mary thought of the piano her heart beat faster, her fingers twitched, the full, sensitive tips tingled and ached to play. When she couldn't play she lay awake at night thinking of the music.

She was trying to learn the Sonato *Appassionata,* going through it bar by bar, slowly and softly, so that nobody outside the room should hear it. That was better than not playing it at all. But sometimes you would forget, and as soon as you struck the loud chords in the first movement

Papa would come in and stop you. And the Sonata would go on sounding inside you, trying to make you play it, giving you no peace.

Towards six o'clock she listened for his feet in the flagged passage. When the front door slammed behind him she rushed to the piano. There might be a whole hour before Roddy fetched him from the Buck Hotel. If you could only reach the last movement, the two thundering chords, and then — the *Presto*.

The music beat on the thick stone walls of the room and was beaten back, its fine, live throbbing blunted by overtones of discord. You longed to open all the doors and windows of the house, to push back the stone walls and let it out.

Terrible minutes to six when Mamma's face watched and listened, when she knew what you were thinking. You kept on looking at the clock, you wondered whether this time Papa would really go. You hoped —

Mamma's eyes hurt you. They said, " She doesn't care what becomes of him so long as she can play."

II

Sometimes the wounded, mutilated *Allegro* would cry inside you all day, imploring you to finish it, to let it pour out its life in joy.

When it left off the white sound patterns of poems came instead. They floated down through the dark as she lay on her back in her hard, narrow bed. Out of doors, her feet, muffled in wet moor grass, went to a beat, a clang.

She would never play well. At any minute her father's voice or her mother's eyes would stiffen her fingers and stop them. She knew what she would do ; she had always known. She would make poems. They couldn't hear you making poems. They couldn't see your thoughts falling into sound patterns.

Only part of the pattern would appear at once while the rest of it went on sounding from somewhere a long way off. When all the parts came together the poem was made. You felt as if you had made it long ago, and had forgotten it and remembered.

III

The room held her close, cold and white, a nun's cell. If you counted the window-place it was shaped like a cross. The door at the foot, the window at the head, bookshelves at the end of each arm. A kitchen lamp with a tin reflector, on a table, stood in the breast of the cross. Its flame was so small that she had to turn it on to her work like a lantern.

"Dumpetty, dumpetty dum. Tell them that Bion is dead ; he is dead, young Bion, the shepherd. And with him music is dead and Dorian poetry perished — "

She had the conceited, exciting thought : " I am translating Moschus, the Funeral Song for Bion."

Moschus was Bion's friend. She wondered whether he had been happy or unhappy, making his funeral song.

If you could translate it all : if you could only make patterns out of English sounds that had the hardness and stillness of the Greek.

"'Archetë, Sikelikai, to pentheos, archetë Moisai, adones hai pukinoisin oduramenai poti phullois.'"

The wind picked at the pane. Through her thick tweed coat she could feel the air of the room soak like cold water to her skin. She curved her aching hands over the hot globe of the lamp.

— Oduromenai. Mourning? No. You thought of black crape, bunched up weepers, red faces.

The wick spluttered; the flame leaned from the burner, gave a skip and went out.

Oduromenai — Grieving ; perhaps.

Suddenly she thought of Maurice Jourdain.

She saw him standing in the field path. She heard him say " Talk to *me*. I'm alive. I'm here. I'll listen. I'll never misunderstand." She saw his worn eyelids; his narrow, yellowish teeth.

Supposing he was dead —

She would forget about him for months together ; then suddenly she would remember him like that. Being happy and excited made you remember. She tried not to see his eyelids and his teeth. They didn't matter.

IV

The season of ungovernable laughter had begun.

"Roddy, they'll hear us. We m-m-mustn't."

"I'm not. I'm blowing my nose."

"I wish *I* could make it sound like that."

They stood on the Kendals' doorstep, in the dark, under the snow. Snow powdered the flagstone path swept ready for the New Year's party.

"Think," she said, "their poor party. It would be awful of us."

Roddy rang. As they waited they began to laugh again. Helpless, ruinous, agonising laughter.

"Oh — oh — I can hear Martha coming. *Do* something. You might be unbuckling my snow-shoes."

The party was waiting for them in the drawing-room. Dr. Charles. Miss Louisa Wright, stiff fragility. A child's face blurred and delicately weathered; features in innocent, low relief. Pale hair rolled into an insubstantial puff above each ear. Speedwell eyes, fading milkily. Hurt eyes, disappointed eyes. Dr. Charles had disappointed her.

Dorsy Heron, tall and straight. Shy hare's face trying to look austere.

Norman Waugh, sulky and superior, in a corner.

As Roddy came in everybody but Norman Waugh turned round and stared at him with sudden, happy smiles. He was so beautiful that it made people happy to look at him. His very name, Rodney Olivier, sounded more beautiful than other people's names.

Dorsy Heron's shy hare's eyes tried to look away and couldn't. Her little high, red nose got redder.

And every now and then Dr. Charles looked at Rodney, a grave, considering look, as if he knew something about him that Rodney didn't know.

V

"She shall play what she likes," Mr. Sutcliffe said. He had come in late, without his wife.

She was going to play to them. They always asked you to play.

She thought: "It'll be all right. They won't listen; they'll go on talking. I'll play something so soft and slow that they won't hear it. I shall be alone, listening to myself."

She played the first movement of the Moonlight Sonata. A beating heart, a grieving voice; beautiful, quiet grief; it couldn't disturb them.

Suddenly they all left off talking. They were listening. Each note sounded pure and sweet, as if it went out into an empty room. They came close up, one by one, on tiptoe, with slight creakings and rustlings, Miss Kendal, Louisa Wright, Dorsy Heron. Their eyes were soft and quiet like the music.

Mr. Sutcliffe sat where he could see her. He was far away from the place where she heard herself playing, but she could feel his face turned on her like a light.

The first movement died on its two chords. Somebody was saying "How beautifully she plays." Life and warmth flowed into her. Exquisite, tingling life and warmth. "Go on. Go on." Mr. Sutcliffe's voice sounded miles away beyond the music.

She went on into the lovely *Allegretto*. She could see their hushed faces leaning nearer. You could make them happy by playing to them. They loved you because you made them happy.

Mr. Sutcliffe had got up; he had come closer.

She was playing the *Presto agitato*. It flowed smoothly under her fingers, at an incredible pace, with an incredible certainty.

Something seemed to be happening over there, outside the place where she heard the music. Martha came in and whispered to the Doctor. The Doctor whispered to Roddy. Roddy started up and they went out together.

She thought: "Papa again." But she was too happy to care. Nothing mattered so long as she could listen to herself playing the Moonlight Sonata.

Under the music she was aware of Miss Kendal stooping over her, pressing her shoulder, saying something. She stood up. Everybody was standing up, looking frightened.

Outside, in the hall, she saw Catty, crying. She went

past her over the open threshold where the snow lay like a light. She couldn't stay to find her snow-shoes and her coat.

The track across the Green struck hard and cold under her slippers. The tickling and trickling of the snow felt like the play of cold light fingers on her skin. Her fear was a body inside her body; it ached and dragged, stone cold and still.

VI

The basin kept on slipping from the bed. She could see its pattern — reddish flowers and green leaves and curlykews — under the splashings of mustard and water. She felt as if it must slip from her fingers and be broken. When she pressed it tighter to the edge of the mattress the rim struck against Papa's breast.

He lay stretched out on the big yellow birchwood bed. The curtains were drawn back, holding the sour smell of sickness in their fluted folds.

Papa's body made an enormous mound under the green eiderdown. It didn't move. A little fluff of down that had pricked its way through the cover still lay where it had settled ; Papa's head still lay where it had dropped ; the forefinger still pointed at the fluff of down.

Papa's head was thrown stiffly back on the high pillows ; it sank in, weighted with the blood that flushed his face. Around it on the white linen there was a spatter and splash of mustard and water. His beard clung to his chin, soaked in the yellowish stain. He breathed with a loud, grating and groaning noise.

Her ears were so tired with listening to this noise that sometimes they would go to sleep for a minute or two. Then it would wake them suddenly and she would begin to cry again.

You could stop crying if you looked steadily at the little fluff of down. At each groaning breath it quivered and sank and quivered.

Roddy sat by the dressing-table. He stared, now at his clenched hands, now at his face in the glass, as if he hated it, as if he hated himself.

Mamma was still dressed. She had got up on the bed beside Papa and crouched on the bolster. She had left off crying. Every now and then she stroked his hair with tender, desperate fingers. It struck out between the white ears of the pillow-slip in a thin, pointed crest.

Papa's hair. His poor hair. These alterations of the familiar person, the blood-red flush, the wet, clinging beard, the pointed hair, stirred in her a rising hysteria of pity.

Mamma had given him the mustard and water. She could see the dregs in the tumbler on the night-table, and the brown hen's feather they had tickled his throat with.

They oughtn't to have done it. Dr. Charles would not have let them do it if he had been there. They should have waited. They might have known the choking and the retching would kill him. Catty ought to have known. Somewhere behind his eyes his life was leaking away through the torn net of the blood vessels, bleeding away over his brain, under his hair, under the tender, desperate fingers.

She fixed her eyes on the pattern of the wall-paper. A purplish rose-bud in a white oval on a lavender ground. She clung to it as to some firm, safe centre of being.

VII

The first day. The first evening.

She went on hushed feet down the passage to let Dan in. The squeak of the latch picked at her taut nerves.

She was glad of the cold air that rushed into the shut-up, soundless house, the sweet, cold air that hung about Dan's face and tingled in the curling frieze of his overcoat.

She took him into the lighted dining-room where Roddy and Mamma waited for him. The callous fire crackled and spurted brightness. The table was set for Dan's supper.

Dan knew that Papa was dead. He betrayed his knowledge by the cramped stare of his heavy, gentle eyes and by the shamed, furtive movements of his hands towards the fire. But that was all. His senses were still uncontaminated by *their* knowledge. He had not seen Papa. He had not heard him.

" What was it? "

"Apoplexy."

His eyes widened. Innocent, vague eyes that didn't see. Their minds fastened on Dan, to get immunity for themselves out of his unconsciousness. As long as they could keep him downstairs, in his innocence, their misery receded from them a little way.

But Mamma would not have it so. She looked at Dan. Her eyes were dull and had no more thought in them. Her mouth quivered. They knew that she was going to say something. Their thread of safety tightened. In another minute it would snap.

"Would you like to see him?" she said.

They waited for Dan to come down from the room. He would not be the same Dan. He would have seen the white sheet raised by the high mound of the body and by the stiff, upturned feet, and he would have lifted the handkerchief from the face. He would be like them, and his consciousness would put a sharper edge on theirs. He would be afraid to look at them, as they were afraid to look at each other, because of what he had seen.

VIII

She lay beside her mother in the strange spare room.

She had got into bed straight from her undressing. On the other side of the mattress she had seen her mother's kneeling body like a dwarfed thing trailed there from the floor, and her hands propped up on the edge of the eiderdown, ivory-white against the red and yellow pattern, and her darling bird's head bowed to her finger-tips.

The wet eyelids had lifted and the drowned eyes had come to life again in a brief glance of horror. Mamma had expected her to kneel down and pray. In bed they had turned their backs on each other, and she had the feeling that her mother shrank from her as from somebody unclean who had omitted to wash herself with prayer. She wanted to take her mother in her arms and hold her tight. But she couldn't. She couldn't.

Suddenly her throat began to jerk with a hysterical spasm. She thought: "I wish I had died instead of Papa."

She forced back the jerk of her hysteria and lay still, listening to her mother's sad, obstructed breathing and her soft, secret blowing of her nose.

Presently these sounds became a meaningless rhythm and ceased. She was a child, dreaming. She stood on the nursery staircase at Five Elms; the coffin came round the turn and crushed her against the banisters; only this time she was not afraid of it; she made herself wake because of something that would happen next. The flagstones of the passage were hard and cold to her naked feet; that was how you could tell you were awake. The door of the Morfe drawing-room opened into Mamma's old bedroom at Five Elms, and when she came to the foot of the bed she saw her father standing there. He looked at her with a mocking, ironic animosity, so that she knew he was alive. She thought:

"It's all right. I only dreamed he was dead. I shall tell Mamma."

When she really woke, two entities, two different and discordant memories, came together with a shock.

Her mother was up and dressed. She leaned over her, tucking the blankets round her shoulders and saying, "Lie still and go to sleep again, there's a good girl."

Her memory cleared and settled, filtering, as the light filtered through the drawn blinds. Mamma and she had slept together because Papa was dead.

IX

"Mary, do you know why you're crying?"

Roddy's face was fixed in a look of anger and resentment, and of anxiety as if he were afraid that at any minute he would be asked to do something that he couldn't do.

They had come down together from the locked room, and gone into the drawing-room where the yellow blinds let in the same repulsive, greyish, ochreish light.

Her tears did not fall. They covered her eyes each with a shaking lens; the chairs and tables floated up to her as if she stood in an aquarium of thick, greyish, ochreish light.

"You think it's because you care," he said. "But it's

because you don't care. . . . You're not as bad as I am.
I don't care a bit."

"Yes, you do, or you wouldn't think you didn't."

"No. None of us really cares. Except Mamma. And
even she doesn't as much as she thinks she does. If we
cared we'd be glad to sit in there, doing nothing, thinking
about him. . . . That's why we keep on going upstairs to
look at him, to make ourselves feel as if we cared."

She wondered. Was that really why they did it? She
thought it was because they couldn't bear to leave him
there, four days and four nights, alone. She said so. But
Roddy went on in his hard, flat voice, beating out his truth.

"We never did anything to make him happy."

"He *was* happy," she said. "When Mark went. He
had Mamma."

"Yes, but he must have known about us. He must have
known about us all the time."

"What did he know about us?"

"That we didn't care.

"Don't you remember," he said, "the things we used to
say about him?"

She remembered. She could see Dan in the nursery at
Five Elms, scowling and swearing he would kill Papa. She
could see Roddy, and Mark with his red tight face, laughing at him. She could see herself, a baby, kicking and
screaming when he took her in his arms. For months she
hadn't thought about him except to wish he wasn't there
so that she could go on playing. When he was in the fit
she had been playing on the Kendals' piano, conceited and
happy, not caring.

Supposing all the time, deep down, in his secret mysterious life, *he* had cared?

"We must leave off thinking about him," Roddy said.
"If we keep on thinking we shall go off our heads."

"We *are* off our heads," she said.

Their hatred of themselves was a biting, aching madness.
She hated the conceited, happy self that hadn't cared. The
piano, gleaming sombrely in the hushed light, reminded her
of it.

She hated the piano.

They dragged themselves back into the dining-room where Mamma and Dan sat doing nothing, hiding their faces from each other. The afternoon went on. Utter callousness, utter weariness came over them.

Their mother kept looking at the clock. "Uncle Victor will have got to Durlingham," she said. An hour ago she had said, "Uncle Victor will have got to York." Their minds clung to Uncle Victor as they had clung, four days ago, to Dan, because of his unconsciousness.

X

Uncle Victor had put his arm on her shoulder. He was leaning rather heavily.

He saw what she saw: the immense coffin set up on trestles at the foot of the bed; the sheeted body packed tight in the padded white lining, the hands, curling a little, smooth and stiff, the hands of a wax figure; the firm, sallowish white face; the brown stains, like iodine, about the nostrils; the pale under lip pushed out, proudly.

A cold, thick smell, like earth damped with stagnant water, came up to them, mixed with the sharp, piercing smell of the coffin. The vigilant, upright coffin-lid leaned with its sloping shoulders against the chimney-piece, ready.

In spite of his heavy hand she was aware that Uncle Victor's consciousness of these things was different from hers. He did not appear to be in the least sorry for Papa. On his face, wistful, absorbed, there was a faint, incongruous smile. He might have been watching a child playing some mysterious game.

He sighed. His eyes turned from the coffin to the coffin-lid. He stared at the black letters on the shining brass plate.

Emilius Olivier.
Born November 13th, 1827.
Died January 2nd, 1881.

The grip on her shoulder tightened.
"He was faithful, Mary."
He said it as if he were telling her something she couldn't possibly have known.

XI

The funeral woke her. A line of light slid through the chink of the door, crooked itself and staggered across the ceiling, a blond triangle throwing the shadows askew. That was Catty, carrying the lamp for the bearers.

It came again. There was a shuffling of feet in the passage, a secret muttering at the head of the stairs, the crack of a banister, a thud as the shoulder of the coffin butted against the wall at the turn. Then the grinding scream of the brakes on the hill, the long " Shr-issh " of the checked wheels ploughing through the snow.

She could see her mother's face on the pillow, glimmering, with shut eyes. At each sound she could hear her draw a shaking, sobbing breath. She turned to her and took her in her arms. The small, stiff body yielded to her, helpless, like a child's.

" Oh Mary, what shall I do? To send him away like that — in a train — all the way. . . . Your Grandmamma Olivier tried to keep him from me, and now he's gone back to her."

" You've got Mark."

" What's that you say? "

" Mark. Mark. Nobody can keep Mark from you. He'll never want anybody but you. He said so."

How small she was. You could feel her little shoulder-blades, weak and fine under your fingers, like a child's; you could break them. To be happy with her either you or she had to be broken, to be helpless and little like a child. It was a sort of happiness to lie there, holding her, hiding her from the dreadful funeral dawn.

Five o'clock.

The funeral would last till three, going along the road to Reyburn Station, going in the train from Reyburn to Dur-lingham, from Durlingham to King's Cross. She wondered whether Dan and Roddy would keep on feeling the funeral all the time. The train was part of it. Not the worst part. Not so bad as going through the East End to the City of London Cemetery.

When it came to the City of London Cemetery her mind stopped with a jerk and refused to follow the funeral any further.

Ten o'clock. Eleven.

They had shut themselves up in the dining-room, in the yellow-ochreish light. Mamma sat in her arm-chair, tired and patient, holding her Bible and her Church Service on her knees, ready. Every now and then she dozed. When this happened Mary took the Bible from her and read where it opened: "And he made the candlestick of pure gold: of beaten work made he the candlestick; his shaft, and his branch, his bowls, his knops, and his flowers, were of the same. . . . And in the candlestick were four bowls made like almonds, his knops and his flowers: And a knop under two branches of the same, and a knop under two branches of the same, and a knop under two branches of the same, according to the six branches going out of it. Their knops and their branches were of the same: all of it was one beaten work of pure gold."

At two o'clock the bell of Renton Church began to toll. Her mother sat up in a stiff, self-conscious attitude and opened the Church Service. The bell went on tolling. For Papa.

It stopped. Her mother was saying something.

"Mary — I can't see with the blind down. Do you think you could read it to me?"

* * * * * *

"'I am the Resurrection and the Life — '"

A queer, jarring voice burst out violently in the dark quiet of the room. It carried each sentence with a rush, making itself steady and hard.

"'. . . He that believeth in me, though he were dead, yet shall he live. . . .

"'I said, I will take heed to my ways: that I offend not with my tongue — '"

"Not that one," her mother said.

"'O Lord, Thou hast been our refuge; from one generation to another.

"'Before the mountains were brought forth, or ever the earth and the world were made — '"

(Too fast. Much too fast. You were supposed to be following Mr. Propart; but if you kept up that pace you would have finished the Service before he had got through the Psalm.)

" ' Lord God most holy — ' "

" I can't *hear* you, Mary."

" I'm sorry. ' O Lord most mighty, O holy and most merciful Saviour, deliver us not into the bitter pains of eternal death.

" ' Thou knowest, Lord, the secrets of our hearts: shut not Thy merciful ears to our prayers: but spare us, Lord most holy, O God most mighty, O holy and merciful Saviour — ' "

(Prayers, abject prayers for themselves. None for him. Not one word. They were cowards, afraid for themselves, afraid of death; their funk had made them forget him. It was as if they didn't believe that he was there. And, after all, it was *his* funeral.)

" ' Suffer us not, at our last hour — ' "

The hard voice staggered and dropped, picked itself and continued on a note of defiance.

" ' . . . For any pains of death, to fall from Thee. . . .' "

(They would have come to the grave now, by the black pointed cypresses. There would be a long pit of yellow clay instead of the green grass and the white curb. Dan and Roddy would be standing by it.)

" ' Forasmuch as it hath pleased Almighty God of His mercy to take unto Himself the soul of our dear brother — ' "

The queer, violent voice stopped.

" I can't — I can't."

Mamma seemed gratified by her inability to finish the Order for the Burial of the Dead.

XII

" You can say *that,* with your poor father lying in his grave — "

It was the third evening after the funeral. A minute ago they were at perfect peace, and now the everlasting dispute about religion had begun again. There had been no Prayers since Papa died, because Mamma couldn't trust herself to read them without breaking down. At the same time, it was inconceivable to her that there should be no Prayers.

"I should have thought, if you could read the Burial Service — "

"I only did it because you asked me to."

"Then you might do this because I ask you."

"It isn't the same thing. You haven't got to believe in the Burial Service. But either you believe in Prayers or you don't believe in them. If you don't you oughtn't to read them. You oughtn't to be asked to read them."

"How are we going on, I should like to know? Supposing I was to be laid aside, are there to be no Prayers, ever, in this house because you've set yourself up in your silly self-conceit against the truth?"

The truth. The truth about God. As if anybody really knew it; as if it mattered; as if anything mattered except Mamma.

Yet it did matter. It mattered more than anything in the whole world, the truth about God, the truth about anything; just the truth. Papa's death had nothing to do with it. It wasn't fair of Mamma to talk as if it had; to bring it up against you like that.

"Let's go to bed," she said.

Her mother took no notice of the suggestion. She sat bolt upright in her chair; her face had lost its look of bored, weary patience; it flushed and flickered with resentment.

"I shall send for Aunt Bella," she said.

"Why Aunt Bella?"

"Because I must have someone. Someone of my own."

XIII

It was three weeks now since the funeral.

Mamma and Aunt Bella sat in the dining-room, one on each side of the fireplace. Mamma looked strange and sunken and rather yellow in a widow's cap and a black knitted shawl, but Aunt Bella had turned herself into a large, comfortable sheep by means of a fleece of white shawl and an ice-wool hood peaked over her cap.

There was a sweet, inky smell of black things dyed at Pullar's. Mary picked out the white threads and pretended to listen while Aunt Bella talked to Mamma in a woolly voice about Aunt Lavvy's friendship with the Unitarian minister, and Uncle Edward's lumbago, and the unreasonableness of the working classes.

She thought how clever it was of Aunt Bella to be able to keep it up like that. " I couldn't do it to save my life. As long as I live I shall never be any good to Mamma."

The dining-room looked like Mr. Metcalfe, the undertaker. Funereal hypocrisy. She wondered whether Roddy would see the likeness.

She thought of Roddy's nervous laugh when Catty brought in the first Yorkshire cakes. His eyes had stared at her steadily as he bit into his piece. They had said: " You don't care. You don't care. If you really cared you couldn't eat."

There were no more threads to pick.

She wondered whether she would be thought unfeeling if she were to take a book and read.

Aunt Bella began to talk about Roddy. Uncle Edward said Roddy ought to go away and get something to do.

If Roddy went away there would be no one. No one.

She got up suddenly and left them.

XIV

The air of the drawing-room braced her like the rigour of a cold bath. Her heartache loosened and lost itself in the long shiver of chilled flesh.

The stone walls were clammy with the sweat of the thaw; they gave out a sour, sickly smell. Grey smears of damp dulled the polished lid of the piano.

They hadn't used the drawing-room since Papa died. It was so bright, so heartlessly cheerful compared with the other rooms, you could see that Mamma would think you unfeeling if you wanted to sit in it when Papa was dead. She had told Catty not to light the fire and to keep the door shut, for fear you should be tempted to sit in it and forget.

The piano. Under the lid the keys were stiffening with

the damp. The hammers were swelling, sticking together. She tried not to think of the piano.

She turned her back on it and stood by the side window that looked out on to the garden. Mamma's garden. It mouldered between the high walls blackened by the thaw. On the grass-plot the snow had sunk to a thin crust, black-pitted. The earth was a black ooze through ulcers of grey snow.

She had a sudden terrifying sense of desolation.

Her mind clutched at this feeling and referred it to her father. It sent out towards him, wherever he might be, a convulsive emotional cry.

" You were wrong. I do care. Can't you see that I can never be happy again? Yet, if you could come back I would be happy. I wouldn't mind your — your little funny ways."

It wasn't true. She *would* mind them. If he were really there he would know it wasn't true.

She turned and looked again at the piano. She went to it. She opened the lid and sat down before it. Her fingers crept along the keyboard; they flickered over the notes of the Sonata *Appassionata:* a ghostly, furtive playing, without pressure, without sound.

And she was ashamed as if the piano were tempting her to some cruel, abominable sin.

XXII

I

THE consultation had lasted more than an hour.

From the cobbled square outside you could see them through the window, Mamma, Uncle Edward, Uncle Victor and Farmer Alderson, sitting round the dining-room table and talking, talking, talking about Roddy.

It was awful to think that things — things that concerned you — could go on and be settled over your head without your knowing anything about it. She only knew that Papa had made Uncle Victor and Uncle Edward the trustees and

guardians of his children who should be under age at his
death (she and Roddy were under age), and that Mamma
had put the idea of farming in Canada into Uncle Edward's
head, and that Uncle Victor had said he wouldn't hear of
letting Roddy go out by himself, and that the landlord of
the Buck Hotel had told Victor that Farmer Alderson's
brother Ben had a big farm somewhere near Montreal and
young Jem Alderson was going out to him in March and
they might come to some arrangement.

They were coming to it now.

Roddy and she, crouching beside each other on the hearth-
rug in the drawing-room, waited till it should be over.
Through the shut doors they could still distinguish Uncle
Edward's smooth, fat voice from Uncle Victor's thin one.
The booming and baying were the noises made by Farmer
Alderson.

" I can't think what they want to drag *him* in for," Roddy
said. " It'll only make it more unpleasant for them."

Roddy's eyes had lost their fear; they were fixed in a
wise, mournful stare. He stared at his fate.

" They don't know yet quite *how* imbecile I am. If I
could have gone out quietly by myself they never need have
known. Now they'll *have* to. Alderson'll tell them. He'll
tell everybody. . . . I don't care. It's their own look-out.
They'll soon see I was right."

" Listen," she said.

The dining-room door had opened. Uncle Edward's voice
came out first, sounding with a sort of complacent finality.
They must have settled it. You could hear Farmer Alderson stumping his way to the front door. His voice boomed
from the step.

" Ah doan't saay, look ye, 'e'll mak mooch out of en t'
farst ye-ear — "

" Damn him, you can hear his beastly voice all over the
place."

" Ef yore yoong mon's dead set to larn fa-armin', an' ef
'e've got a head on 'is shoulders our Jem can larn 'en. Ef
'e 'aven't, ah tall yo stra-aight, Mr. Ollyveer, ye med joost's
well tak yore mooney and trow it in t' mistal."

Roddy laughed. " *I* could have told them that," he said.

"Money?"

"Rather. They can't do it under two hundred pounds. I suppose Victor'll stump up as usual."

"Poor Victor."

"Victor won't mind. He'll do anything for Mamma. They can call it a premium if it makes them any happier, but it simply means that they're paying Alderson to get rid of me."

"No. They've got it into their heads that it's bad for you sticking here doing nothing."

"So it is. But being made to do what I can't do's worse. . . . I'm not likely to do it any better with that young beast Alderson looking at me all the time and thinking what a bloody fool I am. . . . They ought to have left it to me. It would have come a lot cheaper. I was going anyhow. I only stayed because of Papa. But I can't tell *them* that. After all, I was the only one who looked after him. If I'd gone you'd have had to."

"Yes."

"It would even come cheaper," he said, "if I stayed. I can prove it."

He produced his pocket sketch-book. The leaves were scribbled over with sums, sums desperately begun and left unfinished, sums that were not quite sure of themselves, sums scratched out and begun again. He crossed them all out and started on a fresh page.

"Premium, two hundred. Passage, twenty. Outfit, say thirty. Two hundred and fifty.

"Land cheap, lumber cheap. Labour expensive. Still, Alderson would be so pleased he might do the job himself for a nominal sum and only charge you for the wood. Funeral expenses, say ten dollars.

"How much does it cost to keep me here?"

"I haven't an idea."

"No, but think."

"I can't think."

"Well, say I eat ten shillings' worth of food per week, that's twenty-six pounds a year. Say thirty. Clothes, five. Thirty-five. Sundries, perhaps five. Forty. But I do the garden. What's a gardener's wages? Twenty? Fifteen?

Say fifteen. Fifteen from forty, fifteen from forty —
twenty-five. How much did Papa's funeral come to? "
"Oh — Roddy — I don't know."
"Say thirty. Twenty-five from two hundred and fifty,
two hundred and twenty-five. Deduct funeral. One hun-
dred and ninety-five.
"There you are. One hundred and ninety-five pounds
for carting me to Canada."
"If you feel like that about it you ought to tell them.
They can't make you go if you don't want to."
"They're not making me go. I'm going. I couldn't possibly stay after the beastly things they've said."
"What sort of things? "
"About my keep and my being no good and making work
in the house."
"They didn't — they couldn't."
"Edward did. He said if it wasn't for me Mamma
wouldn't have to have Maggie. Catty could do all the
work. And when Victor sat on him and said Mamma
was to have Maggie whatever happened, he jawed back and
said she couldn't afford both Maggie and me."
"Catty could do Maggie's work and I could do Catty's,
if you'd stop. It would be only cleaning things. That's
nothing. I'd rather clean the whole house and *have* you."
"You wouldn't. You only think you would."
"I would, really. I'll tell them."
"It's no use," he said. "They won't let you."
"I'll make them. I'll go and tell Edward and Victor
now."
She had shot up from the floor with sudden energy, and
stood looking down at Roddy as he still crouched there.
Her heart ached for him. He didn't want to go to Canada;
he wanted to stay with Mamma, and Mamma was driving
him away from her, for no reason except that Uncle Edward
said he ought to go.
She could hear the dining-room door open and shut again.
They were coming.
Roddy rose from the floor. He drew himself up, stretch-
ing out his arms in a crucified attitude, and grinned at her.
"Do you suppose," he said, "I'd let you? "

He grinned at Uncle Edward and Uncle Victor as they came in.

"Uncle Victor," she said, "Why should Roddy go away? If it's Maggie, we don't really want her. I'll do Catty's work and he'll do the garden. So he can stay, can't he?"

"He *can*, Mary, but I don't think he will."

"Of course I won't. If you hadn't waited to mix me up with Alderson I could have cleared out and got there by this time. You don't suppose I was going to sponge on my mother for ever, do you?"

He stood there, defying Uncle Edward and Uncle Victor, defying their thoughts of him. She wondered whether he had forgotten the two hundred pounds and whether they were thinking of it. They didn't answer, and Roddy, after fixing on them a look they couldn't meet, strode out of the room.

She thought: How like Mark he is, with his tight, squared shoulders, holding his head high. His hair was like Mark's hair, golden brown, close clipped to the nape of his neck. When he had gone it would be like Mark's going.

"It's better he should go," Uncle Victor said. "For his own sake."

Uncle Edward said, "Of course it is."

His little blue eyes glanced up from the side of his nose, twinkling. His mouth stretched from white whisker to white whisker in a smile of righteous benevolence. But Uncle Victor's eyes slunk away as if he were ashamed of himself.

It was Uncle Victor who had paid the two hundred pounds.

IJ

"Supposing there's something the matter with him, will he still have to go?"

"I don't see why you should suppose there's anything the matter with him," her mother said. "Is it likely your Uncle Victor would be paying all that money to send him out if he wasn't fit to go?"

It didn't seem likely that Victor would have done

anything of the sort; any more than Uncle Edward would
have let Aunt Bella give him an overcoat lined with black
jennet.

They were waiting for Roddy to come back from the
doctor's. Before Uncle Victor left Morfe he had made
Roddy promise that for Mamma's satisfaction he would go
and be overhauled. And it was as if he had said " You'll
see then how much need there is to worry."

You might have kept on hoping that something would
happen to prevent Roddy's going but for the size and solidity
and expensiveness of the preparations. You might forget
that his passage was booked for the first Saturday in March,
that to-day was the first Wednesday, that Victor's two hundred pounds had been paid to Jem Alderson's account at
the bank in Montreal, and still the black jennet lining of the
overcoat shouted at you that nothing *could* stop Roddy's
going now. Uncle Victor might be reckless, but Uncle Edward and Aunt Bella took no risks.

Unless, after all, Dr. Kendal stopped it — if he said
Roddy mustn't go.

She could hear Roddy's feet coming back. They sounded
like Mark's feet on the flagged path outside.

He came into the room quickly. His eyes shone, he
looked pleased and excited.

Mamma stirred in her chair.

" That's a bright face. We needn't ask if you've got
your passport," she said.

He looked at her, a light, unresting look.

" How right you are," he said. " And wise."

" Well, I didn't suppose there was much the matter with
you."

" There isn't."

He went to the bookshelf where he kept his drawing-
blocks.

" I wouldn't sit down and draw if I were you. There
isn't time."

" There'll be less after Saturday."

He sat down and began to draw. He was as absorbed
and happy as if none of them had ever heard of Canada.

He chanted:

> " ' Cannon to right of them,
>   Cannon to left of them,
>   Cannon in front of them
>   Volleyed and thundered.' "

The pencil moved excitedly. Volumes of smoke curled and rolled and writhed on the left-hand side of the sheet. The guns of Balaclava.

> " ' Into the jaws of Death,
>   Into the mouth of Hell,
>   Rode the six hundred.' "

A rush of hoofs and heads and lifted blades on the right hand. The horses and swords of the Light Brigade.

> " ' Theirs not to make reply,
>   Theirs not to reason why,
>   Theirs but to do and die ' " —

" You ought to be a soldier, Roddy, like Mark, not a farmer."
" Oh wise!   Oh right!

> " ' Forward, the Light Brigade!
>   Was there a man dismayed?
>   Not though the soldier knew
>   Someone had blundered.' "

III

She was going up the schoolhouse lane towards Karva, because Roddy and she had gone that way together on Friday, his last evening.

It was Sunday now; six o'clock: the time he used to bring Papa home. His ship would have left Queenstown, it would be steering to the west.

She wondered how much he had really minded going. Perhaps he had only been afraid he wouldn't be strong enough; for after he had seen the doctor he had been different. Pleased and excited. Perhaps he didn't mind so very much.

If she could only remember how he had looked and what he had said. He had talked about the big Atlantic liner, and the Canadian forests. With luck the voyage might last eleven or twelve clear days. You could shoot moose and wapiti. Wapiti and elk. Elk. With his eyes shining. He was not quite sure about the elk. He wished he had written to the High Commissioner for Canada about the elk. That was what the Commissioner was there for, to answer questions, to encourage you to go to his beastly country.

She could hear Roddy's voice saying these things as they walked over Karva. He was turning it all into an adventure, his imagination playing round and round it. And on Saturday morning he had been sick and couldn't eat his breakfast. Mamma had been sorry, and at the same time vexed and irritable as if she were afraid that the arrangements might, after all, be upset. But in the end he had gone off, pleased and excited, with Jem Alderson in the train.

She could see Jem's wide shoulders pushing through the carriage door after Roddy. He had a gentle, reddish face and long, hanging moustaches like a dying Gladiator. Little eyes that screwed up to look at you. He would be good to Roddy.

It would be all right.

She stood still in the dark lane. A disturbing memory gnawed its way through her thoughts that covered it: the way Roddy had looked at Mamma, that Wednesday, the way he had spoken to her. " Oh wise. Oh right! "

That was because he believed she wanted him to go away. He couldn't believe that she really cared for him; that Mamma really cared for anybody but Mark; he couldn't believe that anybody cared for him.

> " ' Into the jaws of Death,
> Into the mouth of Hell,
> Rode the six hundred.' "

Roddy's chant pursued her up the lane.

The gate at the top fell to behind her. Moor grass showed grey among black heather. She half saw, half felt her way along the sheep tracks. There, where the edge of the round pit broke away, was the place where Roddy had stopped suddenly in front of her.

" I wouldn't mind a bit if I hadn't been such a brute to
little Mamma.   Why *are* we such brutes to her? "   He had
turned in the narrow moor-track and faced her with his
question: " Why? "

> " ' Forward, the Light Brigade!
> Was there a man dismayed?
> Not though the soldier knew
> Someone had blundered ' " —

Hunderd — blundered.   Did Tennyson really call hundred
hunderd?

The grey curve of the high road glimmered alongside the
moor.   From the point where her track joined it she could
see three lights, two moving, one still.   The still light at the
turn came from the Aldersons' house.   The moving lights
went with the klomp-klomp of hoofs on the road.

Down in the darkness beyond the fields Garthdale lay
like a ditch under the immense wall of Greffington Edge.
Roddy hated Greffington Edge.   He hated Morfe.   He
wanted to get away.

It would be all right.

The klomp-klomping sounded close behind her.   Two
shafts of light shot out in front, white on the grey road.
Dr. Kendal drove past in his dog-cart.   He leaned out over
the side, peering.   She heard him say something to himself.

The wheels slowed down with a grating noise.   The lights
stood still.   He had pulled up.   He was waiting for her.

She turned suddenly and went back up the moor by the
way she had come.   She didn't want to see Dr. Kendal.
She was afraid he would say something about Roddy.

XXIII

I

THE books stood piled on the table by her window, the
books Miss Wray of Clevehead had procured for her, had
given and lent her.   Now Roddy had gone she had time
enough to read them: Hume's *Essays*, the fat maroon
Schwegler, the two volumes of Kant in the hedgesparrow-
green paper covers.

"*Kritik der reinen Vernunft. Kritik der reinen Vernunft.*" She said it over and over to herself. It sounded nicer than "*The Critique of Pure Reason.*" At the sight of the thick black letters on the hedgesparrow-green ground her heart jumped up and down with excitement. Lucky it was in German, so that Mamma couldn't find out what Kant was driving at. The secret was hidden behind the thick black bars of the letters.

In Schwegler, as you went on you went deeper. You saw thought folding and unfolding, thought moving on and on, thought drawing the universe to itself, pushing the universe away from itself to draw it back again, closer than close.

Space and Time were forms of thought. They were infinite. So thought was infinite; it went on and on for ever, carrying Space, carrying Time.

If only you knew what the Thing-in-itself was.

II

"Mamma —"

The letter lay between them on the hall table by the study door. Her mother put her hand over it, quick. A black, long-tailed M showed between her forefinger and her thumb.

They looked at each other, and her mother's mouth began to pout and smile as it used to when Papa said something improper. She took the letter and went, with soft feet and swinging haunches like a cat carrying a mouse, into the study. Mary stared at the shut door.

Maurice Jourdain. Maurice Jourdain. What on earth was he writing to Mamma for?

Five minutes ago she had been quiet and happy, reading Kant's *Critique of Pure Reason.* Now her heart beat like a hammer, staggering with its own blows. The blood raced in her brain.

III

"Mamma, if you don't tell me I shall write and ask him." Her mother looked up, frightened.

"You wouldn't do that, Mary?"

" Oh, wouldn't I though!   I'd do it like a shot."

She wondered why she hadn't thought of it an hour ago.

" Well — If there's no other way to stop you — "

Her mother gave her the letter, picking it up by one corner, as though it had been a dirty pocket-handkerchief.

" It'll show you," she said, " the sort of man he is."

Mary held the letter in both her hands, gently.   Her heart beat gently now with a quiet feeling of happiness and satisfaction.   She looked a long time at the characters, the long-tailed M's, the close, sharp v's, the t's crossed with a savage, downward stab.   She was quiet as long as she only looked. When she read the blood in her brain raced faster and confused her.   She stopped at the bottom of the first page.

" I can't think what he means."

" It's pretty plain what he means," her mother said.

" About all those letters.   What letters? "

" Letters he's been writing to your father and me and your Uncle Victor."

" When? "

" Ever since you left school.   You were sent to school to keep you out of his way; and you weren't back before he began his persecuting.   If you want to know why we left Ilford, *that's* why.   He persecuted your poor father.   He persecuted your Uncle Victor.   And now he's persecuting me."

" Persecuting? "

" What is it but persecuting?   Threatening that he won't answer for the consequences if he doesn't get what he wants. He's mistaken if he thinks that's the way to get it."

" What — *does* he want? "

" I suppose," her mother said, " he thinks he wants to marry you."

" Me?   He doesn't say that.   He only says he wants to come and see me.   Why shouldn't he? "

" Because your father didn't wish it, and your uncle and I don't wish it."

" You don't like him."

" Do *you?* "

" I — love him."

" Nonsense.   You don't know what you're talking about.

You'd have forgotten all about him if you hadn't seen that letter."

"I thought he'd forgotten me. You ought to have told me. It was cruel not to tell me. He must have loved me all the time. He said I was to wait three years and I didn't know what he meant. He must have loved me then and I didn't know it."

The sound of her voice surprised her. It came from her whole body; it vibrated like a violin.

"How could he love you? You were a child then."

"I'm not a child now. You'll have to let him marry me."

"I'd rather see you in your coffin. I'd rather see you married to poor Norman Waugh. And goodness knows I wouldn't like that."

"Your mother didn't like your marrying Papa."

"You surely don't compare Maurice Jourdain with your father?"

"He's faithful. Papa was faithful. I'm faithful too."

"Faithful! To a horrid man like that!"

"He isn't horrid. He's kind and clever and good. He's brave, like Mark. He'd have been a soldier if he hadn't had to help his mother. And he's honourable. He said he wouldn't see me or write to me unless you let him. And he hasn't seen me and he hasn't written. You can't say he isn't honourable."

"I suppose," her mother said, "he's honourable enough."

"You'll have to let him come. If you don't, I *shall go to him*."

"I declare if you're not as bad as your Aunt Charlotte."

IV

Incredible; impossible; but it had happened.

And it was as if she had known it — all the time, known that she would come downstairs that morning and see Maurice Jourdain's letter lying on the table. She always had known that something, some wonderful, beautiful, tremendous thing would happen to her. This was it.

It had been hidden in all her happiness. Her happiness was it. Maurice Jourdain.

When she said " Maurice Jourdain " she could feel her voice throb in her body like the string of a violin. When she thought of Maurice Jourdain the stir renewed itself in a vague, exquisite vibration. The edges of her mouth curled out with faint throbbing movements, suddenly sensitive, like eyelids, like finger-tips.

Odd memories darted out at her. The plantation at Ilford. Jimmy's mouth crushing her face. Jimmy's arms crushing her chest. A scarlet frock. The white bridge-rail by the ford. Bertha Mitchison, saying things, things you wouldn't think of if you could help it. But she was mainly aware of a surpassing tenderness and a desire to immolate herself, in some remarkable and noble \fashion, for Maurice Jourdain. If only she could see him, for ten minutes, five minutes, and tell him that she hadn't forgotten him. He belonged to her real life. Her self had a secret place where people couldn't get at it, where its real life went on. He was the only person she could think of as having a real life at all like her own. She had thought of him as mixed up for ever with her real life, so that whether she saw him or not, whether she remembered him or not, he would be there. He was in the songs she made, he was in the Sonata *Appassionata;* he was in the solemn beauty of Karva under the moon. In the *Critique of Pure Reason* she caught the bright passing of his mind.

Perhaps she had forgotten a little what he looked like. Smoky black eyes. Tired eyelids. A crystal mind, shining and flashing. A mind like a big room, filled from end to end with light. Maurice Jourdain.

V

" I don't think I should have known you, Mary."

Maurice Jourdain had come. In the end Uncle Victor had let him. He was sitting there, all by himself, on the sofa in the middle of the room.

It was his third evening. She had thought it was going to pass exactly like the other two, and then her mother had got up, with an incredible suddenness, and left them.

Through the open window you could hear the rain falling

in the garden; you could see the garden grey and wet with rain.

She sat on the edge of the fender, and without looking up she knew that he was watching her from under half-shut eyelids.

His eyelids were so old, so tired, so very tired and old.

" What did you cut it all off for? "

" Oh, just for fun."

Without looking at him she knew that he had moved, that his chin had dropped to his chest; there would be a sort of puffiness in his cheeks and about his jaw under the black, close-clipped beard. When she saw it she felt a little creeping chill at her heart.

But that was unfaithfulness, that was cruelty. If he knew it — poor thing — how it would hurt him! But he never would know. She would behave as though she hadn't seen any difference in him at all.

If only she could set his mind moving; turn the crystal about; make it flash and shine.

" What have they been doing to you? " he said. " You used to be clever. I wonder if you're clever still."

" I don't think I am, very."

She thought: " I'm stupid. I'm as stupid as an owl. I never felt so stupid in all my life. If only I could *think* of something to say to him."

" Did they tell you what I've come for? "

" Yes."

" Are you glad? "

" Very glad."

" Why do you sit on the fender? "

" I'm cold."

" Cold and glad."

A long pause.

" Do you know why your mother hates me, Mary? "

" She doesn't. She only thought you'd killed Papa."

" I didn't kill him. It wasn't my fault if he couldn't control his temper. . . . That isn't what she hates me for. . . . Do you know why you were sent to school — the school my aunt found for you? "

" Well — to keep me from seeing you."

" Yes. And because I asked your father to let me educate
you, since he wasn't doing it himself. I wanted to send you
to a school in Paris for two years."

" I didn't know. They never told me. What made you
want to do all that for me? "

" It wasn't for you. It was for the little girl who used
to go for walks with me. . . . She was the nicest little girl.
She said the jolliest things in the dearest little voice. ' How
can a man like *you* care to talk to a child like *me?* ' "

" Did I say that? I don't remember."

" *She* said it."

" It sounds rather silly of her."

" She wasn't silly. She was clever as they make them.
And she was pretty too. She had lots of hair, hanging down
her back. Curling. . . . And they take her away from
me and I wait three years for her. She knew I was waiting.
And when I come back to her she won't look at me. She
sits on the fender and stares at the fire. She wears horrible
black clothes."

" Because Papa's dead."

" She goes and cuts her hair all off. That isn't because
your father's dead."

" It'll grow again."

" Not for another three years. And I believe I hear your
mother coming back."

His chin dropped to his chest again. He brooded
morosely. Presently Catty came in with the coffee.

The next day he was gone.

VI

" It seems to me," her mother said, " you only care for
him when he isn't there."

He had come again, twice, in July, in August. Each time
her mother had said, " Are you sure you want him to come
again? You know you weren't very happy the last time."
And she had answered, " I know I'm going to be this time."

" You see," she said, " when he *isn't* there you remember,
and when he *is* there he makes you forget."

" Forget what? "

"What it used to feel like."

Mamma had smiled a funny, contented smile. Mamma was different. Her face had left off being reproachful and disapproving. It had got back the tender, adorable look it used to have when you were little. She hated Maurice Jourdain, yet you felt that in some queer way she loved you because of him. You loved her more because of Maurice Jourdain.

The engagement happened suddenly at the end of August. You knew it would happen some day; but you thought of it as happening to-morrow or the day after rather than to-day. At three o'clock you started for a walk, never knowing how you might come back, and at five you found yourself sitting at tea in the orchard, safe. He would slouch along beside you, for miles, morosely. You thought of his mind swinging off by itself, shining where you couldn't see it. You broke loose from him to run tearing along the road, to jump water-courses, to climb trees and grin down at him through the branches. Then he would wake up from his sulking. Sometimes he would be pleased and sometimes he wouldn't. The engagement happened just after he had not been pleased at all.

She could still hear his voice saying "What do you *do* it for?" and her own answering.

"You must do *something*."

"You needn't dance jigs on the parapets of bridges."

They slid through the gap into the fields. In the narrow path he stopped suddenly and turned.

"How can a child like *you* care for a man like *me?*" Mocking her sing-song.

He stooped and kissed her. She shut her eyes so as not to see the puffiness.

"Will you marry me, Mary?"

VII

After the engagement, the quarrel. It lasted all the way up the schoolhouse lane.

"I *do* care for you, I do, really."

"You don't know what you're talking about. You may

care for me as a child cares. You don't care as a woman does. No woman who cared for a man would write the letters you do. I ask you to tell me about yourself — what you're feeling and thinking — and you send me some ghastly screed about Spinoza or Kant. Do you suppose any man wants to hear what his sweetheart thinks about Space and Time and the Ding-an-sich? "

"You used to like it."

"I don't like it now. No woman would wear those horrible clothes if she cared for a man and wanted him to care for her. She wouldn't cut her hair off."

"How was I to know you'd mind so awfully? And how do you know what women do or don't do? "

"Has it never occurred to you that I might know more women than you know men? That I might have women friends? "

"I don't think I've thought about it very much."

"*Haven't* you? Men don't live to be thirty-seven without getting to know women; they can't go about the world without meeting them. . . . There's a little girl down in Sussex. A dear little girl. She's everything a man wants a woman to be."

"Lots of hair? "

"Lots of hair. Stacks of it. And she's clever. She can cook and sew and make her own clothes and her sisters'. She's kept her father's house since she was fifteen. Without a servant."

"How awful for her. And you like her? "

"Yes, Mary."

"I'm glad you like her. Who else? "

"A Frenchwoman in Paris. And a German woman in Hamburg. And an Englishwoman in London; the cleverest woman I know. She's unhappy, Mary. Her husband behaves to her like a perfect brute."

"Poor thing. I hope you're nice to her."

"She thinks I am."

Silence. He peered into her face.

"Are you jealous of her, Mary? "

"I'm not jealous of any of them. You can marry them all if you want to."

"I was going to marry one of them."

"Then why didn't you?"

"Because the little girl in Essex wouldn't let me."

"Little beast!"

"So you're jealous of *her*, are you? You needn't be. She's gone. She tried to swallow the *Kritik der reinen Vernunft* and it disagreed with her and she died.

> "'Nur einmal doch möcht' ich dich sehen,
> Und sinken vor dir auf's Knie,
> Und sterbend zu dir sprechen,
> Madam, ich liebe Sie!'"

"What's that? Oh, what's that?"

"*That* — Madam — is Heine."

VIII

"My dearest Maurice — "

It was her turn for writing. She wondered whether he would like to hear about the tennis party at the Vicarage. Mr. Spencer Rollitt's nephew, Harry Craven, had been there, and the two Acroyd girls from Renton Lodge, and Norman Waugh.

Harry Craven's fawn face with pointed chin; dust-white face with black accents. Small fawn's mouth lifting upwards. Narrow nostrils slanting upwards. Two lobes of white forehead. Half-moons of parted, brushed-back hair.

He smiled: a blunt V opening suddenly on white teeth, black eyes fluttering. He laughed: all his features made sudden, upward movements like raised wings.

The Acroyds. Plump girls with pink, blown cheeks and sulky mouths. You thought of sullen, milk-fed babies, of trumpeting cherubs disgusted with their trumpets. They were showing their racquets to Harry Craven, bending their heads. You could see the backs of their privet-white necks, fat, with no groove in the nape, where their hair curled in springy wires, Minna's dark, Sophy's golden. They turned their backs when you spoke and pretended not to hear you.

She thought she would like Maurice to know that Harry

Craven and she had beaten Minna Ackroyd and Norman
Waugh. A love set.

Afterwards — Harry Craven playing hide-and-seek in the
dark. The tennis net, coiled like a grey snake on the black
lawn. "Let's hide together." Harry Craven, hiding,
crouching beside you under the currant bushes. The
scramble together up the water-butt and along the scullery
roof. The last rush across the lawn.

"I say, you run like the wind."

He took your hand. You ran faster and faster. You
stood together, under the ash tree, panting, and laughing,
safe. He still held your hand.

Funny that you should remember it when you hadn't
noticed it at the time. Hands were funny things. His
hand had felt like Mark's hand, or Roddy's. You didn't
think of it as belonging to him. It made you want to have
Mark and Roddy back again. To play with them.

Perhaps, after all, it wouldn't be kind to tell Maurice
about the tennis party. He couldn't have played like that.
He couldn't have scrambled up the water-butt and run with
you along the scullery roof.

"My dearest Maurice: Nothing has happened since you
left, except that there was a tennis party at the Vicarage
yesterday. You know what tennis parties are like. You'll
be shocked to hear that I wore my old black jersey — the
one you hated so — "

IX

" ' Mein Kind, wir waren Kinder.' "

She shut her eyes. She wanted nothing but his voice.
His voice was alive. It remembered. It hadn't grown old
and tired. "My child, we once were children, two children
happy and small; we crept in the little hen-house and hid
ourselves under the straw."

> "Kikeriküh! sie glaubten
> Es wäre Hahnen geschrei."

" . . . It's all very well, Mary, I can't go on reading Heine
to you for ever. And — *après?* "

He had taken her on his knees. That happened sometimes. She kept one foot on the floor so as not to press on
him with her whole weight. And she played with his watch
chain. She liked to touch the things he wore. It made her
feel that she cared for him; it staved off the creeping, sicken-
ing fear that came when their hands and faces touched.

" Do you know," he said, " what it will be like — afterwards? "

She began, slowly, to count the buttons of his waistcoat.

" Have you ever tried to think what it will be like? "

" Yes."

Last night, lying awake in the dark, she had tried to
think. She had thought of shoulders heaving over her, of
arms holding her, of a face looking into hers, a honey-white,
beardless face, blue eyes, black eyebrows drawn close down
on to the blue. Jimmy's face, not Maurice Jourdain's.

That was in September. October passed. She began to
wonder when he would come again.

He came on the last day of November.

X

" Maurice, you're keeping something from me. Something's happened. Something's made you unhappy."

" Yes. Something's made me unhappy."

The Garthdale road. Before them, on the rise, the white
highway showed like a sickle curving into the moor. At the
horn of the sickle a tall ash tree in the wall of the Aldersons'
farm. Where the road dipped they turned.

He slouched slowly, his head hung forward, loosening the
fold of flesh about his jaw. His eyes blinked in the soft
November sunshine. His eyelids were tight as though they
had been tied with string.

" Supposing I asked you to release me from our engagement? "

" For always? "

" Perhaps for always. Perhaps only for a short time.
Till I've settled something. Till I've found out something
I want to know. Would you, Mary? "

" Of course I would. Like a shot."

" And supposing — I never settled it? "

" That would be all right. I can go on being engaged to you; but you needn't be engaged to me."

" You dear little thing. . . . I'm afraid, I'm afraid that wouldn't do."

" It would do beautifully. Unless you're really keeping something back from me."

" I am keeping something back from you. . . . I've no right to worry you with my unpleasant affairs. I was fairly well off when I asked you to marry me, but, the fact is, it looks as if my business was going to bits. I may be able to pull it together again. I may not — "

" Is *that* all? I'm glad you've told me. If you'd told me before it would have saved a lot of bother."

" What sort of bother? "

" Well, you see, I wasn't quite sure whether I really wanted to marry you — just yet. Sometimes I thought I did, sometimes I thought I didn't. And now I know I do."

" That's it. I may not be in a position to marry you. I can't ask you to share my poverty."

" I shan't mind that. I'm used to it."

" I may not be able to keep a wife at all."

" Of course you will. You're keeping a housekeeper now. And a cook and a housemaid."

" I may have to send two of them away."

" Send them all away. I'll work for you all my life. I shall never want to do anything else. It's what I always wanted. When I was a child I used to imagine myself doing it for you. It was a sort of game I played."

" It's a sort of game you're playing now, my poor Mary. . . . No. No. It won't do."

" What do you think I'm made of? No woman who cared for a man could give him up for a thing like that."

" There are other things. Complications. . . . I think I'd better write to your mother. Or your brother."

" Write to them — write to them. They won't care a rap about your business. We're not like that, Maurice."

XI

" You'd better let me see what he says, Mamma."

Her mother had called to her to come into the study. She
had Maurice Jourdain's letter in her hand. She looked sad
and at the same time happy.

" My darling, he doesn't want you to see it."

" Is it as bad as all that? "

" Yes. If I'd had my way you should never have had
anything to do with him. I'd have forbidden him the house
if your Uncle Victor hadn't said that was the way to make
you mad about him. He seemed to think that seeing him
would cure you. And so it ought to have done. . . .

" He says you know he wants to break off the engagement,
but he doesn't think he has made you understand why."

" Oh, yes, he did. It's because of his business."

" He doesn't say a word about his business. I'm to
break it to you that he doesn't care for you as he thought
he cared. As if he wasn't old enough to know what he
wanted. He might have made up his mind before he drove
your father into his grave."

" Tell me what he says."

" He just says that. He says he's in an awful position,
and whatever he does he must behave dishonourably. . . .
I admit he's sorry enough. And he's doing the only honourable thing."

" He *would* do that."

She fixed her mind on his honour. You could love that.
You could love that always.

" He *says* he asked you to release him. Did he? "

" Yes."

" Then why on earth didn't you? "

" I did. But I couldn't release myself."

" But that's what you ought to have done. Instead of
leaving him to do it."

" Oh, no. That would have been dishonourable to myself."

" You'd rather be jilted? "

" Much rather. It's more honourable to be jilted than to
jilt."

"That's not the world's idea of honour."

"It's my idea of it. . . . And, after all, he *was* Maurice Jourdain."

XII

The pain hung on to the left side of her head, clawing. When she left off reading she could feel it beat like a hammer, driving in a warm nail.

Aunt Lavvy sat on the parrot chair, with her feet on the fender. Her fingers had left off embroidering brown birds on drab linen.

In the dying light of the room things showed fuzzy, headachy outlines. It made you feel sick to look at them.

Mamma had left her alone with Aunt Lavvy.

"I suppose you think that nobody was ever so unhappy as you are," Aunt Lavvy said.

"I hope nobody is. I hope nobody ever will be."

"Should you say *I* was unhappy?"

"You don't look it. I hope you're not."

"Thirty-three years ago I was miserable, because I couldn't have my own way. I couldn't marry the man I cared for."

"Oh — *that*. Why didn't you?"

"My mother and your father and your Uncle Victor wouldn't let me."

"I suppose he was a Unitarian?"

"Yes. He was a Unitarian. But whatever he'd been I couldn't have married him. I couldn't do anything I liked. I couldn't go where I liked or stay where I liked. I wanted to be a teacher, but I had to give it up."

"*Why?*"

"Because your Uncle Victor and I had to look after your Aunt Charlotte."

"You could have got somebody else to look after Aunt Charlotte. Somebody else has to look after her now."

"Your Grandmamma made us promise never to send her away as long as it was possible to keep her. That's why your Uncle Victor never married."

"And all the time Aunt Charlotte would have been better

and happier with Dr. Draper. Aunt Lavvy — it's too horrible."

"It wasn't as bad as you think. Your Uncle Victor couldn't have married in any case."

"Didn't he love anybody?"

"Yes, Mary; he loved your mother."

"I see. And she didn't love him."

"He wouldn't have married her if she had loved him. He was afraid."

"Afraid?"

"Afraid of going like your Aunt Charlotte. Afraid of what he might hand on to his children."

"Papa wasn't afraid. He grabbed. It was poor little Victor and you who got nothing."

"Victor has got a great deal."

"And you — you?"

"I've got all I want. I've got all there is. When everything's taken away, then God's there."

"If he's there, he's there anyhow."

"Until everything's taken away there isn't room to *see* that he's there."

When Catty came in with the lamp Aunt Lavvy went out quickly.

Mary got up and stretched herself. The pain had left off hammering. She could think.

Aunt Lavvy — to live like that for thirty-three years and to be happy at the end. She wondered what happiness there could be in that dull surrender and acquiescence, that cold, meek love of God.

> "Kikeriküh! sie glaubten
> Es wäre Hahnen geschrei."

XXIV

I

EVERYBODY in the village knew you had been jilted. Mrs. Waugh and Miss Frewin knew it, and Mr. Horn, the grocer, and Mr. Oldshaw at the bank. And Mr. Belk, the

Justice of the Peace — little pink and flaxen gentleman, carrying himself with an air of pompous levity — eyes slewing round as you passed; and Mrs. Belk — hard, tight rotundity, little iron-grey eyes twinkling busily in a snub face, putty-skinned with a bilious gleam; curious eyes, busy eyes saying, " I'd like to know what she did to be jilted."

Minna and Sophy Acroyd, with their blown faces and small, disgusted mouths: you could see them look at each other; they were saying, " Here's that awful girl again." They were glad you were jilted.

Mr. Spencer Rollitt looked at you with his hard, blue eyes. His mouth closed tight with a snap when he saw you coming. He had disapproved of you ever since you played hide-and-seek in his garden with his nephew. He thought it served you right to be jilted.

And there was Dr. Charles's kind look under his savage, shaggy eyebrows, and Miss Kendal's squeeze of your hand when you left her, and the sudden start in Dorsy Heron's black hare's eyes. They were sorry for you because you had been jilted.

Miss Louisa Wright was sorry for you. She would ask you to tea in her little green-dark drawing-room; she lived in the ivy house next door to Mrs. Waugh; the piano would be open, the yellow keys shining; from the white title page enormous black letters would call to you across the room: " Cleansing Fires." That was the song she sang when she was thinking about Dr. Charles. First you played for her the Moonlight Sonata, and then she sang for you with a feverish exaltation:

> " For as gold is refined in the fi-yer,
> So a heart is tried by pain."

She sang it to comfort you.

Her head quivered slightly as she shook the notes out of her throat in ecstasy.

She was sorry for you; but she was like Aunt Lavvy; she thought it was a good thing to be jilted; for then you were purified; your soul was set free; it went up, writhing and aspiring, in a white flame to God.

" Mary, why are you always admiring yourself in the glass? "

" I'm not admiring myself. I only wanted to see if I was better-looking than last time."

" Why are you worrying about it? You never used to."

" Because I used to think I was pretty."

Her mother smiled. " You were pretty." And took back her smile. " You'd be pretty always if you were happy, and you'd be happy if you were good. There's no happiness for any of us without Christ."

She ignored the dexterous application.

" Do you mean I'm *not*, then, really, so very ugly? "

'" Nobody said you were ugly."

" Maurice Jourdain did."

" You don't mean to say you're still thinking of that man? "

" Not thinking exactly. Only wondering. Wondering what it was he hated so."

" You wouldn't wonder if you knew the sort of man he is. A man who could threaten you with his infidelity."

" He never threatened me."

" I suppose it was me he threatened, then."

" What did he say? "

" He said that if his wife didn't take care to please him there were other women who would."

" He ought to have said that to me. It was horrible of him to say it to you."

She didn't know why she felt that it was horrible.

" I can tell you *one* thing," said her mother, as if she had not told her anything. " It was those books you read. That everlasting philosophy. He said it was answerable for the whole thing."

" Then it was the — *the whole thing* he hated."

" I suppose so," her mother said, dismissing a matter of small interest. "You'd better change that skirt if you're going with me to Mrs. Waugh's."

" Do you mind if I go for a walk instead? "

" Not if it makes you any more contented."

" It might. Are you sure you don't mind? "
" Oh, go along with you! "
Her mother was pleased. She was always pleased when
she scored a point against philosophy.

III

Mr. and Mrs. Belk were coming along High Row. She
avoided them by turning down the narrow passage into
Mr. Horn's yard and the Back Lane. From the Back Lane
you could get up through the fields to the school-house lane
without seeing people.

She hated seeing them. They all thought the same
thing: that you wanted Maurice Jourdain and that you
were unhappy because you hadn't got him. They thought
it was awful of you. Mamma thought it was awful, like —
like Aunt Charlotte wanting to marry the piano-tuner, or
poor Jenny wanting to marry Mr. Spall.

Maurice Jourdain knew better than that. He knew you
didn't want to marry him any more than he wanted to
marry you. He nagged at you about your hair, about philosophy — she could hear his voice nag-nagging now as she
went up the lane — he could nag worse than a woman, but
he knew. *She* knew. As far as she could see through the
working of his dark mind, first he had cared for her, cared
violently. Then he had not cared.

That would be because he cared for some other woman.
There were two of them. The girl and the married woman.
She felt no jealousy and no interest in them beyond wonder-
ing which of them it would be and what they would be like.
There had been two Mary Oliviers; long-haired — short-
haired, and she had been jealous of the long-haired one.
Jealous of herself.

There had been two Maurice Jourdains, the one who said,
" I'll understand. I'll never lose my temper "; the one with
the crystal mind, shining and flashing, the mind like a big
room filled from end to end with light. But he had never
existed.

Maurice Jourdain was only a name. A name for intellectual beauty. You could love that. Love was " the

cle-eansing *fi*-yer!'" There was the love of the body and
the love of the soul. Perhaps she had loved Maurice Jourdain with her soul and not with her body. No. She had
not loved him with her soul, either. Body and soul; soul
and body. Spinoza said they were two aspects of the same
thing. *What* thing? Perhaps it was silly to ask what
thing; it would be just body *and* soul. Somebody talked
about a soul dragging a corpse. Her body wasn't a corpse;
it was strong and active; it could play games and jump; it
could pick Dan up and carry him round the table; it could
run a mile straight on end. It could excite itself with its
own activity and strength. It dragged a corpse-like soul,
dull and heavy; a soul that would never be excited again,
never lift itself up again in any ecstasy.

If only he had let her alone. If only she could go back
to her real life. But she couldn't. She couldn't feel any
more her sudden, secret happiness. Maurice Jourdain had
driven it away. It had nothing to do with Maurice Jourdain. He ought not to have been able to take it from you.

She might go up to Karva Hill to look for it; but it
would not be there. She couldn't even remember what it
had been like.

IV

New Year's night. She was lying awake in her white
cell.

She hated Maurice Jourdain. His wearily searching
eyes made her restless. His man's voice made her restless
with its questions. "Do you know what it will be like —
afterwards?" "Do you really want me?"

She didn't want him. But she wanted Somebody. Somebody. Somebody. He had left her with this ungovernable
want.

Somebody. If you lay very still and shut your eyes he
would come to you. You would see him. You knew what
he was like. He had Jimmy's body and Jimmy's face, and
Mark's ways. He had the soul of Shelley and the mind
of Spinoza and Immanuel Kant.

They talked to each other. Her reverie ran first into
long, fascinating conversations about Space and Time and

the Thing-in-itself, and the Transcendental Ego. He could tell you whether you were right or wrong; whether Substance and the Thing-in-itself were the same thing or different.

" Die — If thou wouldst be with that which thou dost seek." He wrote that. He wrote all Shelley's poems except the bad ones. He wrote Swinburne's *Atalanta in Calydon*. He could understand your wanting to know what the Thing-in-itself was. If by dying to-morrow, to-night, this minute, you could know what it was, you would be glad to die. Wouldn't you?

The world was built up in Space and Time. Time and Space were forms of thought — ways of thinking. If there was thinking there would be a thinker. Supposing — supposing the Transcendental Ego was the Thing-in-itself?

That was *his* idea. She was content to let him have the best ones. You could keep him going for quite a long time that way before you got tired.

The nicest way of all, though, was not to be yourself, but to be him; to live his exciting, adventurous, dangerous life. Then you could raise an army and free Ireland from the English, and Armenia from the Turks. You could go away to beautiful golden cities, melting in sunshine. You could sail in the China Sea; you could get into Central Africa among savage people with queer, bloody gods. You could find out all sorts of things.

You were he, and at the same time you were yourself, going about with him. You loved him with a passionate, self-immolating love. There wasn't room for both of you on the raft, you sat cramped up, huddled together. Not enough hard tack. While he was sleeping you slipped off. A shark got you. It had a face like Dr. Charles. The lunatic was running after him like mad, with a revolver. You ran like mad. Morfe Bridge. When he raised his arm you jerked it up and the revolver went off into the air. The fire was between his bed and the door. It curled and broke along the floor like surf. You waded through it. You picked him up and carried him out as Sister Dora carried the corpses with the small-pox. A screw loose somewhere. A tap turned on. Your mind dribbled imbecilities.

She kicked. " I won't think. I won't think about it any more! "

Restlessness. It ached. It gnawed, stopping a minute, beginning again, only to be appeased by reverie, by the running tap.

Restlessness. That was desire. It must be.

Desire: ἵμερος. Ἔρως. There was the chorus in the Antigone:

$$\text{`` Ἔρως ἀνίκατε μάχαν,}$$
$$\text{Ἔρως ὃς ἐν κτήμασι πίπτεις.''}$$

There was Swinburne:

" . . . swift and subtle and blind as a flame of fire,
Before thee the laughter, behind thee the tears of desire."

There was the song Minna Acroyd sang at the Sutcliffes' party. " Sigh-ing and sad for des-ire *of* the bee." How could anybody sing such a silly song?

Through the wide open window she could smell the frost; she could hear it tingle. She put up her mouth above the bedclothes and drank down the clear, cold air. She thought with pleasure of the ice in her bath in the morning. It would break under her feet, splintering and tinkling like glass. If you kept on thinking about it you would sleep.

V

Passion Week.

Her mother was reading the Lessons for the Day. Mary waited till she had finished.

" Mamma — what was the matter with Aunt Charlotte? "

" I'm sure I don't know. Except that she was always thinking about getting married. Whatever put Aunt Charlotte in your head? "

Her mother looked up from the Prayer Book as she closed it. Sweet and pretty; sweet and pretty; young almost, as she used to look, and tranquil.

" It's my belief," she said, " there wouldn't have been anything the matter with her if your Grandmamma Olivier hadn't spoiled her. Charlotte was as vain as a little pea-

cock, and your Grandmamma was always petting and prais-
ing her and letting her have her own way."

" If she'd had her own way she'd have been married, and
then perhaps she wouldn't have gone mad."

" She might have gone madder," said her mother. " It
was a good thing for *you*, my dear, you didn't get your
way. I'd rather have seen you in your coffin than married
to Maurice Jourdain."

" Whoever it had been, you'd have said that."

" Perhaps I should. I don't want my only daughter to
go away and leave me. It would be different if there were
six or seven of you."

Her mother's complacence and tranquillity annoyed her.
She hated her mother. She adored her and hated her.
Mamma had married for her own pleasure, for her own passion.
She had brought you into the world, without asking your
leave, for her own pleasure. She had brought you into the
world to be unhappy. She had planned for you to do the
things that she did. She cared for you only as long as you
were doing them. When you left off and did other things
she left off caring.

" I shall never go away and leave you," she said.

She hated her mother and she adored her.

An hour later, when she found her in the garden kneeling
by the violet bed, weeding it, she knelt down beside her, and
weeded too.

VI

April, May, June.

One afternoon before post-time her mother called her
into the study to show her Mrs. Draper's letter.

Mrs. Draper wrote about Dora's engagement and Effie's
wedding. Dora was engaged to Hubert Manisty who
would have Vinings. Effie had broken off her engagement
to young Tom Manisty; she was married last week to Mr.
Stuart-Gore, the banker. Mrs. Draper thought Effie had
been very wise to give up young Manisty for Mr. Stuart-
Gore. She wrote in a postscript: " Maurice Jourdain has
just called to ask if I have any news of Mary. I think he

would like to know that that wretched affair has not made
her unhappy."

Mamma was smiling in a nervous way. "What am I to
say to Mrs. Draper?"

"Tell her that Mr. Jourdain was right and that I am not
at all unhappy."

She was glad to take the letter to the post and set his
mind at rest.

It was in June last year that Maurice Jourdain had come
to her: June the twenty-fourth. To-day was the twenty-
fifth. He must have remembered.

The hayfields shone, ready for mowing. Under the wind
the shimmering hay grass moved like waves of hot air, up
and up the hill.

She slipped through the gap by Morfe Bridge and went
up the fields to the road on Greffington Edge. She lay
down among the bracken in the place where Roddy and she
had sat two years ago when they had met Mr. Sutcliffe
coming down the road.

The bracken hid her. It made a green sunshade above
her head. She shut her eyes.

> "Kikeriküh! sie glaubten
> Es wäre Hahnen geschrei."

That was all nonsense. Maurice Jourdain would never
have crept in the little hen-house and hidden himself under
the straw. He would never have crowed like a cock. Mark
and Roddy would. And Harry Craven and Jimmy. Jimmy
would certainly have hidden himself under the straw.

Supposing Jimmy had had a crystal mind. Shining and
flashing. Supposing he had never done that awful thing
they said he did. Supposing he had had Mark's ways, had
been noble and honourable like Mark —

The interminable reverie began. He was there beside
her in the bracken. She didn't know what his name would
be. It couldn't be Jimmy or Harry or any of those names.
Not Mark. Mark's name was sacred.

Cecil, perhaps.

Why Cecil? *Cecil?*—You ape! You drivelling, drib-
bling idiot! That was the sort of thing Aunt Charlotte
would have thought of.

She got up with a jump and stretched herself. She would
have to run if she was to be home in time for tea.

From the top hayfield she could see the Sutcliffes' tennis
court; an emerald green space set in thick grey walls.
She drew her left hand slowly down her right forearm.
The muscle was hardening and thickening.

Mamma didn't like it when you went by yourself to play
singles with Mr. Sutcliffe. But if Mr. Sutcliffe asked you
you would simply have to go. You would have to play a
great many singles against Mr. Sutcliffe if you were to be
in good form next year when Mark came home.

VII

She was always going to the Sutcliffes' now. Her mother
shook her head when she saw her in her short white skirt
and white jersey, slashing at nothing with her racquet,
ready. Mamma didn't like the Sutcliffes. She said they
hadn't been nice to poor Papa. They had never asked him
again. You could see she thought you a beast to like them.

"But, Mamma darling, I can't help liking them."

And Mamma would look disgusted and go back to her
pansy bed and dig her trowel in with little savage thrusts,
and say she supposed you would always have your own way.

You would go down to Greffington Hall and find Mr.
Sutcliffe sitting under the beech tree on the lawn, in white
flannels, looking rather tired and bored. And Mrs. Sutcliffe, a long-faced, delicate-nosed Beauty of Victorian
Albums, growing stout, wearing full skirts and white cashmere shawls and wide mushroomy hats when nobody else
did. She had an air of doing it on purpose, to be different,
like royalty. She would take your hand and press it gently
and smile her downward, dragging smile, and she would
say, "How is your mother? Does she mind the hot
weather? She must come and see me when it's cooler."
That was the nice way she had, so that you mightn't think
it was Mamma's fault, or Papa's, if they didn't see each
other often. And she would look down at her shawl and
gather it about her, as if in spirit she had got up and gone
away.

And Mr. Sutcliffe would be standing in front of you, looking suddenly years younger, with his eyes shining and clean as though he had just washed them.

And after tea you would play singles furiously. For two hours you would try to beat him. When you jumped the net Mrs. Sutcliffe would wave her hand and nod to you and smile. You had done something that pleased her.

To-day, when it was all over, Mr. Sutcliffe took her back into the house, and there on the hall table were the books he had got for her from the London Library: The Heine, the Goethe's *Faust*, the Sappho, the Darwin's *Origin of Species*, the Schopenhauer, *Die Welt als Wille und Vorstellung*.

" Five? All at once? "

" I get fifteen. As long as we're here you shall have your five."

He walked home with her, carrying the books. Five. Five. And when you had finished them there would be five more. It was unbelievable.

" Why are you so nice to me? Why? *Why?* "

" I think it must be because I like you, Mary."

Utterly unbelievable.

" Do — you — *really* — like me? "

" I liked you the first day I saw you. With your brother. On Greffington Edge."

" I wonder why." She wondered what he was thinking, what, deep down inside him, he was really thinking.

" Perhaps it was because you wanted something I could give you. . . . Tennis. . . . You wanted it so badly. Everything you want you want so badly."

" And I never knew we were going to be such friends."

" No more did I. And I don't know now how long it's going to last."

" Why shouldn't it last? "

" Because next year ' Mark ' will have come home and you'll have nothing to say to me."

" Mark won't make a scrap of difference."

" Well — if it isn't ' Mark ' . . . You'll grow up, Mary, and it won't amuse you to talk to me any more. I shan't know you. You'll wear long skirts and long hair done in the fashion."

"I shall always want to talk to you. I shall never do
up my hair. I cut it off because I couldn't be bothered
with it. But I was sold. I thought it would curl all over
my head, and it didn't curl."

"It curls at the tips," Mr. Sutcliffe said. "I like it.
Makes you look like a jolly boy, instead of a dreadful, un-
approachable young lady. A little San Giovanni. A little
San Giovanni."

That was his trick: caressing his own words as if he
liked them.

She wondered what, deep down inside him, he was really
like.

"Mr. Sutcliffe — if you'd known a girl when she was
only fourteen, and you liked her and you never saw her
again till she was seventeen, and then you found that she'd
gone and cut her hair all off, would it give you an awful
shock?"

"Depends on how much I liked her."

"If you'd liked her awfully — would it make you leave
off liking her?"

"I think my friendship could stand the strain."

"If it wasn't just friendship? Supposing it was Mrs.
Sutcliffe?"

"I shouldn't like my wife to cut her hair off. It wouldn't
be at all becoming to her."

"No. But when she was young?"

"Ah — when she was young — "

"Would it have made any difference?"

"No. No. It wouldn't have made any difference at all."

"You'd have married her just the same?"

"Just the same, Mary. Why?"

"Oh, nothing. I thought you'd be like that. I just
wanted to make sure."

He smiled to himself. He had funny, secret thoughts
that you would never know.

"Well," she said, "I didn't beat you."

"Form not good enough yet — quite."

He promised her it should be perfect by the time Mark
came home.

VIII

" The pale pearl-purple evening — " The words rushed together. She couldn't tell whether they were her own or somebody else's.

There was the queer shock of recognition that came with your own real things. It wasn't remembering though it felt like it.

Shelley — " The pale purple even." Not pearl-purple. Pearl-purple was what you saw. The sky to the east after sunset above Greffington Edge. Take out " pale," and " pearl-purple evening " was your own.

The poem was coming by bits at a time. She could feel the rest throbbing behind it, an unreleased, impatient energy.

Her mother looked in at the door. " What are you doing it for, Mary? "

" Oh — for nothing."

" Then for pity's sake come down into the warm room and do it there. You'll catch cold."

She hated the warm room.

The poem would be made up of many poems. It would last a long time, through the winter and on into the spring. As long as it lasted she would be happy. She would be free from the restlessness and the endless idiotic reverie of desire.

IX

" From all blindness of heart ; from pride, vain-glory and hypocrisy ; from envy, hatred, and malice, and all uncharitableness,

" *Good Lord, deliver us.*"

Mary was kneeling beside her mother in church.

" From fornication, and all other deadly sin — "

Happiness, the happiness that came from writing poems; happiness that other people couldn't have, that you couldn't give to them; happiness that was no good to Mamma, no good to anybody but you, secret and selfish; that was your happiness. It was deadly sin.

She felt an immense, intolerable compassion for everybody who was unhappy. A litany of compassion went on inside her: For old Dr. Kendal, sloughing and rotting in his chair; for Miss Kendal; for all women labouring of child; for old Mrs. Heron; for Dorsy Heron; for all prisoners and captives; for Miss Louisa Wright; for all that were desolate and oppressed; for Maggie's sister, dying of cancer; and for Mamma, kneeling there, praying.

Sunday after Sunday.

And she would work in the garden every morning, digging in leaf mould and carrying the big stones for the rockery; she would go to Mrs. Sutcliffe's sewing parties; she would sit for hours with Maggie's sister, trying not to look as if she minded the smell of the cancer. You were no good unless you could do little things like that. You were no good unless you could keep on doing them.

She tried to keep on.

Some people kept on all day, all their lives. Still, it was not you so much as the world that was wrong. It wasn't fair and right that Maggie's sister should have cancer while you had nothing the matter with you. Or even that Maggie had to cook and scrub while you made poems.

Not fair and right.

X

" Mamma, what is it? Why are you in the dark? "

By the firelight she could see her mother sitting with her eyes shut, and her hands folded in her lap.

" I can't use my eyes. I think there must be something the matter with them."

" Your eyes? . . . Do they hurt? "

(You might have known — you might have known that something would happen. While you were upstairs, writing, not thinking of her. You might have known.)

" *Something* hurts. Just there. When I try to read. I must be going blind."

" Are you sure it isn't your glasses? "

" How can it be my glasses? They never hurt me before."

But the oculist in Durlingham said it *was* her glasses.
She wasn't going blind. It wasn't likely that she ever
would go blind.

For a week before the new glasses came Mamma sat,
patient and gentle, in her chair, with her eyes shut and her
hands folded in her lap. And you read aloud to her: the
Bible and *The Times* in the morning, and Dickens in the
afternoon. And in the evening you played draughts and
Mamma beat you.

Mamma said, "I shall be quite sorry when the new
glasses come."

Mary was sorry too. They had been so happy.

XI

April. Mark's ship had left Port Said nine days ago.
Mamma had come in with the letter.

"I've got news for you. Guess."

"Mark's coming to-day."

"No. . . . Mr. Jourdain was married yesterday."

"Who — to?"

"Some girl he used to see in Sussex."

(That one. She was glad it was the little girl, the poor
one. Nice of Maurice to marry her.)

"Do you mind, Mary?"

"No, not a bit. I hope they'll be happy. I *want* them
to be happy. . . . Now, you see — *that* was why he didn't
want to marry me."

Her mother sat down on the bed. There was something
she was going to say.

"Well — thank goodness that's the last of it."

"Does Mark know?"

"No, he does not. You surely don't imagine anybody
would tell him a thing like that about his sister?"

"Like what?"

"Well — he wouldn't think it very nice of you."

"You talk as if I was Aunt Charlotte. . . . Do you think
I'm like her?"

"I never said you were like her. . . ."

"You think — you think and won't say."

" Well, if you don't want to be thought like your Aunt Charlotte you should try and behave a little more like other people. For pity's sake, do while Mark's here, or he won't like it, I can tell you."

" I don't do anything Mark wouldn't like."

" You do very queer things sometimes, though you mayn't think so. . . . I'm not the only one that notices. If you really want to know, that was what Mr. Jourdain was afraid of — the queer things you say and do. You told me yourself you'd have gone to him if he hadn't come to you."

She remembered. Yes, she had said that.

" Did he know about Aunt Charlotte? "

" You may be sure he did."

Mamma didn't know. She never would know what it had been like, that night. But there were things you didn't know, either.

"What did Aunt Charlotte *do?* "

" Nothing. She just fell in love with every man she met. If she'd only seen him for five minutes she was off after him. Ordering her trousseau and dressing herself up. She was no more mad than I am except just on that one point."

" Aunt Lavvy said that was why Uncle Victor never married. He was afraid of something — something happening to his children. What do you think he thought would happen? "

Her mother's foot tapped on the floor.

" I'm sure I can't tell you what he thought. And I don't know what there was to be afraid of. I wish you wouldn't throw your stockings all about the room."

Mamma picked up the stockings and went away. You could see that she was annoyed. Annoyed with Uncle Victor for having been afraid to marry.

A dreadful thought came to her. " Does Mamma really think I'm like Aunt Charlotte? I won't be like her. I won't. . . . I'm not. There was Jimmy and there was Maurice Jourdain. But I didn't fall in love with the Proparts or the Manistys, or Norman Waugh, or Harry Craven, or Dr. Charles. Or Mr. Sutcliffe. . . . She *said* I was as bad as Aunt Charlotte. Because I said I'd go to Maurice.

... I meant, just to see him. What did she think I meant? ... Oh, not *that.* ... Would I really have gone? Got into the train and gone? *Would* I? "

She would never know.

" I wish I knew what Uncle Victor was afraid of."

Wondering what he had been afraid of, she felt afraid.

XXV

I

SHE waited.

Mamma and Mark had turned their backs to her as they clung together. But there was his sparrow-brown hair, clipped close into the nape of his red-brown neck. If only Mamma wouldn't cry like that —

" Mark — "

" Is that Minky? "

They held each other and let go in one tick of the clock, but she had stood a long time seeing his eyes arrested in their rush of recognition. Disappointed.

The square dinner-table stretched itself into an immense white space between her and Mark. It made itself small again for Mark and Mamma. Across the white space she heard him saying things: about Dan meeting him at Tilbury, and poor Victor coming to Liverpool Street, and Cox's. Last night he had stayed at Ilford, he had seen Bella and Edward and Pidgeon and Mrs. Fisher and the Proparts. " Do you remember poor Edward and his sheep? And Mary's lamb! "

Mark hadn't changed, except that he was firmer and squarer, and thinner, because he had had fever. And his eyes — He was staring at her with his disappointed eyes.

She called to him. " You don't know me a bit, Mark."

He laughed. " I thought I'd see somebody grown up. Victor said Mary was dreadfully mature. What did he mean? "

Mamma said she was sure she didn't know.

" What do you do with yourself all day, Minky? "

" Nothing much. Read — work — play tennis with Mr. Sutcliffe."

" Mr. — Sutcliffe? "

" Never mind Mr. Sutcliffe. Mark doesn't want to hear about him."

" Is there a *Mrs.* Sutcliffe? "

" Yes."

" Does *she* play? "

" No., She's too old. Much older than he is."

" That'll do, Mary."

Mamma's eyes blinked. Her forehead was pinched with vexation. Her foot tapped on the floor.

Mark's eyes kept up their puzzled stare.

" What's been happening? " he said. " What's the matter? Everywhere I go there's a mystery. There was a mystery at Ilford. About Dan. And about poor Charlotte. I come down here and there's a mystery about some people called Sutcliffe. And a mystery about Mary." He laughed again. " Minky seems to be in disgrace, as if she'd done something. . . . It's awfully queer. Mamma's the only person something hasn't happened to."

"I should have thought everything had happened to me," said Mamma.

" That makes it queerer."

Mamma went up with Mark into his room. Papa's room. You could hear her feet going up and down in it, and the squeaking wail of the wardrobe door as she opened and shut it.

She waited, listening. When she heard her mother come downstairs she went to him.

Mark didn't know that the room had been Papa's room. He didn't know that she shivered when she saw him sitting on the bed. She had stood just there where Mark's feet were and watched Papa die. She could feel the basin slipping, slipping from the edge of the bed.

Mark wasn't happy. There was something he missed, something he wanted. She had meant to say, " It's all right. Nothing's happened. I haven't done anything," but she couldn't think about it when she saw him sitting there.

" Mark — what is it? "

" I don't know, Minky."

" *I* know. You've come back, and it isn't like what you thought it would be."

"No," he said, "it isn't. . . . I didn't think it would be so awful without Papa."

II

The big package in the hall had been opened. The tiger's skin lay on the drawing-room carpet.

Mark was sorry for the tiger.

"He was only a young cat. You'd have loved him, Minky, if you'd seen him, with his shoulders down — very big cat — shaking his haunches at you, and his eyes shining and playing ; cat's eyes, sort of swimming and shaking with his fun."

"How did you feel? "

"Beastly mean to go and shoot him when he was happy and excited."

"Five years without any fighting. . . . Anything else happen? "

"No. No polo. No fighting. Only a mutiny in the battery once."

"What was it like? "

"Oh, it just tumbled into the office and yelled and waved jabby things and made faces at you till you nearly burst with laughing."

"You laughed? " Mamma said. "At a mutiny? "

"Anybody would. Minky'd have laughed if she'd been there. It frightened them horribly because they didn't expect it. The poor things never know when they're being funny."

"What happened," said Mary, "to the mutiny? "

"That."

"Oh — Mark — " She adored him.

She went to bed, happy, thinking of the tiger and the mutiny. When Catty called her in the morning she jumped out of bed, quickly, to begin another happy day. Everything was going to be interesting, to be exciting.

At any minute anything might happen, now that Mark had come home.

III

" Mark, are you coming? "

She was tired of waiting on the flagstones, swinging her
stick. She called through the house for him to come. She
looked through the rooms, and found him in the study with
Mamma. When they saw her they stopped talking suddenly, and Mamma drew herself up and blinked.

Mark shook his head. After all, he couldn't come.

Mamma wanted him. Mamma had him. As long as
they lived she would have him. Mamma and Mark were
happy together ; their happiness tingled, you could feel it
tingling, like the happiness of lovers. They didn't want
anybody but each other. You existed for them as an object
in some unintelligible time and in a space outside their space.
The only difference was that Mark knew you were there and
Mamma didn't.

She chose the Garthdale road. Yesterday she had gone
that way with Mamma and Mark. She had not talked to
him, for when she talked the pinched, vexed look came into
Mamma's face though she pretended she hadn't heard you.
Every now and then Mark had looked at her over his
shoulder and said, " Poor Minx." It was as if he said,
" I'm sorry, but you see how it is. I can't help it."

And just here, where the moor track touched the road,
she had left them, clearing the water-courses, and had gone
up towards Karva.

She had looked back and seen them going slowly towards
the white sickle of the road, Mark very upright, taut muscles
held in to his shortened stride ; Mamma pathetic and fragile,
in her shawl, moving with a stiff, self-hypnotised air.

Her love for them was a savage pang that cut her eyes
and drew her throat tight.

Then suddenly she had heard Mark whooping, and she
had run back, whooping and leaping, down the hill to walk
with them again.

She turned back now, at the sickle. Perhaps Mark
would come to meet her.

He didn't come. She found them sitting close on the
drawing-room sofa ; the tea-table was pushed aside ; they

were looking at Mark's photographs. She came and stood
by them to see.

Mark didn't look up or say anything. He went on giving
the photographs to Mamma, telling her the names. " Dicky
Carter. Man called St. John. Man called Bibby — Jonas
Bibby. Allingham. Peters. Gunning, Stobart Hamilton.
Sir George Limond, Colonel Robertson."

Photographs of women. Mamma's fingers twitched as
she took them, one by one. Women with smooth hair and
correct, distinguished faces. She looked at each face a
long time; her mouth half-smiled, half-pouted at them. She
didn't hand on the photographs to you, but laid them down
on the sofa, one by one, as if you were not there.

A youngish woman in a black silk gown; Mrs. Robertson,
the Colonel's wife. A girl in a white frock; Mrs. Dicky
Carter, she had nursed Mark through his fever. A tall
woman in a riding habit and a solar topee, standing very
straight, looking very straight at you, under the shadow of
the topee. Mamma didn't mind the others so much, but
she was afraid of this one. There was danger under the
shadow of the topee.

" Lady Limond. " Mark had stayed with them at Simla.

" Oh. Very handsome face."

" Very handsome."

You could see by Mark's face that he didn't care about
Lady Limond.

Mamma had turned again to the girl in the white frock
who had nursed him.

" Are those all, Mark? "

" Those are all."

She took off her glasses and closed her eyes. Her face
was smooth now: her hands were quiet. She had him.
She would always have him.

But when he went away for a fortnight to stay with the
man called St. John, she was miserable till he had come
back, safe.

IV

Whit Sunday morning. She would walk home with
Mark after church while Mamma stayed behind for the
Sacrament.

But it didn't happen. Mark scowled as he turned out into the aisle to make way for her. He went back into the pew and sat there, looking stiff and stubborn. He would go up with Mamma to the altar rails. He would eat the bread and drink the wine.

That afternoon she took her book into the garden. Mark came to her there. Mamma, tired with the long service, dozed in the drawing-room.

Mark read over her shoulder: "'Wir haben in der Transcendentalen Æsthetik hinreichend bewiesen.' Do it in English."

"'In the Transcendental Æsthetic we have sufficiently proved that all that is perceived in space or time, and with it all objects of any experience possible to us are mere Vorstellungen — Vorstellungen — ideas — presentations, which, so far as they are presented, whether as extended things or series of changes, have no existence grounded in themselves outside our thoughts — '"

"Why have you taken to that dreadful stodge?"

"I'm driven to it. It's like drink; once you begin you've got to go on."

"What on earth made you begin?"

"I wanted to know things — to know what's real and what isn't, and what's at the back of everything, and whether there *is* anything there or not. And whether you can know it or not. And how you can know anything at all, anyhow. I'd give anything. . . . Are you listening?"

"Yes, Minky, you'd give anything — "

"I'd give everything — everything I possess — to know what the Thing-in-itself is."

"I'd rather know Arabic. Or how to make a gun that would find its own range and feed itself with bullets sixty to the minute."

"That would be only knowing a few more things. I want *the* thing. Reality, Substance, the Thing-in-itself. ·Spinoza calls it God. Kant doesn't; but he seems to think it's all the God you'll ever get, and that, even then, you can't know it. Transcendental Idealism is just another sell."

"Supposing," Mark said, "there isn't any God at all."

"Then I'd rather know *that* than go on thinking there was one when there wasn't."

" But you'd feel sold? "

" Sort of sold. But it's the risk — the risk that makes
it so exciting. . . . Why? Do *you* think there isn't any
God? "

" I'm afraid I think there mayn't be."

" Oh, Mark — and you went to the Sacrament. You ate
it and drank it."

" Why shouldn't I? "

" You don't believe in it any more than I do."

" I never said anything about believing in it."

" *You ate and drank it.*"

" Poor Jesus said he wanted you to do that and remember
him. I did it and remembered Jesus."

" I don't care. It was awful of you."

" Much more awful to spoil Mamma's pleasure in God
and Jesus. I did it to make her happy. Somebody had to
go with her. You wouldn't, so I did. . . . It doesn't matter,
Minky. Nothing matters except Mamma."

" Truth matters. You'd die rather than lie or do anything dishonourable. Yet that was dishonourable."

" I'd die rather than hurt Mamma. . . . If you make her
unhappy, Minky, I shall hate you."

V

" You can't go in that thing."

They were going to the Sutcliffes' dance. Mamma hadn't
told Mark she didn't like them. She wanted Mark to go to
the dance. He had said Morfe was an awful hole and it
wasn't good for you to live in it.

The frock was black muslin, ironed out. Mamma's black
net Indian scarf, dotted with little green and scarlet flowers,
was drawn tight over her hips to hide the place that Catty
had scorched with the iron. The heavy, brilliant, silk-
embroidered ends, green and scarlet, hung down behind.
She felt exquisitely light and slender.

Mamma was shaking her head at Mark as he stared at
you.

" If you knew," he said, " what you look like. . . . That's

the way the funny ladies dress in the bazaars — If you'd only take that awful thing off."

"She can't take it off," Mamma said. "He's only teasing you."

Funny ladies in the bazaars — Funny ladies in the bazaars. Bazaars were Indian shops. . . . Shop-girls. . . . Mark didn't mean shop-girls, though. You could tell that by his face and by Mamma's. . . . Was *that* what you really looked like? Or was he teasing? Perhaps you would tell by Mrs. Sutcliffe's face. Or by Mr. Sutcliffe's.

Their faces were nicer than ever. You couldn't tell. They would never let you know if anything was wrong.

Mrs. Sutcliffe said, "What a beautiful scarf you've got on, my dear."

"It's Mamma's. She gave it me." She wanted Mrs. Sutcliffe to know that Mamma had beautiful things and that she would give them. The scarf *was* beautiful. Nothing could take from her the feeling of lightness and slenderness she had in it.

Her programme stood: Nobody. Nobody. Norman Waugh. Dr. Charles. Mr. Sutcliffe. Mr. Sutcliffe. Nobody. Nobody again, all the way down to Mr. Sutcliffe, Mr. Sutcliffe, Mr. Sutcliffe. Then Mark. Mr. Sutcliffe had wanted the last dance, the polka; but she couldn't give it him. She didn't want to dance with anybody after Mark.

The big, long dining-room was cleared; the floor waxed. People had come from Reyburn and Durlingham. A hollow square of faces. Faces round the walls. Painted faces hanging above them: Mr. Sutcliffe's ancestors looking at you.

The awful thing was she didn't know how to dance. Mark said you didn't have to know. It would be all right. Perhaps it would come, suddenly, when you heard the music. Supposing it came like skating, only after you had slithered a lot and tumbled down?

The feeling of lightness and slenderness had gone. Her feet stuck to the waxed floor as if they were glued there. She was frightened.

It had begun. Norman Waugh was dragging her round the room. Once. Twice. She hated the feeling of his short, thick body moving a little way in front of her. She hated his sullen bull's face, his mouth close to hers, half open, puffing. From the walls Mr. Sutcliffe's ancestors looked at you as you shambled round, tied tight in your Indian scarf, like a funny lady in the bazaars. Raised eyebrows. Quiet, disdainful faces. She was glad when Norman Waugh left her on the window-seat.

Dr. Charles next. He was kind. You trod on his feet and he pretended he had trodden on yours.

" My dancing days are over."

" And mine haven't begun."

They sat out and she watched Mark. He didn't dance very well: he danced tightly and stiffly as if he didn't like it; but he danced: with Miss Frewin and Miss Louisa Wright, because nobody else would; with the Acroyds because Mrs. Sutcliffe made him; five dances with Dorsy Heron, because he liked her, because he was sorry for her, because he found her looking sad and shy in a corner. You could see Dorsy's eyes turn and turn, restlessly, to look at Mark, and her nose getting redder as he came to her.

Dr. Charles watched them. You knew what he was thinking. " She's in love with him. She can't take her eyes off him."

Supposing you told her the truth? " He won't marry you. He won't care for you. He won't care for anybody but Mamma. Can't you see, by the way he looks at you, the way he holds you? It's no *use* your caring for him. It'll only make your little nose redder."

He wouldn't mind her red nose; her little proud, high-bridged nose. He liked her small face, trying to look austere with shy hare's eyes; her vague mouth, pointed at the corners in a sort of sharp tenderness; her smooth, otter-brown hair brushed back and twisted in a tight coil at the nape of her neck. Dorsy was sweet and gentle and unselfish. He might have cared for Dorsy if it hadn't been for Mamma. Anyhow, for one evening in her life Dorsy was happy, dancing round and round, with her wild black hare's eyes shining.

Mr. Sutcliffe. She stood up. She would have to tell him. " I can't dance."

"Nonsense. You can run and you can jump. Of course you can dance."

"I don't know how to."

"The sooner you learn the better. I'll teach you in two minutes."

He steered her into the sheltered bay behind the piano. They practised.

"Mark's looking at us."

"Is he? What has he done to you, Mary? We'll go where he can't look at us."

They went out into the hall.

"That's it; your feet between mine. In and out. Don't throw your shoulders back. Don't keep your elbows in. It's not a hurdle race."

"I wish it was."

"You won't in a minute. Don't count your steps. Listen for the beat. It's the beat that does it."

She began to feel light and slender again.

"Now you're off. You're all right."

Off. Turning and turning. You steered through the open door, in and out among the other dancers; you skimmed; you swam, whirling, to the steady tump-tump of the piano, and the queer, exciting squeak of the fiddles —

Whirling together, you and Mr. Sutcliffe and the piano and the two fiddles. One animal, one light, slender animal, whirling and playing. Every now and then his arm tightened round your waist with a sort of impatience. When it slackened you were one light, slender animal again, four feet and four arms whirling together, the piano was its heart, going tump-tump, and the fiddles —

"Why did I think I couldn't do it?"

"Funk. Pure funk. You wanted to dance — you wanted to so badly that it frightened you."

His arm tightened.

As they passed she could see Mrs. Sutcliffe sitting in an arm-chair pushed back out of the dancers' way. She looked tired and bored and a little anxious.

When the last three dances were over he took her back to Mark.

Mark scowled after Mr. Sutcliffe.

"What does he look at you like that for?"

"Perhaps he thinks I'm — a funny lady in a bazaar."

"*That's* the sort of thing you oughtn't to say."

"*You* said it."

"All the more reason why you shouldn't."

He put his arm round her and they danced. They danced.

"You can do it all right now," he said.

"I've learnt. He taught me. He took me outside and taught me. I'm not frightened any more."

Mark was dancing better now. Better and better. His eyes shone down into yours. He whispered.

"Minky — Poor Minky — Pretty Minky."

He swung you. He lifted you off your feet. He danced like mad, carrying you on the taut muscle of his arm.

Somebody said, "That chap's waked up at last. Who's the girl?"

Somebody said, "His sister."

Mark laughed out loud. You could have sworn he was enjoying himself.

But when he got home he said he hadn't enjoyed himself at all. And he had a headache the next day. It turned out that he hadn't wanted to go. He hated dancing. Mamma said he had only gone because he thought you'd like it and because he thought it would be good for you to dance like other people.

VI

"Why are you always going to the Sutcliffes'?" Mark said suddenly.

"Because I like them."

They were coming down the fields from Greffington Edge in sight of the tennis court.

"You oughtn't to like them when they weren't nice to poor Papa. If Mamma doesn't want to know them you oughtn't to."

Mark, too. Mark saying what Mamma said. Her heart swelled and tightened. She didn't answer him.

"Anyhow," he said, "you oughtn't to go about all over the place with old Sutcliffe." When he said "old Sutcliffe" his eyes were merry and insolent as they used to be. " What do you do it for? "

" Because I like him. And because there's nobody else who wants to go about with me."

" There's Miss Heron."

" Dorsy isn't quite the same thing."

" Whether she is or isn't you've got to chuck it."

" Why? "

" Because Mamma doesn't like it and I don't like it. That ought to be enough." (Like Papa.)

" It isn't enough."

" Minky — why are you such a brute to little Mamma? "

" Because I can't help it. . . . It's all very well for you — "

Mark turned in the path and looked at her; his tight, firm face tighter and firmer. She thought: " He doesn't know. He's like Mamma. He won't see what he doesn't want to see. It would be kinder not to tell him. But I can't be kind. He's joined with Mamma against me. They're two to one. Mamma must have said something to make him hate me." . . . Perhaps she hadn't. Perhaps he had only seen her disapproving, reproachful face. . . . " If he says another word — if he looks like that again, I shall tell him."

" It's different for you," she said. " Ever since I began to grow up I felt there was something about Mamma that would kill me if I let it. I've had to fight for every single thing I've ever wanted. It's awful fighting her, when she's so sweet and gentle. But it's either that or go under."

" Minky — you talk as if she hated you."

" She does hate me."

" You lie." He said it gently, without rancour.

" No. I found that out years ago. She doesn't *know* she hates me. She never knows that awful sort of thing. And of course she loved me when I was little. She'd love me now if I stayed little, so that she could do what she liked with me; if I'd sit in a corner and think as she thinks, and feel as she feels and do what she does."

" If you did you'd be a much nicer Minx."

" Yes. Except that I *should* be lying then, the whole time. Hiding my real self and crushing it. It's your *real*

self she hates — the thing she can't see and touch and get
at — the thing that makes you different. Even when I was
little she hated it and tried to crush it. I remember
things — "

"You don't love her. You wouldn't talk like that about
her if you loved her."

"It's *because* I love her. Her self. *Her* real self. When
she's working in the garden, planting flowers with her
blessed little hands, doing what she likes, and when she's
reading the Bible and thinking about God and Jesus, and
when she's with *you*, Mark, happy. That's her real self. I
adore it. Selves are sacred. You ought to adore them.
Anybody's self. Catty's. . . . I used to wonder what the
sin against the Holy Ghost was. They told you nobody
knew what it was. *I* know. It's that. Not adoring the self
in people. Hating it. Trying to crush it."

"I see. Mamma's committed the sin against the Holy
Ghost, has she?"

"Yes."

He laughed. "You mustn't go about saying those things.
People will think you mad."

"Let them. I don't care — I don't care if *you* think I'm
mad. I only think it's beastly of you to say so."

"You're not madder than I am. We're all mad. Mad
as hatters. You and me and Dank and Roddy and Uncle
Victor. Poor Charlotte's the sanest of the lot, and she's
the only one that's got shut up."

"Why do you say she's the sanest?"

"Because she knew what she wanted."

"Yes. She knew what she wanted. She spent her whole
life trying to get it. She went straight for that one thing.
Didn't care a hang what anybody thought of her."

"So they said poor Charlotte was mad."

"She was only mad because she didn't get it."

"Yes, Minx. . . . Would poor Minky like to be
married?"

"No. I'm not thinking about that. I'd like to write
poems. And to get away sometimes and see places. To
get away from Mamma."

"You little beast."

" Not more beast than you. You got away. Altogether.
I believe you knew."

" Knew what? "

Mark's face was stiff and red. He was angry now.

" That if you stayed you'd be crushed. Like Roddy.
Like me."

" I knew nothing of the sort."

" Deep down inside you you knew. You were afraid.
That's why you wanted to be a soldier. So as not to be
afraid. So as to get away altogether."

" You little devil. You're lying. Lying."

He threw his words at you softly, so as not to hurt you.
" Lying. Because you're a beast to Mamma you'd like to
think I'm a beast, too."

" No — no." She could feel herself making it out more
and more. Flash after flash. Till she knew him. She knew
Mark.

" You *had* to. To get away from her, to get away from
her sweetness and gentleness so that you could be yourself;
so that you could be a man."

She had a tremendous flash.

" You haven't got away altogether. Half of you still
sticks. It'll never get away. . . . You'll never love anybody. You'll never marry."

" No, I won't. You're right there."

" Yes. Papa never got away. That was why he was so
beastly to us."

" He wasn't beastly to us."

" He was. You know he was. You're only saying that
because it's what Mamma would like you to say. . . . He
couldn't help being beastly. He couldn't care for us. He
couldn't care for anybody but Mamma."

" That's why I care for *him*," Mark said.

" I know. . . . None of it would have mattered if we'd
been brought up right. But we were brought up all wrong.
Taught that our selves were beastly, that our wills were
beastly and that everything we liked was bad. Taught to
sit on our wills, to be afraid of our selves and not trust them
for a single minute. . . . Mamma was glad when I was
jilted, because that was one for *me*."

" Were you jilted? "

" Yes. She thought it would make me humble. I always
was. I am. I'm afraid of my self *now*. I can't trust it. I
keep on asking people what they think when *I* ought to
know. . . . But I'm going to stop all that. I'm going to
fight."

" Fight little Mamma? "

" No. Myself. The bit of me that claws on to her and
can't get away. My body'll stay here and take care of her
all her life, but my *self* will have got away. It'll get away
from all of them. It's got bits of them sticking to it, bits
of Mamma, bits of Papa, bits of Roddy, bits of Aunt Charlotte. Bits of you, Mark. I don't *want* to get away from
you, but I shall have to. You'd kick me down and stamp
on me if you thought it would please Mamma. There
mayn't be much left when I'm done, but at least it'll be me."

" Mad. Quite mad, Minx. You ought to be married."

" And leave little Mamma? . . . I'll race you from the
bridge to the top of the hill."

He raced her. He wasn't really angry. Deep down
inside him he knew.

VII

November, and Mark's last morning. He had got pro-
motion. He was going back to India with a new battery.
He would be stationed at Poona, a place he hated. Nothing
ever happened as he wanted it to happen.

She was in Papa's room, helping him to pack. The
wardrobe door gave out its squeaking wail again and again
as he opened it and threw his things on to the bed. Her
mother had gone away because she couldn't bear to see
them, his poor things.

They were all folded now and pressed down into the
boxes and portmanteaus. She sat on the bed with Mark's
sword across her knees, rubbing vaseline on the blade.
Mark came and stood before her, looking down at her.

" Minky, I don't like going away and leaving Mamma
with you. . . . When I went before you promised you'd
be kind to her."

" What do I do? "

There was a groove down the middle of the blade for the blood to run in.

" Do? You do nothing. Nothing. You don't talk to her. You don't want to talk to her. You behave as if she wasn't there."

The blade was blunt. It would have to be sharpened before Mark took it into a battle. Mark's eyes hurt her. She tried to fix her attention on the blade.

" What makes you? "

" I don't know," she said. " Whatever it is it was done long ago."

" She hasn't got anybody," he said. " Roddy's gone. Dan's no good to her. She won't have anybody but you."

" I know, Mark. I shall never go away and leave her."

" Don't talk about going away and leaving her! "

.   .   .   .

He didn't want her to see him off at the train. He wanted to go away alone, after he had said good-bye to Mamma. He didn't want Mamma to be left by herself after he had gone.

They stood together by the shut door of the drawing-room. She and her mother stood between Mark and the door. She had said good-bye a minute ago, alone with him in Papa's room. But there was something they had missed —

She thought: " We must get it now, this minute. He'll say good-bye to Mamma last. He'll kiss her last. But I must kiss him again, first. "

She came to him, holding up her face. He didn't see her; but when his arm felt her hand it jerked up and pushed her out of his way, as he would have pushed anything that stood there between him and Mamma.

XXVI

I

OLD Mr. Peacock of Sarrack was dead, and Dr. Kendal was the oldest man in the Dale. He was not afraid of death;

he was only afraid of dying before Mr. Peacock died.
Mamma had finished building the rockery in the garden.
You had carried all the stones. There were no more stones
to carry. That was all that had happened in the year and
nine months since Mark had gone.

To you nothing happened. Nothing ever would happen.
At twenty-one and a half you were old too, and very wise.
You had given up expecting things to happen. You put 1883
on your letters to Mark and Dan and Roddy, instead of
1882. Then 1884. You measured time by the poems you
wrote and by the books you read and by the Sutcliffes' going
abroad in January and coming back in March.

You had advanced from the Critique of Pure Reason to
the Critique of Practical Reason, and the Critique of Judgment and the Prolegomena. And in the end you were
cheated. You would never know the only thing worth
knowing. Reality. For all you knew there was no Reality,
no God, no freedom, no immortality. Only doing your duty.
" You can because you ought." Kant, when you got to
the bottom of him, was no more exciting than Mamma.
" *Du kannst, weil du sollst.*"

Why not " You can because you shall "? It would never
do to let Mamma know what Kant thought. She would say
" Your Bible could have told you that."

There was Schopenhauer, though. *He* didn't cheat you.
There was " *reine Anschauung,* " pure perception ; it happened when you looked at beautiful things. Beautiful things
were crystal; you looked through them and saw Reality.
You saw God. While the crystal flash lasted "*Wille und
Vorstellung,*" the Will and the Idea, were not divided as
they are in life; they were one. That was why beautiful
things made you happy.

And there was Mamma's disapproving, reproachful face.
Sometimes you felt that you couldn't stand it for another
minute. You wanted to get away from it, to the other end
of the world, out of the world, to die. When you were
dead perhaps you would know. Or perhaps you wouldn't.
Perhaps death would cheat you, too.

II

" Oh — have I come too soon? "

She had found Mr. Sutcliffe at his writing-table in the
library, a pile of papers before him. He turned in his chair
and looked at her above the fine, lean hand that passed over
his face as if it brushed cobwebs.

" They didn't tell me you were busy."

" I'm not. I ought to be, but I'm not."

" You *are*. I'll go and talk to Mrs. Sutcliffe till you've
finished."

" No. You'll stay here and talk to me. Mrs. Sutcliffe
really *is* busy."

" Sewing-party? "

" Sewing-party."

She could see them sitting round the dining-room: Mrs.
Waugh and Miss Frewin, Mrs. Belk with her busy eyes, and
Miss Kendal and Miss Louisa, Mrs. Oldshaw and Dorsy;
and Mrs. Horn, the grocer's wife, very stiff in a corner by
herself, sewing unbleached calico and hot red flannel, hot
sunlight soaking into them. The library was dim, and
leathery and tobaccoey and cool.

The last time she came on a Wednesday Mrs. Sutcliffe
had popped out of the dining-room and made them go round
to the tennis court by the back, so that they might not be
seen from the windows. She wondered why Mrs. Sutcliffe
was so afraid of them being seen, and why she had not
looked quite pleased.

And to-day — there was something about Mr. Sutcliffe.

" You don't want to play? "

" After tea. When it's cooler. We'll have it in here.
By ourselves." He got up and rang the bell.

The tea-table between them, and she, pouring out the tea.
She was grown up. Her hair was grown up. It lay like a
wreath, plaited on the top of her head.

He was smoothing out the wrinkles of one hand with
the other, and smiling. " Everybody busy except you and
me, Mary. . . . How are you getting on with Kant? "

" I've done with him. It's taken me four years. You
see, either the German's hard or I'm awfully stupid."

" German hard, I should imagine. Do you *like* Kant? "

" I like him awfully when he says exciting things about Space and Time. I don't like him when he goes maundering on about his old Categorical Imperative. You can because you ought — putting you off, like a clergyman."

" Kant said that, did he? That shows what an old humbug he was. . . . And it isn't true, Mary, it isn't true."

" If it was it wouldn't prove anything. That's what bothers me."

" What bothers me is that it isn't true. If I did what I ought I'd be the busiest man in England. I wouldn't be sitting here. If I even did what I want — Do you know what I should like to do? To farm my own land instead of letting it out to these fellows here. I don't suppose you think me clever, but I've got ideas."

" What sort of ideas? "

" Practical ideas. Ideas that can be carried out. That ought to be carried out because they can. Ideas about cattle-breeding, cattle-feeding, chemical manuring, housing, labour, wages, everything that has to do with farming."

Two years ago you talked and he listened. Now that you were grown up he talked to you and you listened. He had said it would make a difference. That was the difference it made.

" Here I am, a landowner who can't do anything with his land. And I can't do anything for my labourers, Mary. If I keep a dry roof over their heads and a dry floor under their feet I'm supposed to have done my duty. . . . People will tell you that Mr. Sootcliffe's the great man of the place, but half of them look down on him because he doesn't farm his own land, and the other half kow-tow to him because he doesn't, because he's the landlord. And they all think I'm a dangerous man. They don't like ideas. They're afraid of 'em. . . . I'd like to sell every acre I've got here and buy land — miles and miles of it — that hasn't been farmed before. I'd show them what farming is if you bring brains to it."

" I see. You *could* do that."

" Could I? The land's entailed. I can't sell it away from my son. And *he*'ll never do anything with it."

" Aren't there other things you could have done? "

" I suppose I could have got the farmers out. Turned them off the land they've sweated their lives into. Or I could have sold my town house instead of letting it and bought land."

" Of course you could. Oh — why didn't you? "

" Why didn't I? Ah — now you've got me. Because I'm a lazy old humbug, Mary. All my farming's in my head when it isn't on my conscience."

" You don't really like farming: you only think you ought to. What do you really like? "

" Going away. Getting out of this confounded country into the South of France. I'm not really happy, Mary, till I'm pottering about my garden at Agaye."

She looked where he was looking. Two drawings above the chimney-piece. A chain of red hills swung out into a blue sea. The Estérel. A pink and white house on the terrace of a hill. House and hill blazing out sunshine.

Agaye. Agaye. Pottering about his garden at Agaye. He was happy there.

" Well, you *can* get away. To Agaye."

" Not as much as I should like. My wife can't stand more than six weeks of it."

" So that you aren't really happy at Agaye. . . . I thought I was the only person who felt like that. Miserable because I've been doing my own things instead of sewing, or reading to Mamma."

" That's the way conscience makes cowards of us all."

" If it was even *my* conscience. But it's Mamma's. And her conscience was Grandmamma's. And Grandmamma's — "

" And mine? "

" Isn't yours a sort of landlord's conscience? Your father's? "

" No. No. It's mine all right. My youth had a conscience."

" Are you sure it wasn't put off with somebody else's? "

" Perhaps. At Oxford we were all social reformers. The collective conscience of the group, perhaps. I wasn't strong enough to rise to it. Wasn't strong enough to resist it. . . .

Don't you do that, my child. Find out what you want, and when you see your chance coming, take it. Don't funk it."

" I don't see *any* chance of getting away."

" Where do you want to get away to? "

" There. Agaye."

He leaned forward. His eyes glittered. " You'd like that? "

" I'd like it more than anything on earth."

" Then," he said, " some day you'll go there."

" No. Don't let's talk about it. I shall never go."

" I don't see why not. I don't really see why not."

She shook her head. " No. That sort of thing doesn't happen."

III

She stitched and stitched, making new underclothing.

It was going to happen. Summer and Christmas and the New Year had gone. In another week it would happen. She would be sitting with the Sutcliffes in the Paris-Lyons-Méditerranée express, going with them to Agaye. She had to have new underclothing. They would be two days in Paris. They would pass, in the train, through Dijon, Avignon, Toulon and Cannes, then back to Agaye. She had no idea what it would be like. Only the sounds, Agaye, rose up out of the other sounds, like a song, a slender foreign song, bright and clear, that you could sing without knowing what it meant. She would stay there with the Sutcliffes, for weeks and weeks, in the pink and white house on the terrace. Perhaps they would go on into Italy.

Mr. Sutcliffe was going to send to Cook's for the tickets to-morrow. Expensive, well-fitting clothes had come from Durlingham, so that nothing could prevent it happening.

Mr. Sutcliffe was paying for her ticket. Uncle Victor had paid for the clothes. He had kept on writing to Mamma and telling her that she really ought to let you go. Aunt Bella and Uncle Edward had written, and Mrs. Draper, and in the end Mamma had given in.

At first she had said, " I won't hear of your going abroad with the Sutcliffes," and, " The Sutcliffes seem to think they've a right to take you away from me. They've only to say ' Come ' and you'll go." Then, " I suppose you'll have to go," and, " I don't know what your Uncle Victor thinks they'll do for you, but he shan't say I've stood in your way." And suddenly her face left off disapproving and reproaching and behaved as it did on Christmas Days and birthdays.

She smiled now as she sat still and sewed, as she watched you sitting still and sewing, making new underclothes.

Aunt Bella would come and stay with Mamma, then Aunt Lavvy, then Mrs. Draper, so that she would not be left alone.

Stitch — stitch. She wondered: Supposing they weren't coming? Could she have left her mother alone, or would she have given up going and stayed? No. She couldn't have given it up. She had never wanted anything in her life as she wanted to go to Agaye with the Sutcliffes. With Mr. Sutcliffe. Mrs. Sutcliffe didn't count; she wouldn't do anything at Agaye, she would just trail about in the background, kind and smiling, in a shawl. She might almost as well not be there.

The happiness was too great. She could not possibly have given it up.

She went on stitching. Mamma went on stitching. Catty brought the lamp in.

Then Roddy's telegram came. From Queenstown.

" Been ill. Coming home. Expect me to-morrow. Rodney."

She knew then that she would not go to Agaye.

IV

But not all at once.

When she thought of Roddy it was easy to say quietly to herself, " I shall have to give it up." When she thought of Mr. Sutcliffe and the Paris-Lyons-Mediterranée train and the shining, gold-white, unknown towns, it seemed to her that it was impossible to give up going to Agaye. You simply could not do it.

She shut her eyes. She could feel Mr. Sutcliffe beside her in the train and the carriage rocking. Dijon, Avignon,

Cannes. She could hear his voice telling her the names. She would stand beside him at the window, and look out. And Mrs. Sutcliffe would sit in her corner, and smile at them kindly, glad because they were so happy.

"Roddy doesn't say he *is* ill," her mother said. "I wonder what he's coming home for."

Supposing you had really gone? Supposing you were at Agaye when Roddy —

The thought of Roddy gave her a pain in her heart. The thought of not going to Agaye dragged at her waist and made her feel weak, suddenly, as if she were trying to stand after an illness.

She went up to her room. The shoulder line of Greffington Edge was fixed across the open window, immovable, immutable. Her knees felt tired. She lay down on her bed, staring at the immovable, immutable white walls. She tried to think of Substance, of the Reality behind appearances. She could feel her mind battering at the walls of her body, the walls of her room, the walls of the world. She could hear it crying out.

She was kneeling now beside her bed. She could see her arms stretched out before her on the counterpane, and her hands, the finger-tips together. She pressed her weak, dragging waist tighter against the bed.

"If Anything's there — if Anything's there — make me give up going. Make me think about Roddy. Not about myself. About Roddy. *Roddy*. Make me not want to go to Agaye."

She didn't really believe that anything would happen.

Her mind left off crying. Outside, the clock on the Congregational Chapel was striking six. She was aware of a sudden checking and letting go, of a black stillness coming on and on, hushing sound and sight and the touch of her arms on the rough counterpane, and her breathing and the beating of her heart. There was a sort of rhythm in the blackness that caught you and took you into its peace. When the thing stopped you could almost hear the click.

She stood up. Her white room was grey. Across the window the shoulder of the hill had darkened. Out there the night crouched, breathing like an immense, quiet animal.

She had a sense of exquisite security and clarity and joy. She was not going to Agaye. She didn't want to go.

She thought: "I shall have to tell the Sutcliffes. Now, this evening. And Mamma. They'll be sorry and Mamma will be glad."

But Mamma was not glad. Mamma hated it when you upset arrangements. She said, "I declare I never saw anybody like you in my life. After all the trouble and expense."

But you could see it was Roddy she was thinking about. She didn't want to believe there was anything the matter with him. If you went that would look as though he was all right.

"What do you suppose the Sutcliffes will think? And your Uncle Victor? With all those new clothes and that new trunk?"

"He'll understand."

"*Will* he!"

"Mr. Sutcliffe, I mean."

v

She went down to Greffington Hall that night and told him. He understood.

But not quite so well as Mrs. Sutcliffe. She gave you a long look, sighed, and smiled. Almost you would have thought she was glad. *He* didn't look at you. He looked down at his own lean fine hands hanging in front of him. You could see them trembling slightly. And when you were going he took you into the library and shut the door.

"Is this necessary, Mary?" he said.

"Yes. We don't quite know what's wrong with Roddy."

"Then why not wait and see?"

"Because I *do* know. And Mamma doesn't. There's something, or he wouldn't have come home."

A long pause. She noticed little things about him. The proud, handsome corners of his mouth had loosened; his eyelids didn't fit nicely as they used to do; they hung slack from the eyebone.

"You care more for Roddy than you do for Mark," he said.

"I don't care for him half so much. But I'm sorry for him. You can't be sorry for Mark. . . . Roddy wants me and Mark doesn't. He wants nobody but Mamma."

"He knows what he wants. . . . Well. It's my fault. I should have known what I wanted. I should have taken you a year ago."

"If you had," she said, "it would have been all over now."

"I wonder, would it?"

For the life of her she couldn't imagine what he meant.

When she got home she found her mother folding up the work in the work-basket.

"Well, anyhow," Mamma said, "you've laid in a good stock of underclothing."

VI

She was sitting in the big leather chair in the consulting-room. The small grey-white window panes and the black crooked bough of the apple tree across them made a pattern in her brain. Dr. Charles stood before her on the hearth-rug. She saw his shark's tooth, hanging sharp in the snap of his jaws. He was powerful, savage and benevolent.

He had told her what was wrong with Roddy.

"What — does — it — mean?"

The savage light went out of his eyes. They were dull and kind under his red shaggy eyebrows.

"It means that you won't have him with you very long, Mary."

That Roddy would die. That Roddy would die. *Roddy.* That was what he had come home for.

"He ought never to have gone out with his heart in that state. It beats me how he's pulled through those five years. Five weeks of it were enough to kill him. . . . Jem Alderson must have taken mighty good care of him."

Jem Alderson. She remembered. The big shoulders, the little screwed up eyes, the long moustaches, the good, gladiator face. Jem Alderson had taken care of him. Jem Alderson had cared.

"I don't know what your mother could have been thinking of to let him go."

"Mamma doesn't think of things. It wasn't her fault. She didn't know. Uncle Edward and Uncle Victor made him."

"They ought to be hung for it."

"They didn't know, either. It was my fault. *I* knew."

It seemed to her that she had known, that she had known all the time, that she remembered knowing.

"Did he tell you?"

"He didn't tell anybody. . . . Did he know?"

"Yes, Mary. He came to me to be overhauled. I told him he wasn't fit to go."

"I did *try* to stop him."

"Why?"

He looked at her sharply, as if he were trying to find out something, to fix responsibility.

"Because I *knew*."

"You couldn't have known if nobody told you."

"I did know. If he dies I shall have killed him. I ought to have stopped him. I was the only one who knew."

"You couldn't have stopped him. You were only a child yourself when it happened. If anybody was to blame it was his mother."

"It wasn't. She didn't know. Mamma never knows anything she doesn't want to know. She can't see that he's ill now. She talks as if he ought to do something. She can't stand men who don't do things like Mark and Dan."

"What on earth does she suppose he could do? He's no more fit to do anything than my brother James. . . . You'll have to take care of him, Mary."

A sharp and tender pang went through her. It was like desire; like the feeling you had when you thought of babies; painful and at the same time delicious.

"Could you?" said Dr. Charles.

"Of course I can."

"If he's taken care of he might live — "

She stood up and faced him. "How long?"

"I don't know. Perhaps — " He went with her to the door. "Perhaps," he said, "quite a long time."

(But if he didn't live she would have killed him. She had known all the time, and she had let him go.)

Through the dining-room window she could see Roddy as he crouched over the hearth, holding out his hands to the fire.

He was hers, not Mamma's, to take care of. Sharp, delicious pain!

VII

"Oh, Roddy — look! Little, little grouse, making nice noises."

The nestlings went flapping and stumbling through the roots of the heather. Roddy gazed at them with his fixed and mournful eyes. He couldn't share your excitement. He drew back his shoulders, bracing himself to bear it; his lips tightened in a hard, bleak grin. He grinned at the absurdity of your supposing that he could be interested in anything any more.

Roddy's beautiful face was bleached and sharpened; the sallow, mauve-tinted skin stretched close over the bone; but below the edge of his cap you could see the fine spring of his head from his neck, like the spring of Mark's head.

They were in April now. He was getting better. He could walk up the lower slopes of Karva without panting.

"Why are we ever out?" he said. "Supposing we went home?"

"All right. Let's."

He was like that. When he was in the house he wanted to be on the moor; when he was on the moor he wanted to be back in the house. They started to go home, and he turned again towards Karva. They went on till they came to the round pit sunk below the track. They rested there, sitting on the stones at the bottom of the pit.

"Mary," he said, "I can't stay here. I shall have to go back. To Canada, I mean."

"You shall never go back to Canada," she said.

"I must. Not to the Aldersons. I can't go there again, because — I can't tell you why. But if I could I wouldn't. I was no good there. They let you know it."

"Jem?"

"No. *He* was all right. That beastly woman."

"What woman?"

"His aunt. She didn't want me there. I wasn't fit for anything but driving cattle and cleaning out their stinking pigsties. . . . She used to look at me when I was eating. You could see she was thinking 'He isn't worth his keep.' . . . Her mouth had black teeth in it, with horrible gummy gaps between. The women were like that. I wanted to hit her on the mouth and smash her teeth. . . . But of course I couldn't."

"It's all over. You mustn't think about it."

"I'm not. I'm thinking about the other thing. . . . The thing I did. And the dog, Mary; the dog."

She knew what was coming.

"You can't imagine what that place was like. Their sheep-run was miles from the farm. Miles from anything. You had to take it in turns to sleep there a month at a time, in a beastly hut. You couldn't sleep because of that dog. Jem *would* give him me. He yapped. You had to put him in the shed to keep him from straying. He yapped all night. The yapping was the only sound there was. It tore pieces out of your brain. . . . I didn't think I could hate a dog. . . . But I did hate him. I simply couldn't stand the yapping. And one night I got up and hung him. I hung him."

"You didn't, Roddy. You know you didn't. The first time you told me that story you said you found him hanging. Don't you remember? He was a bad dog. He bit the sheep. Jem's uncle hung him."

"No. It was me. Do you know what he did? He licked my hands when I was tying the rope round his neck. He played with my hands. He was a yellow dog with a white breast and white paws. . . . And that isn't the worst. That isn't It."

"It?"

"The other thing. What I did. . . . I haven't told you that. You couldn't stand me if you knew. It was why I had to go. Somebody must have known. Jem must have known."

"I don't believe you did anything. Anything at all."

"I tell you I did."

"No, Roddy. You only think you did. You only think
you hung the dog."

They got up out of the pit. They took the track to the
schoolhouse lane. A sheep staggered from its bed and
stalked away, bleating, with head thrown back and shaking
buttocks. Plovers got up, wheeling round, sweeping close.
"Pee-vit — Pee-vit. Pee-vitt!"

"This damned place is full of noises," Roddy said.

VIII

"The mind can bring it about, that all bodily modifications or images of things may be referred to the idea of
God."

The book stood open before her on the kitchen table,
propped against the scales. As long as you were only strip-
ping the strings from the French beans you could read.

The mind can bring it about. The mind can bring it
about. "He who clearly and distinctly understands himself and his emotions loves God, and so much the more in
proportion as he more understands himself and his
emotions."

Fine slices of French beans fell from the knife, one by
one, into the bowl of clear water. Spinoza's thought beat
its way out through the smell of steel, the clean green smell
of the cut beans, the crusty, spicy smell of the apple pie you
had made. "He who loves God cannot endeavour that
God should love him in return."

"'Shall we gather at the river — '" Catty sang as she
went to and fro between the kitchen and the scullery. Catty
was happy now that Maggie had gone and she had only you
and Jesus with her in the kitchen. Through the open door
you could hear the clack of the hatchet and the thud on the
stone flags as Roddy, with slow, sorrowful strokes, chopped
wood in the backyard.

"Miss Mary — " Catty's thick, loving voice and the
jerk of her black eyes warned her.

Mamma looked in at the door.

"Put that book away," she said. She hated the two

brown volumes of Elwes's Spinoza you had bought for your birthday. "The dinner will be ruined if you read."

"It'll be ruined if I don't read."

For then your mind raged over the saucepans and the fragrant, floury pasteboard, hungry and unfed. It couldn't bring anything about. It snatched at the minutes left over from Roddy and the house and Mamma and the piano. You knew what every day would be like. You would get up early to practise. When the cooking and the housework was done Roddy would want you. You would play tennis together with Mr. Sutcliffe and Dorsy Heron. Or you would go up on to the moors and comfort Roddy while he talked about the "things" he had done in Canada and about getting away and about the dog. You would say over and over again, "You know you didn't hang him. It was Jem's uncle. He was a bad dog. He bit the sheep." In the winter evenings you would sew or play or read aloud to Mamma and Roddy, and Roddy would crouch over the fender, with his hands stretched out to the fire, not listening.

But Roddy was better. The wind whipped red blood into his cheeks. He said he would be well if it wasn't for the bleating of the sheep, and the crying of the peewits and the shouting of the damned villagers. And people staring at him. He would be well if he could get away.

Then — he would be well if he could marry Dorsy.

So the first year passed. And the second. And the third year. She was five and twenty. She thought: "I shall die before I'm fifty. I've lived half my life and done nothing."

IX

Old Dr. Kendal was dead. He had had nothing more to live for. He had beaten Mr. Peacock of Sarrack. Miss Kendal was wearing black ribbons in her cap instead of pink. And Maggie's sister was dead of her cancer.

The wall at the bottom of the garden had fallen down and Roddy had built it up again.

He had heaved up the big stones and packed them in mortar; he had laid them true by the plumb-line; Blenkiron's brother, the stonemason, couldn't have built a better wall.

It had all happened in the week when she was ill and went to stay with Aunt Lavvy at Scarborough. Yesterday evening, when she got home, Roddy had come in out of the garden to meet her. He was in his shirt sleeves; glass beads of sweat stood out on his forehead, his face was white with excitement. He had just put the last dab of mortar to the last stone.

In the blue and white morning Mary and her mother stood in the garden, looking at the wall. In its setting of clean white cement, Roddy's bit showed like the map of South Africa. They were waiting for him to come down to breakfast.

"I must say," Mamma said, "he's earned his extra half-hour in bed."

She was pleased because Roddy had built the wall up and because he was well again.

They had turned. They were walking on the flagged path by the flower-border under the house. Mamma walked slowly, with meditative pauses, and bright, sidelong glances for her flowers.

"If only," she said, "he could work without trampling the flowers down."

The sun was shining on the flagged path. Mamma was stooping over the bed; she had lifted the stalk of the daffodil up out of the sunk print of Roddy's boot. Catty was coming down the house passage to the side door. Her mouth was open. Her eyes stared above her high, sallow cheeks. She stood on the doorstep, saying something in a husky voice.

"Miss Mary — will you go upstairs to Master Roddy? I think there's something the matter with him. I think — "

Upstairs, in his narrow iron bed, Roddy lay on his back, his lips parted, his eyes — white slits under half-open lids — turned up to the ceiling. His arms were squared stiffly above his chest as they had pushed back the bedclothes. The hands had been clenched and unclenched; the fingers still curled in towards the palms. His face had a look of innocence and candour.

Catty's thick, wet voice soaked through his mother's crying. "Miss Mary — he went in his first sleep. His hair's
as smooth as smooth."

x

She was alone with Dan in the funeral carriage.

Her heart heaved and dragged with the grinding of the
brakes on the hill; the brake of the hearse going in front;
the brake of their carriage; the brake of the one that followed with Dr. Charles in it.

When they left off she could hear Dan crying. He had
begun as soon as he got into the carriage.

She tried to think of Dr. Charles, sitting all by himself
in the back carriage, calm and comfortable among the
wreaths. But she couldn't. She couldn't think of anything
but Dan and the black hearse in front of them. She could
see it when the road turned to the right; when she shut her
eyes she could see the yellow coffin inside it, heaped with
white flowers; and Roddy lying deep down in the coffin.
The sides were made high to cover his arms, squared over
his chest as if he had been beating something off. She could
see Roddy's arms beating off his thoughts, and under the
fine hair Roddy's face, innocent and candid.

Dr. Charles said it wasn't that. He had just raised them
in surprise. A sort of surprise. He hadn't suffered.

Dan's dark head was bowed forward, just above the level
of her knees. His deep, hot eyes were inflamed with grief;
they kept on blinking, gushing out tears over red lids. He
cried like a child, with loud sobs and hiccoughs that shook
him. *Her* eyes were dry; burning dry; the lids choked with
something that felt like hot sand, and hurt.

(If only the carriage didn't smell of brandy. That was
the driver. He must have sat in it while he waited.)

Dan left off crying and sat up suddenly.

"What's that hat doing there?"

He had taken off his tall hat as he was getting into the
carriage and laid it on the empty seat. He pointed at the
hat.

"That isn't my hat," he said.

"Yes, Dank. You put it there yourself."

"I didn't. My hat hasn't got a beastly black band on it."

He rose violently, knocking his head against the carriage roof.

"Here — I must get out of this."

He tugged at the window-strap, hanging on to it and swaying as he tugged. She dragged him back into his seat.

"Sit down and keep quiet."

She put her hand on his wrist and held it. Down the road the bell of Renton Church began tolling. He turned and looked at her unsteadily, his dark eyes showing bloodshot as they swerved.

"Mary — is Roddy really dead?"

A warm steam of brandy came and went with his breathing.

"Yes. That's why you must keep quiet."

Mr. Rollitt was standing at the open gate of the churchyard. He was saying something that she didn't hear. Then he swung round solemnly. She saw the flash of his scarlet hood. Then the coffin.

She began to walk behind it, between two rows of villagers, between Dorsy Heron and Mr. Sutcliffe. She went, holding Dan tight, pulling him closer when he lurched, and carrying his tall hat in her hand.

Close before her face the head of Roddy's coffin swayed and swung as the bearers staggered.

XI

"Roddy ought never to have gone to Canada."

Her mother had turned again, shaking the big bed. They would sleep together for three nights; then Aunt Bella would come, as she came when Papa died.

"But your Uncle Victor would have his own way."

"He didn't know."

She thought: "But *I* knew. I knew and I let him go. Why did I?"

It seemed to her that it was because, deep down inside her, she had wanted him to go. Deep down inside her she had been afraid of the unhappiness that would come through Roddy.

" And I don't think," her mother said presently, " it *could* have been very good for him, building that wall."

" You didn't know."

She thought: " I'd have known. If I'd been here it wouldn't have happened. I wouldn't have let him. I'd no business to go away and leave him. I might have known."

" Lord, if Thou hadst been here our brother had not died."

The yellow coffin swayed before her eyes, heaped with the white flowers. Yellow and white. Roddy's dog. His yellow dog with a white breast and white paws. And a rope round his neck. Roddy thought he had hanged him.

At seven she got up and dressed and dusted the drawing-room. She dusted everything very carefully, especially the piano. She would never want to play on it again.

The side door stood open. She went out. In the bed by the flagged path she saw the sunk print of Roddy's foot and the dead daffodil stalk lying in it. Mamma had been angry.

She had forgotten that. She had forgotten everything that happened in the minutes before Catty had come down the passage.

She filled in the footprint and stroked the earth smooth above it, lest Mamma should see it and remember.

XXVII

I

POTNIA, Potnia Nux —

Lady, our Lady,
Night,
You who give sleep to men, to men labouring and suffering—
Out of the darkness, come,
Come with your wings, come down
On the house of Agamemnon.

Time stretched out behind and before you, time to read, to make music, to make poems in, to translate Euripides, while Mamma looked after her flowers in the garden;

Mamma, sowing and planting and weeding with a fixed, vehement passion. You could hear Catty and little Alice, Maggie's niece, singing against each other in the kitchen as Alice helped Catty with her work. You needn't have been afraid. You would never have anything more to do in the house. Roddy wasn't there.

Agamemnon — that was where you broke off two years ago. He didn't keep you waiting long to finish. You needn't have been afraid.

Uncle Victor's letter came on the day when the gentians flowered. One minute Mamma had been happy, the next she was crying. When you saw her with the letter you knew. Uncle Victor was sending Dan home. Dan was no good at the office; he had been drinking since Roddy died. Three months.

Mamma was saying something as she cried. " I suppose he'll be here, then, all his life, doing nothing."

II

Mamma had given Papa's smoking-room to Dan. She kept on going in and out of it to see if he was there.

" When you've posted the letters you might go and see what Dan's doing."

Everybody in the village knew about Dan. The postmistress looked up from stamping the letters to say, " Your brother was here a minute ago." Mr. Horn, the grocer, called to you from the bench at the fork of the roads, " Ef yo're lookin' for yore broother, he's joost gawn oop daale."

If Mr. Horn had looked the other way when he saw you coming you would have known that Dan was in the Buck Hotel.

The white sickle of the road; a light at the top of the sickle; the Aldersons' house.

A man was crossing from the moor-track to the road. He carried a stack of heather on his shoulder: Jem's brother, Ned. He stopped and stared. He was thicker and slower than Jem; darker haired; fuller and redder in the face; he looked at you with the same little, kind, screwed-up eyes.

" Ef yo're lookin' for yore broother, 'e's in t' oose long

o' us. Wull yo coom in? T' missus med gev yo a coop
o' tea."

She went in. There was dusk in the kitchen, with a grey
light in the square of the window and a red light in the
oblong of the grate. A small boy with a toasting-fork knelt
by the hearth. You disentangled a smell of stewed tea and
browning toast from thick, deep smells of peat smoke and
the sweat drying on Ned's shirt. When Farmer Alderson
got up you saw the round table, the coarse blue-grey
teacups and the brown glazed teapot on a brown glazed
cloth.

Dan sat by the table. Dumpling, Ned's three-year-old
daughter, sat on Dan's knee; you could see her scarlet
cheeks and yellow hair above the grey frieze of his coat-
sleeve. His mournful black-and-white face stooped to her in
earnest, respectful attention. He was taking a piece of but-
terscotch out of the silver paper. Dumpling opened her wet,
red mouth.

Rachel, Ned's wife, watched them, her lips twisted in a
fond, wise smile, as she pressed the big loaf to her breast
and cut thick slices of bread-and-jam. She had made a
place for you beside her.

"She sengs ersen to slape wid a li'l' song she maakes,"
Rachel said. "Tha'll seng that li'l' song for Mester Dan,
wuntha?"

Dumpling hid her face and sang. You had to stoop to
hear the cheeping that came out of Dan's shoulder.

> "Aw, dinny, dinny dy-Doomplin',
> Dy-Doomplin', dy-Doomplin',
> Dinny, dinny dy-Doomplin',
> Dy-Doomplin' daay."

"Ef tha'll seng for Mester Dan," Farmer Alderson said,
"tha'llt seng for tha faather, wuntha, Doomplin'?"

"Naw."

"For Graffer then?"

"Naw."

Dumpling put her head on one side, butting under Dan's
chin like a cat. Dan's arm drew her closer. He was happy
there, in the Aldersons' kitchen, holding Dumpling on his

knee. There was something in his happiness that hurt you as Roddy's unhappiness had hurt. All your life you had never really known Dan, the queer, scowling boy who didn't notice you, didn't play with you as Roddy played or care for you as Mark had cared. And suddenly you knew him; better even than Roddy, better than Mark.

III

The grey byre was warm with the bodies of the cows and their grassy, milky breath. Dan, in his clean white shirt sleeves, crouched on Ned's milking stool, his head pressed to the cow's curly red and white flank. His fingers worked rhythmically down the teat and the milk squirted and hissed and pinged against the pail. Sometimes the cow swung round her white face and looked at Dan, sometimes she lashed him gently with her tail. Ned leaned against the stall post and watched.

" Thot's t' road, thot's t' road. Yo're the foorst straanger she a' let milk 'er. She's a narvous cow. 'Er teats is tander."

When the milking was done Dan put on his well-fitting coat and they went home over Karva to the schoolhouse lane.

Dan loved the things that Roddy hated: the crying of the peewits, the bleating of the sheep, the shouts of the village children when they saw him and came running to his coat pockets for sweets. He liked to tramp over the moors with the shepherds; he helped them with the dipping and shearing and the lambing.

" Dan, you ought to be a farmer."

" I know," he said, " that's why they stuck me in an office."

IV

" If the killer thinks that he kills, if the killed thinks that he is killed, they do not understand; for this one does not kill, nor is that one killed."

Passion Week, two years after Roddy's death; Roddy's death the measure you measured time by still.

Mamma looked up from her Bible; she looked over her glasses with eyes tired of their everlasting reproach.

" What have you got there, Mary? "

" The Upanishads from the Sacred Book of the East."

" Tchtt! It was that Buddhism the other day."

" Religion."

" Any religion except your own. Or else it's philosophy. You're destroying your soul, Mary. I shall write to your Uncle Victor and tell him to ask Mr. Sutcliffe not to send you any more books from that library."

" I'm seven and twenty, Mamma ducky."

" The more shame for you then," her mother said.

The clock on the Congregational Chapel struck six. They put down their books and looked at each other.

" Dan not back? " Mamma knew perfectly well he wasn't back.

" He went to Reyburn."

" T't! " Mamma's chin nodded in queer, vexed resignation. She folded her hands on her knees and waited, listening.

Sounds of wheels and of hoofs scraping up the hill. The Morfe bus, back from Reyburn. Catty's feet, running along the passage. The front door opening, then shutting. Dan hadn't come with the bus.

" Perhaps," Mamma said, " Ned Anderson'll bring him."

" Perhaps. . . . (' There is one eternal thinker, thinking non-eternal thoughts, who, though one, fulfils the desires of many, . . .') Mamma — why won't you let him go to Canada? "

" It was Canada that killed poor Roddy."

" It won't kill Dan. He's different."

" And what good would he be there? If your Uncle Victor can't keep him, who will, I should like to know? "

" Jem Alderson would. He'd take him for nothing. He told Ned he would. To make up for Roddy."

" Make up! He thinks that's the way to make up! I won't have Dan's death at my door. I'd rather keep him for the rest of my life."

" How about Dan? "

" Dan's safe here."

"He's safe on the moor with Alderson looking after the sheep, and he's safe in the cowshed milking the cows; but he isn't safe when Ned drives into Reyburn market."

"Would it be safer in Canada?"

"Yes. He'd be thirty miles from the nearest pub. He'd be safer here if you didn't give him money."

"The boy has to have money to buy clothes."

"I could buy them."

"I daresay! You can't treat a man of thirty as if he was a baby of three."

She thought. "No. You can only treat a woman. . . . 'There is one eternal thinker'—"

A knock on the door.

"There," her mother said, "that's Dan."

Mary went to the door. Ned Alderson stood outside; he stood slantways, not looking at her.

"Ah tried to maake yore broother coom back long o' us, but 'e would na."

"Hadn't I better go and meet him?"

"Naw. Ah would na. Ah wouldn' woorry; there's shepherds on t' road wi' t' sheep. Mebbe 'e'll toorn oop long o' they. Dawn' woorry ef tes laate like."

He went away.

They waited, listening while the clock struck the hours, seven; eight; nine. At ten her mother and the servants went to bed. She sat up, and waited, reading.

". . . My son, that subtle essence which you do not perceive there, of that very essence this great Nyagrodha tree exists. . . . That which is the subtile essence. in it all that exists has its self. It is the True. It is the Self, and thou, O Svetaketu, art it."

Substance, the Thing-in-itself — You were It. Dan was It. You could think away your body, Dan's body. One eternal thinker, thinking non-eternal thoughts. Dreaming horrible dreams. Dan's drunkenness. Why?

Eleven. A soft scuffle. The scurry of sheep's feet on the Green. A dog barking. The shepherds were back from Reyburn.

Feet shuffled on the flagstone. She went to the door. Dan leaned against the doorpost, bent forward heavily; his

chin dropped to his chest. Something slimy gleamed on his
shoulder and hip. Wet mud of the ditch he had fallen in.
She stiffened her muscles to his weight, to the pull and push
of his reeling body.

Roddy's room. With one lurch he reached Roddy's white
bed in the corner.

She looked at the dressing-table. A strip of steel flashed
under the candlestick. The blue end of a matchbox stuck up
out of the saucer. There would be more matches in Dan's
coat pocket. She took away the matches and the razor.

Her mother stood waiting in the doorway of her room,
small and piteous in her nightgown. Her eyes glanced off
the razor, and blinked.

" Is Dan all right? "

" Yes. He came back with the sheep."

v

The Hegels had come: The *Logik*. Three volumes. The
bristling Gothic text an ambush of secret, exciting, formid-
able things. The titles flamed; flags of strange battles;
signals of strange ships; challenging, enticing to the dangerous adventure.

After the first enchantment, the Buddhist Suttas and the
Upanishads were no good. Nor yet the Vedânta. You
couldn't keep on saying, " This is That," and " Thou art It,"
or that the Self is the dark blue bee and the green parrot
with red eyes and the thunder-cloud, the seasons and the
seas. It was too easy, too sleepy, like lying on a sofa and
dropping laudanum, slowly, into a rotten, aching tooth.
Your teeth were sound and strong, they had to have something hard to bite on. You wanted to think, to keep on
thinking. Your mind wasn't really like a tooth; it was like
a robust, energetic body, happy when it was doing difficult
and dangerous things, balancing itself on heights, lifting
great weights of thought, following the long march into
thick, smoky battles.

" Being and Not-Being are the same " : ironic and
superb defiance. And then commotion; as if the infinite
stillness, the immovable Substance, had got up and begun

moving — Rhythm of eternity: the same for ever: for ever
different: for ever the same.

Thought *was* the Thing-in-itself.

This man was saying, over and over and all the time
what you had wanted Kant to say, what he wouldn't say,
what you couldn't squeeze out of him, however you turned
and twisted him.

You jumped to where the name " Spinoza " glittered like
a jewel on the large grey page.

Something wanting. You knew it, and you were afraid.
You loved him. You didn't want him to be found out and
exposed, like Kant. He had given you the first incompar-
able thrill.

Hegel. Spinoza. She thought of Spinoza's murky, mysterious face. It said, " I live in you, still, as he will never
live. You will never love that old German man. He ran
away from the cholera. He bolstered up the Trinity with
his Triple Dialectic, to keep his chair at Berlin. *I* refused
their bribes. They excommunicated me. You remember?
Cursed be Baruch Spinoza in his going out and his coming
in."

You had tried to turn and twist Spinoza, too; and always
he had refused to come within your meaning. His Substance, his God stood still, in eternity. He, too; before the
noisy, rich, exciting Hegel, he drew back into its stillness;
pure and cold, a little sinister, a little ironic. And you felt
a pang of misgiving, as if, after all, he might have been
right. So powerful had been his hold.

Dan looked up. " What are you reading, Mary? "

" Hegel."

" Haeckel — that's the chap Vickers talks about."

Vickers — she remembered. Dan lived with Vickers when
he left Papa.

" He's clever," Dan said, " but he's an awful ass."

" Who? Haeckel? "

" No. Vickers."

" You mean he's an awful ass, but he's clever."

VI

One Friday evening an unusual smell of roast chicken came through the kitchen door. Mary put on the slender, long-tailed white gown she wore when she dined at the Sutcliffes'.

Dan's friend, Lindley Vickers, was sitting on the sofa, talking to Mamma. When she came in he left off talking and looked at her with sudden happy eyes. She remembered Maurice Jourdain's disappointed eyes, and Mark's. Dan became suddenly very polite and attentive.

All through dinner Mr. Vickers kept on turning his eyes away from Mamma and looking at her; every time she looked she caught him looking. His dark hair sprang in two ridges from the parting. His short, high-bridged nose seemed to be looking at you, too, with its wide nostrils, alert. His face did all sorts of vivid, interesting things; you wondered every minute whether this time it would be straight and serious or crooked and gay, whether his eyes would stay as they were, black crystals, or move and show grey rings, green speckled.

He was alive, running over with life; no, not running over, vibrating with it, holding it in; he looked as if he expected something delightful to happen, and waited, excited, ready.

He began talking, about Hegel. " ' Plus ça change, plus c'est la même chose.' "

She heard herself saying something. Dan turned and looked at her with a sombre, thoughtful stare. Mamma smiled, and nodded her chin as much as to say " Did you ever hear such nonsense? " She knew that was the way to stop you.

Mr. Vickers's eyes were large and attentive. When you stopped his mouth gave such a sidelong leap of surprise and amusement that you laughed. Then he laughed.

Dan said, " What's the joke? " And Mr. Vickers replied that it wasn't a joke.

In the drawing-room Mamma said, " I won't have any of those asides between you and Mr. Vickers, do you hear? "

Mary thought that so funny that she laughed. She knew what Mamma was thinking, but she was too happy to care. Her intelligence had found its mate.

You played, and at the first sound of the piano he came in and stood by you and listened.

You had only to play and you could make him come to you. He would get up and leave Dan in the smoking-room; he would leave Mamma in the garden. When you played the soft Schubert *Impromptu* he would sit near you, very quiet; when you played the *Appassionata* he would get up and stand close beside you. When you played the loud, joyful Chopin *Polonaise* he would walk up and down; up and down the room.

Saturday evening. Sunday evening. (He was going on Monday very early.)

He sang,

> " ' Es ist bestimmt in Gottes Rath
> Das man vom liebsten was man hat
> Muss scheiden.' "

Dan called out from his corner, " Translate. Let's know what it's all about."

He pounded out the accompaniment louder. " We won't, will we? " He jumped up suddenly. " Play the *Appassionata.*"

She played and he talked.

" I can't play if you talk."

" Yes, you can. I wish I hadn't got to go to-morrow."

" Have you " (false note) " got to go? "

" I suppose so."

" If Dan asked you, would you stop? "

" Yes."

He slept in Papa's room. When she heard his door shut she went to Dan.

" Dan, why don't you ask him to stay longer? "

" Because I don't want him to."

" I thought he was your friend."

" He is my friend. The only one I've got."

" Then — why —— ? "

" That's why." He shut the door on her.

She got up early. Dan was alone in the dining-room.
He said, " What have you come down for? "
" To give you your breakfasts."
" Don't be a little fool. Go back to your room."
Mr. Vickers had come in. He stood by the doorway,
looking at her and smiling. " Why this harsh treatment? "
he said. He had heard Dan.

Now and then he smiled again at Dan, who sat sulking
over his breakfast.

Dan went with him to Durlingham. He was away all
night.

Next day, at dinner-time, they appeared again together.
Mr. Vickers had brought Dan back. He was going to stay
for another week. At the Buck Hotel.

VII

" Es ist bestimmt in Gottes Rath." He had no business
to sing it, to sing it like that, so that you couldn't get the
thing out of your head. That wouldn't have mattered if you
could have got his voice out of your heart. It hung there,
clawing, hurting. She resented this pain.

" Das man vom liebsten was man hat," the dearest that
we have, " muss schei-ei-eden, muss schei-ei-eden."

Her fingers pressed and crept over the keys, in guilty,
shamed silence; it would be awful if he heard you playing it
if Dan heard you or Mamma.

You had only to play and you could make him come.

Supposing you played the Schubert *Impromptu* — She
found herself playing it.

He didn't come. He wasn't coming. He was going into
Reyburn with Dan. And on Monday he would be gone.
This time he would really go.

When you left off playing you could still hear him singing
in your head. " Das man vom liebsten was man hat."
" Es ist bestimmt — " But if you felt like that about it,
then —

Her hands dropped from the keys.

It wasn't possible. He only came on Friday evening last
week. This was Saturday morning. Seven days. It

couldn't happen in seven days. He would be gone on Monday morning. Not ten days.

"I can't — I don't."

Something crossing the window pane made her start and turn. Nannie Learoyd's face, looking in. Naughty Nannie. You could see her big pink cheeks and her scarlet mouth and her eyes sliding and peering. Poor pretty, naughty Nannie. Nannie smiled when she met you on the Green, as if she trusted you not to tell how you saw her after dark slinking about the Back Lane waiting for young Horn to come out to her.

The door opened. Nannie slid away. It was only Mamma.

"Mary," she said, "I wish you would remember that Mr. Vickers has come to see Dan, and that he has only got two days more."

"It's all right. He's going into Reyburn with him."

"I'm sure," her mother said, "I wish he'd stay here."

She pottered about the room, taking things up and putting them down again. Presently Catty came for her and she went out.

Mary began to play the Sonata *Appassionata*. She thought: "I don't care if he doesn't come. I want to play it, and I shall."

He came. He stood close beside her and listened. Once he put his hand on her arm. "Oh no," he said. "*Not* like that."

She stood up and faced him. "Tell me the truth, shall I ever be any good? Shall I ever play?"

"Do you really want the truth?"

"Of course I do."

Her mind fastened itself on her playing. It hid and sheltered itself behind her playing.

"Let's look at your hands."

She gave him her hands. He lifted them; he felt the small bones sliding under the skin, he bent back the padded tips, the joints of the fingers.

"There's no reason why you shouldn't have played magnificently," he said.

"Only I don't. I never have."

" No, you never have."

He came closer; she didn't know whether he drew her to him or whether he came closer. A queer, delicious feeling, a new feeling, thrilled through her body to her mouth, to her finger-tips. Her head swam slightly. She kept her eyes open by an effort.

He gave her back her hands. She remembered. They had been talking about her playing.

" I knew," she said, " it was bad in places."

" I don't care whether it's bad or good. It's you. The only part of you that can get out. You're very bad in places, but you do something to me all the same."

" What do I do? "

" You know what you do."

" I don't. I don't really. Tell me."

" If you don't know, I can't tell you — dear — "

He said it so thickly that she was not sure at the time whether he had really said it. She remembered afterwards.

" There's Dan," she whispered.

He swung himself off from her and made himself a rigid figure at the window. Dan stood in the doorway. He was trying to took as if she wasn't there.

" I say, aren't you coming to Reyburn? "

" No, I'm not."

" Why not? "

" I've got a headache."

" *What?* "

" Headache."

Outside on the flagstones she saw Nannie pass again and look in.

VIII

An hour later she was sitting on the slope under the hill road of Greffington Edge. He lay on his back beside her in the bracken. Lindley Vickers.

Suddenly he pulled himself up into a sitting posture like her own. She was then aware that Mr. Sutcliffe had gone up the road behind them; he had lifted his hat and passed her without speaking.

" What does Sutcliffe talk to you about? "

" Farming."

" And what do you do? "

" Listen."

Below them, across the dale, they could see the square of Morfe on its platform.

" How long have you lived in that place? "

" Ten years. No; eleven."

" Women," he said, " are wonderful. I can't think where you come from. I knew your father, I know Dan and your mother, and Victor Olivier and your aunt — "

" Which aunt? "

" The Unitarian lady; and I knew Mark — and Rodney. They don't account for you."

" Does anybody account for anybody else? "

" Yes. You believe in heredity? "

" I don't know enough about it."

" You should read Haeckel — *The History of Evolution,* and Herbert Spencer and Ribot's *Heredity.* It would interest you. . . . No, it wouldn't. It wouldn't interest you a bit."

" It sounds as if it would rather."

" It wouldn't. . . . Look here, promise me you won't think about it, you'll let it alone. Promise me."

He was like Jimmy making you promise not to hang out of top-storey windows.

" No good making promises."

" Well," he said, " there's nothing in it. . . . I wish I hadn't said that about your playing. I only wanted to see whether you'd mind or not."

" I don't mind. What does it matter? When I'm making music I think there's nothing but music in all the world; when I'm doing philosophy I think there's nothing but philosophy in all the world; when I'm writing verses I think there's nothing but writing in all the world; and when I'm playing tennis I think there's nothing but tennis in all the world."

" I see. And when you suffer you think there's nothing but suffering in all the world."

" Yes."

" And when — and when — "

His face was straight and serious and quiet. His eyes covered her; first her face, then her breasts; she knew he could see her bodice quiver with the beating of her heart. She felt afraid.

" Then," he said, " you'll not think; you'll know."

She thought: " He didn't say it. He won't. He can't. It isn't possible."

" Hadn't we better go? "

He sprang to his feet.

" Much better," he said.

IX

She would not see him again that day. Dan was going to dine with him at the Buck Hotel.

When Dan came back from Reyburn he said he wouldn't go. He had a headache. If Vickers could have a headache, so could he. He sulked all evening in the smoking-room by himself; but towards nine o'clock he thought better of it and went round, he said, to look Vickers up.

Her mother yawned over her book; and the yawns made her impatient; she wanted to be out of doors, walking, instead of sitting there listening to Mamma.

At nine o'clock Mamma gave one supreme yawn and dragged herself to bed.

She went out through the orchard into the Back Lane. She could see Nannie Learoyd sitting on the stone stairs of Horn's granary, waiting for young Horn to come round the corner of his yard. Perhaps they would go up into the granary and hide under the straw. She turned into the field track to the schoolhouse and the highway. In the dark bottom the river lay like a broad, white, glittering road.

She stopped by the schoolhouse, considering whether she would go up to the moor by the high fields and come back down the lane, or go up the lane and come back down the fields.

" Too dark to find the gaps if I come back by the fields."

She had forgotten the hidden moon.

There was a breaking twilight when she reached the lane.

She came down at a swinging stride. Her feet went on the grass borders without a sound.

At the last crook of the lane she came suddenly on a man and woman standing in her path by the stone wall. It would be Nannie Learoyd and young Horn. They were fixed in one block, their faces tilted backwards, their bodies motionless. The woman's arms were round the man's neck, his arms round her waist. There was something about the queer back-tilted faces — queer and ugly.

As she came on she saw them break loose from each other and swing apart: Nannie Learoyd and Lindley Vickers.

x

She lay awake all night. Her brain, incapable of thought, kept turning round and round, showing her on an endless rolling screen the images of Lindley and Nannie Learoyd, clinging together, loosening, swinging apart, clinging together. When she came down on Sunday morning breakfast was over.

Sunday — Sunday. She remembered. Last night was Saturday night. Lindley Vickers was coming to Sunday dinner and Sunday supper. She would have to get away somewhere, to Dorsy or the Sutcliffes. She didn't want to see him again. She wanted to forget that she ever had seen him.

Her mother and Dan had shut themselves up in the smoking-room; she found them there, talking. As she came in they stopped abruptly and looked at each other. Her mother began picking at the pleats in her gown with nervous, agitated fingers. Dan got up and left the room.

"Well, Mary, you'll not see Mr. Vickers again. He's just told Dan he isn't coming."

Then he knew that she had seen him in the lane with Nannie.

"I don't want to see him," she said.

"It's a pity you didn't think of that before you put us in such a position."

She understood Lindley; but she wasn't even trying to understand her mother. The vexed face and picking fingers meant nothing to her. She was saying to herself, "I can't tell Mamma I saw him with Nannie in the lane. I oughtn't to have seen him. He didn't know anybody was there. He didn't want me to see him. I'd be a perfect beast to tell her."

Her mother went on: "I don't know what to do with you, Mary. One would have thought my only daughter would have been a comfort to me, but I declare you've given me more trouble than any of my children."

"More than Dan?"

"Dan hadn't a chance. He'd have been different if your poor father hadn't driven him out of the house. He'd be different now if your Uncle Victor had kept him. . . . It's hard for poor Dan if he can't bring his friends to the house any more because of you."

"Because of me?"

"Because of your folly."

She understood. Her mother believed that she had frightened Lindley away. She was thinking of Aunt Charlotte.

It would have been all right if she could have told her about Nannie; then Mamma would have seen why Lindley couldn't come.

"I don't care," she thought. "She may think what she likes. I can't tell her."

XI

Lindley Vickers had gone. Nothing was left of him but Mamma's silence and Dan's, and Nannie's flush as she slunk by and her obscene smirk of satisfaction.

Then Nannie forgot him. As if nothing had happened she hung about Horn's yard and the Back Lane, waiting for young Horn. She smiled her trusting smile again. As long as you lived in Morfe you would remember.

Mary didn't blame her mother and Dan for their awful attitude. She couldn't blink the fact that she had begun to care for a man who was no better than young Horn, who had shown her that he didn't care for her by going to Nannie. If he could go to Nannie he was no better than young Horn.

She thought of Lindley's communion with Nannie as a part of him, essential, enduring. Beside it, her own communion with him was not quite real. She remembered his singing; she remembered playing to him and sitting beside him on the bracken as you remember things that have happened to you a long time ago (if they had really happened). She remembered phrases broken from their context (if they had ever had a context): " Das man vom liebsten was man hat. . . . " " If you don't know I can't tell you — Dear." . . . " And when — when — Then you won't think, you'll *know*."

She said to herself, " I must have been mad. It couldn't have happened. I must have made it up."

But, if you made up things like that you *were* mad. It was what Aunt Charlotte had done. She had lived all her life in a dream of loving and being loved, a dream that began with clergymen and ended with the piano-tuner and the man who did the clocks. Mamma and Dan knew it. Uncle Victor knew it and he had been afraid. Maurice Jourdain knew it and he had been afraid. Perhaps Lindley Vickers knew it, too.

There must be something in heredity. She thought: " If there is I'd rather face it. It's cowardly not to."

Lindley Vickers had told her what to read. Herbert Spencer she knew. Haeckel and Ribot were in the London Library Catalogue at Greffington Hall. And Maudsley: she had seen the name somewhere. It was perhaps lucky that Mr. Sutcliffe had gone abroad early this year; for he had begun to follow her through Balzac and Flaubert and Maupassant, since when he had sometimes interfered with her selection.

The books came down in two days: Herbert Spencer's *First Principles*, the *Principles of Biology*, the *Principles of Psychology*; Haeckel's *History of Evolution*; Maudsley's *Body and Mind, Physiology and Pathology of Mind, Responsibility in Mental Disease*; and Ribot's *Heredity*. Your instinct told you to read them in that order, controlling personal curiosity.

For the first time in her life she understood what Spinoza meant by " the intellectual love of God." She saw how all things work together for good to those who, in Spinoza's sense, love God. If it hadn't been for Aunt Charlotte and Lindley Vickers she might have died without knowing anything about the exquisite movements and connections of the live world. She had spent most of her time in the passionate pursuit of things under the form of eternity, regardless of their actual behaviour in time. She had kept on for fifteen years trying to find out the reality — if there *was* any reality — that hid behind appearances, piggishly obtuse to the interest of appearances themselves. She had cared for nothing in them but their beauty, and its exciting play on her emotions. When life brought ugly things before her she faced them with a show of courage, but inwardly she was sick with fear.

For the first time she saw the ugliest facts take on enchantment, a secret and terrible enchantment. Dr. Mitchell's ape-faced idiot; Dr. Browne's girl with the goose-face and goose-neck, billing her shoulders like a bird.

There was something in Heredity. But the sheer interest of it made you forget about Papa and Mamma and Aunt Charlotte; it kept you from thinking about yourself. You could see why Ribot was so excited about his *laws* of Heredity: "They it is that are real. . . ." "To know a fact thoroughly is to know the quality and quantity of the laws that compose it . . . facts are but appearances, laws the reality."

There was Darwin's *Origin of Species*. According to Darwin, it didn't seem likely that anything so useless as insanity could be inherited at all; according to Maudsley and Ribot, it seemed even less likely that sanity could survive. To be sure, after many generations, insanity was stamped out; but not before it had run its course through imbecility to idiocy, infecting more generations as it went.

Maudsley was solemn and exalted in his desire that there should be no mistake about it. "There is a destiny made for a man by his ancestors, and no one can elude, were he able to attempt it, the tyranny of his organisation."

You had been wrong all the time. You had thought of your family, Papa and Mamma, perhaps Grandpapa and Grandmamma, as powerful, but independent and separate

entities, in themselves sacred and inviolable, working against
you from the outside: either with open or secret and in-
scrutable hostility, hindering, thwarting, crushing you down.
But always from the outside. You had thought of yourself
as a somewhat less powerful, but still independent and
separate entity, a sacred, inviolable self, struggling against
them for completer freedom and detachment. Crushed
down, but always getting up and going on again; fighting a
more and more successful battle for your own; beating them
in the end. But it was not so. There were no independent,
separate entities, no sacred, inviolable selves. They were
one immense organism and you were part of it; you were
nothing that they had not been before you. It was no
good struggling. You were caught in the net; you couldn't
get out.

And so were they. Mamma and Papa were no more in-
dependent and separate than you were. Dan had gone like
Papa, but Papa had gone like Grandpapa and Grandmamma
Olivier. Nobody ever said anything about Grandpapa
Olivier; so perhaps there had been something queer about
him. Anyhow, Papa couldn't help drinking any more than
Mamma could help being sweet and gentle; they hadn't had
a choice or a chance.

How senseless you had been with your old angers and
resentments. Now that you understood, you could never
feel anger or resentment any more. As long as you lived
you could never feel anything but love for them and compassion. Mamma, Papa and Aunt Charlotte, Dan and
Roddy, they were caught in the net. They couldn't get out.

Dan and Roddy — But Mark had got out. Why not
you?

They were not all alike. Papa and Uncle Victor were
different; and Aunt Charlotte and Aunt Lavvy. Papa had
married and handed it on; he hadn't cared. Uncle Victor
hadn't married; he had cared too much; he had been afraid.

And Maurice Jourdain and Lindley Vickers had been
afraid; everybody who knew about Aunt Charlotte would
be afraid, and if they didn't know you would have to tell
them, supposing —

You would be like Aunt Lavvy. You would live in Morfe

with Mamma for years and years as Aunt Lavvy had lived
with Grandmamma. First you would be like Dorsy Heron;
then like Louisa Wright; then like Aunt Lavvy.

No; when you were forty-five you would go like Aunt
Charlotte.

XII

Anyhow, she had filled in the time between October and
March when the Sutcliffes came back.

If she could talk to somebody about it — But you
couldn't talk to Mamma; she would only pretend that she
hadn't been thinking about Aunt Charlotte at all. If Mark
had been there — But Mark wasn't there, and Dan would
only call you a little fool. Aunt Lavvy? She would tell
you to love God. Even Aunt Charlotte could tell you that.

She could see Aunt Charlotte sitting up in the big white
bed and saying "Love God and you'll be happy," as she
scribbled letters to Mr. Marriott and hid them under the
bedclothes.

Uncle Victor? Uncle Victor was afraid himself.

Dr. Charles — He looked at you as he used to look at
Roddy. Perhaps he knew about Aunt Charlotte and wondered whether you would go like her. Or, if he didn't wonder, he would only give you the iron pills and arsenic he
gave to Dorsy.

Mrs. Sutcliffe? You couldn't tell a thing like that to Mrs.
Sutcliffe. She wouldn't know what you were talking about;
or if she did know she would gather herself up, spiritually,
in her shawl, and trail away.

Mr. Sutcliffe — He would know. If you could tell him.
You might take back Maudsley and Ribot and ask him if he
knew anything about heredity, and what he thought of it.

She went to him one Wednesday afternoon. He was
always at home on Wednesday afternoons. She knew how
it would be. Mrs. Sutcliffe would be shut up in the dining-
room with the sewing-party. You would go in. You would
knock at the library door. He would be there by himself,
in the big arm-chair, smoking and reading; the small arm-
chair would be waiting for you on the other side of the

fireplace. He would be looking rather old and tired, and
when he saw you he would jump up and pull himself
together and be young again.

The library door closed softly. She was in the room
before he saw her.

He was older and more tired than you could have believed.
He stooped in his chair; his long hands rested on his knees,
slackly, as they had dropped there. Grey streaks in the
curly lock of hair that *would* fall forward and be a whisker.

His mouth had tightened and hardened. It held out; it
refused to become old and tired.

" It's Mary," she said.

" My dear — "

He dragged himself to his feet, making his body very
straight and stiff. His eyes glistened; but they didn't smile.
Only his eyelids and his mouth smiled. His eyes were different, their blue was shrunk and flattened and drawn back
behind the lense.

When he moved, pushing forward the small arm-chair,
she saw how lean and stiff he was.

" I've been ill," he said.

" Oh — ! "

" I'm all right now."

" No. You oughtn't to have come back from Agaye."

" I never do what I ought, Mary."

She remembered how beautiful and strong he used to be,
when he danced and when he played tennis, and when he
walked up and down the hills. His beauty and his strength
had never moved her to anything but a happy, tranquil
admiration. She remembered how she had seen Maurice
Jourdain tired and old (at thirty-three), and how she had
been afraid to look at him. She wondered, " Was that my
fault, or his? If I'd cared should I have minded? If I
cared for Mr. Sutcliffe I wouldn't mind his growing tired
and old. The tireder and older he was the more I'd care."

Somehow you couldn't imagine Lindley Vickers growing
old and tired.

She gave him back the books: Ribot's *Heredity* and
Maudsley's *Physiology and Pathology of Mind*. He held
them in his long, thin hands, reading the titles. His strange

eyes looked at her over the tops of the bindings. He smiled.

" When did you order these, Mary? "

" In October."

" That's the sort of thing you do when I'm away, is it? "

" Yes — I'm afraid you won't care for them very much."

He still stood up, examining the books. He was dipping into Maudsley now and reading him.

" You don't mean to say you've *read* this horrible stuff? "

" Every word of it. I *had* to."

" You had to? "

" I wanted to know about heredity."

" And insanity? "

" That's part of it. I wanted to see if there was anything in it. Heredity, I mean. Do you think there is? "

She kept her eyes on him. He was still smiling.

" My dear child, you know as much as I do. Why are you worrying your poor little head about madness? "

" Because I can't help thinking I may go mad."

" I should think the same if I read Maudsley. I shouldn't be quite sure whether I was a general paralytic or an epileptic homicide."

" You see — I'm not afraid because I've been reading him; I've been reading him because I was afraid. Not even afraid, exactly. As a matter of fact while you're reading about it you're so interested that you forget about yourself. It's only when you've finished that you wonder."

" What makes you wonder? "

He threw Maudsley aside and sat down in the big armchair.

" That's just what I don't think I can tell you."

" You used to tell me things, Mary. I remember a little girl with short hair who asked me whether cutting off her hair would make me stop caring for her."

" Not *you* caring for *me*."

" Precisely. So, if you can't tell me who *can* you tell? "

" Nobody."

" Come, then. . . . Is it because of your father? Or Dan? "

She thought: " After all, I can tell him."

" No. Not exactly. But it's somebody. One of Papa's

sisters — Aunt Charlotte. You see, Mamma seems to think I'm rather like her."

"Does Aunt Charlotte read Kant and Hegel and Schopenhauer, to find out whether the Thing-in-itself is mind or matter? Does she read Maudsley and Ribot to find out what's the matter with her mind?"

"I don't think she ever read anything."

"What *did* she do?"

"Well — she doesn't seem to have done much but fall in love with people."

"She'd have been a very abnormal lady if she'd never fallen in love at all, Mary."

"Yes; but then she used to think people were in love with her when they weren't."

"How old is Aunt Charlotte?"

"She must be ages over fifty now."

"Well, my dear, you're just twenty-eight, and I don't think you've been in love yet."

"That's it. I have."

"No. You've only thought you were. Once? Twice, perhaps? You may have been very near it — for ten minutes. But a man might be in love with you for ten years, and you wouldn't be a bit the wiser, if he held his tongue about it. . . . No. People don't go off their heads because their aunts do, or we should all of us be mad. There's hardly a family that hasn't got somebody with a tile loose."

"Then you don't think there's anything in it?"

"I don't think there's anything in it in your case. Anything at all."

"I'm glad I told you."

She thought: "It isn't so bad. Whatever happens he'll be here."

XIII

The sewing-party had broken up. She could see them going before her on the road, by the garden wall, by the row of nine ash-trees in the field, round the curve and over Morfe Bridge.

Bobbing shoulders, craning necks, stiff, nodding heads in funny hats, turning to each other.

When she got home she found Mrs. Waugh, and Miss Frewin in the drawing-room with Mamma. They had brought her the news.

The Sutcliffes were going. They were trying to let Greffington Hall. The agent, Mr. Oldshaw, had told Mr. Horn. Mr. Frank, the Major, would be back from India in April. He was going to be married. He would live in the London house and Mr. and Mrs. Sutcliffe would live abroad.

Mamma said, " If their son's coming back they've chosen a queer time to go away."

XIV

It couldn't be true.

You knew it when you dined with them, when you saw the tranquil Regency faces looking at you from above the long row of Sheraton chairs, the pretty Gainsborough lady smiling from her place above the sideboard.

As you sat drinking coffee out of the dark blue coffee cups with gold linings you knew it couldn't be true. You were reassured by the pattern of the chintzes — pink roses and green leaves on a pearl-grey ground — by the crystal chains and pendants of the chandelier, by the round black mirror sunk deep in the bowl of its gilt frame.

They couldn't go; for if they went, the quiet, gentle life of these things would be gone. The room had no soul apart from the two utterly beloved figures that sat there, each in its own chintz-covered chair.

" It isn't true," she said, " that you're going? "

She was sitting on the polar bear hearthrug at Mrs. Sutcliffe's feet.

" Yes, Mary."

The delicate, wrinkled hand came out from under the cashmere shawl to stroke her arm. It kept on stroking, a long, loving, slow caress. It made her queerly aware of her arm — white and slender under the big puff of the sleeve — lying across Mrs. Sutcliffe's lap.

" He'll be happier in his garden at Agaye."

She heard herself assenting. " *He'*ll be happier." And breaking out. " But I shall never be happy again."

"You mustn't say that, my dear."

The hand went on stroking.

"There's no place on earth," she said, "where I'm so happy as I am here."

Suddenly the hand stopped; it stiffened; it drew back under the cashmere shawl.

She turned her head towards Mr. Sutcliffe in his chair on the other side of the hearthrug.

His face had a queer, strained look. His eyes were fixed, fixed on the white, slender arm that lay across· his wife's lap.

And Mrs. Sutcliffe's eyes were fixed on the queer, strained face.

XV

Uncle Victor's letter was almost a relief.

She had not yet allowed herself to imagine what Morfe would be like without the Sutcliffes. And, after all, they wouldn't have to live in it. If Dan accepted Uncle Victor's offer, and if Mamma accepted his conditions.

Uncle Victor left no doubt as to his conditions. He wouldn't take Dan back unless Mamma left Morfe and made a home for him in London. He wanted them all to live together at Five Elms.

The discussion had lasted from a quarter-past nine till half-past ten. Mamma still sat at the breakfast-table, crumpling and uncrumpling the letter.

"I wish I knew what to do," she said.

"Better do what you want," Dan said. "Stay here if you want to. Go back to Five Elms if you want to. But for God's sake don't say you're doing it on my account."

He got up and went out of the room.

"Goodness knows I don't want to go back to Five Elms. But I won't stand in Dan's way. If your Uncle Victor thinks I ought to make the sacrifice, I shall make it."

"And Dan," Mary said, "will make the sacrifice of going back to Victor's office. It would be simpler if he went to Canada."

"Your uncle can't help him to go to Canada. He won't hear of it. . . . I suppose we shall have to go."

They were going. You could hear Mrs. Belk buzzing round the village with the news. " The Oliviers are going."

One day Mrs. Belk came towards her, busily, across the Green.

She stopped to speak, while her little iron-grey eyes glanced off sideways, as if they saw something important to be done.

The Sutcliffes were not going, after all.

XVI

When it was all settled and she thought that Dan had gone into Reyburn a fortnight ago to give notice to the landlord's solicitors, one evening, as she was coming home from the Aldersons' he told her that he hadn't been to the solicitors at all.

He had arranged yesterday for his transport on a cattle ship sailing next week for Montreal.

He said he had always meant to go out to Jem Alderson when he had learnt enough from Ned.

" Then why," she said, " did you let Mamma tell poor Victor — "

" I wanted her to have the credit of the sacrifice," he said. And then: " I don't like leaving you here — "

An awful thought came to her.

" Are you sure you aren't going because of me? "

" You? What on earth are you thinking of? "

" That time — when you wouldn't ask Lindley Vickers to stop on."

" Oh . . . I didn't ask him because I knew he wanted to stop altogether. And I don't approve of him."

She turned and stared at him. " Then it wasn't that you didn't approve of *me?* "

" What put that in your head? "

" Mamma. She told me you couldn't ask anybody again because of me. She said I'd frightened Lindley Vickers away. Like Aunt Charlotte."

Dan smiled, a sombre, reminiscent smile.

" You don't mean to say you still take Mamma seriously? *I* never did."

"But — Mark — "
"Or him either."
It hurt her like some abominable blasphemy.

XVII

Nothing would ever happen.   She would stay on in Morfe,
she and Mamma: without Mark, without Dan, without the
Sutcliffes. . . .
They were going. . . .
They were gone.

XXVIII

I

SHE lay out on the moor, under the August sun.   Her
hands were pressed like a bandage over her eyes.   When she
lifted them she caught the faint pink glow of their flesh.
The light throbbed and flickered as she pressed it out, and
let it in.
The sheep couched, panting, in the shade of the stone
covers.   She lay so still that the peewits had stopped their
cry.
Something bothered her. . . .
And in the east one pure, prophetic star — one pure prophetic star — *Trembles between the darkness and the dawn.*
What you wrote last year.   No reason why you shouldn't
write modern plays in blank verse if you wanted to.   Only
people didn't say those things.   You couldn't do it that way.
Let the thing go.   Tear it to bits and burn them in the
kitchen fire.
If you lay still, perfectly still, and stopped thinking the
other thing would come back.

> *In dreams He has made you wise,*
> *With the wisdom of silence and prayer,*
> *God, who has blinded your eyes,*
> *With the dusk of your hair.*

The Mother.   The Mother.   Mother and Son.

You and he are near akin.
Would you slay your brother-in-sin?
What he does yourself shall do —

That was the Son's hereditary destiny.

Lying on her back under Karva, she dreamed her "Dream-Play"; saying the unfinished verses over and over again, so as to remember them when she got home. She was unutterably happy.

She thought: "I don't care what happens so long as I can go on."

She jumped up to her feet. "I must go and see what Mamma's doing."

Her mother was sewing in the drawing-room and waiting for her to come to tea. She looked up and smiled.

"What are you so pleased about?" she said.

"Oh, nothing."

Mamma was adorable, sitting there like a dove on its nest, dressed in a dove's dress, grey on grey, turning dove's eyes to you in soft, crinkly lids. She held her head on one side, smiling at some secret that she kept. Mamma was happy, too.

"What are you looking such an angel for?"

Mamma lifted up her work, showing an envelope that lay on her lap, the crested flap upwards, a blue gun-carriage on a white ground, and the motto: *"Ubique."*

Catty had been into Reyburn to shop and had called for the letters. Mark was coming home in April.

"Oh — Mamma — "

"There's a letter for you, Mary."

(Not from Mark.)

"If he gets that appointment he won't go back." She thought: "She'll never be unhappy again. She'll never be afraid he'll get cholera."

For a minute their souls met and burned together in the joy they shared.

Then broke apart.

"Aren't you going to show me Mr. Sutcliffe's letter?"

"Why should I?"

"You don't mean to say there's anything in it I can't see?"

"You can see it if you like. There's nothing in it."

That was why she hadn't wanted her to see it. For anything there was in it you might never have known him. But Mrs. Sutcliffe had sent her love.

Mamma looked up sharply.

" Did you write to him, Mary? "

" Of course I did."

" You'll not write again. He's let you know pretty plainly he isn't going to be bothered."

(It wasn't that. It couldn't be that.)

" Did they say anything more about your going there? "

" No."

" That ought to show you then. . . . But as long as you live you'll give yourself away to people who don't want you."

" I'd rather you didn't talk about them."

" I should like to know what I *can* talk about," said Mamma.

She folded up her work and laid it in the basket.

Her voice dropped from the sharp note of resentment.

" I wish you'd go and see if those asters have come."

II

The asters had come. She had carried out the long, shallow boxes into the garden. She had left her mother kneeling beside them, looking with adoration into the large, round, innocent faces, white and purple, mauve and magenta and amethyst and pink. If the asters had not come the memory of the awful things they had said to each other would have remained with them till bed-time; but Mamma would be happy with the asters like a child with its toys, planning where they were to go and planting them.

She went up to her room. After thirteen years she had still the same childish pleasure in the thought that it was hers and couldn't be taken from her, because nobody else wanted it.

The bookshelves stretched into three long rows on the white wall above her bed to hold the books Mr. Sutcliffe had given her; a light blue row for the Thomas Hardys; a dark blue for the George Merediths; royal blue and gold for the Rudyard Kiplings. And in the narrow upright bookcase in the arm of the T facing her writing-table, Mark's books: the Homers and the Greek dramatists. Their backs had faded from puce colour to drab.

Mark's books.— When she looked at them she could still feel her old, childish lust for possession, her childish sense of insecurity, of defeat. And something else. The beginning of thinking things about Mamma. She could see herself standing in Mark's bedroom at Five Elms and Mamma with her hands on Mark's books. She could hear herself saying, " You're afraid."

" What did I think Mamma was afraid of? "

Mamma was happy out there with the asters.

There would be three hours before dinner.

She began setting down the fragments of the " Dream-Play " that had come to her: then the outlines. She saw very clearly and precisely how it would have to be. She was intensely happy.

. . . . . .

She was still thinking of it as she went across the Green to the post office, instead of wondering why the postmistress had sent for her, or why Miss Horn waited for her by the house door at the side, or why she looked at her like that, with a sort of yearning pity and fear. She followed her into the parlour behind the post office.

Suddenly she was awake to the existence of this parlour and its yellow cane-bottomed chairs and round table with the maroon cloth and the white alabaster lamp that smelt. The orange envelope lay on the maroon cloth. Miss Horn covered it with her hand.

" It's for Mr. Dan," she said. " I daren't send it to the house lest your mother should get it."

She gave it up with a slow, unwilling gesture.

" It's bad news, Miss Mary."

. . . " *Your Brother Died This Evening.*" . . .

Her heart stopped, staggered and went on again.

" *Poona* "—Mark—

" *Your Brother Died This Evening.* — SYMONDS."

" This evening " was yesterday. Mark had died yesterday.

Her heart stopped again. She had a sudden feeling of
suffocation and sickness.

Her mind left off following the sprawl of the thick grey-
black letters on the livid pink form.

It woke again to the extraordinary existence of Miss
Horn's parlour. It went back to Mark, slowly, by the way
it had come, by the smell of the lamp, by the orange envelope on the maroon cloth.

Mark. And something else.

Mamma — Mamma. She would have to know.

Miss Horn still faced her, supporting herself by her
spread hands pressed down on to the table. Her eyes had
a look of gentle, helpless interrogation, as if she said, " What
are you going to do about it? "

She did all the necessary things; asked for a telegram
form, filled it in: " *Send Details*, MARY OLIVIER "; and ad-
dressed it to Symonds of " E " Company. And all the time,
while her hand moved over the paper, she was thinking, " I
shall have to tell Mamma."

III

The five windows of the house stared out at her across
the Green. She avoided them by cutting through Horn's
yard and round by the Back Lane into the orchard. She
was afraid that her mother would see her before she had
thought how she would tell her that Mark was dead. She
shut herself into her room to think.

She couldn't think.

She dragged herself from the window seat to the chair by
the writing-table and from the chair to the bed.

She could still feel her heart staggering and stopping.
Once she thought it was going to stop altogether. She had
a sudden pang of joy. " If it would stop altogether — I
should go to Mark. Nothing would matter. I shouldn't
have to tell Mamma that he's dead." But it always went
on again.

She thought of Mark now without any feeling at all except that bodily distress. Her mind was fixed in one centre of burning, lucid agony. Mamma.

"I can't tell her. I can't. It'll kill her. . . . I don't see how she's to live if Mark's dead. . . . I shall send for Aunt Bella. She can do it. Or I might ask Mrs. Waugh. Or Mr. Rollitt."

She knew she wouldn't do any of these things. She would have to tell her.

She heard the clock strike the half hour. Half-past five. Not yet. "When it strikes seven I shall go and tell Mamma."

She lay down on her bed and listened for the strokes of the clock. She felt nothing but an immense fatigue, an appalling heaviness. Her back and arms were loaded with weights that held her body down on to the bed.

"I shall never be able to get up and tell her."

Six. Half-past. At seven she got up and went downstairs. Through the open side door she saw her mother working in the garden.

She would have to get her into the house.

"Mamma — darling."

But Mamma wouldn't come in. She was planting the last aster in the row. She went on scooping out the hole for it, slowly and deliberately, with her trowel, and patting the earth about it with wilful hands. There was a little smudge of grey earth above the crinkles in her soft, sallow-white forehead.

"You wait," she said.

She smiled like a child pleased with itself for taking its own way.

Mary waited.

She thought: "Three hours ago I was angry with her. I was angry with her. And Mark was dead then. And when she read his letter. He was dead yesterday."

IV

Time was not good to you. Time was cruel. Time made you see.

Yet somehow they had gone through time. Nights of August and September when you got up before daybreak to listen at her door. Days when you did nothing. Mamma sat upright in her chair with her hands folded on her lap. She kept her back to the window: you saw her face darkening in the dusk. When the lamp came she raised her arm and the black shawl hung from it and hid her face. Nights of insane fear when you *had* to open her door and look in to see whether she were alive or dead. Days when you were afraid to speak, afraid to look at each other. Nights when you couldn't sleep for wondering how Mark had died. They might have told you. They might have told you in one word. They didn't, because they couldn't; because the word was too awful. They would never say how Mark died. Mamma thought he had died of cholera.

You started at sounds, at the hiss of the flame in the grate, the fall of the ashes on the hearth, the tinkling of the front door bell.

You heard Catty slide back the bolt. People muttered on the doorstep. You saw them go back past the window, quietly, their heads turned away. They were ashamed.

You began to go out. You walked slowly, weighted more than ever by your immense, inexplicable fatigue. When you saw people coming you tried to go quicker; when you spoke to them you panted and felt absurd. A coldness came over you when you saw Mrs. Waugh and Miss Frewin with their heads on one side and their shocked, grieved faces. You smiled at them as you panted, but they wouldn't smile back. Their grief was too great. They would never get over it.

You began to watch for the Indian mail.

One day the letter came. You read blunt, jerky sentences that told you Mark had died suddenly, in the mess room, of heart failure. Captain Symonds said he thought you would want to know exactly how it happened. . . . " Well, we were ' cock-fighting,' if you know what that is, after dinner. Peters is the heaviest man in our battery, and Major Olivier was carrying him on his back. We oughtn't to have let him do it. But we didn't know there was anything wrong with his heart. He didn't know it himself. We thought he was fooling when he dropped on the floor.

. . . Everything was done that could be done. . . . He couldn't have suffered. . . . He was happy up to the last minute of his life — shouting with laughter."

She saw the long lighted room. She saw it with yellow walls and yellow lights, with a long, white table and clear, empty wine-glasses. Men in straw-coloured bamboo arm-chairs turning round to look. She couldn't see their faces. She saw Mark's face. She heard Mark's voice, shouting with laughter. She saw Mark lying dead on the floor. The men stood up suddenly. Somebody without a face knelt down and bent over him.

It was as if she had never known before that Mark was dead and knew it now. She cried for the first time since his death, not because he was dead, but because he had died like that — playing.

He should have died fighting. Why couldn't he? There was the Boer War and the Khyber Pass and Chitral and the Soudan. He had missed them all. He had never had what he had wanted.

And Mamma who had cried so much had left off crying. "The poor man couldn't have liked writing that letter, Mary. You needn't be angry with him."

"I'm not angry with him. I'm angry because Mark died like that."

"Heigh-h — " The sound in her mother's throat was like a sigh and a sob and a laugh jerking out contempt.

"You don't know what you're talking about. He's gone, Mary. If you were his mother it wouldn't matter to you how he died so long as he didn't suffer. So long as he didn't die of cholera."

"If he could have got what he wanted — "

"What's that you say?"

"If he could have got what he wanted."

"None of us ever get what we want in this world," said Mamma.

She thought: "It was her son — *her* son she loved, not Mark's real, secret self. He's got away from her at last — altogether."

V

She sewed.

Every day she went to the linen cupboard and gathered up all the old towels and sheets that wanted mending, and she sewed.

Her mother had a book in her lap. She noticed that if she left off sewing Mamma would take up the book and read, and when she began again she would put it down.

Her thoughts went from Mamma to Mark, from Mark to Mamma. She used to be pleased when she saw you sewing. "Nothing will ever please her now. She'll never be happy again. . . . I ought to have died instead of Mark. . . . That's Anthony Trollope she's reading."

The long sheet kept slipping. It dragged on her arm. Her arms felt swollen, and heavy like bars of lead. She let them drop to her knees. . . . Little Mamma.

She picked up the sheet again.

"Why are you sewing, Mary?"

"I must do *something*."

"Why don't you take a book and read?"

"I can't read."

"Well — why don't you go out for a walk?"

"Too tired."

"You'd better go and lie down in your room."

She hated her room. Everything in it reminded her of the day after Mark died. The rows of new books reminded her; and Mark's books in the narrow bookcase. They were hers. She would never be asked to give them back again. Yesterday she had taken out the Æschylus and looked at it, and she had forgotten that Mark was dead and had felt glad because it was hers. To-day she had been afraid to see its shabby drab back lest it should remind her of that, too.

Her mother sighed and put her book away. She sat with her hands before her, waiting.

Her face had its old look of reproach and disapproval, the drawn, irritated look you saw when you came between her and Mark. As if your grief for Mark came between her and her grief, as if, deep down inside her, she hated your grief as she had hated your love for him, without knowing that she hated it.

Suddenly she turned on you her blurred, wounded eyes.

" Mary, when you look at me like that I feel as if you knew everything I'm thinking."

" I don't. I shall never know."

Supposing all the time she knew what you were thinking? Supposing Mark knew? Supposing the dead knew?

She was glad of the aching of her heart that dragged her thought down and numbed it.

The January twilight crept between them. She put down her sewing. At the stroke of the clock her mother stirred in her chair.

" What day of the month is it? " she said.

" The twenty-fifth."

" Then — yesterday was your birthday. . . . Poor Mary. I forgot. . . . I sit here, thinking. My own thoughts. They make me forget. . . . Come here."

She went to her, drawn by a passion stronger than her passion for Mark, her hard, proud passion for Mark.

Her mother put up her face. She stooped down and kissed her passionately, on her mouth, her wet cheeks, her dove's eyes, her dove's eyelids. She crouched on the floor beside her, leaning her head against her lap. Mamma's hand held it there.

" Are you twenty-nine or thirty? "

" Thirty. "

" You don't look it. You've always been such a little thing. . . . You remember the silly question you used to ask me? ' Mamma — would you love me better if I was two? ' "

She remembered. Long ago. When she came teasing for kisses. The silly question.

" You remember *that?* "

" Yes. I remember."

Deep down inside her there was something you would never know.

XXIX

I

MAMMA was planting another row of asters in the garden in the place of those that had died last September.

The outline of the map of South Africa had gone from the wall at the bottom. Roddy's bit was indistinguishable from the rest.

And always you knew what would happen. Outside, on the Green, the movements of the village repeated themselves like the play of a clock-work toy. Always the same figures on the same painted stand, marked with the same pattern of slanting roads and three-cornered grass-plots. Half-way through prayers the Morfe bus would break loose from High Row with a clatter, and the brakes would grind on the hill. An hour after tea-time it would come back with a mournful tapping and scraping of hoofs.

She had left off watching for the old red mail-cart to come round the corner at the bottom. Sometimes, at long intervals, there would be a letter for her from Aunt Lavvy or Dan or Mrs. Sutcliffe. She couldn't tell when it would come, but she knew on what days the long trolleys would stop by Mr. Horn's yard loaded with powdery sacks of flour, and on what days the brewer's van would draw up to the King's Head and the Farmers' Arms. When she looked out across the Green she caught the hard stare of the Belks' house, the tall, lean, grey house blotched with iron stains. It stood on the sheer edge where the platform dropped to the turn of the road. Every morning at ten o'clock its little door would open and Mr. Belk would come out and watch for his London paper. Every evening at ten minutes past ten the shadow of Mr. Belk would move across the yellow blind of the drawing-room window on the right; the light would go out, and presently a blond blur would appear behind the blind of the bedroom window on the left.

Every morning at twelve Mrs. Belk would hurry along, waddling and shaking, to leave the paper with her aunt, old Mrs. Heron, in the dark cottage that crouched at the top of the Green. Every afternoon at three Dorsy would bring it back again.

When Mary came in from the village Mamma would look up and say "Well?" as if she expected her to have something interesting to tell. She wished that something would happen so that she might tell Mamma about it. She tried to think of something, something to say that would interest Mamma.

" I met Mr. James on the Garthdale Road. Walking like
anything. "

" Did you? " Mamma was not interested in Mr. James.
She wondered, " Why can't I think of things like other
people? " She had a sense of defeat, of mournful incapacity.

One day Catty came bustling in with the tea-things, looking important. She had brought news from the village.

Mrs. Heron had broken her thigh. She had slipped on
the landing. Mrs. Belk was with her and wouldn't go away.

Catty tried to look sorry, but you could see she was
pleased because she had something to tell you.

They talked about it all through tea-time. They were
sorry for Mrs. Heron. They wondered what poor Dorsy
would do if anything should happen to her. And through all
their sorrow there ran a delicate, secret thrill of satisfaction.
Something had happened. Something that interested
Mamma.

Two days later Dorsy came in with her tale; her nose
was redder, her hare's eyes were frightened.

" Mrs. Belk's there still," she said. " She wants to take
Aunt to live with her. She wants her to send me away. She
says it wouldn't have happened if I'd looked after her properly. And so it wouldn't, Mary, if I'd been there. But
I'd a bad headache, and I was lying down for a minute when
she fell. . . . She won't go. She's sitting there in Aunt's
room all the time, talking and tiring her. Trying to
poison Aunt's mind against me. Working on her to send
me away."

Dorsy's voice dropped and her face reddened.

" She thinks I'm after Aunt's money. She's always been
afraid of her leaving it to me. I'm only her husband's
nephew's daughter. Mrs. Belk's her real niece. . . .

" I'd go to-morrow, Mary, but Aunt wants me there.
She doesn't like Mrs. Belk; I think she's afraid of her. And
she can't get away from her. She just lies there with her
poor leg in the splints; there's the four-pound weight from
the kitchen scales tied on to keep it on the stretch. If you
could *see* her eyes turning to me when I come. . . .

" One thing — Mrs. Belk's afraid for her life of me.
That's why she's trying to poison Aunt's mind."

When they saw Mrs. Belk hurrying across the Green to Mrs. Heron's house they knew what she was going for.

" Poor Dorsy ! " they said.

" Poor Dorsy ! "

They had something to talk to each other about now.

II

Winter and spring passed. The thorn-trees flowered on Greffington Edge: dim white groves, magically still under the grey, glassy air.

May passed and June. The sleek waves of the hay-fields shone with the brushing of the wind, ready for mowing.

The elder tree by the garden wall was a froth of greenish white on green.

At the turn of the schoolhouse lane the flowers began: wild geraniums and rose campion, purple and blue and magenta, in a white spray of cow's parsley: standing high against the stone walls, up and up the green lane.

Down there, where the two dales spread out at the bottom, a tiny Dutch landscape. Flat pastures. Trees dotted about. A stiff row of trees at the end. No sky behind them. Trees green on green, not green on blue. The great flood of the sky dammed off by the hills.

She shut her eyes and saw the flat fields of Ilford, and the low line of flying trees; a thin, watery mirage against the hill.

Since Mark died she had begun to dream about Ilford. She would struggle and break through out of some dream about Morfe and find herself in Ley Street, going to Five Elms. She would get past the corner and see the red brick gable end. Sometimes, when she came up to the gate, the house would turn into Greffington Hall. Sometimes it would stand firm with its three rows of flat windows; she would go up the flagged path and see the sumach tree growing by the pantry window; and when the door was opening she would wake.

Sometimes the door stood open. She would go in. She would go up the stairs and down the passages, trying to find the schoolroom. She would know that Mark was in the

schoolroom. But she could never find it. She never saw
Mark. The passages led through empty, grey-lit rooms to
the bottom of the kitchen stairs, and she would find a dead
baby lying among the boots and shoes in the cat's cupboard.

Autumn and winter passed. She was thirty-two.

III

When your mind stopped and stood still it could feel
time. Time going fast, going faster and faster. Every year
its rhythm swung on a longer curve.

Your mind stretched to the span of time. There was
something exciting about this stretch, like a new sense
growing. But in your dreams your mind shrank again; you
were a child, a child remembering and returning; haunting
old stairs and passages, knocking at shut doors. This child
tried to drag you back, it teased you to make rhymes about
it. You were not happy till you had made the rhymes.

There was something in you that went on, that refused
to turn back, to look for happiness in memory. Your happiness was *now*, in the moment that you lived, while you made
rhymes; while you looked at the white thorn-trees; while the
black-purple cloud passed over Karva.

Yesterday she had said to Dorsy Heron, "What I can't
stand is seeing the same faces every day."

But the hill world had never the same face for five minutes. Its very form changed as the roads turned. The
swing of your stride put in play a vast, mysterious scene-
shifting that disturbed the sky. Moving through it you
stood still in the heart of an immense being that moved.
Standing still you were moved, you were drawn nearer and
nearer to its enclosing heart.

She swung off the road beyond the sickle to the last moor-
track that led to the other side of Karva. She came back
by the southern slope, down the twelve fields, past the four-
farms.

The farm of the thorn-tree, the farm of the ash, the farm
of the three firs and the farm all alone.

Four houses. Four tales to be written.

There was something in you that would go on, whatever

happened.   Whatever happened it would still be happy.   Its happiness was not like the queer, sudden, uncertain ecstasy. She had never known *what* that was.   It came and went; it had gone so long ago that she was sure that whatever it had been it would never come again.   She could only remember its happening as you remember the faint ecstasies of dreams.   She thought of it as something strange and exciting.   Sometimes she wondered whether it had really happened, whether there wasn't a sort of untruthfulness in supposing it had.

But that ecstasy and this happiness had one quality in common; they belonged to some part of you that was free. A you that had no hereditary destiny; that had got out of the net, or had never been caught in it.

You could stand aside and look on at its happiness with horror, it didn't care.   It was utterly indifferent to your praise or blame, and the praise or blame of other people; or to your happiness and theirs.   It was open to you to own it as your self or to detach yourself from it in your horror. It was stronger and saner than you.   If you chose to set up that awful conflict in your soul that was your own affair.

Perhaps not your own.   Supposing the conflict in you was the tug of the generations before you, trying to drag you back to them?   Supposing the horror was *their* horror, their fear of defeat?

She had left off being afraid of what might happen to her.   It might never happen.   And supposing it did, supposing it had to happen when you were forty-five, you had still thirteen years to write in.

"It shan't happen.   I won't let it.   I won't let them beat me."

IV

Last year the drawer in the writing-table was full.   This year it had overflowed into the top left-hand drawer of the dressing-table.   She had to turn out all the handkerchiefs and stockings.

Her mother met her as she was carrying them to the wardrobe in the spare room.   You could see she felt that there was something here that must be enquired into.

" I should have thought," she said, " that writing-table drawer was enough."

" It isn't."

" Tt-t — " Mamma nodded her head in a sort of exasperated resignation.

" Do you mean to say you're going to *keep* all that? "

" All that? You should see what I've burnt."

" I should like to know what you're going to do with it! "

" So should I. That's just it — I don't know."

That night the monstrous thought came to her in bed: Supposing I published those poems — I always meant to do it some day. Why haven't I? Because I don't care? Or because I care too much? Because I'm afraid? Afraid that if somebody reads them the illusion they've created would be gone?

How do I know my writing isn't like my playing?

This is different. There's nothing else. If it's taken from me I shan't want to go on living.

You didn't want to go on living when Mark died. Yet you went on. As if Mark had never died. . . . And if Mamma died you'd go on — in your illusion.

If it is an illusion I'd rather know it.

How *can* I know? There isn't anybody here who can tell me. Nobody you could believe if they told you —

I can believe *myself*. I've burnt everything I've written that was bad.

You believe yourself to-day. You believed yesterday. How do you know you'll believe to-morrow?

To-morrow —

V

Aunt Lavvy had come to stay.

When she came you had the old feeling of something interesting about to happen. Only you knew now that this was an illusion.

She talked to you as though, instead of being thirty-three, you were still very small and very young and ignorant of all the things that really mattered. She was vaguer and greyer, more placid than ever, and more content with God.

Impossible to believe that Papa used to bully her and
that Aunt Lavvy had revolted.

" For thirty-three years, Emilius, thirty-three years " —
Sunday supper at Five Elms; on the table James
Martineau's *Endeavours After the Christian Life.*

She wondered why she hadn't thought of Aunt Lavvy.
Aunt Lavvy knew Dr. Martineau. As long as you could
remember she had always given a strong impression of
knowing him quite well.

But when Mary had made it clear what she wanted her
to ask him to do, it turned out that Aunt Lavvy didn't know
Dr. Martineau at all.

And you could see she thought you presumptuous.

VI

When old Martha brought the message for her to go to
tea with Miss Kendal, Mary slunk out through the orchard
into the Back Lane. At that moment the prospect of talking
two hours with Miss Kendal was unendurable.

And there was no other prospect. As long as she lived
in Morfe there would be nothing — apart from her real,
secret life there would be nothing — to look forward to but
that. If it was not Miss Kendal it would be Miss Louisa or
Dorsy or old Mrs. Heron. People talked about dying of
boredom who didn't know that you could really die of it.

If only you didn't keep on wanting somebody — somebody
who wasn't there. If, before it killed you, you could kill
the desire to know another mind, a luminous, fiery crystal,
to see it turn, shining and flashing. To talk to it, to listen
to it, to love the human creature it belonged to.

She envied her youth its capacity for day-dreaming, for
imagining interminable communions. Brilliant hallucina-
tions of a mental hunger. Better than nothing. . . . If
this went on the breaking-point must come. Suddenly you
would go smash. Smash. Your mind would die in a de-
lirium of hunger.

VII

" It's a pity we can't go to his lecture, " said Miss Kendal.
The train was moving out of Reyburn station. It was
awful to think how nearly they had missed it. If Dr.
Charles had stayed another minute at the harness-maker's.

Miss Kendal sat on the edge of the seat, very upright in
her black silk mantle with the accordion-pleated chiffon
frills. She had sat like that since the train began to pull,
ready to get out the instant it stopped at Durlingham.

" I feel sure it's going to be all right," she said.

The white marabou feather nodded.

Her gentle mauve and sallow face was growing old, with
soft curdlings and puckerings of the skin; but she still
carried her head high, nodding at you with her air of gaiety,
of ineffable intrigue.

" I wouldn't bring you, Mary, if I didn't feel sure."

If she had not felt sure she wouldn't have put on the
grey kid gloves, the mantle and the bonnet with the white
marabou feather. You don't dress like that to go shopping
in Durlingham.

" You mean," Mary said, " that we shall see him."

Her heart beat calmly, stilled by the sheer incredibility
of the adventure.

" Of course we shall see him." Mrs. Smythe-Caulfield
will manage that. It might have been a little difficult if the
Professor had been staying anywhere else. But I know
Mrs. Smythe-Caulfield very well. No doubt she's arranged
for you to have a long talk with him."

" Does she know what I want to see him about? "

" Well — yes — I thought it best, my dear, to tell her just
what you told me, so that she might see how important
it is. . . . There's no knowing what may come of it. . . .
Did you bring them with you? "

" No, I didn't. If he won't look at them I should feel
such an awful fool."

",Perhaps," said Miss Kendal, " it is wiser not to assume
beforehand. Nothing may come of it. Still, I can't help
feeling something will. . . . When you're famous, Mary,
I shall think of how we went into Durlingham together."

"Whatever comes of it I shall think of *you.*"

The marabou feather quivered slightly.

"How long have we known each other?"

"Seventeen years."

"Is it so long? . . . I shall never forget the first day you came with your mother. I can see you now, Mary, sitting beside my poor father with your hand on his chair. . . . And that evening when you played to us, and dear Mr. Roddy was there. . . ."

She thought: "Why can't I be kind — always? Kindness matters more than anything. Some day she'll die and she'll never have said or thought one unkind thing in all her poor, dreadful little life. . . . Why didn't I go to tea with her on Wednesday?"

On Wednesday her mind had revolted against its destiny of hunger. She had hated Morfe. She had felt angry with her mother for making her live in it, for expecting her to be content, for thinking that Dorsy and Miss Louisa and Miss Kendal were enough. She had been angry with Aunt Lavvy for talking about her to Miss Kendal.

Yet if it weren't for Miss Kendal she wouldn't be going into Durlingham to see Professor Lee Ramsden.

Inconceivable that she should be taken by Miss Kendal to see Professor Lee Ramsden. Yet this inconceivable thing appeared to be happening.

She tried to remember what she knew about him. He was Professor of English literature at the University of London. He had edited Anthologies and written Introductions. He had written a *History of English Literature* from Chaucer to Tennyson and a monograph on Shelley.

She thought of his mind as a luminous, fiery crystal, shining.

Posters on the platform at Durlingham announced in red letters that Professor Lee Ramsden, M.A., F.R.S.L., would lecture in the Town Hall at 8 P.M. She heard Miss Kendal saying, "If it had been at three instead of eight we could have gone." She had a supreme sense of something about to happen.

Heavenly the long, steep-curved glass roof of the station, the iron arches and girders, the fanlights. Foreign and beautiful the black canal between the purplish rose-red walls, the white swans swaying on the black water, the red shaft of the clock-tower. It shot up high out of the Market-place, topped with the fantastically large, round, white eye of its clock.

She kept on looking up to the clock-tower. At four she would see him.

They walked about the town. They lunched and shopped. They sat in the Park. They kept on looking at the clock-tower.

At the bookseller's in the Market-place she bought a second-hand copy of Walt Whitman's *Leaves of Grass*. . . .

A black-grey drive between bushes of smutty laurel and arbutus. A black-grey house of big cut stones that stuck out. Gables and bow windows with sharp freestone facings that stuck out. You waited in a drawing-room stuffed with fragile mahogany and sea-green plush. Immense sea-green acanthus leaves, shaded in myrtle green, curled out from the walls. A suggestion of pictures heaved up from their places by this vigorous, thrusting growth.

Curtains, cream-coloured net, sea-green plush, veiled the black-grey walks and smutty lawns of the garden.

While she contemplated these things the long hand of the white marble tombstone clock moved from the hour to the quarter.

She was reading the inscription, in black letters, on the golden plinth: " Presented to Thomas Smythe-Caulfield, Esqr., M.P., by the Council and Teachers of St. Paul's Schools, Durlingham "—" Presented "— when Mrs. Smythe-Caulfield came in.

A foolish, overblown, conceited face. Grey hair arranged with art and science, curl on curl. Three-cornered eyelids, hutches for small, malevolently watching eyes. A sharp, insolent nose. Fish's mouth peering out above the backward slope of casca :ng chins.

Mrs. Smythe-Caulfield shook hands at a sidelong arm's-length, not looking at you, holding Miss Kendal in her sharp pointed stare. They were Kate and Eleanor: Eleanor and Kate.

" You're going to the lecture? "

" If it had been at three instead of eight — "

" The hour was fixed for the townspeople's convenience."

In five minutes you had gathered that you would not be
allowed to see Professor Lee Ramsden; that Professor Lee
Ramsden did not desire to see or talk to anybody except
Mrs. Smythe-Caulfield; that he kept his best things for her;
that *all sorts of people* were trying to get at him, and that
he trusted her to protect him from invasion; that you had
been admitted in order that Mrs. Smythe-Caulfield might
have the pleasure of telling you these things.

Mary saw that the moment was atrocious; but it didn't
matter. A curious tranquillity possessed her: she felt something there, close to her, like a person in the room, giving
her a sudden security. The moment that was mattering so
abominably to her poor, kind friend belonged to a time that
was not her time.

She heard the tinkle of tea cups outside the hall; then
a male voice, male footsteps. Mrs. Smythe-Caulfield made
a large encircling movement towards the door. Something
interceptive took place there.

As they went back down the black-grey drive between
the laurel and arbutus Miss Kendal carried her head higher
than ever.

" That is the first time in my life, Mary, that I've asked
a favour."

" You did it for me." (" She hated it, but she did it for
me.")

" Never mind. We aren't going to mind, are we? We'll
do without them. . . . That's right, my dear. Laugh. I'm
glad you can. I dare say I shall laugh myself to-morrow."

" I don't *want* to laugh," Mary said. She could have
cried when she looked at the grey gloves and the frilled
mantle, and the sad, insulted face in the bonnet with the
white marabou feather. (And that horrible woman hadn't
even given her tea.)

The enormous eye of the town clock pursued them to the
station.

As they settled into their seats in the Reyburn train Miss
Kendal said, " It's a pity we couldn't go to the lecture."

She leaned back, tired, in her corner. She closed her
eyes.

Mary openea Walt Whitman's *Leaves of Grass.*
The beginning had begun.

XXX

I

" WHAT are you reading, Mary? "
" The New Testament. . . .   Extraordinary how interest-
ing it is."
" Interesting! "
" Frightfully interesting."
" You may say what you like, Mary; you'll change your
mind some day.   I pray every night that you may come to
Christ; and you'll find in the end you'll have to come." . . .
No.   No.   Still, he said, " The Kingdom of God is within
you." If the Greek would bear it — within you.
Did they understand their Christ?   Had anybody ever
understood him?   Their " Prince of Peace " who said he
hadn't come to send peace, but a sword?   The sword of the
Self. He said he had come to set a man against his father
and the daughter against her mother, and that because of
him a man's foes should be those of his own household.
" Gentle Jesus, meek and mild. "
He was not meek and mild.   He was only gentle with
children and women and sick people.   He was brave and
proud and impatient and ironic.   He wouldn't stay with his
father and mother. He liked happy people who could amuse
themselves without boring him.   He liked to get away from
his disciples, and from Lazarus and Martha and Mary of
Bethany, and go to the rich, cosmopolitan houses and hear
the tax-gatherer's talk and see the young Roman captains
swaggering with their swords and making eyes at Mary of
Magdala.
He was the sublimest rebel that ever lived.
He said, " The spirit blows where it wills.   You hear the
sound of it, but you can't tell where it comes from or where
it goes to.   Everybody that is born from the spirit is like
that."   The spirit blows where it wants to.
He said it was a good thing for them that he was going

away. If he didn't the Holy Ghost wouldn't come to them; they would never have any real selves; they would never be free. They would set him up as a god outside themselves and worship Him, and forget that the Kingdom of God was within them, that God was their real self.

Their hidden self was God. It was their Saviour. Its existence was the hushed secret of the world.

Christ knew — he must have known — it was greater than he was.

It was a good thing for them that Christ died. That was how he saved them. By going away. By a proud, brave, ironic death. Not at all the sort of death you had been taught to believe in.

And because they couldn't understand a death like that, they went and made a god of him just the same.

But the Atonement was that — Christ's going away.

II

February: grey, black-bellied clouds crawling over Greffington Edge, over Karva, swelling out: swollen bodies crawling and climbing, coming together, joining. Monstrous bodies ballooning up behind them, mounting on top of them, flattening them out, pressing them down on to the hills; going on, up and up the sky, swelling out overhead, coming together.

One cloud, grey as sink water, over all the sky, shredded here and there, stirred by slight stretchings, and spoutings of thin steam.

Then the whole mass coming down, streaming grey sink water.

She came down the twelve fields on the south slope of Karva: she could say them by heart: the field with the big gap, the field above the four firs farm, the field below the farm of the ash-tree, the bare field, the field with the thorn tree, the field with the sheep's well, the field with the wild rose bush, the steep field of long grass, the hillocky field, the haunted field with the ash grove, the field with the big barn, the last field with the gap to the road.

She thought of her thirty-four years; of the verses she

had sent to the magazines and how they had come back
again; of the four farms on the hill, of the four tales not
written.

The wet field grasses swept, cold, round her ankles.

Mamma sat waiting in her chair, in the drawing-room,
in the clear, grey, glassy dusk of the cross-lights. She
waited for the fine weather to come when she would work
again in the garden. She waited for you to come to her.
Her forehead unknitted itself; her dove's eyes brightened;
she smiled, and the rough feathers of her eyebrows lay
down, appeased.

At the opening of the door she stirred in her chair. She
was glad when you came.

Catty brought in the lamp. When she turned up the
wick the rising flame carved Mamma's face out of the dusk.
Her pretty face, delicately dinted, whitened with a powdery
down; stained with faint bistres of age. Her little, high-
bridged nose stood up from the softness, clear and young,
firm as ivory.

The globed light showed like a ball of fire, hung out in
the garden, on the black, glassy darkness, behind the pane.
Catty drew down the blind and went. You heard the click
of the latch falling to behind her. The evening had begun.

They took up their books. Mamma hid her face behind
Anthony Trollope, Mary hers behind Thomas Hardy. Presently she would hear Mamma sigh, then yawn.

Horrible tension.

Under the edge of her book she would see Anthony
Trollope lying in Mamma's lap and Mamma's fingers playing with the fringe of her shawl. She would put Thomas
Hardy down and take up Anthony Trollope and read aloud
till Mamma's head began bowing in a doze. Then she would
take up Thomas Hardy. When Mamma waked Hardy
would go down under Trollope; when she dozed he would
come to the top again.

After supper Mamma would be wide awake. She would
sit straight up in her chair, waiting, motionless, ready. You
would pick up your book but you would have no heart in it.
You knew what she wanted. She knew that you knew.
You could go on trying to read if you chose; but she would

still sit there, waiting. You would know what she was thinking of.

The green box in the cabinet drawer.

The green box. You began to think of it, too, hidden, hidden in the cabinet drawer. You were disturbed by the thought of the green box, of the little figures inside it, white and green. You would get up and go to the cabinet drawer.

Mamma would put out her hands on the table, ready. She smiled with shut lips, pouting, half ashamed, half delighted. You would set out the green and white chequer board, the rows of pawns. And the game of halma would begin. White figures leap-frogging over green, green over white. Your hand and your eyes playing, your brain hanging inert, remembering, forgetting.

In the pauses of the game you waited; for the clock to strike ten, for Catty to bring in the Bible and the Prayer-book, for the evening to end. Old verses, old unfinished verses, coming and going.

In the long pauses of the game, when Mamma sat stone-still, hypnotised by the green and white chequers, her curved hand lifted, holding her pawn, her head quivering with indecision.

> *In dreams He has made you wise*
> *With the wisdom of silence and prayer. . . .*

Coming and going, between the leap-frogging of the green figures and the white.

> *God, Who has blinded your eyes*
> *With the dusk of your hair. . . .*

Brown hair, sleek and thin, brown hair that wouldn't go grey.

And the evening would go on, soundless and calm, with soft, annihilating feet, with the soft, cruel feet of oblivion.

III

One day, when she came in, she heard the sound of the piano. The knocking of loose hammers on dead wires, the

light, hacking clang of chords rolling like dead drum taps:
Droom — Droom, Droom-era-room.

Alone in the dusk, Mamma was playing the Hungarian
March, bowing and swaying as she played.

When the door opened she started up, turning her back
on the piano, frightened, like a child caught in a play it is
ashamed of. The piano looked mournful and self-conscious.

Then suddenly, all by itself, it shot out a cry like an
arrow, a pinging, stinging, violently vibrating cry.

"I'm afraid," Mamma said, "something's happened to the
piano."

IV

They were turning out the cabinet drawer, when they
found the bundle of letters. Mamma had marked it in her
sharp, three cornered hand-writing: "Correspondence.
Mary."

"Dear me," she said, "I didn't know I'd kept those
letters."

She slipped them from the rubber band and looked at
them. You could see Uncle Victor's on the top, then
Maurice Jourdain's. You heard the click of her tongue that
dismissed those useless, unimportant things. The slim, yellowish letter at the bottom was Miss Lambert's.

"Tt-tt —"

"Oh, let me see that."

She looked over her mother's shoulder. They read
together.

"We don't want her to go. . . . She made us love her
more in one fortnight than girls we've had with us for
years. . . . Perhaps some day we may have her again."

The poor, kind woman. The kind, dead woman. Years
ago dead; her poor voice rising up, a ghostlike wail over
your "unbelief."

That was only the way she began.

"I say — I say!"

The thin voice was quivering with praise. Incredible,
bewildering praise. "Remarkable — remarkable " — You
would have thought there had never been such a remarkable
child as Mary Olivier.

It came back to her. She could see Miss Lambert talking to her father on the platform at Victoria. She could see herself, excited, running up the flagged walk at Five Elms. And Mamma coming down the hall. And what happened then. The shock and all the misery that came after.

" That was the letter you wouldn't let me read."

" What do you mean? "

" The day I came back. I asked you to let me read it and you wouldn't."

" Really, Mary, you accuse me of the most awful things. I don't believe I wouldn't let you read it."

" You didn't. I remember. You didn't want me to know — "

" Well," her mother said, giving in suddenly, " if I didn't, it was because I thought it would make you even more conceited than you were. I don't suppose I was very well pleased with you at the time."

" Still — you kept it."

But her mother was not even going to admit that she had kept it.

She said, " I must have overlooked it. But we can burn it now."

She carried it across the room to the fire. She didn't want even now — even now. You saw again the old way of it, her little obstinate, triumphant smile, the look that paid you out, that said, " See how I've sold you."

The violet ashen sheet clung to the furred soot of the chimney: you could still see the blenched letters.

She couldn't really have thought it would make you conceited. That was only what she wanted to think she had thought.

" It wasn't easy to make you pleased with me all the time. . . . Still, I can't think why on earth you weren't pleased."

She knelt before the fire, watching the violet ashen bit of burnt-out paper, the cause, the stupid cause of it all.

Her mother had settled again, placidly, in her chair.

" Even if I was a bit conceited. . . . I don't think I was, really. I only wanted to know whether I could do things. I wanted people to tell me just because I didn't know. But even if I was, what did it matter? You must have known I loved you — desperately — all the time."

"I didn't know it, Mary."

"Then you were stup — "

"Oh, say I was stupid. It's what you think. It's what you always have thought."

"You were — you were, if you didn't see it."

"See what?"

"How I cared — I can remember — when I was a kid — the awful feeling. It used to make me ill."

"I didn't know that. If you did care you'd a queer way of showing it."

"That was because I thought you didn't."

"Who told you I didn't care for you?"

"I didn't need to be told. I could see the difference."

Her mother sat fixed in a curious stillness. She held her elbows pressed tight against her sides. Her face was hard and still. Her eyes looked away across the room.

"You were different," she said. "You weren't like any of the others. I was afraid of you. You used to look at me with your little bright eyes. I felt as if you knew everything I was thinking. I never knew what you'd say or do next."

No. Her face wasn't hard. There was something else. Something clear. Clear and beautiful.

"I suppose I — I didn't like your being clever. It was the boys I wanted to do things. Not you."

"Don't — Mamma darling — *don't.*"

The stiff, tight body let go its hold of itself. The eyes turned to her again.

"I was jealous of you, Mary. And I was afraid for my life you'd find it out."

v

Eighteen ninety-eight. Eighteen ninety-nine. Nineteen hundred. Thirty-five — thirty-six — thirty-seven. Three years. Her mind kept on stretching; it held three years in one span like one year. The large rhythm of time appeased and exalted her.

In the long summers while Mamma worked in the garden she translated *Euripides.*

The *Bacchæ.* You could do it after you had read Walt
Whitman. If you gave up the superstition of singing; the
little tunes of rhyme. If you left off that eternal jingling
and listened, you could hear what it ought to be.

Something between talking and singing. If you wrote
verse that could be chanted: that could be whispered,
shouted, screamed as they moved. Agave and her Maenads.
Verse that would go with a throbbing beat, excited, exciting;
beyond rhyme. That would be nearest to the Greek verse.

    .   .   .   .

September, nineteen hundred.

Across the room she could see the pale buff-coloured
magazine, on the table where, five minutes ago, Mamma had
laid it down. She could see the black letters of its title
and the squat column of the table of contents. The magazine with her poem in it.

And Mamma, sitting very straight, very still.

You would never know what she was thinking. She
hadn't said anything. You couldn't tell whether she was
glad or sorry; or whether she was afraid.

The air tingled with the thought of the magazine with
your poem in it. But you would never know what she was
thinking.

VI

A long letter from Uncle Edward. Uncle Edward was
worrying Mamma.

"He never could get on with your poor father. Or your
Uncle Victor. He did his best to prevent him being made
trustee. . . . And now he comes meddling, wanting to upset
all their arrangements."

"Why?"

"Just because poor Victor's business isn't doing quite so
well as it did."

"Yes, but why's he bothering *you* about it?"

"Well, he says I ought to make another will, leaving half
the boys' money to you. That would be taking it from
Dan. He always had a grudge against poor Dan."

"But you mustn't do anything of the sort."

"Well — he knows your father provided for you. You're to have the Five Elms money that's in your Uncle Victor's business. You'd suppose, to hear him talk, that it wasn't safe there."

"Just tell him to mind his own business," Mary said.

"Actually," Mamma went on, "advising me not to pay back any more of Victor's money. I shall tell him I sent the last of it yesterday."

There would be no more debts to Uncle Victor. Mark had paid back his; Mamma had paid back Roddy's, scraping and scraping, Mark and Mamma, over ten years, over twenty.

A long letter from Uncle Victor. Uncle Victor was worrying Mamma.

"Don't imagine that I shall take this money. I have invested it for you, in sound securities. Not in my own business. That, I am afraid I ought to tell you, is no longer a sound security."

"Poor Victor — "

"It almost looks," Mamma said, "as if Edward might be right."

So right that in his next letter Uncle Victor prepared you for his bankruptcy.

"It will not affect you and Mary," he wrote. "I may as well tell you now that all the Five Elms money has been reinvested, and is safe. As for myself, I can assure you that, after the appalling anxiety of the last ten years, the thought of bankruptcy is a relief. A blessed relief, Caroline."

All through September and October the long letters came from Uncle Victor.

Then Aunt Lavvy's short letter that told you of his death.

Then the lawyer's letters.

It seemed that, after all, Uncle Victor had been mistaken. His affairs were in perfect order.

Only the Five Elms money was gone; and the money Mark and Mamma had paid back to him. He had taken it all out of his own business, and put it into the Sheba Mines and Joe's Reef, and the Golconda Company where he thought it would be safe.

The poor dear. The poor dear.

VII

So that you knew —

Mamma might believe what Aunt Lavvy told her, that he had only gone to look out of the window and had turned giddy. Aunt Lavvy might believe that he didn't know what he was doing.

But you knew.

He had been afraid. Afraid. He wouldn't go up to the top-landing after they took Aunt Charlotte away; because he was afraid.

Then, at last, after all those years, he had gone up. When he knew he was caught in the net and couldn't get out. He had found that they had moved the linen cupboard from the window back into the night nursery. And he had bolted the staircase door on himself. He had shut himself up. And the great bare, high window was there. And the low sill. And the steep, bare wall, dropping to the lane below.

END OF BOOK FOUR

BOOK FIVE

MIDDLE-AGE

1900-1910

BOOK FIVE

MIDDLE-AGE

XXXI

I

SHE must have been sitting there twenty minutes.

She was afraid to look up at the clock, afraid to move an eyelid lest she should disturb him.

The library had the same nice, leathery, tobaccoey smell. Rough under her fingers the same little sharp tongue of leather scratched up from the arm of her chair. The hanging, half-open fans of the ash-tree would be making the same Japanese pattern in the top left hand pane of the third window. She wanted to see it again to make sure of the pattern, but she was afraid to look up.

If she looked up she would see him.

She mustn't. It would disturb him horribly. He couldn't write if he thought you were looking at him.

It was wonderful that he could go on like that, with somebody in the room, that he let you sit in it when he was writing. The big man.

She had asked him whether she hadn't better go away and come back again, and he had said No, he didn't want her to go away. He wouldn't keep her waiting more than five minutes.

It was unbelievable that she should be sitting there, in that room, as if nothing had happened; as if *they* were there; as if they might come in any minute; as if they had never gone. A week ago she would have said it was impossible, she couldn't do it, for anybody, no matter how big or how celebrated he was.

Why, after ten years — it must be ten years — she

couldn't even bear to go past the house while other people were in it. She hated them, the people who took Greffington Hall for the summer holidays and the autumn shooting. She would go round to Renton by Jackson's yard and the fields so as not to see it. But when the brutes were gone and the yellow blinds were down in the long rows of windows that you saw above the grey garden wall, she liked to pass it and look up and pretend that the house was only waiting for them, only sleeping its usual winter sleep, resting till they came back.

It *was* ten years since they had gone.

No. If Richard Nicholson hadn't been Mr. Sutcliffe's nephew, she couldn't, no matter how big and how celebrated he was, or how badly he wanted her help or she wanted his money.

No matter how wonderful and important it would feel to be Richard Nicholson's secretary.

It wasn't really his money that she wanted. It would be worth while doing it for nothing, for the sake of knowing him. She had read his *Euripides*.

She wondered: Supposing he kept her, how long would it last? He was in the middle of his First Series of *Studies in Greek Literature;* and there would be two, or even three if he went on.

He had taken Greffington Hall for four months. When he went back to London he would have to have somebody else.

Perhaps he would tell her that, after thinking it over, he had found he didn't want her. Then to-day would be the end of it.

If she looked up she would see him.

She knew what she would see: the fine, cross upper lip lifted backwards by the moustache, the small grizzled brown moustache, turned up, that made it look crosser. The narrow, pensive lower lip, thrust out by its light jaw. His nose — quite a young nose — that wouldn't be Roman, wouldn't be Sutcliffe; it looked out over your head, tilted itself up to sniff the world, obstinate, alert. His eyes, young too, bright and dark, sheltered, safe from age under the low straight eyebrows. They would never have shabby, wrinkled

sagging lids. Dark brown hair, grey above his ears, clipped
close to stop its curling like his uncle's. He liked to go
clipped and clean. You felt that he liked his own tall,
straight slenderness.

The big library rustled with the quick, irritable sound of
his writing.

It stopped. He had finished. He looked at the clock.
She heard a small, commiserating sound.

"Forgive me. I really thought it would only take five
minutes. How on earth do you manage to keep so quiet?
I should have known if a mouse had moved."

He turned towards her. He leaned back in his chair.
"You don't mind my smoking?"

He was settling himself. Now she would know.

"Well," he said, "if I did keep you waiting forty minutes,
it was a good test, wasn't it?"

He meditated.

"I'm always changing my secretaries because of something. The last one was admirable, but I couldn't have
stood her in the room when I was writing. . . . Besides,
you work better."

"Can you tell? In a week?"

"Yes. I can tell. . . . Are you sure you can spare me
four months?"

"Easily."

"Five? Six?"

"If you were still here."

"I shan't be. I shall be in London. . . . Couldn't you
come up?"

"I couldn't, possibly."

His cross mouth and brilliant, irritated eyes questioned
her.

"I couldn't leave my mother."

II

Five weeks of the four months gone. And to-morrow
he was going up to London.

Only till Friday. Only for five days. She kept on
telling herself he would stay longer. Once he was there you

couldn't tell how many days he might stay. But say he
didn't come back till the middle of July, still there would
be the rest of July and all August and September.

To-day he was walking home with her, carrying the
books. She liked walking with him, she liked to be seen
walking with him, as she used to like being seen walking
with Roddy and Mark, because she was proud of them,
proud of belonging to them. She was proud of Richard
Nicholson because of what he had done.

The Morfe people didn't know anything about what he
had done; but they knew he was something wonderful and
important; they knew it was wonderful and important that
you should be his secretary. They were proud of you, glad
that they had provided him with you, proud that he should
have found what he was looking for in Morfe.

Mr. Belk, for instance, coming along the road. He used
to pass you with a jaunty, gallant, curious look as if you
were seventeen and he were saying, " There's a girl who
ought to be married. Why isn't she? " He had just sidled
past them, abashed and obsequious, a little afraid of the
big man. Even Mrs. Belk was obsequious.

And Mr. Spencer Rollitt. He was proud because Richard
Nicholson had asked him about a secretary and he had
recommended you. Funny that people could go on disapproving of you for twenty years, and then suddenly
approve because of Richard Nicholson.

And Mamma. Mamma thought you wonderful and important, too.

Mamma liked Mr. Nicholson. Ever since that Sunday
when he had called and brought the roses and stayed to tea.
She had gone out of the room and left them abruptly because
she was afraid of his " cleverness," afraid that he would
begin to talk about something that she didn't understand.

And he had said, " How beautiful she is — "

After he had gone she had told Mamma that Richard
Nicholson had said she was beautiful; and Mamma had
pretended that it didn't matter what he said; but she had
smiled all the same.

He carried himself like Mr. Sutcliffe when he walked,
straight and tall in his clean cut grey suit. Only he was

lighter and leaner. His eyes looked gentle and peaceable now under the shadow of the Panama hat.

The front door stood open. She asked him to come in for tea.

" May I? . . . What are you doing afterwards? "

" Going for a walk somewhere."

" Will you let me come too? " . . .

He was standing by the window looking at the garden. She saw him smile when he heard Catty say that Mamma had gone over to Mrs. Waugh's and wouldn't be back for tea. He smiled to himself, a secret, happy smile, looking out into the garden. . . . She took him out through the orchard. He went stooping under the low apple boughs and laughing. Down the Back Lane and through the gap in the lower fields, along the flagged path to the Bottom Lane and through the Rathdale fields to the river. Over the stepping stones.

She took the stones at a striding run. He followed, running and laughing.

Up the Rathdale fields to Renton Moor. Not up the schoolhouse lane, or on the Garthdale Road, or along the fields by the beck. Not up Greffington Edge or Karva. Because of Lindley Vickers and Maurice Jourdain; and Roddy and Mark.

No. She was humbugging herself. Not up Karva because of her secret happiness. She didn't want to mix him up with *that* or with the self that had felt it. She wanted to keep him in the clear spaces of her mind, away from her memories, away from her emotions.

They sat down on the side of the moor in the heather.

Indoors when he was working he was irritable and restless. You would hear a gentle sighing sound: " D-amn "; and he would start up and walk about the room. There would be shakings of his head, twistings of his eyebrows, shruggings of his shoulders, and tormented gestures of his hands. But not out here. He sat in the heather as quiet, as motionless as you were, every muscle at rest. His mind was at rest.

The strong sunlight beat on him; it showed up small surface signs. Perhaps you could see now that he might really be forty, or even forty-five.

No, you couldn't. You couldn't see or feel anything but
the burning, inextinguishable youth inside him. The little grey
streaks and patches might have been powder put on for fun.

"I want to finish with all my Greek stuff," he said suddenly. "I want to go on to something else — studies in
modern French literature. Then English. I want to get
everything clean and straight in five pages where other
people would take fifty. . . . I want to go smash through
some of the traditions. The tradition of the long, grey
paragraph. . . . We might learn things from France.
But we're a proud island people. We won't learn. . . .
We're a proud island people, held in too tight, held in
till we burst. That's why we've no æsthetic restraint. No
restraint of any sort. Take our economics. Take our
politics. We've had to colonise, to burst out over conti-
nents. When our minds begin moving it's the same thing.
They burst out. All over the place. . . . When we've
learned restraint we shall take our place inside Europe, not
outside it."

"We do restrain our emotions quite a lot."

"We do. We do. That's precisely why we don't restrain our expression of them. Really unrestrained emotion
that forces its way through and breaks down your intellectual defences and saturates you with itself — it hasn't any
words. . . . It hasn't any words; or very few."

. . . .

The mown fields over there, below Greffington Edge, were
bleached with the sun: the grey cliffs quivered in the hot
yellow light.

"It might be somewhere in the South of France."

"*Not* Agaye."

"No. Not Agaye. The limestone country. . . . I can't
think why I never came here. My uncle used to ask me
dozens of times. I suppose I funked it. . . . What the
poor old chap must have felt like shut up in that house all
those years with my aunt — "

"Please don't. I — I liked her."

"You mean you liked him and put up with her because
of him. We all did that."

"She was kind to me."

"Who wouldn't be?"

" Oh, but you don't know how kind."

" Kind? Good Lord, yes. There are millions of kind people in the world. It's possible to be kind and at the same time not entirely brainless."

" He wouldn't mind that. He wouldn't think she was brainless — "

" He wasn't in love with her — there was another woman — a girl. It was so like the dear old duffer to put it off till he was forty-five and then come a cropper over a little girl of seventeen."

" That isn't true. I knew him much better than you do. He never cared for anybody but her. . . . Besides, if it *was* true you shouldn't have told me. I've no business to know it." . . .

" Everybody knew it. The poor dear managed so badly that everybody in the place knew it. *She* knew, that's why she dragged him away and made him live abroad. She hated living abroad, but she liked it better than seeing him going to pieces over the girl."

" I don't believe it. If there was anything in it I'd have been sure to have heard of it. . . . Why, there wasn't anybody here but me — "

" It must have been years before your time," he said. " You could hardly even have come in for the sad end of it."

. . . .

Dorsy Heron said it was true.

" It was you he was in love with. Everybody saw it but you."

She remembered. His face when she came to him. In the library. And what he had said.

" A man might be in love with you for ten years and you wouldn't know about it if he held his tongue."

And *her* face. Her poor face, so worried when people saw them together. And that last night when she stroked your arm and when she saw him looking at it and stopped. And her eyes. Frightened. Frightened.

" How I must have hurt him. How I must have hurt them both."

. . . .

Mr. Nicholson had come back on Friday as he had said.

III

He put down his scratching pen and was leaning back in his chair, looking at her.

She wondered what he was thinking. Sometimes the space of the room was enormous between her table by the first tall window and his by the third; sometimes it shrank and brought them close. It was bringing them close now.

"You can't see the text for the footnotes," she said. "The notes must go in the Appendix."

She wanted to make herself forget that all her own things, the things she had saved from the last burning, were lying there on his table, staring at her. She was trying not to look that way, not to let herself imagine for a moment that he had read them.

"Never mind the notes and the Appendix."

He had got up. He was leaning now against the tall shutter of her window, looking down at her.

"Why didn't you tell me? Before I let you in for that horrible drudgery? All that typing and indexing — If I'd only known you were doing anything like this. . . . Why couldn't you have told me? "

"Because I wasn't doing it. It was done ages ago."

"It's my fault. I ought to have known. I did know there was something. I ought to have attended to it and found out what it was."

He began walking up and down the room, turning on her again and again, making himself more and more excited.

"That translation of the *Bacchœ* — what made you think of doing it like that? "

"I'd been reading Walt Whitman — It showed me you *could* do without rhyme. I knew it must sound as if it was all spoken — chanted — that they mustn't sing. Then I thought perhaps that was the way to do it."

"Yes. Yes. It *is* the way to do it. The only way. . . . You see, that's what my Euripides book's about. The very thing I've been trying to ram down people's throats, for years. And all the time you were doing it — down here — all by yourself — for fun. . . . I wish I'd known. . . . What are you going to do about it? "

"I didn't think anything could be done."
He sat down to consider that part of it.

.   .   .   .   .   .

He was going to get it published for her.
He was going to write the Introduction.
"And — the other things?"
"Oh, well, that's another matter. There's not much of
it that'll stand."
He knew. He would never say more or less than he
meant.
Not much of it that would stand. Now that she knew,
it was extraordinary how little she minded.
"Still, there are a few things. They must come out first.
In the spring. Then the *Bacchæ* in the autumn. I want it
to be clear from the start that you're a poet translating; not
the other way on."
He walked home with her, discussing gravely how it
would be done.

IV

It had come without surprise, almost without excitement;
the quiet happening of something secretly foreseen, present
to her mind as long as she could remember.
"I always meant that this should happen: something
like this."
Now that it had happened she was afraid, seeing, but not
so clearly, what would come afterwards: something that
would make her want to leave Morfe and Mamma and go
away to London and know the people Richard Nicholson had
told her about, the people who would care for what she had
done; the people who were doing the things she cared about.
To talk to them; to hear them talk. She was afraid of
wanting that more than anything in the world.
She saw her fear first in Mamma's eyes when she told
her.
And there was something else. Something to do with
Richard Nicholson. Something she didn't want to think
about. Not fear exactly, but a sort of uneasiness when she
thought about him.
His mind really was the enormous, perfect crystal she

had imagined. It had been brought close to her; she had turned it in her hand and seen it flash and shine. She had looked into it and seen beautiful, clear things in it: nothing that wasn't beautiful and clear. She was afraid of wanting to look at it again when it wasn't there. Because it had made her happy she might come to want it more than anything in the world.

In two weeks it would be gone. She would want it and it would not be there.

V

When she passed the house and saw the long rows of yellow blinds in the grey front she thought of him. He would not come back. He had never come before, so it wasn't likely he would come again.

His being there was one of the things that only happened once. Perhaps those were the perfect things, the things that would never pass away; they would stay for ever, beautiful as you had seen them, fixed in their moment of perfection, wearing the very air and light of it for ever.

You would see them *sub specie œternitatis*. Under the form of eternity.

So that Richard Nicholson would always be like that, the same whenever you thought of him.

Look at the others: the ones that hadn't come back and the ones that had. Jimmy Ponsonby, Harry Craven, Mr. Sutcliffe. And Maurice Jourdain and Lindley Vickers. If Maurice Jourdain had never come back she would always have seen him standing in the cornfield. If Lindley Vickers had never come back she wouldn't have seen him with Nannie Learoyd in the schoolhouse lane; the moment when he held her hands in the drawing-room, standing by the piano, would have been their one eternal moment.

Because Jimmy Ponsonby had gone away she had never known the awful thing he had done. She would go through the Ilford fields for ever and ever with her hot hand in his; she happy and he innocent; innocent for ever and ever. Harry Craven, her playmate of two hours, he would always be playing, always laughing, always holding her hand, like Roddy, without knowing that he held it.

Suppose Mr. Sutcliffe had come back. She would have hurt them more and more. Mrs. Sutcliffe would have hated her. They would have been miserable, all three. All three damned for ever and ever.

She was not sure she wanted Richard Nicholson to come back.

She was not sure he wasn't spoiling it by writing. She hadn't thought he would do that.

A correspondence? Prolonging the beautiful moment, stretching it thin; thinner and thinner; stretching it so thin that it would snap? You would come to identify him with his letters, so that in the end you would lose what had been real, what had been perfect. You would forget. You would have another and less real kind of memory.

But his letters were not thin; they were as real as his voice. They *were* his voice talking to you; you could tell which words would take the stress of it. "I don't know how *much* there is of you, whether this is all of it or only a little bit. You gave me an impression — you made me feel that there might be any *amount* gone under that you can't get at, that you may *never* get at if you go on staying where you are. I believe if you got clean away it might come to the top again.

"But I don't *know*. I don't know whether you're at the end or the beginning. I could tell better if you were here."

She counted the months till April when her poems would come out. She counted the days till Tuesday when there might be a letter from Richard Nicholson.

If only he would not keep on telling you you ought to come to London. That was what made you afraid. He might have seen how impossible it was. He had seen Mamma.

"Don't try to dig me out of my 'hole.' I *can* 'go on living in it for ever' if I'm never taken out. But if I got out once it would be awful coming back. It isn't awful now. Don't make it awful."

He only wrote: "I'll make it awfuller and *aw*fuller, until out you come."

XXXII

I

THINGS were happening in the village.

The old people were dying. Mr. James had died in a fit the day after Christmas Day. Old Mrs. Heron had died of a stroke in the first week of January. She had left Dorsy her house and furniture and seventy pounds a year. Mrs. Belk got the rest.

The middle-aged people were growing old. Louisa Wright's hair hung in a limp white fold over each ear, her face had tight lines in it that pulled it into grimaces, her eyes had milky white rings like speedwell when it begins to fade. Dorsy Heron's otter brown hair was striped with grey; her nose stood up sharp and bleak in her red, withering face; her sharp, tender mouth drooped at the corners. She was forty-nine.

It was cruel, cruel, cruel; it hurt you to see them. Rather than own it was cruel they went about pulling faces and pretending they were happy. Their gestures had become exaggerated, tricks that they would never grow out of, that gave them the illusion of their youth.

The old people were dying and the middle-aged people were growing old. Nothing would ever begin for them again.

Each morning when she got out of bed she had the sacred, solemn certainty that for her everything was beginning. At thirty-nine.

What was thirty-nine? A time-feeling, a feeling she hadn't got. If you haven't got the feeling you are not thirty-nine. You can be any age you please, twenty-nine, nineteen.

But she had been horribly old at nineteen. She could remember what it had felt like, the desperate, middle-aged sadness, the middle-aged certainty that nothing interesting would ever happen. She had got hold of life at the wrong end.

And all the time her youth had been waiting for her at the other end, at the turn of the unknown road, at thirty-nine. All through the autumn and winter Richard Nicholson had kept on writing. Her poems would be out on the tenth of April.

On the third the note came.

" Shall I still find you at Morfe if I come down this week-end? — R. N."

" You will never find me anywhere else. — M. O."

" I shall bike from Durlingham. If you've anything to do in Reyburn it would be nice if you met me at The King's Head about four. We could have tea there and ride out together. — R. N."

II

" I'm excited. I've never been to tea in an hotel before."

She was chattering like a fool, saying anything that came into her head, to break up the silence he made.

She was aware of something underneath it, something that was growing more and more beautiful every minute. She was trying to smash this thing lest it should grow more beautiful than she could bear.

" You see how I score by being shut up in Morfe. When I do get out it's no end of an adventure." (Was there ever such an idiot?)

Suddenly she left off trying to smash the silence.

The silence made everything stand out with a supernatural clearness, the square, white-clothed table in the bay of the window, the Queen Anne fluting on the Britannia metal teapot, the cups and saucers and plates, white with a gentian blue band, The King's Head stamped in gold like a crest.

Sitting there so still he had the queer effect of creating for both of you a space of your own, more real than the space you had just stepped out of. There, there and not anywhere else, these supernaturally clear things had reality, a unique but impermanent reality. It would last as long as you sat there and would go when you went. You knew that whatever else you might forget you would remember this.

The rest of the room, the other tables and the people

sitting at them were not quite real. They stood in another space, a different and inferior kind of space.

"I came first of all," he said, "to bring you *that*."

He took out of his pocket and put down between them the thin, new white parchment book of her *Poems*.

"Oh . . . Poor thing, I wonder what'll happen to it?"

Funny — it was the least real thing. If it existed at all it existed somewhere else, not in this space, not in this time. If you took it up and looked at it the clearness, the unique, impermanent reality would be gone, and you would never get it again.

    ·   ·   ·   ·   ·   ·   ·

They had finished the run down Reyburn hill. Their pace was slackening on the level.

He said, "That's a jolly bicycle of yours."

"Isn't it? I'm sure you'll like to know I bought it with the wonderful cheque you gave me. I should never have had it without that."

"I'm glad you got something out of that awful time."

"Awful? It was one of the nicest times I've ever had. . . . Nearly all my nice times have been in that house."

"I know," he said. "My uncle would let you do anything you liked if you were young enough. He ought to have had children of his own. They'd have kept him out of mischief."

"I can't think," she said to the surrounding hills, "why people get into mischief, or why they go and kill themselves. When they can ride bicycles instead."

III

Mamma was sitting upright and averted, with an air of self-conscious effacement, holding the thin white book before her like a fan.

Every now and then you could see her face swinging round from behind the cover and her eyes looking at Richard Nicholson, above the rims of her glasses. Uneasy, frightened eyes.

IV

The big pink roses of the chintzes and the gold bordered bowls of the black mirrors looked at you rememberingly.

There was a sort of brutality about it. To come here and be happy, to come here in order to be happy, when *they* were gone; when you had hurt them both so horribly.

" I'm sitting in her chair," she thought.

Richard Nicholson sat, in a purely temporary attitude, by the table in the window. Against the window-pane she could see his side face drawn in a brilliant, furred line of light. His moustache twitched under the shadow of his nose. He was smiling to himself as he wrote the letter to Mamma.

There was a brutality about that, too. She wondered if he had seen old Baxter's pinched mouth and sliding eyes when he took the letter. He was watching him as he went out, waiting for the click of the latch.

"It's all right," he said. " They expect you. They think it's work."

He settled himself (in Mr. Sutcliffe's chair).

" It's the best way," he said. " I want to see you and I don't want to frighten your mother. She *is* afraid of me."

" No. She's afraid of the whole thing. She wishes it hadn't happened. She's afraid of what'll happen next. I can't make her see that nothing need happen next."

" She's cleverer than you think. She sees that something's got to happen next. I couldn't stand another evening like the last."

" You couldn't," she agreed. " You couldn't possibly."

" We can't exactly go on like — like this, you know."

" Don't let's think about it. Here we are. Now this minute. It's an hour and a half till dinner time. Why, even if I go at nine we've got three hours."

" That's not enough. . . . You talk as though we could think or not think, as we chose. Even if we left off thinking we should have to go on living. Your mother knows that."

" I don't think she knows more than we do."

" She knows enough to frighten her. She knows what *I* want. . . . I want to marry you, Mary."

(This then was what she had been afraid of. But Mamma wouldn't have thought of it.)

"I didn't think you wanted to do that. Why should you?"

"It's the usual thing, isn't it? When you care enough."

"*Do* you care enough?"

"More than enough. Don't you? . . . It's no use saying you don't. I know you do."

"Can you tell?"

"Yes."

"Do I go about showing it?"

"No; there hasn't been time. You only began yesterday."

"When? *When?*"

"In the hotel. When you stopped talking suddenly. And when I gave you your book. You looked as though you wished I hadn't. As though I'd dragged you away from somewhere where you were happy."

"Yes. . . . If it only began yesterday we can stop it. Stop it before it gets worse."

"I can't. I've been at it longer than that."

"How long?"

"Oh — I don't know. It might have been that first week. After I'd found out that there was peace when you came into the room; and no peace when you went out. When you're there peace oozes out of you and soaks into me all the time."

"Does it feel like that?"

"Just like that."

"But — if it feels like that now, we should spoil it by marrying."

"Oh no we shouldn't."

"Yes. . . . If it's peace you want. There won't be *any* peace. . . . Besides, you don't know. Do you remember telling me about your uncle?"

"What's he got to do with it?"

"And that girl. You said I couldn't have known anything about it. . . . You said I couldn't even have come in for the sad end of it."

"Well?"

"Well. . . . I did. . . . I *was* the sad end of it. . . . The girl was me."

" But you told me it wasn't true."

. . . He had got up. He wanted to stand. To stand up high above you.

" You *know*," he said, " you told me it wasn't true."

.   .   .   .

They would have to go through with it. Dining. Drinking coffee. Talking politely; talking intelligently; talking. Villiers de L'Isle Adam, Villiers de L'Isle Adam. " The symbolistes are finished. . . . Do you know Jean Richepin? ' Il était une fois un pauvre gars Qui aimait celle qui ne l'aimait pas '? . . . ' Le cœur de ta mère pour mon chien.' " He thinks I lied. " You ought to read Henri de Regnier and Remy de Gourmont. You'd like them." . . . Le cœur de ta mère. He thinks I lied. Goodness knows what he doesn't think.

The end of it would come at nine o'clock.

.   .   .   .

" Are you still angry? "

He laughed. A dreadful sniffling laugh that came through his nostrils.

" *I'm* not. If I were I should let you go on thinking I lied. You see, I didn't know it was true. I didn't know I was the girl."

" You didn't *know?* "

" How could I when he never said a word? "

" I can't understand your not seeing it."

" Would you like me better if I had seen it? "

" N-no. . . . But I wish you hadn't told me. Why did you? "

" I was only trying to break the shock. You thought I couldn't be old enough to be that girl. I meant you to do a sum in your head: ' If she was that girl and she was seventeen, then she must be thirty-nine now.' "

" Is *that* what you smashed up our evening for? "

" Yes."

" I shouldn't care if you were fifty-nine. I'm forty-five."

" You're sorry. You're sorry all the same."

" I'm sorry because there's so little time, Mary. Sorry
I'm six years older than you. . . ."

Nine o'clock.

She stood up. He turned to her. He made a queer
sound. A sound like a deep, tearing sigh.

.   .   .   .

" If I were twenty I couldn't marry you, because of
Mamma. That's one thing. You can't marry Mamma."

" We can talk about your mother afterwards."

" No. Now. There isn't any afterwards. There's only
this minute that we're in. And perhaps the next. . . .
You haven't thought what it'll be like. You can't leave
London because of your work. I can't leave this place
because of Mamma. She'd be miserable in London. I can't
leave her. She hasn't anybody but me. I promised my
brother I'd look after her. . . .

" She'd have to live with me."

" Why not? "

" You couldn't live with her."

" I could, Mary."

" Not you. You said you couldn't stand another evening
like yesterday. . . . *All the evenings would be like yesterday.* . . . Please. . . . Even if there wasn't Mamma,
you don't want to marry. If you'd wanted to you'd have
done it long ago, instead of waiting till you're forty-five.
Think of two people tied up together for life whether they
both like it or not. It isn't even as if one of them could
be happy. How could you if the other wasn't? Look at
the Sutcliffes. Think how he hated it. . . . And *he* was
a kind, patient man. You know you wouldn't dream of
marrying me if you didn't think it was the only possible
way."

" Well — isn't it? "

" No. The one impossible way. I'd do anything for you
but that. . . . Anything."

" Would you, Mary? Would you have the courage? "

" It would take infinitely more courage to marry you.
We should be risking more. All the beautiful things. If
it wasn't for Mamma. . . . But there *is* Mamma. So — you
see."

She thought: "He *hasn't* kissed me. He *hasn't* held me in his arms. He'll be all right. It won't hurt him."

V

That was Catty's white apron.

Catty stood on the cobbled square by the front door, looking for her. When she saw them coming she ran back into the house.

She was waiting in the passage as Mary came in.

"The mistress is upset about something," she said. "After she got Mr. Nicholson's letter."

"There wasn't anything to upset her in that, Catty."

"P'raps not, Miss Mary; but I thought I'd tell you."

Mamma had been crying all evening. Her pocket-handkerchief lay in her lap, a wet rag.

"I thought you were never coming back again," she said.

"Why, where did you think I'd gone?"

"Goodness knows where. I believe there's nothing you wouldn't do. I've no security with you, Mary. . . . Staying out till all hours of the night. . . . Sitting up with that man. . . . You'll be the talk of the place if you don't take care."

(She thought: "I must let her go on. I won't say anything. If I do it'll be terrible.")

"I can't think what possessed you. . . ."

("Why did I do it? *Why* did I smash it all up? Uncle Victor suicided. That's what I've done. . . . I've killed myself. . . . This isn't me.")

"If that's what comes of your publishing I'd rather your books were sunk to the bottom of the sea. I'd rather see you in your coffin."

"I *am* in my coffin."

"I wish I were in mine," her mother said.

. . . .

Mamma was getting up from her chair, raising herself slowly by her arms.

Mary stooped to pick up the pocket-handkerchief.

"Don't, Mamma; I've got it."

Mamma went on stooping. Sinking, sliding down sideways, clutching at the edge of the table.

Mary saw terror, bright, animal terror, darting up to her out of Mamma's eyes, and in a place by themselves the cloth sliding, the lamp rocking and righting itself.

She was dragging her up by her armpits, holding her up. Mamma's arms were dangling like dolls' arms.

And like a machine wound up, like a child in a passion, she still struggled to walk, her knees thrust out, doubled up, giving way, her feet trailing.

VI

Not a stroke. Well, only a slight stroke, a threatening, a warning. " Remember she's getting old, Mary."

Any little worry or excitement would do it.

She was worried and excited about me. Richard worried and excited her.

If I could only stay awake till she sleeps. She's lying there like a lamb, calling me " dear " and afraid of giving me trouble. . . . Her little hands dragged the bedclothes up to her chin when Dr. Charles came. She looked at him with her bright, terrified eyes.

She isn't old. She can't be when her eyes are so bright.

She thinks it's a stroke. She won't believe him. She thinks she'll die like Mrs. Heron.

Perhaps she knows.

Perhaps Dr. Charles really thinks she'll die and won't tell me. Richard thought it. He was sorry and gentle, because he knew. You could see by his cleared, smoothed face and that dreadfully kind, dreadfully wise look. He gave in to everything — with an air of insincere, provisional acquiescence, as if he knew it couldn't be for very long. Dr. Charles must have told him.

Richard wants it to happen. . . . Richard's wanting it can't make it happen.

It might, though. Richard might get at her. His mind and will might be getting at her all the time, making her die. He might do it without knowing he was doing it, because he couldn't help it. He might do it in his sleep.

But I can stop that. . . . If Richard's mind and will can make her die, my mind and will can keep her from dying. . . . There was something I did before.

That time I wanted to go away with the Sutcliffes. When Roddy was coming home. Something happened then. . . . If it happened then it can happen now.

If I could remember how you do it. Flat on your back with your eyes shut; not tight shut. You mustn't feel your eyelids. You mustn't feel any part of you at all. You think of nothing, absolutely nothing; not even think. You keep on not feeling, not thinking, not seeing things till the blackness comes in waves, blacker and blacker. That's how it was before. Then the blackness was perfectly still. You couldn't feel your breathing or your heart beating. . . . It's coming all right. . . . Blacker and blacker.

It wasn't like this before.

This is an awful feeling. Dying must be like this. One thing going after another. Something holding down your heart, stopping its beat; something holding down your chest, crushing the breath out of it. . . . Don't think about the feeling. Don't feel. Think of the blackness. . . .

It isn't the same blackness. There are specks and shreds of light in it; you can't get the light away. . . . Don't think about the blackness and the light. Let everything go except yourself. Hold on to yourself. . . . But you felt your self going.

Going and coming back; gathered together; incredibly free; disentangled from the net of nerves and veins. It didn't move any more with the movement of the net. It was clear and still in the blackness; intensely real.

Then it willed. Your self willed. It was free to will. You knew that it had never been free before except once; it had never willed before except once. Willing was *this*. Waves and waves of will, coming on and on, making your will, driving it through empty time. . . . " The time of time ": that was the Self. . . . Time where nothing happens except this. Where nothing happens except God's will. God's will in your will. Self of your self. Reality of reality. . . . It had felt like that.

Mamma had waked up. She was saying she was better.

*   *   *   *   *   *   *   *

Mamma was better. She said she felt perfectly well. She could walk across the room. She could walk without your holding her.

It couldn't have been that. It couldn't, possibly. It was a tiny hæmorrhage and it had dried up. It would have dried up just the same if you hadn't done anything. Those things *don't happen*.

What did happen was extraordinary enough. The queer dying. The freedom afterwards. The intense stillness, the intense energy; the certainty.

Something was there.

.　　.　　.　　.　　.　　.　　.

That horrible dream. Dorsy oughtn't to have made me go and see the old woman in the workhouse. A body without a mind. That's what made the dream come. It was Mamma's face; but she was doing what the old woman did.

"Mamma!"—That's the second time I've dreamed Mamma was dead.

The little lamb, lying on her back with her mouth open, making that funny noise: "Cluck-cluck," like a hen.

Why can't I dream about something I *want* to happen? Why can't I dream about Richard? . . . Poor Richard, how can he go on believing I shall come to him?

VII

Dear Dr. Charles, with his head sticking out between the tubes of the stethoscope, like a ram. His poor old mouth hung loose as he breathed. He was out late last night; there was white stubble on his chin.

"It won't do it when you want it to."

"It's doing quite enough. . . . Let me see, it's two years since your mother had that illness. You must go away, Mary. For a month at least. Dorsy'll come and take care of your mother."

"Does it matter where I go?"

"N-no. Not so much. Go where you'll get a thorough

change, my dear. I wouldn't stay with relations, if I were you."

"All right, I'll go if you'll tell me what's the matter with me."

"You've got your brother Rodney's heart. But it won't kill you if you'll take care of yourself."

(Roddy's heart, the net of flesh and blood drawing in a bit of your body.)

XXXIII

I

RICHARD had gone up into his own flat and left her to wash and dress and explore. He had told her she was to have Tiedeman's flat. Not knowing who Tiedeman was made it more wonderful that God should have put it into his head to go away for Easter and lend you his flat.

If you wanted anything you could ring and they would come up from the basement and look after you.

She didn't want them to come up yet. She wanted to lie back among her cushions where Richard had packed her, and turn over the moments and remember what they had been like: getting out of the train at King's Cross and finding Richard there; coming with him out of the thin white April light into the rich darkness and brilliant colours of the room; the feeling of Richard's hands as they undid her fur stole and peeled the sleeves of her coat from her arms; seeing him kneel on the hearthrug and make tea with an air of doing something intensely interesting, an air of security and possession. He went about in Tiedeman's rooms as if they belonged to him.

She liked Tiedeman's flat: the big outer room, curtained with thick gentian blue and thin violet. There was a bowl of crimson and purple anemones on the dark oval of the oak table.

Tiedeman's books covered the walls with their coloured bands and stripes and the illuminated gold of their tooling. The deep bookcases made a ledge all round half-way up the wall, and the shallow bookcases went on above it to the ceiling.

But — those white books on the table were Richard's
books. *Mary Olivier* — *Mary Olivier*. *My* books that I
gave him. . . . They're Richard's rooms.

She got up and looked about. That long dark thing was
her coat and fur stretched out on the flat couch in the corner
where Richard had laid them; stretched out in an absolute
peace and rest.

She picked them up and went into the inner room that
showed through the wide square opening. The small brown
oak-panelled room. No furniture but Richard's writing
table and his chair. A tall narrow French window looking
to the backs of houses, and opening on a leaded balcony.
Spindle-wood trees, green balls held up on ramrod stems in
green tubs. Richard's garden.

Curtains of thin silk, brilliant magenta, letting the light
through. The hanging green bough of a plane tree, high
up on the pane, between. A worn magentaish rug on the
dark floor.

She went through the door on the right and found a
short, narrow passage. Another French window opening
from it on to the balcony. A bathroom on the other side;
a small white panelled bedroom at the end.

She had no new gown. Nothing but the black chiffon
one (black because of Uncle Victor) she had bought two
years ago with Richard's cheque. She had worn it at
Greffington that evening when she dined with him. It had
a long, pointed train. Its thin, open, wide spreading sleeves
fell from her shoulders in long pointed wings. It made her
feel slender.

.   .   .   .

There was no light in the inner room. Clear glassy dark
twilight behind the tall window. She stood there waiting
for Richard to come down.

Richard loved all this. He loved beautiful books, beautiful things, beautiful anemone colours, red and purple with
the light coming through them, thin silk curtains that let
the light through like the thin silky tissues of flowers. He
loved the sooty brown London walls, houses standing back
to back, the dark flanks of the back wings jutting out,

almost meeting across the trenches of the gardens, making the colours in his rooms brilliant as stained glass.

He loved the sound of the street outside, intensifying the quiet of the house.

It was the backs that were so beautiful at night; the long straight ranges of the dark walls, the sudden high dark cliffs and peaks of the walls, hollowed out into long galleries filled with thick, burning light, rows on rows of oblong casements opening into the light. Here and there a tree stood up black in the trenches of the gardens.

The tight strain in her mind loosened and melted in the stream of the pure new light, the pure new darkness, the pure new colours.

Richard came in. They stood together a long time, looking out; they didn't say a word.

Then, as they turned back to the lighted outer room, " I thought I was to have had Tiedeman's flat?"

" Well, he's up another flight of stairs and the rain makes a row on the skylight. It was simpler to take his and give you mine. I want you to have mine."

II

She turned off the electric light and shut her eyes and lay thinking. The violent motion of the express prolonged itself in a ghostly vibration, rocking the bed. In still space, unshaken by this tremor, she could see the other rooms, the quiet, beautiful rooms.

I wonder how Mamma and Dorsy are getting on. . . . I'm not going to think about Mamma. It isn't fair to Richard. I shan't think about anybody but Richard for this fortnight. One evening of it's gone already. It might have lasted quite another hour if he hadn't got up and gone away so suddenly. What a fool I was to let him think I was tired.

There will be thirteen evenings more. Thirteen. You can stretch time out by doing a lot of things in it; doing something different every hour. When you're with Richard every minute's different from the last, and he brings you the next all bright and new.

Heaven would be like that. Imagine an eternity of heaven; being with Richard for ever and ever. But nobody ever did imagine an eternity of heaven. People only talk about it because they can't imagine it. What they mean is that if they had one minute of it they would remember that for ever and ever.

.   .   .   .

This is Richard's life. This is what I'd have taken from him if I'd let him marry me.

I daren't even think what it would have been like if I'd tried to mix up Mamma and Richard in the same house. . . . And poor little Mamma in a strange place with nothing about it that she could remember, going up and down in it, trying to get at me, and looking reproachful and disapproving all the time. She'd have to be shut in her own rooms because Richard wouldn't have her in his. Sitting up waiting to be read aloud to and played halma with when Richard wanted me. Saying the same things over and over again. Sighing.

Richard would go off his head if he heard Mamma sigh.

He wants to be by himself the whole time, " working like blazes." He likes to feel that the very servants are battened down in the basement so that he doesn't know they're there. He couldn't stand Tiedeman and Peters if they weren't doing the same thing. Tiedeman working like blazes in the flat above him and Peters working like blazes in the flat below.

Richard slept in this room last night. He will sleep in it again when I'm gone.

She switched the light on to look at it for another second: the privet-white panelled cabin, the small wine-coloured chest of drawers, the small golden-brown wardrobe, shining.

My hat's in that wardrobe, lying on Richard's waistcoat, fast asleep.

If Tiedeman's flat's up there, that's Richard walking up and down over my head. . . . If it rains there'll be a row on the skylight and he won't sleep. He isn't sleeping now.

III

It would be much nicer to walk home through Kensington Gardens and Hyde Park.

She was glad that they were going to have a quiet evening. After three evenings at the play and Richard ruining himself in hansoms and not sleeping. . . . After this unbelievable afternoon. All those people, those terribly important people.

It was amusing to go about with Richard and feel important yourself because you were with him. And to see Richard's ways with them, his nice way of behaving as if *he* wasn't important in the least, as if it was you they had made all that fuss about.

To think that the little dried up schoolmasterish man was Professor Lee Ramsden, prowling about outside the group, eager and shy, waiting to be introduced to you, nobody taking the smallest notice of him. The woman who had brought him making soft, sentimental eyes at you through the gaps in the group, and trying to push him in a bit nearer. Then Richard asking you to be kind for one minute to the poor old thing. It hurt you to see him shy and humble and out of it.

And when you thought of his arrogance at Durlingham.

It was the women's voices that tired you so, and their nervous, snapping eyes.

The best of all was going away from them quietly with Richard into Kensington Gardens.

" Did you like it, Mary? "

" Frightfully. But not half so much as this."

IV

She was all alone in the front room, stretched out on the flat couch in the corner facing the door.

He was still writing his letter in the inner room. When she heard him move she would slide her feet to the floor and sit up.

She wanted to lie still with her hands over her shut eyes,

making the four long, delicious days begin again and go
on in her head.

Richard *would* take hansoms. You couldn't stop him.
Perhaps he was afraid if you walked too far you would
drop down dead. When it was all over your soul would
still drive about London in a hansom for ever and ever,
through blue and gold rain-sprinkled days, through poignant
white evenings, through the streaming, steep, brown-purple
darkness and the streaming flat, thin gold of the wet nights.

They were not going to have any more tiring parties.
There wasn't enough time.

When she opened her eyes he was sitting on the chair
by the foot of the couch, leaning forward, looking at her.
She saw nothing but his loose, hanging hands and straining
eyes.

" Oh, Richard — what time is it? " She swung her feet
to the floor and sat up suddenly.

" Only nine."

" *Only* nine. The evening's nearly gone."

    ·   ·   ·   ·   ·   · ·   ·

" Is that why you aren't sleeping, Richard? . . . I didn't
know. I didn't *know* I was hurting you."

" What-did-you-think? What-did-you-think? Isn't it
hurting *you?* "

" Me? I've got used to it. I was so happy just being
with you."

" So happy and so quiet that I thought you didn't care.
. . . Well, what was I to think? If you won't marry me."

" That's because I care so frightfully. Don't let's rake
that up again."

" Well, there it is."

She thought: " I've no business to come here to his rooms,
turning him out, making him so wretched that he can't
sleep. No business. . . . Unless — "

" And we've got to go on living with it," he said.

He thinks I haven't the courage. . . . I can't *tell* him.

" Yes," she said, " there it is."

Why shouldn't I tell him? . . . We've only ten days.
As long as I'm here nothing matters but Richard. . . . If

I keep perfectly still, still like this, if I don't say a word
he'll think of it. . . .

"Richard — would you rather I hadn't come? "

" No."

" You remember the evening I came — you got up so
suddenly and left me? What did you do that for? "

" Because if I'd stayed another minute I couldn't have
left you at all."

He stood up.

" And you're only going now because you can't see that
I'm not a coward."

.   .   .   .

This wouldn't last, the leaping and knocking of her
heart, the eyelids screwing themselves tight, the jerking of
her nerves at every sound: at the two harsh rattling screams
of the curtain rings along the pole, at the light click of the
switches. Only the small green-shaded lamp still burning
on Richard's writing table in the inner room. She could
hear him moving about, softly and secretly, in there.

He was Richard. That was Richard, moving about in
there.

V

Richard thought his flat was a safe place. But it wasn't.
People creeping up the stairs every minute and standing still
to listen. People would come and try the handle of the
door.

" They won't, dear. Nobody ever comes in. It has
never happened. It isn't going to happen now."

Yet you couldn't help thinking that just this night it
would happen.

She thought that Peters knew. He wouldn't come out
of his door till you had turned the corner of the stairs.

She thought the woman in the basement knew. She
remembered the evening at Greffington: Baxter's pinched
mouth and his eyes sliding sideways to look at you. She
knew now what Baxter had been thinking. The woman's
look was the female of Baxter's.

As if that could hurt you!

VI

"Mary, do you know you're growing younger every minute?"

"I shall go on growing younger and younger till it's all over."

"Till what's all over?"

"This. So will you, Richard."

"Not in the same way. My hair isn't young any more. My face isn't young any more."

"I don't want it to be young. It wasn't half so nice a face when it was young. . . . Some other woman loved it when it was young."

"Yes. Another woman loved it when it was young."

"Is she alive and going about?"

"Oh, yes; she's alive and she goes about a lot."

"Does she love you now?"

"I suppose she does."

"I wish she didn't."

"You needn't mind her, Mary. She was never anything to me. She never will be."

"But I do mind her. I mind her awfully. I can't bear to think of her going about and loving you. She's no business to. . . . Why do I mind her loving you more than I'd mind your loving her?"

"Because you like loving more than being loved."

"How do you know?"

"I know every time I hold you in my arms."

There have been other women then, or he wouldn't know the difference. There must have been a woman that he loved.

I don't care. It wasn't the same thing.

"What are you thinking?"

"I'm thinking nothing was ever the same thing as this."

"No. . . . Whatever we do, Mary, we mustn't go back on it. . . . If we could have done anything else. But I can't see. . . . It's not as if it could last long. Nothing lasts long. Life doesn't last long."

He sounded as if he were sorry, as if already, in his mind, he had gone back on it. After three days.

" You're not *sorry*, Richard? "

" Only when I think of you. The awful risks I've made you take."

" Can't you see I *like* risks? I always have liked risks. When we were children my brothers and I were always trying to see just how near we could go to breaking our necks."

" I know you've courage enough for anything. But that was rather a different sort of risk."

" No. No. There are no different sorts of risk. All intense moments of danger are the same. It's always the same feeling. I don't know whether I've courage or not, but I do know that when danger comes you don't care. You're hoisted up above caring."

" You *do* care, Mary."

" About my ' reputation '? You wouldn't like to think I didn't care about it. . . . Of course, I care frightfully. If I didn't, where's the risk? "

" I hate your having to take it all. I don't risk anything."

" I wish you did. Then you'd be happier. Poor Richard — so safe in his man's world. . . . You can be sorry about that, if you like. But not about me. I shall never be sorry. Nothing in this world can make me sorry. . . . I shouldn't like Mamma to know about it. But even Mamma couldn't make me sorry. . . . I've always been happy about the things that matter, the real things. I hate people who sneak and snivel about real things. . . . People who have doubts about God and don't like them and snivel. I had doubts about God once, and they made me so happy I could hardly bear it. . . . Mamma couldn't bear it making me happy. She wouldn't have minded half so much if I had been sorry and snivelled. She wouldn't mind so much if I was sorry and snivelled about this."

" You *said* you weren't going to think about your mother."

" I'm not thinking about her. I'm thinking about how happy I have been and am and shall be."

Even thinking about Mamma couldn't hurt you now. Nothing could hurt the happiness you shared with Richard. What it was now it would always be. Pure and remorseless.

VII

Delicious, warm, shining day. She had her coat and hat on ready to go down with him. The hansom stood waiting in the street.

They were looking up the place on the map, when the loud double knock came.

"That's for Peters. He's always getting wires —"

"If we don't go to-day we shall never go. We've only got five more now."

The long, soft rapping on the door of the room. Knuckles rapping out their warning. "You can't say I don't give you time."

Richard took the orange envelope.

"It's for you, Mary."

"Oh, Richard, '*Come at once. Mother ill. — DORSY.*'"

She would catch the ten train. That was what the hansom was there for.

"I'll send your things on after you."

The driver and the slog-slogging horse knew that she would catch the train. Richard knew.

He had the same look on his face that was there before when Mamma was ill. Sorrow that wasn't sorrow. And the same clear thought behind it.

XXXIV

I

Dorsy's nerves were in a shocking state. You could see she had been afraid all the time; from the first day when Mamma had kept on saying, "Has Mary come back?"

Dorsy was sure that was how it began; but she couldn't tell you whether it was before or afterwards that she had forgotten the days of the week.

Anybody could forget the days of the week. What frightened Dorsy was hearing her say suddenly, "Mary's *gone.*" She said it to herself when she didn't know Dorsy was in the room. Then she had left off asking and wondering. For five days she hadn't said anything about you.

Not anything at all. When she heard your name she stared at them with a queer, scared look.

Catty said that yesterday she had begun to be afraid of Dorsy and couldn't bear her in the room. That was what made them send the wire.

* * * * * * *

What had she been thinking of those five days? It was as though she knew.

Dorsy said she didn't believe she was thinking anything at all. Dorsy didn't know.

II

Somebody knew. Somebody had been talking. She had found Catty in the room making up the bed for her in the corner. Catty was crying as she tucked in the blankets. " There's some people," she said, " as had ought to be poisoned." But she wouldn't say why she was crying.

You could tell by Mr. Belk's face, his mouth drawn in between claws of nose and chin; by Mrs. Belk's face and her busy eyes, staring. By the old men sitting on the bench at the corner, their eyes coming together as you passed.

And Mr. Spencer Rollitt, stretching himself straight and looking away over your head and drawing in his breath with a " Fivv-vv-vv " when he asked how Mamma was. His thoughts were hidden behind his bare, wooden face. He was a just and cautious man. He wouldn't accept any statement outside the Bible without proof.

You had to go down and talk to Mrs. Waugh. She had come to see how you would look. Her mouth talked about Mamma but her face was saying all the time, " I'm not going to ask you what you were doing in London in Mr. Nicholson's flat, Mary. I'm sure you wouldn't do anything you'd be sorry to think of with your poor mother in the state she's in."

I don't care. I don't care what they think.

There would still be Catty and Dorsy and Louisa Wright

and Miss Kendal and Dr. Charles with their kind eyes that loved you. And Richard living his eternal life in your heart. And Mamma would never know.

III

Mamma was going backwards and forwards between the open work-table and the cabinet. She was taking out the ivory reels and thimbles and button boxes, wrapping them in tissue paper and hiding them in the cabinet. When she had locked the doors she waited till you weren't looking to lift up her skirt and hide the key in her petticoat pocket.

She was happy, like a busy child at play.

She was never ill, only tired like a child that plays too long. Her face was growing smooth and young and pretty again; a pink flush under her eyes. She would never look disapproving or reproachful any more. She couldn't listen any more when you read aloud to her. She had forgotten how to play halma.

One day she found the green box in the cabinet drawer. She came to you carrying it with care. When she had put it down on the table she lifted the lid and looked at the little green and white pawns and smiled.

" Roddy's soldiers," she said.

. . . .

Richard doesn't know what he's talking about when he asks me to give up Mamma. He might as well ask me to give up my child. It's no use his saying she " isn't there." Any minute she may come back and remember and know me.

She must have known me yesterday when she asked me to go and see what Papa was doing.

As for " waiting," he may have to wait years and years. And I'm forty-five now.

IV

The round black eye of the mirror looked at them. Their figures would be there, hers and Richard's, at the bottom of the black crystal bowl, small like the figures in the wrong end of a telescope, very clear in the deep, clear swirl of the glass.

They were sitting close together on the old rose-chintz-covered couch. *Her* couch. You could see him putting the cushions at her back, tucking the wide Victorian skirt in close about the feet in the black velvet slippers. And she would lie there with her poor hands folded in the white cashmere shawl.

Richard knew what you were thinking.

" You can't expect me," he was saying, " to behave like my uncle. . . . Besides, it's a little too late, isn't it? . . . We said, whatever we did we wouldn't go back on it. If it wasn't wrong then, Mary, it isn't wrong now."

" It isn't that, Richard."

(No. Not that. Pure and remorseless then. Pure and remorseless now.)

She wondered whether he had heard it. The crunching on the gravel walk under the windows, stopping suddenly when the feet stepped on to the grass. And the hushed growl of the men's voices. Baxter and the gardener. They had come to see whether the light would go out again behind the yellow blinds as it had gone out last night.

If you were a coward; if you had wanted to get off scot-free, it was too late.

Richard knows I'm not a coward. Funk wouldn't keep me from him. It isn't *that.*

" What is it, then? "

" Can't you see, can't you *feel* that it's no use coming again, just for this? It'll never be what it was then. It'll always be like last night, and you'll think I don't care. Something's holding me back from you. Something that's happened to me. I don't know yet what it is."

" Nerves. Nothing but nerves."

" No. I thought it was nerves last night. I thought it was this room. Those two poor ghosts, looking at us. I even thought it might be Mark and Roddy — all of them — tugging at me to get me away from you. . . . But it isn't that. It's something in me."

" You're trying to tell me you don't want me."

" I'm trying to tell you what happened. I did want you,

all last year. It was so awful that I had to stop it. You couldn't go on living like that. . . . I willed and willed not to want you."

"So did I. All the willing in the world couldn't stop me."

"It isn't that sort of willing. You might go on all your life like that and nothing would happen. You have to find it out for yourself; and even that might take you all your life. . . . It isn't the thing people call willing at all. It's much queerer. Awfully queer."

"How — *queer?* "

"Oh — the sort of queerness you don't like talking about."

"I'm sorry, Mary. You seem to be talking about something, but I haven't the faintest notion what it is. But you can make yourself believe anything you like if you keep on long enough."

"No. Half the time I'm doing it I don't believe it'll come off. . . . But it always does. Every time it's the same. Every time; exactly as if something had happened."

"Poor Mary."

"But, Richard, it makes you absolutely happy. That's the queer part of it. It's how you know."

"Know *what?* "

He was angry.

"That there's something there. That it's absolutely real."

"Real? "

"Why not? If it makes you happy without the thing you care most for in the whole world. . . . There must be something there. It must be real. Real in a way that nothing else is."

"You aren't happy now," he said.

"No. And you're with me. And I care for you more than anything in the whole world."

"I thought you said that was all over."

"No. It's only just begun."

"I can't say I see it."

"You'll see it all right soon. . . . When you've gone."

V

It was no use not marrying him, no use sending him away, as long as he was tied to you by his want.

You had no business to be happy. It wasn't fair. There was he, tied to you tighter than if you *had* married him. And there you were in your inconceivable freedom. Supposing you could give him the same freedom, the same happiness? Supposing you could "work" it for him, make It (whatever it was) reach out and draw him into your immunity, your peace?

VI

Whatever It was It was there. You could doubt away yourself and Richard, but you couldn't doubt away It.

It might leave you for a time, but it came back. It came back. Its going only intensified the wonder of its return. You might lose all sense of it between its moments; but the thing was certain while it lasted. Doubt it away, and still what had been done for you lasted. Done for you once for all, two years ago. And that wasn't the first time.

Even supposing you could doubt away the other times. — You might have made the other things happen by yourself. But not that. Not giving Richard up and still being happy. That was something you couldn't possibly have done yourself. Or you might have done it in time — time might have done it for you — but not like that, all at once, making that incredible, supernatural happiness and peace out of nothing at all, in one night, and going on in it, without Richard. Richard himself didn't believe it was possible. He simply thought it hadn't happened.

Still, even then, you might have said it didn't count so long as it was nothing but your private adventure; but not now, never again now when it had happened to Richard.

His letter didn't tell you whether he thought there was anything in it. He saw the "queerness" of it and left it there:

"Something happened that night after you'd gone. You know how I felt. I couldn't stop wanting you. My mind

was tied to you and couldn't get away. Well — that night
something let go — quite suddenly. Something went.

"It's a year ago and it hasn't come back.

"I didn't know what on earth you meant by 'not
wanting and still caring'; but I think I see now. I don't
'want' you any more and I 'care' more than ever. . . .

"Don't 'work like blazes.' Still I'm glad you like it.
I can get you any amount of the same thing — more than
you'll care to do."

VII

He didn't know how hard it was to "work like blazes."
You had to keep your eyes ready all the time to see what
Mamma was doing. You had to take her up and down
stairs, holding her lest she should turn dizzy and fall. If
you left her a minute she would get out of the room, out
of the house and on to the Green by herself and be
frightened.

Mamma couldn't remember the garden. She looked at
her flowers with dislike.

You had brought her on a visit to a strange, disagreeable
place and left her there. She was angry with you because
she couldn't get away.

Then, suddenly, for whole hours she would be good: a
child playing its delicious game of goodness. When Dr.
Charles came in and you took him out of the room to talk
about her you would tell her to sit still until you came back.
And she would smile, the sweet, serious smile of a child
that is being trusted, and sit down on the parrot chair; and
when you came back you would find her sitting there, still
smiling to herself because she was so good.

Why do I love her now, when she is like this — when
"*this*" is what I was afraid of, what I thought I could not
bear — why do I love her more, if anything, now than I've
ever done before? Why am I happier now than I've ever
been before, except in the times when I was writing and
the times when I was with Richard?

VIII

Forty-five. Yesterday she was forty-five, and to-day. To-morrow she would be forty-six. She had come through the dreadful, dangerous year without thinking of it, and nothing had happened. Nothing at all. She couldn't imagine why she had ever been afraid of it; she could hardly remember what being afraid of it had felt like.

Aunt Charlotte — Uncle Victor —

If I were going to be mad I should have gone mad long ago: when Roddy came back; when Mark died; when I sent Richard away. I should be mad now.

It was getting worse.

In the cramped room where the big bed stuck out from the wall to within a yard of the window, Mamma went about, small and weak, in her wadded lavender Japanese dressing-gown, like a child that can't sit still, looking for something it wants that nobody can find. You couldn't think because of the soft pad-pad of the dreaming, sleep-walking feet in the lamb's-wool slippers.

When you weren't looking she would slip out of the room on to the landing to the head of the stairs, and stand there, vexed and bewildered when you caught her.

IX

Mamma was not well enough now to get up and be dressed. They had moved her into Papa's room. It was bright all morning with the sun. She was happy there. She remembered the yellow furniture. She was back in the old bedroom at Five Elms.

Mamma lay in the big bed, waiting for you to brush her hair. She was playing with her white flannel dressing jacket, spread out before her on the counterpane, ready. She talked to herself.

"Lindley Vickers — Vickers Lindley."

But she was not thinking of Lindley Vickers; she was thinking of Dan, trying to get back to Dan.

"Is Jenny there? Tell her to go and see what Master

Roddy's doing." She thought Catty was Jenny. . . . "Has Dan come in?"

Sometimes it would be Papa; but not often; she soon left him for Dan and Roddy.

Always Dan and Roddy. And never Mark.

Never Mark and never Mary. Had she forgotten Mark or did she remember him too well? Or was she afraid to remember? Supposing there was a black hole in her mind where Mark's death was, and another black hole where Mary had been? Had she always held you together in her mind so that you went down together? Did she hold you together now, in some time and place safer than memory?

She was still playing with the dressing-jacket. She smoothed it, and patted it, and folded it up and laid it beside her on the bed. She took up her pocket-handkerchief and shook it out and folded it and put it on the top of the dressing-jacket.

"What are you doing, you darling?"

"Going to bed."

She looked at you with a half-happy, half-frightened smile, because you had found her out. She was putting out the baby clothes, ready. Serious and pleased and frightened.

"Who will take care of my little children when I'm laid aside?"

She knew what she was lying in the big bed for.

x

It was really bedtime. She was sitting up in the arm-chair while Catty who was Jenny made her bed. The long white sheet lay smooth and flat on the high mattress; it hung down on the floor.

Mamma was afraid of the white sheet. She wouldn't go back to bed.

"There's a coffin on the bed. Somebody's died of cholera," she said.

Cholera? That was what she thought Mark had died of.

.　　.　　.　　.　　.　　.　　.

She knows who I am now.

XI

Richard had written to say he was married. On the twenty-fifth of February. That was just ten days after Mamma died.

" We've known each other the best part of our lives. So you see it's a very sober middle-aged affair."

He had married the woman who loved him when he was young. " A very sober middle-aged affair." Not what it would have been if you and he — He didn't want you to think that *that* would ever happen again. He wanted you to see that with him and you it had been different, that you had loved him and lived with him in that other time he had made for you where you were always young.

He had only made it for you. She, poor thing, would have to put up with other people's time, time that made them middle-aged, made them old.

You had got to write and tell him you were glad. You had got to tell him Mamma died ten days ago. And he would say to himself, " If I'd waited another ten days — " There was nothing he could say to you.

That was why he didn't write again. There was nothing to say.

XXXV

I

She would never get used to the house.

She couldn't think why she had been such a fool as to take it. On a seven years' lease, too; it would feel like being in prison for seven years.

That was the worst of moving about for a whole year in boats and trains, and staying at hotels; it gave you an unnatural longing to settle down, in a place of your own.

Your own — Undying lust of possession. If you *had* to have things, why a house? Why six rooms when two would have done as well and left you your freedom? After all that ecstasy of space, that succession of heavenly places with singing names: Carcassone and Vezelay; Rome and

Florence and San Gimignano; Marseilles and Arles and Avignon; filling up time, stretching it out, making a long life out of one year.

If you could go moving on and on while time stood still.

Oh this damned house. It would be you sitting still while time tore by, as it used to tear by at Morfe before Richard came, and in the three years after he had gone, when Mamma —

II

It was rather attractive, when you turned the corner and came on it suddenly, flat-roofed and small, clean white and innocent. The spring twilight gave it that look of being somewhere in Italy, the look that made you fall in love with it at first sight.

As for not getting used to it, that was precisely the effect she wanted: rooms that wouldn't look like anything in the house at Morfe, things that she would always come on with a faint, exquisite surprise: the worn magentaish rug on the dark polished floor, the oak table, the gentian blue chair, the thin magenta curtains letting the light through: the things Richard had given her because in their beginning they had been meant for her. Richard knew that you were safe from unhappiness, that you had never once " gone back on it," if you could be happy with his things.

He had thought, too, that if you had a house you would settle down and work.

You would have to; you would have to work like blazes, after spending all the money Aunt Charlotte left you on rushing about, and half the money Aunt Lavvy left you on settling down. It was horrible this living on other people's deaths.

III

Catty couldn't bear it being so different. You could see she thought you were unfaithful not to have kept the piano when Mamma had played on it.

Catty's faithfulness was unsurpassable. She had wanted

to marry Blenkiron, the stonemason at Morfe, but first she wouldn't because of Mamma and then she wouldn't because of Miss Mary. When you told her to go back and marry him at once she would only laugh and say, " There's your husband, and there's your children. You're my child, Miss Mary. Master Roddy was Jenny's child and you was always mine."

You were only ten years younger than Catty, but like Richard she couldn't see that you were old.

You would never know whether Catty knew about Richard; or whether Dorsy knew. Whatever you did they would love you, Catty because you were her child, and Dorsy because you were Mark's sister.

IV

The sun had been shining for a fortnight. She could sit out all day now in the garden.

It was nonsense to talk about time standing still if you kept on moving. Just now, in the garden, when the light came through the thin green silk leaves of the lime tree, for a moment, while she sat looking at the lime tree, time stood still.

Catty had taken away the tea-things and was going down the four steps into the house. It happened between the opening and shutting of the door.

She saw that the beauty of the tree was its real life, and that its real life was in her real self and that her real self was God. The leaves and the light had nothing to do with it; she had seen it before when the tree was a stem and bare branches on a grey sky; and that beauty too was the real life of the tree.

V

If she could only dream about Mark. But if she dreamed about any of them it was always Mamma. She had left her in the house by herself and she had got out of her room to the stair-head. Or they were in London at the crossing by the Bank and Mamma was frightened. She had to get

her through the thick of the traffic. The horses pushed at
Mamma and you tried to hold back their noses, but she
sank down and slid away from you sideways under the
wheel.

Or she would come into this room and find her in it. At
first she would be glad to see that Mamma was still there;
then she would be unhappy and afraid. She would go on to
a clear thought: if Mamma was still there, then she had got
back somehow to Morfe. The old life was still going on;
it had never really stopped. But if that was real, then this
was not real. Her secure, shining life of last year and now
wasn't real; nothing could make it real; her exquisite sense
of it was not real. She had only thought it had happened.

Nothing had happened but what had happened before; it
was happening now; it would go on and on till it frightened
you, till you could not bear it. When she woke up she was
glad that the dream had been nothing but a dream.

But that meant that you were glad Mamma was not there.
The dream showed you what you were hiding from yourself.
Supposing the dead knew? Supposing Mamma knew, and
Mark knew that you were glad —

VI

It came to her at queer times, in queer ways. After that
horrible evening at the Dining Club when the secretary
woman put her as far as possible from Richard, next to the
little Jew financier who smelt of wine.

She couldn't even hear what Richard was saying; the
little wine-lapping Jew went on talking about Women's Suffrage and his collection of Fragonards and his wife's portrait
by Sargent. His tongue slid between one overhanging and
one dropping jaw, in and out like a shuttle.

She tried not to hate him, not to shrink back from his
puffing, wine-sour breath, to be kind to him and listen and
smile and remember that his real secret self was God, and
was holy; not to attend to Richard's voice breaking the beat
of her heart.

She had gone away before Richard could get up and come
to her. She wanted to be back in her house by herself.

She had pushed open the French windows of the study to breathe the air of the garden and see the tall sycamore growing deep into the thick blue night. Half the room, reflected on the long pane, was thrown out into the garden. She saw it thinning away, going off from the garden into another space, existing there with an unearthly reality of its own. She had sat down at last, too tired to go upstairs, and had found herself crying, incredibly crying; all the misery, all the fear, all the boredom of her life gathered together and discharging now.

" If I could get out of it all " — Her crying stopped with a start as if somebody had come in and put a hand on her shoulder. Everything went still. She had a sense of happiness and peace suddenly there with her in the room. Not so much her own as the happiness and peace of an immense, invisible, intangible being of whose life she was thus aware. She knew, somehow through It, that there was no need to get away; she was out of it all now, this minute. There was always a point where she could get out of it and into this enduring happiness and peace.

VII

They were talking to-night about Richard and his wife. They said he wasn't happy; he wasn't in love with her.

He never had been; she knew it; yet she took him, and tied him to her, an old woman, older than Richard, with grey hair.

Oh well — she had had to wait for him longer than he waited for me, and she's in love with him still. She's making it impossible for him to see me.

Then I shan't see him. I don't want him to see me if it hurts her. I don't want her to be hurt.

I wonder if she knows? *They* know. I can hear them talking about me when I've gone.

. . . " Mary Olivier, the woman who translated Euripides."

. . . " Mary Olivier, the woman Nicholson discovered."

. . . " Mary Olivier, the woman who was Nicholson's mistress."

Richard's mistress — I know that's what they say, but I can't feel that they're saying it about *me*. It must be somebody else, some woman I never heard of.

VIII

Mr. Sutcliffe is dead. He died two weeks ago at Agaye.
I can see now how beautiful they were; how beautiful he was, going away like that, letting her take him away so that the sight of me shouldn't hurt her.

I can see that what I thought so ugly was really beautiful, their sticking to each other through it all, his faithfulness and her forgiveness, their long life of faithfulness and forgiveness.

But my short life with Richard was beautiful too; my coming to him and leaving him free. I shall never go back on that; I shall never be sorry for it.

The things I'm sorry for are not caring more for Papa, being unkind to Mamma, not doing enough for her, not knowing what she was really like. I'd give anything to have been able to think about her as Mark thought, to feel about her as he felt. If only I had known what she was really like. Even now I don't know. I never shall.

But going to Richard — No. If it was to be done again to-morrow I'd do it.

And I don't humbug myself about it. If I made Richard happy I made myself happy too; *he* made me happy. Still, if I had had no happiness in it, if I'd hated it, I'd have done it for Richard all the same.

IX

All this religious resignation. And the paradox of prayer: people praying one minute, " Thy will be done," then praying for things to happen or not happen, just as they please.

God's will be done — as if it *wouldn't* be done whatever they did or didn't do. God's will was your fate. The thing was to know it and not waste your strength in the illusion of resistance.

If you were part of God your will was God's will at the

moment when you really willed. There was always a point when you knew it: the flash point of freedom. You couldn't mistake your flash when it came. You couldn't doubt away that certainty of freedom any more than you could doubt away the certainty of necessity and determination. From the outside they were part of the show of existence, the illusion of separation from God. From the inside they were God's will, the way things were willed. Free-will was the reality underneath the illusion of necessity. The flash point of freedom was your consciousness of God.

Then praying would be willing. There would be no such thing as passive prayer. There could be no surrender. . . . And yet there was. Not the surrender of your will, but of all the things that entangle and confuse it; that stand between it and you, between God and you. When you lay still with your eyes shut and made the darkness come on, wave after wave, blotting out your body and the world, blotting out everything but your self and your will, that was a dying to live; a real dying, a real life.

The Christians got hold of real things and turned them into something unreal, impossible to believe. The grace of God was a real thing. It was that miracle of perfect happiness, with all its queerness, its divine certainty and uncertainty. The Christians knew at least one thing about it; they could see it had nothing to do with deserving. But it had nothing to do with believing, either, or with being good and getting into heaven. It *was* heaven. It had to do with beauty, absolutely un-moral beauty, more than anything else.

She couldn't see the way of it beyond that. It had come to her when she was a child in brilliant. clear flashes; it had come again and again in her adolescence, with more brilliant and clearer flashes; then, after leaving her for twenty-three years, it had come like this — streaming in and out of her till its ebb and flow were the rhythm of her life.

Why hadn't she known that this would happen, instead of being afraid that she would " go like " Aunt Charlotte or Uncle Victor? People talked a lot about compensation, but nobody told you that after forty-five life would have this exquisite clearness and intensity.

Why, since it *could* happen when you were young —
reality breaking through, if only in flashes coming and going,
going altogether and forgotten — why had you to wait so
long before you could remember it and be aware of it as one
continuous, shining background? She had never been aware
of it before; she had only thought about and about it, about
Substance, the Thing-in-itself, Reality, God. Thinking was
not being aware.

She made it out more and more. For twenty-three years
something had come between her and reality. She could see
what it was now. She had gone through life wanting things,
wanting people, clinging to the thought of them, not able to
keep off them and let them go.

X

All her life she had gone wrong about happiness. She had
attached it to certain things and certain people: Mamma
and Mark, Jenny, visits to Aunt Bella, the coming of Aunt
Charlotte and Aunt Lavvy and Uncle Victor, the things
people would say and do which they had not said and not
done: when she was older she had attached it to Maurice
Jourdain and to Mark still and Mamma; to going back to
Mamma after Dover; to the unknown houses in Morfe; to
Maurice Jourdain's coming; then to Mark's coming, to
Lindley Vickers. And in the end none of these things had
brought her the happiness she had seemed to foresee in them.

She knew only one thing about perfect happiness: it
didn't hide; it didn't wait for you behind unknown doors.
There were little happinesses, pleasures that came like that:
the pleasure of feeling good when you sat with Maggie's
sister; the pleasure of doing things for Mamma or Dorsy;
all the pleasures that had come through the Sutcliffes. The
Sutcliffes went, and yet she had been happy. They had all
gone, and yet she was happy.

If you looked back on any perfect happiness you saw that
it had not come from the people or the things you thought it
had come from, but from somewhere inside yourself. When
you attached it to people and things they ceased for that
moment to be themselves; the space they then seemed to

inhabit was not their own space; the time of the wonderful event was not their time. They became part of the kingdom of God within you.

Not Richard. He had become part of the kingdom of God without ceasing to be himself.

That was because she had loved him more than herself. Loving him more than herself she had let him go.

Letting go had somehow done the trick.

XI

I used to think there was nothing I couldn't give up for Richard.

Could I give up this? If I had to choose between losing Richard and losing this? (I suppose it would be generally considered that I *had* lost Richard.) If I had had to choose seven years ago, before I knew, I'd have chosen Richard; I couldn't have helped myself. But if I had to choose now — knowing what reality is — between losing Richard in the way I have lost him and losing reality, absolutely and for ever, losing, absolutely and for ever, my real self, knowing that I'd lost it? . . .

If there's anything in it at all, losing my real self would be losing Richard, losing Richard's real self absolutely and for ever. Knowing reality is knowing that you can't lose it. That or nothing.

XII

Supposing there isn't anything in it? Supposing — Supposing —

Last night I began thinking about it again. I stripped my soul; I opened all the windows and let my ice-cold thoughts in on the poor thing; it stood shivering between certainty and uncertainty.

I tried to doubt away this ultimate passion, and it turned my doubt into its own exquisite sting, the very thrill of the adventure.

Supposing there's nothing in it, nothing at all?

That's the risk you take.

XIII

There isn't any risk. This time it was clear, clear as the black pattern the sycamore makes on the sky.

If it never came again I should remember.

THE END

MAY SINCLAIR

was born in Liverpool in 1863, the only daughter and youngest child of the six children of Amelia and William Sinclair. In the 1870s her father's shipowning business went bankrupt and the family moved first to Essex, then to Gloucester, later to Devon. Her parents lived apart, due in part to her father's intermittent alcoholism. Her brothers suffered from inherited heart disease, four dying before their fifties, most of them nursed by their sister. May Sinclair had no formal education until her eighteenth year which she spent at Cheltenham Ladies College, taught by the great educator Dorothea Beale. Under her influence she began to read philosophy, psychology and Greek literature, and to write, first poetry, then fiction. She published her first novel, *Audrey Craven*, in 1897 and with its publication moved to London where she continued to live with her mother until the latter's death in 1901.

From 1908 she was active in the fight for the vote, working with writers such as Violet Hunt and Cicely Hamilton for the suffragist cause. Critically acclaimed in both Britain and America as one of the great writers of the Georgian Age, she was the friend and contemporary of Wells, James, Hardy, Galsworthy, Ford Madox Ford, and of Dorothy Richardson, about whose work she first coined the famous phrase 'stream of consciousness'. She was one of the earliest novelists to be influenced by the work of Freud and Jung, and was influenced too by her friendships with the Imagists Richard Aldington, Ezra Pound and Hilda Doolittle. She wrote poetry, criticism, philosophical works, short stories, and twenty-four novels in all, the best known of which are *The Divine Fire* (1904), *The Tree of Heaven* (1917), *Mary Olivier: A Life* (1919) and *Life and Death of Harriett Frean* (1922) also published by Virago. For the last fifteen years of her life May Sinclair was incapacitated by Parkinson's disease. In 1932 she retired to Buckinghamshire where she died in 1946.